ALLEYCAT

A novel

Sue Armstrong

978-1482328790

© 2013 Sue Armstrong

No part of this publication may be reproduced, stored in a retrieval system, in any form or by any means, electronic, mechanical, photocopy, or otherwise, without prior written permission from the author.

Contact author at www.wordsfromsue.com
or sue_armstrong@yahoo.com

Dedicated to:

Bill Armstrong
Lisette A. Parker
Gary "Doc" Weisgerber

The setting for this story is Monmouth, Oregon—about 20 miles west of Oregon's capital city, Salem. In 1971 the present-day Western Oregon University (WOU) was named Oregon College of Education (OCE). Many places in the story are real, although they may be long gone or changed, and some are completely fictionalized. Characters in the story are just that—none portray actual persons, living or dead.

Acknowledgements

I want to thank the many people who helped shape this story. Without them, it might still be a bundle of hand-scribbled papers stuck in a folder in the back of a file drawer.

First of all, my husband, Bill, who encouraged me from the beginning to put my story on paper. He was my first reader and first supporter of my dream to write a novel.

Next, my incredible friends Lisette and Gary, who, along with Bill, helped in countless ways to keep the integrity of the times and shared with me their memories of living in Monmouth in 1971.

I am grateful for the following people who spent many hours reading and discussing the manuscript as it evolved: Jean Adams, Pearl Anderson, Bill Armstrong, David Armstrong, Cari Becker, Susan Crook, Dennis Davis, Molly Armstrong Falleur, Marguerite Garrison, KatSue Grant, Staci Harris, Lorraine Jarvi, Wendy Armstrong Markt, Katie Nelson, Nancy Nowak, Lisette Parker, Liz Robinson, Diane Williams, and Terry Worley, some of whom read more than one revision. Rhonda Leigh, author of *Through the Veil*, assisted with the psychic experiences depicted in the book. And special thanks to the extraordinary Douglas County writers group, Taking Care of Business, who spent countless hours critiquing individual passages.

Graphic artist Danyal Watkins of Phyre Phoenix Design, KatSue Grant of Seaborne Editing, and Kristen James of Bravado Publishing offered invaluable expertise. Thank you!

August *(1970)*

~ 1 ~

Portland International Airport

Renee stared at the floor, mentally deep breathing. She clenched the strap of her purse; her fingers would ache later when she tried to uncurl them. Her free hand tap-tap-tapped against her thigh, echoing the rhythmic *don't go don't go don't go* in her head. She rubbed the back of her neck, damp with perspiration. Even in her thin sundress she felt too warm. Russ had chosen the dress, a cheerful yellow print, halter back, short full skirt, wide yellow belt cinched around her slender waist. A dancing dress. Innocent and sexy at the same time. A bright yellow bird, ready to fly out of the golden cage.

Breathe.

Several feet away, Russ finished loading his 35 mm camera, snapped the rewind crank back into place, and raised the camera to his eye, turning his body to view images through the lens. Renee could visualize his concentration without looking directly at him. Shoulders slightly hunched, heavy brows lowered over deep brown eyes, lips pursed, stance wide to support his two hundred and fifty pounds. Knowing a photograph was imminent, she removed her glasses and held them loosely at her side, eyes closed. *Breathe.*

"Let's get a picture," Russ said and handed the camera to his father. "Here, Dad, it's all set." He took Renee's hand; when he felt the rigid frames clutched there, he frowned. "You could keep your glasses on, you know." He circled her shoulder with his arm and smiled at his father. "Say 'cheese' Renee." She bared her teeth in what she hoped would be enough of a smile and the shutter clicked. The beginning of a headache gripped the base of her skull.

"Renee, you keep that smile on for our boy here," Russ's father said. "He's going to need that memory to hold him."

"I'll send you a copy when I get the film developed," Russ said. "We can each carry one in our wallets."

"Your mother and I will want one, too," his father said. "Too bad she couldn't see you off today."

Russ shrugged. "Grandma needed her more than me. It's all right." He turned to Renee. "Didn't Kim give you some kind of photo album for your purse?"

"Yes."

"Do you have it? I want to see what you have so far."

Renee pulled a small plastic-covered booklet from her purse. Russ took it and flipped through the pages. "Good, you have our prom picture and the one of us at Silver Falls State Park—that's my favorite. You look happy."

"I was," Renee said. "It was a weekday and hardly anyone was in the park."

"When I get back, we'll go there again."

"I'd like that. We can—"

"You'll be back in no time," his father said. "Let's not rush into homecoming before you even get on the plane. A whole new world is waiting for you, son. I have to admit I'm envious. It's been a long time since I was overseas."

"Flight 286 to Tokyo now boarding." A crackle of anticipation zigzagged through the waiting passengers in the busy Portland airport. Renee scanned the crowded area, taking in all the activity. Suitcases, purses, tote bags were gathered up and juggled for best position so hugs and kisses could be exchanged. Several GIs, ultimately bound for Viet Nam, milled around, creases sharp, scalps shadowed by buzz cuts, postures ramrod straight. A toddler played peek-a-boo around his soldier father's legs, chubby fingers gripping khaki as he giggled and shrieked gleefully. His mother watched with a mournful smile.

Snatches of chatter punctuated the noisy hum in the room. Two young Japanese women, heads together as they talked, sat nearby. One had sleek black hair that hung to her waist. Her t-shirt and hip-hugger pants revealed a lithe, athletic body. *Russ would love that hair. I never should have cut mine.* Renee felt a twinge of uncertainty in her gut. *What if Russ meets someone like her?* She glanced at him, a quick sideways look. His eyes, too, studied the women, a faint smirk on his face. *He won't.* Her right hand clasped the left, then found the diamond glittering on her left ring finger. *He loves me.*

Piped-in music filtered through the noise of the terminal. An orchestral rendition of the Beatles' "All You Need Is Love" floated over the shuffling sounds of people hurrying, the click and rattle of baggage carts, distant roar of jetliners, plaintive cries of small children and their harried parents' impatient voices. The soldier picked up his son and held him close, kissing his cheek, forehead, tip of his nose. He swayed in time to the music and sang to his wife. Her smile brightened and she leaned against him, arms around their child. Renee watched them through a blur of tears. *Breathe, breathe.*

A flash of movement at the edge of her field of vision caught her attention. A whisper. "You'll be all right." Faint whiff of leather, tobacco. *A man. Watching me.* Turning her head, looking in all directions, she saw nothing unusual. No man standing alone. And certainly no one observing her. A tiny prickle shot up her spine. *What the heck?*

Russ put the camera back in its leather case and slung the strap over one shoulder. Renee fussed with his shirt collar, smoothed back his hair that had fallen over one eyebrow. He reached down for his briefcase, giving her a quick peck on the lips. A heavy duffel bag, hooked over his other shoulder, caused his stance to be off-kilter just a fraction.

"I wish you weren't going," she said softly.

"We've been through this enough," he answered, his voice firm and she sensed a hint of irritation. Her shoulders sagged. "Besides, you'll be back in school and that will keep you busy. New roommate, too. Aren't you looking forward to that?"

She shrugged. "Yeah, I guess so."

"It's neat you'll be in the new dorm this year."

"It'll be different. My roommate's name is Judy. I got a letter from her yesterday. A transfer from Mt. Hood Community College, psych major, a sophomore like us. She's never been away from home."

"Well, there you go. You can show her all around campus and help her make friends—"

"You sound like my mother." Renee shook her head and sighed.

Russ beamed at her, his eyes traveling over her body. He took her hand and twirled her around once. "You sure don't look like your mother. That dress is perfect on you."

"I love it. You do have good taste."

"Thank you. I know what I like." He pulled her close and ran his hand down her arm. She leaned into him. "So, your new roommate?"

"She said she doesn't know anybody going to Monmouth and she's kind of worried about settling in."

"Then you won't even miss me. You'll be too busy acclimating Judy to the college culture at a big school."

"Oh, sure. Campus is what? Three blocks long and two blocks wide? Probably the smallest state school in Oregon." Renee shut her eyes, shoulders bowed, fingers tightening on the purse strap. "How will I manage without you, Russ?"

"*I'm* the one leaving, facing the unknown, not you. Come on, Renee, I need to see your smile." She looked up at him, attempting a smile, eyes full of tears. "That's better. Hey, did you notice our song playing a minute ago?"

"Yes. 'All We Need—'"

"Time to go!" Russ's father spoke in his booming voice, stepping between Renee and Russ. He patted his son on the back, a hearty slap that caused the duffel bag to slip. Russ set down his briefcase to pull the duffel bag strap back up. With his now-free arm, he reached past his father to pull Renee close in a tight embrace.

"It's only until July," he said, stroking her hair. "One year."

Breathe.

January (1971)

~~ 2 ~~

Oregon College of Education

"Wait up, Savannah!" Renee yelled to a coed walking through the lobby of the student center. She trotted the last few yards to catch up with her best friend. "Let's get a locker for our stuff, okay? I don't want to haul all these books to dinner."

"I hate Mondays. I had every one of my classes today." Savannah ducked into an alcove filled with stacked rows of square lockers, a red key for each one. "Do you have a quarter?"

Renee dropped her load of books on the floor and dug in the pocket of her jeans. "Yeah, I think so." She extracted a quarter from a small pile of change and held it up. "We got money! Hey, check the coin return boxes, okay? Maybe we'll find something today." Stacking her books in a vault, she added Savannah's, cramming them to fit in the small space. Savannah walked along the lockers lining three sides of the alcove, reaching down to sweep her fingers into each open slot at the bottom of the vertical rows. Many students didn't realize the money was refunded when the key was returned and left without retrieving their quarters.

"Any luck?" an amused voice asked.

They turned to see a tall, well-dressed young man leaning against the archway, a Sherlock Holmes-style pipe in one hand, aromatic smoke drifting upward. His sandy-colored hair curled around the collar of his tan overcoat and a long, navy blue muffler trailed over his shoulder. The unbuttoned coat revealed a light blue dress shirt, expertly knotted paisley tie, dark slacks, and a belt that matched his well-shined shoes. He didn't look like a student but appeared too young to be a professor. Renee stared at him for a moment, then continued loading the books into the locker.

"No," Savannah said. "Nothing today."

"Too bad." He shook his head sympathetically.

She shrugged. "That's business."

His lively brown eyes appraised the two girls as Renee deposited the money and pocketed the key. As they moved toward the doors leading to the dorm residents' dining room in the next building, he maneuvered so he walked between them, adjusting his stride to match theirs. "Where're you headed?"

"The cafeteria," Savannah said. "You, too?"

"God, no. You think I would live in the dorm? And eat the crap they serve at this school? Not if I can help it."

"Oh!" said Renee. "No, I guess not. It *is* pretty gross."

"But," he said, as he linked his arms through theirs, "I do eat there sometimes." The girls glanced at each other behind his back, both stifling giggles.

"Oh, of course." Savannah nodded, eyes wide. "But why?"

"I get hungry."

"Are you hinting around for a meal? Do you want us to sneak you in?"

"No, no," he said, shaking his head and backing away, a sly smile lighting up his eyes. "Not yet, anyway. I barely know you." With a tip of his head, he raised one hand in a salute. "Enjoy your dinner. See you around, ladies." He took off before they could say good-bye.

"Wow," Savannah said, turning to watch him walk away. "Have you seen him before, Renee?"

There's something familiar... Renee shook her head. "If I have, I don't remember. He was dressed like a teacher but—"

"But sure didn't act like one!"

"Maybe he's a grad student."

"Yeah, that could explain the nice clothes, especially if he's a TA helping a professor." Savannah smiled. "That pipe! I've never seen anyone with a pipe, much less a—what do you call that kind of pipe?"

Renee squinted and wrinkled her nose, thinking. "Meerschaum? It smelled good, didn't it? I'm surprised."

Alleycat

"We'll have to watch for him in the dining room—see who's sneaking him in." They reached the double doors of the cafeteria. "There's Judy."

Renee paused, squared her shoulders, and shifted her purse from one arm to the other. Seeing her roommate caused her stomach to tighten, accompanied by the threat of a headache. She rubbed her fingers against her temples.

"Can you believe this snow?" Judy asked as soon as they were in earshot.

"I love it!" Savannah said. "Did you see that snow sculpture of a wolf in front of Campbell Hall?"

"I did," Judy said. "Whoever made it sure has talent."

"Too bad it won't last," Savannah said.

"If Russ was here, he'd take a picture of it," Renee said.

"Why don't you take one?" Judy asked.

"I don't have a camera, remember? And I wouldn't take it even if I did have one."

"Why not?"

"Because it wouldn't measure up."

"What do you mean?" Judy said. "By whose standards?"

"I just mean I couldn't do justice to the sculpture."

Judy snorted. "That's just silly."

"Not really," Renee said, shaking her head. "I'm not a photographer like Russ." She gestured toward the cafeteria. "Come on, let's get some dinner." The headache began to pulse, like a faint heartbeat inside her skull. *Give me a break today, Judy, please.*

They went through the line, a strong mixture of cafeteria aromas assaulting them as they slid their trays along the metal ledge. Nothing was identifiable by smell and even looking at the assortment made naming some of the choices difficult. Renee selected a dinner salad, some kind of casserole made with noodles, pale sauce and olive-green canned peas, and a buttermilk roll. With a wry frown, Savannah passed on the casserole and instead took the chicken-fried steak. Judy had spinach, cooked to a grayish lump, the casserole, and an apple.

"I can't believe they get away with serving us this slop," Judy said as they handed their meal cards to the student worker at the end of the line. "What kind of meat do you think this is?"

"Tuna or chicken," Renee said, wrinkling her nose. "I'm hoping for tuna."

"At least the apple looks halfway fresh. If it's good, I'll get another one to take back to the room."

As soon as they settled at a table and started eating, Savannah said, "Hey, Judy, we met this interesting guy by the lockers. He just started walking with us, kind of flirty. We thought he wanted us to sneak him into the cafeteria but then he suddenly took off." She laughed. "He actually saluted and called us 'ladies'!"

"So?"

"Oh, you should have seen him! All dressed up—a tie! And a pipe. Not an ordinary guy."

"And good-looking, too," Renee said.

Judy glanced sharply at Renee. "Do you know his name? Or anything about him?"

"Not really," Savannah said. "But he was interesting." She put a lot of emphasis on the last word.

Judy shook her head. "Big deal." Poking her spinach, she grimaced, then tried a small taste. "I can't eat this. How can they even call this food?" She put her fork down and picked up the apple, examined it closely, twisted the stem until it popped off. "Oh, did you get a letter today, Renee?"

"Judy," Savannah said in a warning tone, glancing at Renee.

"Yes, I did, as a matter of fact." Renee continued eating. The pulsing in her head turned to a steady throb.

"Well?" Judy stared at Renee, elbow on the table, chin resting on her hand.

"Well, what?" Renee looked directly at Judy. "You want to read it or something? Too bad—it's private." Although she smiled to soften the sarcasm, inside she seethed. *You've got a lot of nerve, giving me looks like that and acting like I would let you read my mail! Especially the letter I got today.* She sighed. "Russ says hi to you both. He had a great holiday and he's doing fine." *It's none of your damn business.* The letter from Russ had upset her; she wasn't ready to talk about it to anyone, not even Savannah. She concentrated on keeping her breaths measured as she slathered butter on her dinner roll.

"Well, what exciting things did he—"

"Hey, Judy," Savannah said, "how's your science teacher? Dr. Hayes? Didn't you have that class today?" Judy started talking enthusiastically about her favorite professor, and as she rambled on, Renee caught Savannah's eye and gave her a grateful half-smile.

Alleycat

When they first met, Renee wondered how she and Judy would get along. She was anxious to get to school and settle in, but her family all wanted to come along and it took longer than expected to get everyone in the car. By the time Renee arrived at the dorm, Judy had already unpacked most of her things. She had claimed the bed closest to the window; it was neatly made, covers pulled taut and tucked tightly. A decorative pillow placed in the exact center of the bed, corners squared, had **JUDY** embroidered across it. The desk was neatly arranged with matching pencil holder, paper tray, and a little catch-all box.

"You look settled in," Renee had said, smiling.

"I hope you don't mind that I took that bed." Judy paused as she put clothes on hangers. "I need the extra light."

"No, it's fine. I like being close to the door, actually." Renee opened her suitcase and began piling clothes in the drawers next to the closet. "Did your family stay long? I thought mine would never go."

Judy shrugged. "They stayed about thirty minutes. I didn't really want them to hang around."

"I was more than ready for mine to leave, too. I just want to get unpacked and check out the dorm, don't you?"

"I looked around a little." Judy squinted at Renee. "I got here at noon. That's when the letter said to check in. It's after two now. I was wondering if you were ever going to show up."

"My dad wanted us to all to go to church together one last time." Renee couldn't help rolling her eyes. "Like I'm going away forever or something. I'm a whole twenty minutes from home. Whoopee."

"Do they expect you to go home a lot?"

"Mm, not too often. How about yours?"

Judy shrugged. "Once a month, they said." She turned away from her closet and moved the few steps to her study area. She opened a typewriter case and popped the machine out, placed it in the middle of the desk and loaded it with a sheet of paper. "There's a bathroom in the center of each floor of the pod. That's what they call these buildings. We each get a locker in there. Eighteen girls have to share one bathroom. At least the showers are private. I don't think I could do showers again like we had in high school."

"This is where we live, not a locker room," Renee said. "Some of us poked around over here last spring when the dorm was being built but it was hard to tell what it would look like. I can't wait to see the new dining hall."

"I think we're required to attend the orientation at five, down in the lounge."

"It's not a requirement, but yeah, we should go. Meet some other people."

"You're the only person I know." Judy sounded morose.

"It'll be fine. You'll make friends." Renee emptied the suitcase and stowed it in the back of the closet. "Hey, your bed looks nice. That's a cool pillow. Did you make it?"

Judy grimaced. "No, I don't do needlework. My grandmother made it. It's kind of embarrassing, really." She reached over and yanked the pillow off the bed. "She came with us today so I had to put it out." She wrapped her arms around the pillow, looking unsure about what to do with it. Finally she stashed it in the corner. Sitting stiffly in the chair at her desk, she opened a paperback novel. "Do you mind if I read for awhile?"

Renee didn't know what to say. *Oh boy, this could be a long afternoon. I hope she makes some friends soon.* She concentrated on getting her bed made and desk organized.

At five o'clock they headed down the stairs, joining the other residents merging through the double doors into the ground floor lounge area. Judy headed straight for the buffet table set with an array of salads and sandwiches. Renee walked around the room, nodding hello to people she didn't know and chatting briefly with the ones she did. She noticed a girl on the far side of the lounge struggling to balance her plate while she tried to take a bite from an unwieldy sandwich. Renee grabbed a napkin and made her way through the crowd, having to zig-zag past clusters of coeds. The dorm housed over three hundred girls and most were milling around in this one room.

"How about a napkin? I'll be glad to hold the plate for you."

"Thank you. I thought I was going to drop the whole thing. What a horrible first impression on these girls."

Renee laughed. "As my mother would say, it only makes them feel better about their own awkwardness. Hi, I'm Renee."

"Hi, Renee. I'd shake your hand but—"

"Oh, no, please don't! We can do the formalities later."

"My name is Savannah. Yes, my parents wanted a Southern belle for a daughter." She giggled, an infectious sound that charmed Renee.

"Are you a freshman?" Renee asked.

"No, I transferred from Umpqua Community College. One year there was enough. I really wanted to get away from the Roseburg area and meet some new people. How about you?"

"I'm a sophomore, too, but I was here last year."

"So, go get yourself some food and see if you can look more poised than me."

Renee and Savannah found a spot on the floor to sit and talk. They discovered a mutual interest in the music of the Beatles, Bob Dylan, and Simon and Garfunkel, and a love of writing, learning they each kept a folder stuffed with poems and half-written short stories. Renee was thrilled to find a writing friend and she asked if she could read some of Savannah's work.

"How about right now?" Savannah asked. "This party is pretty boring. We could hang out in my room."

That was the beginning of regular evenings spent listening to their favorite songs and studying or working on writing projects. With different majors—Renee wanted to teach primary grades and Savannah was working toward a high school teaching endorsement in English—they had only one or two classes in common. Study sessions invariably ended up being talk sessions late into the night, chatter turning to whispers as their roommates slept.

People often mistook Renee and Savannah for sisters. Both stood just over five feet tall and had shoulder length, chestnut brown hair. Savannah's, thick and wavy, always appeared just brushed and neat while Renee frequently hid hers under a scarf or pulled up into a ponytail to keep the fine strands off her face. Renee liked the "wash'n'wear" style, as she called it, avoiding the frustration of curlers, hairdryers, and other trappings most women relied on. Wanting comfort over fashion, she favored jeans, baggy sweatshirts, and saddle shoes or Keds. She rarely used makeup but didn't need it—her clear skin had a natural glow and her dark-lashed, luminous blue eyes lit up her face. Her fingernails were ragged and bitten-down; she had tried to keep nail polish on them but ended up chewing it off so she no longer bothered with manicures. When she spoke, she gestured broadly, but her soft voice gave the impression of shyness.

Savannah liked to wear colorful dresses that showed off her slender frame. In the winter, she often wore tights with short wool skirts and knee-high leather boots. In her purse, a huge leather bag with multiple pockets and zippers, she carried lipstick, mascara, blush, a nail file, and a small can of hairspray. She hadn't gone out of the house without makeup on since she was sixteen. She had an open, friendly face highlighted by light blue eyes, a small, straight nose, and dimples in both cheeks. Her spirited smile was the first thing that caught people's attention and her bubbling laughter drew them to her. Renee liked Savannah's spontaneity, so different from her own quiet personality.

Judy and Renee shared a room on the second floor of Landers Hall; Savannah and her roommate Molly lived just below them on the first. Using a long length of cord and a spring clothespin, they rigged up a message system between their rooms. When Savannah wanted to send a note, she pounded on the ceiling, alerting Renee to check the string outside her window. Renee's stomps on the floor attracted Savannah's attention. The system saved them countless trips up and down the stairs.

Molly, a freshman, had a large circle of friends, many from high school, and she rarely spent time with Savannah, although the two got along well. For Renee, getting Judy as a roommate was simply the luck of the draw. The girl she had roomed with her freshman year moved off campus and Renee didn't know anyone who needed a roommate.

Renee's first impression of Judy proved true. Meticulous about how she sorted her things and arranged her areas of the room, Judy openly frowned at Renee's casual style. Renee didn't care if her books were lined up spine to shelf edge or if her pens were all capped and stored in a special container. She couldn't stand bedcovers tucked in at night so she simply smoothed out the top of the bed in the morning and left the ends loose. Judy used hospital corners and lined up the hem of the comforter with the floor. When Renee dropped her coat on the bed, Judy invariably hung it up for her, without a word, but her eyes revealed clear annoyance.

She didn't know many people and had a hard time making friends; she latched onto Renee and Savannah, hanging out with them as much as possible, whether she had an interest in what they were doing or not. They put up with Judy because it was easier than trying to avoid her. If they could have figured out a way to switch roommates and live together without hurting Judy's feelings, Renee and Savannah would have done it. But Renee balked against Savannah's suggestion that she simply move to another room, knowing it would impair Judy financially. And Savannah's attempts to convince Molly to trade with Renee were met with "you gotta be kidding" guffaws.

More of a night owl than a morning person, Renee liked to stay up late. Fortunately, Savannah had the same propensity and they enjoyed late-night walks around campus, just the two of them, at least a couple of times a week. It was one activity Judy declined to participate in which made it all the more appealing. And helped make their time with Judy more bearable.

As Judy wound down her monologue, Renee started stacking dishes on her tray. "Are we finished eating? Let's go for a walk. We can see if this town actually shovels snow off sidewalks." Judy scowled but didn't say anything.

"Great idea," Savannah said. "It'll be gone in a couple of days."

"That's right," Renee said. "Oregon rain will wash it away. Besides, the cold will help my headache."

Savannah watched Judy's face. "You don't have to come, Judy."

Judy forced a smile. "Oh, no, I want to. It'll be fun." She checked her pockets. "I don't have my gloves, though. Can we go back to the dorm first?"

"I don't have gloves, either," said Renee. "Come on, we won't be gone that long. If we take time to get gloves, we'll just talk ourselves out of going at all. Jeez, we hardly ever go out anywhere, especially after dinner. We need to live a little."

After dumping their trays, they headed out the front doors of the dining hall, buttoning up against the cold. They walked past the two dorms, Arbuthnot and Maaske, on Monmouth Avenue, then the student center. Scattered groups of people crisscrossed the courtyard to the street, voices floating across the crisp air. The three girls strolled across town, all the way to the highway, then looped back along side streets to the tiny city park facing Main Street. Drifts of crusted snow lay in heaps on either side of the sidewalk that cut through the park; streetlights glimmered in the growing darkness.

"I'm hungry," Judy said. "In fact, I'm starving. And I don't want popcorn. I'm so sick of popcorn—"

"Amen," Renee agreed. "Hot chocolate. French fries. Something like that."

"What?" Savannah said. "We just finished dinner."

"At least an hour ago," Renee reminded her. "Look how far we've walked. Besides, dinner was awful, as usual. It's no wonder that guy didn't want us to sneak him in—he's done that before and knows better."

"How's your headache?" Savannah asked. "You sure you don't want to just go home?"

"No, no, it's gone. I knew the walk would help. You want to go to the Duck-In?"

"Not me," Judy said. "There are hardly any seats inside and I'm cold. It's a drive-in, for pete's sake."

"Oh!" Savannah snapped her fingers. "I know! Let's go to that place on the corner, um, the Alley-something-or-other. What do you think? Have you been there, Renee?"

Renee shook her head. "No, Russ thought it looked like a dive. We never ate anywhere in Monmouth. He likes to eat in 'high-class restaurants.' This from a guy who carried a briefcase in high school!" She laughed. "But it's no worse than Crider's Variety across the street and we shopped there all the time. And that's a dark, strange little store."

"Crider's is dark and a little creepy," Judy said. "But shopping is different from eating."

"Three months we've lived in this dinky town and we've never been there," Savannah said. "Come on, let's check it out."

The Alleycat, a half block from the park, was on the corner of Main Street and Monmouth Avenue, which bisected the campus, and practically the only place in town that stayed open past nine o'clock on weeknights. The front façade was brick with eye-level windows facing both streets. Someone had painted a cheerful snow scene on the glass. Lights from the restaurant shone through the snowflakes. Under the front window was a wooden bench next to a tall, leafless tree rooted in a square of dirt surrounded by concrete. Double glass doors allowed passers-by to see inside the diner; each time one opened, noise poured out to the street and was abruptly cut off when the door swung shut. ALLEYCAT was painted in black and gray lettering on the upper part of the doors and a black cat perched on a fence decorated the lower section.

Alleycat

Inside, Renee, Savannah, and Judy placed their orders at the counter, then surveyed the brightly lit diner crowded with college students. Backless stools with red leatherette seats lined the counter of gold-flecked white Formica edged with polished chrome, and a few tables filled the center of the room. Fluorescent lights ran down the length of the restaurant and above the counter. Along the walls were booths, cozy with high-backed red seats. Each had a hanging lamp positioned overhead so the light pooled in the center of the table. Cigarette smoke floated upward, curling around the light fixtures, mixing with the smells of hot grease, strong coffee, and damp clothes. A group of boys had pushed two tables together and a raucous card game was in progress. The jukebox blared.

Savannah led the way to a big corner booth at the back, next to the jukebox. It had a large rectangular table and u-shaped bench, enough seating for six or seven people. Judy sat in the corner of the booth where she could see the restaurant and stretch her legs out along the seat. Renee settled with her back to the room and Savannah slid in next to her. A few minutes later a waitress delivered a large plate of french fries, a cup of coffee, and two steaming mugs of frothy hot chocolate.

Judy slid the coffee cup over in front of her and measured out a spoonful of sugar from the tall glass dispenser on the table. She added it to her coffee, then poured in a dollop of cream from the little pitcher the waitress had brought with the drinks.

"Hey," she said, stirring the coffee as she looked around the room. "How come we never came in here before? It's a great place. And no more expensive than the drive-in."

"It's sure a lot roomier," Renee said. She ate tiny bites of the whipped cream topping her cocoa. "You know, this is a nice table. Booth. Lots of space. It'd even be good for studying."

"Studying?" Judy shook her head. "It's too noisy in here." She squirted a puddle of ketchup next to the fries.

Renee turned slightly away from the table and scanned the room. "But those guys are studying," she said, pointing to another booth. She turned back to face Judy. "It must be quiet sometimes. We could give it a try. Not stuff that takes a lot of concentration, but there's always some kind of work we could do--you know, quizzing each other or something." She removed her glasses and hooked them on the neckline of her sweatshirt. She picked up a french fry, dipped it in the ketchup, and popped it in her mouth, chewing

21

slowly, enjoying the contrast of salty-hot potato and the ketchup's tangy, smooth sweetness.

"Sure," Savannah said. "Let's come back tomorrow night and see if it's any better. I can't study in the dorm and the library's too quiet." She slid out of the booth and went to the jukebox, now silent. After a moment she dropped in a quarter and punched in her selections—"Hey Jude" and "Let It Be" by the Beatles, and James Taylor's "Fire and Rain." As she turned back to the table, she started to say something but the words caught in her throat. Quickly she sat down next to Judy, eyes wide.

Leaning forward, concern on her face, Renee asked, "What's the matter?"

"Renee, he—he's here!"

"What! You're kidding." Renee shifted in the seat and tried to look discreetly around the room.

"What are you talking about?" Judy demanded. "Who's here?"

"Should we say anything to him?" Savannah whispered.

"Wait," Renee whispered back. "Where is he?" She grabbed her glasses and put them on.

"You wait," Judy said in a loud voice. "Who's here?"

Savannah put a finger to her lips. "Shh. The guy we told you about." She peeked over the top of the seats. "Four tables away. This side. See, by himself."

Judy craned her neck to get a good look at the lone figure. "I don't think he even knows where he is. He's just sitting there and turning his coffee cup around and around. He *is* good looking."

Renee laughed. "Told you so."

"He looks very preoccupied," Judy stated emphatically. "You shouldn't bother him."

"Well, you're probably right," Savannah said with a loud sigh. "He does look like he wants to be alone."

They chatted for awhile, listening to the music that played almost non-stop as other customers fed the jukebox. The card players left and the restaurant quieted. Renee stretched and yawned. She retied the red bandana covering her hair, fluffing her bangs out around the front.

"We should probably go," she said. "It's nine o'clock already."

"Wow," Judy said. "We stayed a long time. I have to get a paper written for tomorrow." Standing, she swung her coat around and pushed her arms into the sleeves. "Just a one pager, thank goodness."

On the way out, Savannah murmured a hello to the man. He raised his head and smiled.

"Good evening, ladies. Did you have a good dinner?"

Renee nodded. "Naturally. Gourmet cafeteria food." She paused then said, "Are you thinking hard?" Instantly, she regretted her comment. *What a dumb thing to say. My God. He must think I'm an idiot.*

He smiled. "Oh, just dreaming." He didn't get up, he didn't ask them to sit down, and he didn't introduce himself. Feeling awkward, the girls said good-bye. When they were almost to the door, he called out, "Coming in tomorrow?"

"Maybe," Savannah replied, a wide smile deepening her dimples.

When they were outside and the door had closed behind them, Renee and Savannah dropped onto the bench and looked at each other, giggling. Judy ignored them and started walking down the street toward campus, but stopped when she realized the others had not followed her.

"Oh my," Savannah said. "I can't believe we saw him again."

"So, Savannah, was that an invitation to come back?"

"I think so!"

"Should we?"

Judy said sourly, "You know you'll go back."

"You want to go, too, Judy, you know you do," Savannah said. Standing, she straightened her coat and patted her hair. As they started walking toward campus, she said to Judy, "I heard you say he's cute!"

"Well, I said good-looking. I don't know if I would call him cute."

"Debonair, maybe?" Renee asked. "Like James Bond."

"Ooh, what if he's a private investigator?" Savannah stopped and looked at the others. "He's been hired by somebody's parents to find out what kind of clandestine events are going on at this college—you know, war protests and such."

They all burst out laughing.

Judy said, "I don't think OCE is aware that a war is going on. Have you ever seen anyone preaching at the Free Speech Platform? And come on, they're showing 'Born Free' at the campus movie night this week. I doubt they would even show 'The Graduate' at

23

this school."

"You're right," Renee said, grinning. "It might give us innocent students too many ideas."

"So we'll go back to the Alleycat after dinner?" Savannah asked.

"You bet," Renee said.

"Okay, sure." Judy resigned herself to the inevitable. "We can at least study there." She wrinkled her nose. "Maybe."

The next evening, armed with books and notes, Renee, Savannah, and Judy entered the restaurant, their eyes sweeping the room in anticipation. But they saw no dashing pipe smokers.

Savannah sighed. "Hmm. Most likely his idea of a joke."

"Yeah," Judy agreed. "So what. Just some brainless guy."

Renee looked at them. "What do we care anyway? We don't even know anything about him. He was probably just passing through and he's already left town."

"Man, he was cute!" Savannah said, then chuckled as Renee pretended to be shocked. "Well, he was. And intriguing, too."

"Cute, available guys are hard to find, that's the truth," Renee said. "But you're right, he was more than cute. Sort of mysterious, huh?"

"Oh God, I've fallen for someone I'll never see again!"

Judy poked Savannah in the arm. "You're so dopey. Come on, let's get something to drink."

After ordering coffee and a side order of buttered toast to share, they settled in the corner booth. Although the restaurant was not crowded or noisy, no one mentioned studying and they left their books piled on one side of the table. Judy chose three songs on the jukebox, all Gordon Lightfoot selections, and the three girls talked for the next hour.

Suddenly the quiet was broken as three young men burst through the door. They paused at the counter, said something that made the waitress blush, then looked around the half-empty restaurant. The tallest one, *him,* pointed toward the girls, spoke to the other two guys and they nodded, following him to the corner table.

"Got room for us?"

With a great commotion, they crowded into the booth from both sides as the girls shifted to the middle. Savannah clutched Renee's hand under the table and they looked at each other, smiling.

Alleycat

"We never got as far as names, did we?" the pipe smoker asked as he removed a gray fedora and set it carefully on the corner ledge behind the booth. "I'm Cal, this is Alex, that's Neil."

Renee ignored the twinge of anxiety that fluttered in her stomach, determined to have a good time. *It's just one night. I'm allowed to have fun for one night.* Pulling her glasses off, she fumbled in her purse for the case. She kept the purse on her lap and her hands folded on top of it. Trying to look casual, she studied the boys. Cal had replaced his pipe with an unfiltered Camel cigarette. Again, he was dressed nicely. With his dress slacks, button-down shirt, tie, hat, and overcoat, he resembled an ad from *GQ*. In contrast, Neil looked typically "hippie." He had a pale mustache and crinkly sideburns, with frizzy, reddish-brown shoulder length hair. A torn Army fatigue jacket covered a blue work shirt, patches adorned faded jeans, his brown hiking boots were scuffed and worn. He gestured wildly with his cigarette as he talked, his voice husky and loud. Renee turned her attention to Alex. *How in the world did three people so different ever get together?* He wore black Converse tennis shoes, jeans, a dark sweater, and a black leather jacket. His wheat-colored hair was cut short with a hint of curl above his broad forehead. His deep-set gray eyes took in the scene with a steady gaze. He nodded once when introduced, his expression reserved. Renee didn't know whether to smile at him or not. *Is he shy? Or wishing he was somewhere else?* She chose the smile and he smiled back. *Nice. He's just a serious guy, I guess.*

"You're students?" Savannah asked.

"Yep," Cal answered. "Sophomores."

"Where are you guys from?" Judy asked.

"Portland," Alex said.

"Hey, I'm from Portland," Judy exclaimed. "What high school did you go to?"

He shook his head. "Not here. My dad's retired military. We came from Gitmo—Guantanamo Bay—in Cuba."

"I'm from Cow Valley," said Cal with a western twang. "Good ole Cow-vallis High."

"Cuba!" Judy said, ignoring Cal. "That's neat. Did you like it there?"

Alex shrugged. "It was okay. Hot."

"I've never been anywhere," she said. "I wish I could travel to another country. Or even around this country. You're so lucky." She sighed loudly, a wistful look on her face. "Where else have you been?"

"Germany, Italy, a bunch of states. Not so many other countries." He looked at Neil. "Tell 'em where you've been, Sparks."

"Sparks?" Judy asked.

"His last name," Savannah said, shaking her head. "You know guys do that, call each other by their last names."

"Actually, it's my nickname. Given to me after I set off cherry bombs in the girls can in high school." He grinned. "Worth every day of suspension. It *is* my last name, too. I just got lucky."

"Well, where have you been?" Judy asked.

"I was born in Canada when my parents were on a trip," Neil said, "and we used to vacation in Mexico every couple of years. When my sister graduated from Reed College, we went to Hawaii. That was four years ago, I think. I traveled around Europe for a month after high school, backpacking, staying in hostels, all that."

"That's a dream I have," Judy said, elbows on the table, chin resting on her clasped hands. "Travel to Europe." She closed her eyes, a dreamy look on her face.

"So what kind of classes are you guys taking?" Savannah asked, sitting back, sipping her coffee.

"I'm majoring in theater and communication," Cal said.

"Yeah, theater of the absurd," said Neil, laughing. "And communication with chicks." He looked the girls over. "You can get a lot of your course work done right here, man. I'm sure these girls will cooperate."

"Neil's taking classes in anything he can pass," Alex said. "He's not too serious about school."

"Speak for yourself! I'm a very serious student. I can't help it if this school doesn't offer classes in enlightenment."

Judy said, "I'm studying psychology but I might change to science. I really like Dr. Hayes, my physics prof. How about you, Alex?"

"Accounting or business administration," Alex answered. "I'm looking at practicality."

"Oh, that's smart." Judy nodded in approval. "There are always jobs for accountants."

"Theater, huh?" Savannah leaned toward Cal. "Have you been in any of the college plays?"

"I played Felix Ungar in 'The Odd Couple' last year. The drama department is putting on 'Harvey' spring term."

"I'm trying out for the part of the rabbit," Neil said.

"Good part for you," said Cal. "Then no one has to look at your ugly face."

"Too bad you didn't get sliced a little lower by that Frisbee last year. It might have improved your looks," Alex said drily.

"What Frisbee?" Savannah asked. "What happened?"

"The dorm—we lived in Maaske Hall—has long hallways," Cal explained. "We played Frisbee handball every chance we got."

"The idea was to throw the Frisbee—" Alex started.

"—as hard as possible," Neil interrupted, "bouncing it off the walls, trying to get it to the other end of the hall."

"You get eight or nine guys in those narrow halls and it's bound to get interesting," Cal said.

"Drunk guys," Neil clarified.

"Only some of us," Alex said, glancing sideways at the girls. "Not *every*body."

"Oh, yeah, of course," Savannah said. "Probably not any of *you*."

"That's right," Neil said. "Some of us were high on other, shall we say, intoxicants."

"What were you on that night?" Cal asked. "Magic mushrooms? Black Beauties?"

"Nah. Just some primo weed. The usual."

Cal said, "Norm Gray had this Frisbee and shot it down the hall to somebody coming out of the bathroom. He yells, 'Catch!' and the guy threw it back pretty wild."

"It hit one of the lights and broke it," Alex said. "Pieces of glass everywhere."

"Doors open, guys come out, there's all this yelling and running," Neil said. "We pushed the broken pieces against the wall and the Frisbee started flying."

"After a couple a minutes, Norm thinks he hears the housemother coming," Neil said. "He yells, 'Duck and cover!' and everybody dives back in their rooms. Doors slam. Dead silence."

"But nothing happened so we all went back in the hall and resumed the game," Cal said.

"We set up rules—the disk had to hit the wall at least once before it could be touched," Alex explained. "One guy stood at each end of the hall, guard positions. It was pretty much a free-for-all for the rest of us. If the Frisbee got past the other team by bouncing off the walls and ceiling, a point was scored."

"Neil played center," said Cal. "Alex and I were guards."

"Not much of one," Neil said. "You'd never dive for the disk."

"Yeah, yeah," Cal said. "I'm not a fool, like some people at the table."

"One guy spins the Frisbee so fast and hard it ricochet's from one side to the other, back and forth," Alex said. "Nobody knew where it was going to hit next."

"Then BAM! The damn thing cracks right into my forehead. It bounces up, hits another light, then—"

"Frisbee?" Cal snorted. "You ran into a doorjamb. You were knocked out and we played a man down. I had—"

"The hell you say, I finished that—"

"It wasn't a Frisbee or a doorjamb." Alex spoke with authority, his arms out. "It was the light fixture. Neil jumped to block the oncoming Frisbee. His hand busted through the light and the whole thing crashed down, splitting his skull. He crumpled to the floor, but at the last second, dazed, gushing blood, he reached up, grabbed the Frisbee, and saved the point."

Everyone stared, mouths open.

"Ooohhh, that's good, damn good." Neil slapped the table. "Light fixture, yeah. It was the light fixture."

Alex nodded, face serious. "That's right. The light fixture."

Cal palmed his face, rolling his eyes. "You see what I put up with? These guys wouldn't know the truth if they stepped in it. Let me tell you the real stor—"

"Shit, were you even there?" Neil shoved Cal. Cal shoved back, knocking Neil against Savannah. "Hey, watch it, buddy." He faked a karate chop and Cal dodged.

Savannah pulled Renee out of the way. "Judy, move over!" Judy slid close to Alex, making more room for Renee. Savannah and Renee giggled and shrieked, trying to keep clear of the boys' flailing arms.

Cal said, "Neil, ya got brains like Caesar."

Neil glowered. "Whaddya mean? He's dead!"

"I know, ya knucklehead."

"Remind me to kill you when we're done here," Neil said in a loud voice.

Alleycat

"I'll make a note of it." Cal turned to Alex. "Got a scrap o' paper on ya, friend?"

"Nah, just knock his brains out. They ain't worth nothing anyhow."

"This is gettin' on my noives," Neil said. He stretched across the table and smacked Alex in the forehead. "Why don't you get a toupee with some brains in it?"

Alex jumped out of the booth, grabbed Cal by the shoulder, and said, "Let's scram! This clown's a wise guy."

Cal grabbed Neil's arm and the three tumbled to the floor, Neil face down, legs still in the booth.

Savannah wiped tears from her eyes as she watched the boys scramble to their feet, dust themselves off, and shake hands, over and over until they began throwing fake punches. "Oh—my—gosh," she said, laughing. "That's straight out of *The Three Stooges*! How do you guys do that?"

"Boredom," Cal said, as the boys sat back in the booth. "Nothing to do on Saturday afternoons in the winter."

Realizing their table had drawn attention from other customers, Renee looked around warily. No familiar faces among the mostly college-aged crowd. Surprisingly, no one appeared annoyed with the racket from the corner booth, maybe because noise was common in the diner. She began to relax a little, wishing she could be as carefree as Savannah, whose laugh rang out cheerfully. It didn't take long for Neil to slide his arm around Savannah's shoulder, pulling her closer to him. Suppressing a smile, she playfully pushed him away. He raised both hands in surrender and she giggled. Renee glanced at Judy who watched the interaction with a solemn look on her face. *It's okay. Relax!* Folding her hands under the table, Renee sat back in the booth. She cleared her throat, then smiled as she looked the boys over.

"I see you guys all planned your wardrobes carefully," she said. "We have the hippie, the lawyer, and the biker."

"Whoa—she talks!" Cal said. "I was beginning to wonder."

Blushing, Renee ducked her head. "Well…"

"It's great," Cal said. "I'm just glad you aren't a mute or something."

"Or one of those people secretly recording the conversation," Alex said. "That would be a drag."

"CIA operative," Neil said, lowering his voice to a whisper.

29

"Hide your stash, Cal."

Cal laughed. "Get your agencies right, man. CIA doesn't care about weed."

"Man, that's a relief," Neil said, wiping his brow in an exaggerated gesture. He cocked his head toward Renee. "Now, what did you call us?"

With a grin, Renee repeated her statement. "The lawyer, the hippie, and the biker."

Neil nodded. "Yep, we never go anywhere without consulting each other first." He struck a model-like pose, one hand arched in the air, the other on his shoulder, head back, lips in an exaggerated pout.

"And sometimes we even switch around and I go as the hippie," said Cal with a deadpan expression.

"That would be a stretch!" Renee chuckled, feeling the tension in her back and shoulders lessening. *It's okay.*

"But I'm always the biker guy." Alex tried to keep a straight face, but a smile broke through.

"I'm glad there's something predictable here," Savannah said. She stared at Cal, then smiled, her dimples deepening as her smile widened. "Ah," she said, tapping the tip of her nose with a forefinger, then pointing at him, "I've figured out who you remind me of. Philip Marlowe. Have you read Raymond Chandler's books?"

Cal grinned. "You know how Dylan emulated Woody Guthrie? Well, I do like Marlowe. He's kind of my ideal, I guess. Sophisticated, chivalrous, and tough."

"You could do worse," Renee said. "Savannah's right. You look like Philip Marlowe. At least, you dress like him."

Savannah reached behind Cal, picked up the hat and put it on, adjusting it so it sat at an angle, her hair fluffed out around it.

"It looks a lot better on you than him," Neil said, nodding in approval. He slid his arm around Savannah's shoulders. She pulled back to look at his face, then smiled and leaned a little into his side.

Cal tipped his head and looked Savannah over, squinting slightly and pursing his lips. "It does look good on you."

"I love *The Big Sleep* with Bogart and Bacall," she said.

"I do, too," said Cal. "I've seen it several times. I own most of Chandler's books."

"Maybe—"

"You could borrow one sometime?" Cal finished Savannah's sentence. She nodded. "Sure. I'll bring one for you next time I go home."

"How did you guys all hook up together, anyway?" Renee asked.

"We knew each other from the dorm last year," Alex explained. "Cal and I talked about getting a place off-campus but he wasn't sure he was coming back to OCE."

"Yeah, I had some big plans that didn't pan out."

Savannah looked at him curiously. "Like what? I mean, what's more important than school?" Her burst of giggles caused a few heads to turn in their direction.

With a rueful chuckle, Cal said, "That's pretty much what my parents said, too. But Alex had already found an apartment with another guy so I figured I was on my own."

Alex picked up the story. "My buddy couldn't scrape up the dough for tuition and rent so he had to drop out of school. I called Cal and asked him if he was still interested. We ran into Neil at a party—"

"I needed a pad and they offered their place," Neil said.

"The only downer," Cal said, "is that it's a one bedroom. A little crowded."

"It works out okay," Alex said.

"So you were already friends," Judy said. "I can sort of see that." She squinted at the three boys, then shook her head.

Cal grinned at her. "Sometimes you gotta find friends where you can." He slapped Alex on the back.

"That's right, man," Neil said. "It's almost impossible to find a place after the term starts." He lit his cigarette, inhaled deeply. "Alex, man, you know I love you."

"Yeah, I know, I know." Alex looked around the table. "Anybody else need a place to crash?"

Laughing, the girls shook their heads. "In a one bedroom apartment?" Renee said. "You're kidding, right?"

"I thought girls like coziness," Cal said.

"We're stuck in the dorm for the year," Judy said. "You know how if you pay up front you get kind of a discount. I need to save money where I can."

"I'd move in with you," Savannah said, "but Molly would kill me."

"Who's Molly?" Neil asked. "Hey, if she's a foxy chick, bring her along next time."

"Is that all you care about? Yes, she's cute and she has a boyfriend. That's all you need to know." She glanced at Renee, rolling her eyes. "One track mind, huh?"

"But who is she?" Neil persisted.

"Savannah's roommate," said Judy.

"Lucky chick," Neil said, with a smirk.

At midnight the restaurant employees began closing up and the group in the corner booth reluctantly bundled into coats and hats, then made their way outside.

"We'll walk you to the dorm," Neil said.

Judy spoke quickly. "Oh, you don't have to do that."

"Yes, we do," Cal said.

"Too early to go home anyway," Alex said.

"You sure?" Savannah asked. "It's a ways."

"What? Half a mile? That's nothing," Alex said. "That's a three minute jog."

"Well, okay," Renee said. "Thank you." *Russ would be more bothered if they let us go home by ourselves.* Hands in her pockets, she ran her thumb over the diamond.

"No way would we let you walk the streets alone," Cal said. "In spite of what you may think, we can be gentlemen."

"Besides," Neil said, "it means we can spend more time with you."

The six of them strolled slowly, walking on the sidewalk and the edge of the street, stretched across the road in a straggly line. The night was quiet, the big buildings lining the main avenue running through campus mere shadows in the dark. Haloed streetlights glowed; a light mist dampened the cold air scented with a faint aroma of wood smoke. The only snow left lay in small, dirty patches under trees.

Cal initiated an impression of W.C. Fields and Savannah quickly picked up the tone of his act and responded with Mae West. They kept the parody going as they crossed the campus, getting louder and more risqué, with the others offering encouragement by cheering and applauding. When they reached Landers Hall, Savannah, slightly out of breath but grinning broadly, held up her hand. "Stop! I can't do any more!"

"Well, my dear," Cal said in his strong Fields' voice, "'Then

Alleycat

quit. There's no point in being a damn fool about it.'" He bowed, one arm sweeping in a deep arc across his body and out to the side. "And that is a direct quote from the great man himself."

"You're good," Savannah said. "That was fun."

"You're good, too. I'm impressed."

The group stood chatting in a loose circle in the dorm parking lot; no one seemed to want the night to end. Between the bright moon and the parking lot lights, the night was almost transformed into day. As Renee swept a few stray ends of hair off her forehead, Cal noticed the diamond on her left hand.

"So you're all set for the little white cottage with a picket fence, two adorable children, preferably a boy and a girl, a dog and a cat and a loving husband."

Renee forced a laugh, feeling a little unsettled. "Well, the husband part anyway."

Neil eyed her curiously. "Where is the lucky man?"

"Oh, Russ is in Japan," Judy piped up. "He left in August, right, Renee? He's coming back in July. He's in an exchange program at some college in Tokyo. What's the name of it, Renee?"

"Waseda University." *But he's coming home early, in March.* She still hadn't told anyone. His last letter was in her purse. Block printing on thin airmail paper. Short and to the point: I CAN'T STAND BEING AWAY FROM YOU. THIS ISN'T WORKING OUT.

Savannah reached out and squeezed Renee's arm reassuringly. "July isn't so long now."

Renee nodded. "Right. Not so long at all."

Neil looked around at each of them. "Any other confessions?"

"Uh, yeah, as a matter of fact," Cal said, incorporating an exaggerated southern drawl into his voice and giving Neil a narrow look. "I de-spise long haired hippie freaks and I don't like the looks of you!" He pushed Neil, palm against his chest, knocking him off balance. "Cain't let perverts out to bother and mo-lest purty young thangs—" he smiled charmingly over his shoulder, "—like y'all." He gripped Neil's shirt in one fist and shook him roughly. "Get outta here 'fore I bust yer head in!"

Neil shoved Cal's hand away, bowed comically, and jogged off across the parking lot, saying over his shoulder, "My apologies, ladies. Good night."

Cal rubbed his hands together. "There. One more weirdo taken care of, eh, Alex?"

Alex chuckled when he saw the looks on the girls' faces. "Ah, Neil's cool."

"He's all right," Cal said. "A hippie, but cool." He grinned. "We ought to get going. It was nice seeing you again." Winking at Renee, he added, "Sleep tight."

"See you around," Alex said as he and Cal headed across the parking lot.

The girls called out good night and went quietly into the dorm lobby. The resident at the desk looked up from the book in front of her and said hello. No one else was around. A large file box on the counter held individual cards for residents to sign in and out, indicating where they would be when off-campus, a requirement that, as sophomores, they all resented. At least they didn't have a curfew like the freshmen. They pulled their cards, quickly scrawled their names, then went back outside. Seven buildings, called pods, faced the center courtyard. One had the upstairs and downstairs lounges, mailboxes, office, housemother's apartment, laundry room, and storage areas. The other six pods had outside staircases leading to the second and third floors. Individual rooms opened off inside corridors.

"That was crazy," Savannah whispered as they stood in the courtyard.

"Shh." Renee stifled a giggle, covering her mouth with her hand. "Speak for yourself, Mae!"

Savannah blushed. "I know, I know. I'm not sure where that came from! And, man, for a second I thought Cal meant it about Neil. That was pretty funny. Jeez, I was cracking up!"

"Me, too!" Renee said.

"Sick humor if you ask me," Judy said as she started for the stairs.

"Oh, come on," Renee said. "You're not serious. They were only laughing at themselves. I thought it was hilarious."

Judy frowned. "I'll tell you what I think. Alex is the only decent one of the bunch."

"Looked more like a hood to me," Renee muttered.

"What did you say?" Judy cocked her head, brow furrowed, and gave Renee a sideways look.

"Never mind. Come on, let's go up." They waved goodnight to Savannah and trotted up the staircase, Judy leading the way.

In their cramped room, Judy sat cross-legged on her bed,

Alleycat

watching as Renee gathered the things she needed for the bathroom down the hall: a flannel nightgown, her laundry bag, locker key, and slippers.

"Renee," Judy said. "About tonight…" Her voice trailed off. She looked straight at Renee, questions clear in her eyes.

"It was fun, wasn't it?"

"I don't know." Judy hesitated. "I guess it was okay. What about Russ? He won't mind that you went to a restaurant with—"

Renee interrupted. "He's in Japan, having his own fun. Besides, we didn't go there *with* them." She gave Judy a quizzical look. "Do you think there's a problem?"

"No, no, not that I know of. If you feel okay—"

"I need to take a shower," Renee said. "Don't wait up for me. I have my room key." She held up the OCE wolf mascot key ring.

Judy let out a loud sigh. "Okay. It's nearly one o'clock anyway." She unbuttoned her blouse, stood, and slipped out of her cords. "I have an early class on Thursdays so I can't go to breakfast with you tomorrow."

"Yeah, I know that. I'm sleeping in. My first class isn't until ten."

"See you at dinner?"

"Yeah, sure, I guess."

Judy hung her blouse in the closet and pulled her nightshirt on. After checking her alarm clock, she sat back down on the bed. "Well, good night." She switched the lamp on and opened a paperback book. Renee turned off the overhead light as she left.

The hot shower steamed around Renee and she stood in the spray for a long time, glad to be alone. She smiled, thinking of the evening, and the afternoon before, when she and Savannah first met Cal. But she had felt Judy watching her closely, disapprovingly. She knew Russ would disapprove as well. Why? Did neither of them want her to have other friends? Sometimes she felt absolutely stifled by Judy. She knew Russ would like Judy and vice versa—both of them were studious, serious, and yes, she had to admit it, they liked to be in charge. *Why do I end up with people like that? Do I want to be bossed around? What's wrong with me?*

Feeling a sense of disquiet, she thought about the friends she and Russ had together their freshman year at OCE. None of them were just her friends. His dorm-mates and their girlfriends, plus Kim, Renee's roommate, comprised their `social group. She rarely saw them since he'd left. She and Kim had never been close and when Kim moved off-campus, they didn't keep in touch. *So I'm making my own friends now. I'm sorry if they aren't the kind you'd choose. Just some crazy guys who had an audience. We had fun, that's all.*

She rubbed a bar of soap across a washcloth, working up a lather. The soap broke in two and dropped from her hand. Squatting to retrieve it, she instead sat on the shower floor, letting the water rain over her head and shoulders. *He's coming back in March. Two months.* She rubbed tears away with a forearm. *Don't cry.*

Rising, she soaped her body and washed her hair. She stepped out of the shower, dried off quickly, and smoothed some gardenia-scented lotion on her legs and elbows before putting on her nightgown. After brushing her teeth, she wound her damp hair up into a knot on top of her head, securing it with several bobby pins. She unlocked the door to her room and entered quietly. The room was dark, Judy fast asleep.

In bed, Renee turned on her side and pulled the covers up over her shoulder. For a long time she lay awake. A sliver of streetlight sliced across her face, shining directly in her eyes. She threw her arm across her forehead to blot it out, and gritted her teeth. Unable to get comfortable in the narrow bed, she tossed back and forth, finally curling into a loose ball. She closed her eyes and inhaled deeply, trying to clear her thoughts. Images flashed in front of her, pictures of Russ interspersed with ones of Cal, Neil, and Alex. Confidence and reason versus ludicrous entertainment. Russ, so sure of things, in control, life planned out.

Russ and Renee are stretched out side by side on the bed in his room at his parents' house, a quilt covering them. "There are too many people in the world, you know," Russ says. "It's totally irresponsible to bring more babies into the mess our parents made."

Renee sits up, pulling the covers up to her shoulders. She can feel the beat of her heart quickening. More than anything, she wants children. Russ knows this. He knows it. She stays quiet, trying to keep her body soft, still.

"We'll find children to adopt," he continues, looking up at the ceiling, arms crossed behind his head. "From China, Africa, Russia, Mexico, Appalachia. We can offer them so much more than they can get otherwise. Seven. We can manage seven."

Adoption. That's good. But...Renee feels an emptiness building in her gut. She does not move, or talk, or think. In a moment, Russ pulls her back down and begins kissing her neck, running his hands over her back, breasts, thighs. "We'll be good parents. Just like mine."

She had made her choice. Russ was her fiancé. With him gone she felt adrift, without direction or purpose. But there was another sense, something she couldn't identify, a vague feeling of uncertainty. She forced herself to ignore it, willing her thoughts toward sleep. Her dreams were disjointed and confusing; she woke up feeling tired.

~~ 3 ~~

Renee and Savannah met in the courtyard in the morning, ready for breakfast. There was a heavy drizzle, the air frigid. Renee pulled her glasses off and stuck them in her jacket pocket to keep them dry. She had forgotten her hat in her haste to get out of the dorm and her hair whipped across her cheeks as she ducked under the umbrella Savannah carried. Savannah held it higher, trying to protect both of them but the wind had kicked up and rain blew sideways, spattering their faces. It was impossible to talk. They raced up the ramp to the dining hall and as soon as the glass doors slammed shut behind them, both girls started talking at once. Laughing, Renee gestured for Savannah to continue. "Go ahead."

Savannah spoke quickly. "Can you believe what happened last night?"

Renee shook her head, a wide smile making crinkles around her eyes. "It was so funny!"

"That Frisbee story was wild! Oh, don't you think Cal is good-looking?"

"Uh huh, he's very cute!"

"What do you think of the other two?" Savannah asked. "I mean, Alex is cute, too, but he looks kind of dangerous."

"Yeah, he does. And Neil! Talk about 'Russian hands and Roman fingers'!"

Savannah laughed and nodded. "Yes, he is very into touching."

"Do you like him?"

"Ha! It was one night. Crazy but fun." She smoothed her hair into place, then extracted her compact from the jumble of things in her purse and quickly checked her makeup. Satisfied, she followed Renee to the cafeteria counter. Picking up trays, they moved along the line choosing from cereal, muffins, fruit, eggs. Selecting a small table near a window, they settled in the straight-backed wooden chairs and began eating.

"They're really different, huh?" Renee asked. "I just about died when Cal said 'Sleep tight.' The way he said it was so—

Alleycat

suggestive!"

Savannah nodded. "Oh gosh, it was! And that whole W.C. Fields thing!" She grinned. "It was fun, though. Do you think we should go back to the Alleycat?"

Renee ate a couple of bites of her blueberry muffin, thinking about the night before. "I want to. Do you?"

"Absolutely! I really had a blast. I just wonder about you—do you feel okay about it?"

"I didn't sleep well, if that's what you mean." Renee put her elbows on the table, rested her chin on her clasped hands. With a sigh, she said, "Russ wouldn't like me going back."

"I figured. That's a problem. But Renee, I have to say..." Savannah's voice drifted off. She looked at her friend, considering how to continue. "I haven't seen you so jazzed in all the months I've known you. Last night you were different. It was good to see you like that."

Renee sat quietly. "I had a good time. It was fun, being sort of flirty and goofy. Maybe it's because we were hanging out with guys, you know?" She sipped her juice. "Not that I *should* be around boys. I mean, I have a boyfriend. But you want a boyfriend, right? Are you attracted to Neil?"

With an amused snort, Savannah wrinkled her nose. "Sure. I'm interested in getting to know him better." She shook her head. "But, I don't know. I just want to have fun. And I want you to have fun. It's really okay, you know."

"Well, they know I'm engaged so they won't be trying to score with me. And Cal and Neil obviously like you."

"They're just typical guys." Savannah laughed. "I know my limits, my line. It won't get crossed."

"You sure?"

"No problem. I've sort of been on hiatus lately because I haven't met anyone intriguing enough." Savannah sighed, watching Renee's face as she exhaled. "But I don't want to put *you* in a tough spot just because I want to go."

Renee sat back in her chair, chewing on a fingernail. After a moment she said, "It's not like I'm going out on a date. Russ probably wouldn't understand, but I need some fun, right?"

"Yes, you do. Of course, I haven't met Russ, but I think if you're worried about his reactions, well—"

"No, it's okay. He just has a way of deciding things and I can't help wondering how he would handle this. He'd probably fit right in with Cal and Neil." *Yeah. In a million years.*

"It's up to you, Renee. The last thing I want to do is cause you problems."

"No, I mean yes, let's go back." She chuckled, a slight blush coloring her cheeks. "I want to see them again."

"Hey, I have to give Cal his hat! I forgot last night." Savannah winked at Renee. "Cool hat, huh?"

"Yeah," Renee agreed. "I had a hat like that once. It was my grandfather's. Russ didn't like it when I wore it."

"That's weird. Why?"

"I don't know. He seemed bothered by it, though, so I never wore it again. Wish I had it now!"

"Oh ho, you'd wear it now that he's gone, huh? You women's libber!"

Renee laughed. "Yeah, I can stand up for myself just fine." Turning serious, she said, "I want to go to the Alleycat tonight but I don't want to make a point of telling Judy. She has her study group. Besides, I don't think she's really interested, know what I mean?"

"She seemed kind of bugged about last night, didn't she?"

"I couldn't tell for sure. She's usually pretty standoffish when we meet new people. She seemed interested in what was going on for awhile, and then she kind of checked out. Did you notice that?"

"Yeah. As soon as the guys started with their outrageous stories, she got quiet."

"She was fine as long as she was asking questions and giving information—like about Russ." Renee sighed. "And I didn't feel like talking when we got to the room. She started to question me as soon as we closed the door. I left and took a shower. She was asleep when I got back."

"What was it she said about Alex?"

"That he's the only 'normal' one. Good Lord! He doesn't seem any more normal than the other two! He's kind of scary-looking with that serious face and the leather jacket and all those black clothes."

"He does look like a biker. Or a beatnik." Savannah snapped her fingers. "Hey, Daddy-o! Remember Dobie Gillis and Maynard G. Krebs? Did you watch that TV show?"

"Oh my gosh! Of course!" Renee giggled. "No, he's nothing like Maynard. Alex might be the real thing!"

Alleycat

"Maybe we'll find out tonight."

After her last class at three, Renee went back to the dorm to change clothes and put her books away. Wanting to do a load of laundry before dinner, she collected her dirty clothes and stuffed them in a pillowcase. As she passed by her desk, she felt Russ's eyes following her. She stopped and picked up his photograph, his senior year portrait in a gold-tone frame. His dark hair was cut a little long, neatly combed from a side part. He wore a white shirt, black tie, and a black suit coat—the required attire for senior pictures. In her own, she had on a black sweater and string of pearls. All supplied by the photographer. Russ did not smile in the picture and his eyes stared straight at the camera. *Intense. He looks like he's in perfect control.*

From the middle drawer of her desk she took a stack of airmail letters. She removed the one on the bottom of the pile and sat at her desk to read it. It was the first letter she had received after he left.

> I THINK LIFE HERE WILL BE INTERESTING. WE HAD A WEEK OF ORIENTATION BEFORE GETTING OUR HOUSING ASSIGNMENTS. I COULDN'T EVEN TAKE TIME TO WRITE TO YOU. I GOT YOUR LETTER, THOUGH, AND YOUR PHOTO. THANK YOU. I WISH YOU HAD SENT A BIGGER PICTURE, LESS CONSERVATIVE. YOU NEED TO FIND SOMEONE TO TAKE ONE OF YOU IN YOUR BIKINI. IT'S GOING TO BE HELL BEING AWAY FROM YOU.

Hell because you can't control what I'm doing? She had never asked anyone to take a photo of her, in her bikini or anything else. He reminded her a couple of times, then seemed to forget about it. *Or maybe he gave up.* She folded the letter and placed it back in the stack. Her hand shook as she put the letters back in her desk. *When he comes back...*

On a small piece of paper she wrote, **Savannah—I'm doing laundry. Want to come? Renee.** She clipped the note to the string in the window, dropped it down, stomped on the floor twice, and waited. No answer. With a sigh, she swung the pillowcase over her shoulder and left the room.

At five-thirty the three girls met in the cafeteria for dinner.

Renee and Savannah purposely did not bring up the subject of the night before, but steered the conversation to other topics. After dinner, as they pulled on jackets and gloves, Judy asked Savannah and Renee about their evening plans.

"Are you going back to the dorm? I'm meeting my study group in the library at six-thirty. I don't know how late I'll be tonight."

Savannah's eyes met Renee's. Renee raised her eyebrows and gave her head a tiny shake. Savannah nodded, saying to Judy, "We might go for a walk or maybe we'll just hang out in the student center for awhile."

"Have fun," Renee told Judy. "Doesn't the library close at nine? I guess I'll see you after that."

"Okie-doke." Judy pushed the door open, then looked back at Renee. "Are you going to be doing any laundry? I have some socks I forgot to add to my wash. Could you toss them in with yours?"

Renee laughed. "Sorry, Judy, but I am *not* doing laundry tonight!"

"Oh. I thought you said this morning—"

"Judy, you can wash them out in the sink if you need them so bad. I already did my clothes this afternoon."

Savannah flicked her hands at Judy. "Go on. Your friends are probably waiting for your expertise in whatever you're working on."

They watched Judy trudge down the ramp to the sidewalk. Before rounding the corner of the dining hall, she turned back to wave. Renee threw her hands up, let out a loud groan, and said to Savannah, "I can't believe it! Wash her socks!" She shook her head. "Thanks for not saying anything about going to the Alleycat."

"Did you think she would skip her study group?"

With a toss of her head, Renee made a *tch* sound. "As if." She rolled her eyes. "No, but she might have cut it short. Even though she wouldn't *really* want to go with us." She pulled her stocking cap over her hair, tucking in the loose ends. "Ready?"

"Let's go. I'm up for some escapism!"

They headed down the ramp and across the parking lot. Renee said, "I like Judy; she can be pretty cool when it's just the three of us." Renee grinned when Savannah snorted. "Well, kind of cool, I guess. But lately, I'm sorry, but she's kind of—"

"Annoying?" Savannah pursed her lips. "Come on, Renee, she's always annoying."

Alleycat

"Yeah, I know, you're right. Maybe the pressure of school is getting to her. Just before winter break she said her parents were hassling her about her choice of classes or something like that."

"Remember how stressed she was during finals week? I about went crazy with her nagging." Savannah shrugged. "I don't mind not telling her we're going to the Alleycat. It'll definitely be more fun without her."

"Very true. She made me feel like I was doing something wrong. I get the feeling sometimes that she's more interested in Russ than I am. She doesn't even know him!" Renee felt her hands balling into fists.

"Yeah, I noticed the way she was watching you every time you said anything last night. It gets old, doesn't it?"

"You know, I'm trying to deal with Russ being gone the best I can," Renee said. "It's hard enough without her making me feel bad. I don't think she means to, it just—"

"She's lonely, she has a hard time making friends, and she wants to be wherever we are." Savannah groaned. "She drives me insane. I don't know how you do it, living with her."

"It's hard sometimes, but mostly I just feel sorry for her. Maybe that's why I put up with some of her, um, oddities. She kind of reminds me of Russ in some ways."

"How?"

"Mm, like being very serious and a little nerdy. He has the same kind of sense of humor."

"You mean no sense of humor?"

Renee laughed. "Good point, Savannah. But let's be kind and say that their idea of a joke is much more serious than ours."

"Sure. I guess you're attracted to that kind of person, huh?"

"Stop!" Renee giggled and cuffed Savannah on the arm. "They have good qualities, too. Russ is a hard worker, he's very involved with his family, he's interested in so many things, he's got lots of hobbies."

"And he loves you."

Renee smiled. "Yes. But I doubt Judy feels that way about either one of us."

"That's a relief. No love lost from my side. I just wish she'd find some other people to hang out with, at least sometimes."

"Yeah, me, too. But she's told me that she really likes the things we do."

"Humph. She should act like it more often, then. Her griping gets old."

They reached the Alleycat. Renee's heart raced as she followed Savannah into the nearly empty restaurant. *Is it okay that I feel excited about seeing them?* She held her breath for a second. *Yes. It's okay to have fun. And if Russ was here, I'd be having fun with him.*

They glanced around the room. The boys were not there. Renee looked at Savannah, giving her a rueful half-smile. They ordered two pots of tea with lemon and honey along with a piece of apple pie to share, then settled in the back corner booth.

"Well, they didn't exactly say they come in every night," Savannah said, dunking her tea bag in the pot of hot water. Dropping the lemon wedge in the cup, she poured the tea over it. "But I have to admit, I'm disappointed."

"Me, too." Renee stirred honey into her tea, then added a squeeze of lemon. She lifted the cup, letting the sweet lemony steam warm her face. Her glasses fogged and she took them off, laying them on the table. "You know, it was just a chancy kind of thing."

"Yeah. Let's forget it," Savannah said cheerfully. "Write a poem, right?"

"Sure," Renee agreed, a big smile on her face. "Let's see, how about 'Three crazy guys sitting with you/Acting all goofy and hugging too.' Take it from there, sister!"

"Hey, only one was doing any hugging, if you want to call it that. I think he was just testing to see if he could cop a feel." Savannah couldn't help giggling. "He *was* persistent, I'll give him that."

"Sure you're okay with it? Russ is like that—hands all over me. Sometimes it's almost embarrassing."

"As long as he keeps it outside the clothes and no lower than my shoulders, yeah. I won't let it get out of hand." She took a compact from her purse and checked her makeup. "Ah well, forget it." She drank some tea and ate a bite of the pie. "Speaking of poems—I'm working on a new one. Would you look at it for me and tell me what you think?"

She pulled a sheet of paper out of her notebook and handed it to Renee. Together they studied the poem, discussing possible changes. When Savannah was satisfied that they had given the piece all they could, she put it away. "Thanks. You always help me so much!"

"Savannah, I—I need to talk to you about something." Renee picked up a napkin and folded it into an accordion shape. "Russ says he's leaving the exchange program."

"Really? That's great!" Savannah studied Renee's face. "Right?"

Renee twisted the napkin, then unfolded and smoothed it out on the table. Picking at a corner of it, she shook her head. "No, actually it isn't."

"I don't understand. You always talk about how much you miss him. Now you don't?"

"I don't know." Crossing her arms, hunching her shoulders, Renee scrunched her face up. "It's just that, um, this is hard to say, but I'm doing things, you know, on my own." She shook her head. "I can't explain it. I love Russ and I'm going to marry him. I was so miserable when he left for Japan. In a way, I was angry." She put emphasis on the last word then shook her head. One hand pressed to her forehead, she squeezed her eyes shut, gritted her teeth. "I'm sorry. I wasn't mad. I was scared."

Savannah reached across the table and gently patted Renee's arm. "I know. You don't get mad, do you?"

"Huh, no." Renee smiled a little. "When I was a kid, even in junior high, I got in trouble for getting mad. That was grounds for punishment. My dad wouldn't tolerate it." She shook her head. "No, I don't get mad."

"Well, maybe you should try it sometime."

Renee shook her head. "I don't think so." She took a sip of tea. "When he comes home, things will go back to what they were."

"And that's bad?"

"I don't know." Renee slowly ripped the napkin into pieces, smaller and smaller, making a pile of shredded paper in the center of the table. Last year she and Russ had lived in a tiny world made up of their dorm rooms, the cafeteria, some classrooms, a few spots around campus, the back seat of his car. He planned every excursion, monitored every move. He kept her dining ID card, requiring her to wait for him for every meal. And he usually made her wait. He hated getting up for breakfast and they had to rush to make their first classes. He arranged their class schedules so that their paths connected or crossed often. He determined who their friends would be—mainly his roommates—and when they would see them. He decided when they would go to Salem to see their families for a weekend. Why did she let him treat her that way? *I don't want to live like that anymore.*

Someone put money in the jukebox and the Beatles' "Hey Jude" filled the diner. Savannah began to sing along, softly, tapping fingers against the table. Renee smiled at her, blinking the threat of tears away, then joined her in song. As the girls swayed to the beat, Cal, Alex and Neil barged through the doors, loud voices booming through the restaurant. Renee and Savannah looked at each other, then simultaneously patted their hair and smoothed their clothes. Savannah snatched Cal's hat from the middle of the table and perched it on her head. The boys yelled for the waitress to bring coffee as they headed straight for the corner. Renee grinned at Savannah when the boys scrambled into the booth from both sides, nudging the girls to the center of the curved bench, Neil shoving ahead of Alex to sit next to Savannah.

"Nice hat," Cal said, nodding at Savannah.

"Thank you. A suave gentleman gave it to me." Savannah adjusted the fedora slightly. "It fits me perfectly."

"Then you should keep it."

"Really?" She tried to keep the excitement out of her voice. "Oh, no, I couldn't. It must be worth a lot of money."

"Marlowe didn't always wear a fedora. I can live without it." He reached across Renee and took Savannah's hand. "You, my dear, I can't live without."

Giggling, she pulled her hand away. "You're so—so—"

"Perfect?" He let go of her hand and smiled. "A gentleman, didn't you say?"

"Okay, so when we break up I'll give the hat back."

"Good enough," Cal said, leaning back, joining the others in laughter.

"Where's that other chick you had with you last night?" Neil asked.

"Judy? She's studying in the library," Renee said. "She's a little more into homework than we are."

"Well, she seemed like a drag—no offense," Neil said. "She had a scowl on her face that would scare a dead man."

Renee giggled. "She's very serious, that's all."

"Yeah," Savannah said. "And we had to practically sneak away tonight."

Alleycat

"That's a bummer," Neil said. "Is she your chaperone or something?"

Renee and Savannah exchanged looks. "Something like that," Savannah said. "In her mind, anyway."

"We'll get her to loosen up," he said as he snagged the plate with the half-eaten pie and finished it in a few bites. When the coffee came, he ordered another piece and asked for extra forks. A couple of minutes later the waitress brought the pie and set the plate in front of him. She refilled the teapots with hot water. Neil gave everyone a fork and passed the pie around. It was gone in seconds, leaving a faint scent of cinnamon drifting around the booth.

"Shoulda ordered a whole pie," Alex said.

"Yeah? Who has the cash to pay for it?" Neil scraped the last crumbs and trace of apple from the plate. "Not me, man."

Cal pulled a pipe and tobacco pouch from his coat pocket. He began filling the pipe, carefully tamping down the tobacco. He worked at lighting it, puffing gently until the flame caught.

"That's a different pipe than the one you had the other day," Savannah said. "How many do you own?"

"Just two. I can't afford more right now. Someday I'll have a collection."

"That tobacco actually smells good," Renee said. "Better than cigarettes anyway."

"It's black cherry," Cal said with a chuckle. "I like it for a change of pace."

"You just like the fact that girls like it," Neil said. "But, shit, a pipe is too much work."

"Huh," Alex said to Neil. "You never say that about rolling a joint."

That's different," Neil said. "It doesn't take all that puffing to get it started. Roll it, light it, take a hit. Easy."

Savannah studied the patches on Neil's jacket. "You've been in the army?"

He ran his hand over the US ARMY insignia sewn above the left breast pocket. "No." His voice took on a serious tone as he pointed to the peace sign button on the collar. "See? I hate this fucking war. Nixon has gotten us deeper and deeper into something that's none of our business. It's wrong to invade another country for no better reason than power. If I—"

Cal cut him off. "Neil."

47

Neil fell silent, smoked his cigarette. He draped one arm across the back of the seat, drummed his fingers on the vinyl.

"Well, why do you wear that jacket?" Renee asked. "Is that a sergeant patch on the shoulder?"

Neil flicked the ash from his cigarette into the glass ashtray on the table. "Yeah, I guess so. I got it this way." He pointed to the strip of cloth over the right pocket. "My last name ain't Kellogg."

"Isn't it kind of, um, wrong," Renee asked, "to wear an army uniform when you're not in the army?"

"That's the whole idea!" He winked at Renee. "Get it?"

She shook her head. "I guess it's a kind of protest, but I don't know if it's effective. People probably think you're a vet."

"Hell, anyone who knows me knows better," Neil said. He stubbed out his cigarette, his face serious. "Actually, this jacket belonged to a buddy of mine who was killed in 'Nam. Josh Kellogg."

"Oh! I'm sorry," Renee murmured.

"Yeah, he was a good guy." Neil shook his head. "Shouldn't have happened."

"None of you were drafted?" Savannah asked.

"Student deferments," Neil said. "And high numbers in the lottery. I'm not sure what I would do if I got called up."

Alex shook his head. "I wanted to go to the Naval Academy or West Point, but coming from Gitmo made that difficult."

"Why?" Renee asked.

"No home state. You have to have a senator recommend you." He waved a hand in a dismissive gesture. "This is so much more fun anyway."

"My little brother is itching to sign up," Renee said. "Marines. My dad is pushing him, too. He wants him to be 'a man.' But he's only seventeen. Maybe the war will be over by the time he's old enough."

"A year? Huh." Neil shook his head. "Don't bet on it."

"My boyfriend is a conscientious objector. We didn't tell my dad, though." Renee began biting a fingernail, then hastily thrust her hands in her lap.

"Would he serve as a medic or would he go to jail for avoiding the draft?" Neil asked.

"He wouldn't go to jail. He refuses to use a gun but he feels service to the country is important, so yeah, he would go as a medic."

"That's cool," Neil said, nodding.

"I wish we could vote," Savannah said. "I know there's a movement to pass legislation for it. If we could have a real say in what happens in this country, maybe the war would end."

"It's gonna take more than a bunch of 18-year-olds voting to make a difference," Alex said.

"Yeah, but it will make a statement and if we can fight, we should have a say," Neil countered.

"C'mon, let's cut the war talk," Cal said. "It's a downer." He turned toward Savannah. "So, Savannah, do you have a boyfriend?"

She opened her mouth to answer, but Neil grabbed her hand across the table. "She's with me. Find your own chick."

Cal spoke softly, gazing into Savannah's eyes. "Savannah, you know he's a lech, right? You'd be much safer with me."

Pulling her hand away from Neil's, Savannah looked sideways at Renee. "Hmm. Do I have to choose?" She looked back at the boys, Cal next to Renee, Neil across the table. "Hmmm."

"I'm smart, funny, I wear clean clothes," Cal said, ticking the words off his fingers one by one. "I am very polite—"

Neil interrupted. "I'm smart, too, and I'm more fun. I can imitate Don Knotts and Elvis Presley." He slapped his hands on the table with a loud snap. "Top that, Clyde."

Both girls giggled and Savannah said, "Yeah, that's a big order, Cal. I'm really impressed with Don Knotts." She tilted her head and batted her eyes at Neil. "So far, you're ahead."

"Too bad you're out of the running," Cal said to Renee with a wink.

Renee shook her head. "No, no, I want no part of this competition." She held up her left hand; the diamond flashed.

Neil looked her up and down. "But," he said in a stage whisper, "the real question is, are you a virgin?"

"That's none of your business," she said, giving him a stern look, her face turning pink.

"Or maybe for you to know and me to find out?" He put his elbows on the table and rested his chin on his hands, staring into her eyes.

She could feel the heat from her face creep down her neck. Savannah nudged her under the table, looking at her questioningly. Renee smiled, shaking her head as if to say, "It's okay, I'm cool."

To Neil, she said, "Ha ha. Just leave that subject alone, buddy."

Neil turned to Savannah. "How about you? Are you—"

"For me to know and you not to," she said, cutting him off.

"So you girls apparently don't have sex," Cal said. "And you obviously don't smoke or you would've been lighting up by now. What vices could you possibly have?"

"Who says we have to have vices?" Renee asked.

"Oh, I get it," Alex said. "You're 'good girls', huh?"

"We don't drink or smoke *anything*," Savannah said. "But tell me what's wrong with being high on life?"

"Oh sure," Neil said, grinning broadly. "High on life. Sorry, but I don't buy it."

Savannah laughed and took his hand. She spread his fingers out and studied his palm. "I see a crooked life line. Oh, and look! It gets thicker here. What do you suppose that means?"

"It's probably a genetic defect," Alex said. "You can't get a true reading off this bum."

"Most likely relates to his many vices. Let me see yours, Cal." Savannah reached for Cal's hand. He held it out. "Hmm, your life line curves around your thumb. That indicates a psychic connection. That's interesting." She looked at her own palm. "Now see, mine is uniform and the head line is just above it. My heart line is straight and definite. I know that means I'm destined to have a good and happy life with my true love." She laughed. "I'm going to have to read up on this to figure you guys out."

Cal said, "Alex, isn't there a Ouija board in that stash of games you have? That would be a trip." He grinned at Renee. "Then we could find out if Renee really *is* available."

"I don't have one," Alex said, "but I could get one. We could find out all sorts of things." He put his hands behind his head, linking his fingers, elbows out. "I have a few questions in mind." His eyes flitted back and forth from Savannah to Renee.

"Dream on, boys," Savannah said, with a flick of her hands. "No Ouija boards for us."

"Tell me about this boyfriend of yours," Cal said to Renee. "How could he leave you unprotected from the wolves at OCE?"

Renee laughed. "Yeah, the wolf mascots are pretty dangerous. That's why I don't go the basketball games."

"You don't need—what's his name again?" Neil looked to Savannah for an answer.

Alleycat

"Russ," Savannah replied, adding pointedly, "Her fiancé."

"Yeah, Russ. You don't need Russ to protect you. You have protection right here." He spread his arms out wide, giving Renee a raised eyebrow and lopsided grin.

"Oh, boy, I'm sure Russ will be forever grateful." She covered her mouth, stifling a giggle, as Savannah rolled her eyes.

"Well, what's he like?" Alex asked. "Do you have a picture of him?"

Renee reached for her purse on the seat beside her. "Of course."

Cal put his hand on her arm. "Wait. Describe him in words."

"Okay." She rested her chin on her folded hands. "He's really smart. He wants to be a teacher, of course, high school math. He's very tall. I don't even come up to his shoulder. He has dark brown hair and brown eyes—"

"Tell us about his eyes," Cal said. "Here, look in mine to help you."

Renee laughed, glanced at Cal's eyes, looked away. "Not the same brown as yours. Darker. Kind of droopy. Sleepy looking. One of my girlfriends calls them bedroom eyes."

"Significant?" Neil asked, eyebrows raised.

"No!" Renee jerked upright as her hands flew out. "Just sleepy-looking."

"What would you call mine?" Cal asked, leaning closer to her, fixing his eyes on hers. She looked away.

"Wolf eyes," Savannah said.

Cal raised his fist, thumb up. "Good call, though untrue. Go on, Renee, more about Rick."

"Russ," she corrected, glancing at Savannah and shaking her head. "What else do you want to know? And nothing that will embarrass me."

"Does he like to cook?" Neil asked.

"What? Yeah, I guess. A little." Renee considered for a moment. "Mostly he likes to tell me how to cook."

"As a good husband should," Neil said. Renee threw a crumpled straw wrapper across the table, hitting him on the arm as Savannah thumped him on the head. Both girls chuckled at Neil's startled look.

"How about books?" Alex asked. "What does he read?"

"Sci-fi like Tolkien, Bradbury, Asimov. History books. He

51

plays chess. He's pretty serious and focused."

"Sounds like a real joy to be around," Neil said sarcastically.

"Hey, those are things I like," Alex said, frowning at Neil. "Are you implying that I'm a drag?" He winked at Renee. She felt her face flush slightly and she resisted the urge to cover it with her hands. Alex sat back and spread his arms along the top of the seat. "I mean, just because *you* don't read books or play anything but Pass Out or strip poker—"

"Nah, you're cool." Neil chuckled. "Definitely not serious and focused."

"Hmm," Cal mused. "I enjoy all those things, too. In fact, Alex and I usually read books about the Civil War while we're playing chess and smokin' a doobie."

"Oh, multi-talented, huh?" Savannah grinned at the boys. "It'll be interesting to see what other skills you have."

Cal and Neil exchanged looks as Alex leaned close to Savannah. "Watch out what you wish for. These two are just waiting for the go-ahead, you know. Consider that a gentle word of caution."

Savannah laughed. "Gentle? I think that was an out-and-out warning. Yes, I'll be ready for whatever comes from these two, thank you very much."

"Don't be fooled by Alexander here," Neil said. "He's just as dangerous."

"Who are you calling dangerous?" Alex said, indignantly. "I'm a nice guy."

"Oh sure, you let the ladies believe that," Cal said. He looked at Renee and Savannah with an earnest expression. "Now, *I* am the most decent man you'll ever meet so don't listen to what these bastards tell you."

Neil tapped the ash from his cigarette into the overflowing ashtray. "I consider myself the best man here. Oh," he added, looking Renee straight in the eye. "Except for Brandon, of course."

Savannah groaned. "Russ! His name is Russ."

"Oh, yeah, how could I forget?" Neil snorted. "So what kind of fun do you have with *Russ*?"

"Russ and I do have fun together," Renee said. "We always go to the state fair, we like to go horseback riding, picnics at the beach—he always has good ideas for things to do."

"But are they things you like to do?" Cal asked, turning

serious."

Renee blushed. "Of course."

"Show us his picture now," Cal said. "I want to see if my mental visual fits the real thing."

"All right." Renee dug in her purse. "He has a great smile. You'll see." She pulled out a small photo album and laid it on the table.

Neil picked it up and flipped through the photos. "Hmmm, such a pretty face."

"Oh, he's fat?" Cal asked. Neil held out the album and Cal took it. "Yep, he's a big boy, all right."

Renee crossed her arms, sitting ramrod straight. "He's tall and muscular. He's not fat."

"I see what you mean," Cal said. He held up a photo for the others to see. It was of Renee and Russ at the airport. "Look at the size of his shoulders. He's built. We better be careful, lads, or we could get seriously hurt."

"Yeah, you better be gentlemen at all times," Savannah said. "No funny stuff."

All three boys crossed their hearts and held up three fingers in a Boy Scout salute. "Promise," they said in unison.

Alex looked closer at the photo. "I've seen him on campus. Might even have had a class with him last year."

"Really?" Renee felt a prickle along her arms.

"Maybe. I think I saw you two in the cafeteria a few times."

"Well, it's a small school. I don't think I ever saw any of you guys before, though."

"From what I remember, he kept a pretty close eye on you."

Eyes averted, Renee scooped up the photo album and slipped it back into her purse with shaking hands. *Stop it. Breathe.* She tucked the purse next to her on the bench, sat back, looked around the table at each of the boys. "Why don't you guys have girlfriends?"

"Aren't you our girlfriends?" Cal asked.

"No, you know we're not." Renee smiled, feeling her heartbeats slow down to a normal rhythm. "I'm serious. Seems like you would be hooked up with someone cute and girly, a party girl."

Neil looked at Savannah. "You're a party girl, right?"

"Oh, sure."

"That's not very convincing," said Cal. "She sounded sarcastic, Neil, old buddy. You're gonna have to work harder on her."

"I'm working damn hard. What about you and Alex?" He dipped his head toward Renee, stroking his mustache with a thumb and forefinger.

Renee folded her hands on the table, left hand over right; her diamond glittered. "I'm engaged. So don't be working on me."

"Yes, we know," Alex said. "To Russ."

"Sorry," Renee said, ducking her head and putting her hands in her lap.

"Hey, don't apologize," Alex said quickly.

"I was nearly engaged once," Neil said. "But then I realized she actually expected to get married."

Renee laughed. "Well, yeah. Isn't that the point?"

"Not really," Neil said. "I had a totally different plan."

"Bet we know what that was." Savannah giggled, shaking her head.

"What time is it?" Renee asked. "We shouldn't stay out too late."

Alex checked his watch. "Almost ten-thirty."

"We better go. Judy'll have a cow."

"Yep," Savannah agreed. "She's most likely waiting up, wondering where we are."

Neil gave a snort. "Oh yeah, I forgot. Don't want to upset the big boss, right?"

Renee sighed. "Sometimes it feels like that. But, really, we need to get home."

"All right, we'll walk you back," Cal said.

After the boys left them at the dorm, Savannah came up to Renee's room with her. Judy had changed into flannel pajamas and lay stretched out on top of her bed reading a book. She checked the clock before marking her place and sitting up.

"Gosh, it's late. I was getting worried."

"No need to be," Renee said. Her neck muscles tightened a fraction. "We're pretty much grown-up girls." She removed her glasses and began polishing the lenses with the edge of her shirt.

"Well, it's okay now," Judy said. "What did you do after dinner?"

Savannah checked her face in the mirror, patting and smoothing her hair into place. "We ended up going to the Alleycat." She watched Judy's reflection.

"You did?" Judy sat up, laying the book face down, pages

open.

"Yeah, we just thought we'd check it out again," Savannah said.

Judy glanced briefly at Renee. "So? Have a good time?"

"We did," Savannah replied. "We had a lot of fun." She turned away from the mirror.

"Well, that's good, I guess."

"We're going tomorrow, too."

"Were those guys there?"

"Yeah."

Judy looked straight at Renee. "You want to go back?"

"Yep," Renee said, with a decisive nod. "I do. Like Savannah said, we had fun and I think that's a good thing."

"Okay," Judy said with a loud sigh. "I guess I'll go with you."

"We're going right after dinner," Savannah said. "So if you want to come, no whining about homework, okay?"

"Or anything else," Renee added. "It's your choice."

Judy scooted under the covers, adjusting the sheet and blanket, smoothing out the wrinkles. "I want to go with you. I won't complain. I promise." She muttered something as she stretched out on her back and closed her eyes.

"What did you say?" Renee asked.

"Nothing." Judy opened her eyes. "I just think—never mind. Good night."

~~ 4 ~~

"Look how much fun you had the last two nights," Savannah said as she and Renee walked across campus to the humanities building. "It's about time."

Renee couldn't help but grin. "Russ would kill me if he knew."

"That's not funny."

"Oh, I'm kidding." Renee waved her hand as if brushing away a fly. "If Russ was here, we'd all be hanging out together."

"Hmm, you sure about that?" Savannah squinted one eye, tilted her head, studying Renee's face. "From what you've told me—"

"I know, I know." They reached the building, joining the crowd entering through double glass doors. "Russ likes to be in charge. It's okay with me. It's easier."

Savannah pulled Renee's arm. "Hey, let's skip class and go for some coffee."

"Skip history?" Renee nodded. "I could do that."

"I have Geography of the World this hour." Savannah rolled her eyes. "Who cares about maps and borders of countries? Not me, not today." She made a ninety degree turn and headed off across the small patch of soggy grass between the humanities and science buildings. Renee followed.

"Alleycat?"

Savannah laughed. "My thought exactly."

The restaurant was nearly empty. They sat in a booth near the front doors and ordered coffee. Renee pulled her bandana off, ran her fingers through her hair, and retied the scarf at the back of her neck. She fluffed her bangs out. The coffee came and both girls added cream, no sugar.

"Feels odd to skip class," Renee said. "I've never done that."

"Really?" Savannah wrapped her hands around the mug, shoulders hunched. "Man, I'm cold!" She sipped her coffee. "I haven't skipped much. But that class is so boring. I'd much rather spend the hour talking!" She grinned. "Especially with you!"

"You're a bad influence," Renee said, chuckling.

Alleycat

"If I'm a bad influence," Savannah said, turning serious, "what do you call Russ?"

Renee didn't answer. She gazed across the room, thinking.

"Proper wife" he says all the time. She struggles to understand what he means. She wears what he tells her to wear, every day. At the high school, he tells her where to wait for him every afternoon so they can drive home together. Sometimes she has to wait for awhile but she never complains. She packs their lunches every morning, getting the kind of bread he likes even though she has to make special trips to the grocery to buy it. He wants his sandwiches kept whole, not cut in half, and wrapped in plastic, not put in waxed paper sandwich bags. She calls him on the phone in the mornings so he won't oversleep. Her last words to him at night are "I love you." He gets mad if she forgets to say it. She studies his parents, looking for clues to a good marriage. His mother is a proper wife. Her own mother is not. He makes the distinction often.

"I remember when I first met you," Savannah said. "You were so quiet. You seemed kind of lost, and all you talked about was Russ."

Renee nodded. "Yeah, I missed him terribly but I also had to fend for myself. Like making new friends, doing things without him. It's different when I'm with Russ. He always takes care of everything." She let out a sigh. "You know, it's what I'm used to. Even growing up, my dad expected us to do whatever he said. I don't even want to go into all that 'bad father' junk. We probably all had dads like that. Ward Cleaver is a figment of some Hollywood writer's imagination."

Her parents had been upset when Renee showed them her engagement ring. Her father had turned red-faced and silent, a sure sign that he did not endorse her relationship, and her mother, eyes cutting away to her husband, stammered a half-hearted congratulations. Later, she implored with Renee to wait before planning a wedding. When Russ decided to enter the exchange program, her parents embraced the opportunity with enthusiasm. Her dad even suggested she might find a more suitable boyfriend with Russ far across the ocean. *But they don't understand what I need, what I want.*

"That's your dad. Your boyfriend isn't supposed to tell you

57

what to do."

"Yeah, I guess. Being on my own is a new experience for me. Kind of liberating, in a way."

"That's good! You know, after a while, you stopped talking about him all the time. It was kind of a relief."

"I'm sorry."

"No, don't be sorry! You are so much fun to be with, especially when you leave Russ out of it." Savannah bit her bottom lip. "Oops. I don't mean to put him down or anything. It's just that sometimes you seem so lost." She reached across the table and put her hand on Renee's. "I just never know how to help you."

"Savannah, being my friend and listening and not questioning everything I do or say—that's how you help me. I've been with Russ for over two years. We've never been apart."

"Are you afraid of being alone?"

Renee hesitated. "I think I am. I dated a lot in high school, before I met Russ—all kinds of guys. One had a motorcycle which really upset my parents. He took me riding once. Then on Halloween, we were supposed to be handing out candy to the trick-or-treaters and instead he had me in a body-lock on the couch. I was trying to push him off. My brother saw us and ran outside with a can of Dad's shaving cream, which he squirted all over this jerk's bike. He comes back in and says, all innocent, 'Somebody touched your precious motorcycle.' Never saw that guy again!"

"Are you telling me you can't handle things yourself?"

"Mmm, maybe. Like I said, I had boyfriends, decent ones and creeps that didn't last more than one date. I had fun. My junior year, before I met Russ, was—exciting. I had some great friends, guys and girls. I went to the prom with a guy who was tutoring me in chemistry—neither one of us had real dates so we decided to go together. It was a blast. You know, no expectations or pressure." Renee poked at her waffle, soggy with syrup. "For some reason, though, I always worried I'd end up alone. I don't know why."

"You just don't trust yourself enough."

"But Russ is smart; he knows what he wants and what's best. I trust *him*."

"Renee, think about it for a minute."

"What do you mean?"

"I mean you've been on your own for months now. Russ hasn't had any say in what you do, who you spend time with, when you study or eat or sleep or get up. Have you had problems with any of that?" Savannah shook her head. "No. You're fine. You have good friends—no, great friends—and you—"

"Okay," Renee said with a laugh. "I get what you're saying. I guess I do trust myself more than I thought. I don't feel like I'm making mistakes."

"Earlier you said something about if Russ was here he'd be part of our group. Now that he'll be back sooner, what do you think is going to happen? Do you want to talk about that?"

"Honesty, right?"

"It's just you and me, no one else. And I won't say anything, you know that."

"Yeah, I do know that." Renee considered how to respond to Savannah's statement. *Russ will not allow this friendship.* "I'd like to say I'm not sure. But…"

"He won't fit in, will he?" Savannah asked.

"He'll be happy about Judy and I know he'll like you."

"But…?"

"Guys are a different matter." Renee twisted her ring absently. "I don't know what will happen."

~~ 5 ~~

The girls were drenched by the time they got to the Alleycat after dinner Friday night. The rain had been falling all day, reaching a peak at six o'clock. The wind had come up, too, and Judy complained all the way across campus. "I hate going out in this weather. This is the fourth night this week. I can't afford to take this much time away from studying."

"Then stay home," Savannah said. She opened the side street door to the restaurant and ducked inside. The corner booth was occupied. "Where do you want to sit?"

Before either Renee or Judy could speak, the boys entered the Alleycat through the other door. Cal strode up to the corner booth and spoke quietly to the high school girls sitting there. They gathered up their things and moved to a table in the front of the restaurant. Cal swept his arm out, nodding to Renee. "Have a seat, m'lady."

"What did you tell those girls?" she asked as she removed her soaking wet jacket.

He took it and hung it on the coat rack near the side door. "I just told them the booth is reserved. They're okay with moving."

"What did you promise them?" Savannah asked. Cal winked at her and didn't answer. He collected her coat and put it with Renee's, adding his to the rack as well.

"It *is* the only table big enough for all of us," Judy mumbled. She scooted along the bench, sitting next to Renee.

"That pie we had the other night was good," Alex said. He opened one of the menus the waitress had brought. "Tonight we should get one of their cinnamon rolls. They're huge."

"I'm not getting anything to eat," Judy said. "I have to watch my money,"

"Hey, man, no prob," Neil said. "We can all share. I got no cooties, do you?"

Judy giggled. "Not me. My brothers have all of them. None left." She raised her hands, palms up. "Three bites of a cinnamon roll sounds just about right."

The waitress brought six stoneware mugs and the coffee pot. Renee wrapped her hands around her cup, letting the heat of the coffee warm her. The diner was busy, more crowded than the first night they had come. The noise helped her feel anonymous. Even surrounded by friends, she felt apart, separate, on her own. Cal and Neil were teasing Savannah about something; she reacted with giggles and flirtatious retorts, clearly enjoying the attention. Judy sat quietly, observing the interactions with a look of envy and annoyance. Alex was quiet, too, but as he drank his coffee he had an amused expression on his face. Renee liked his smile and the way his eyes crinkled as he watched the flirting between Savannah, Neil, and Cal. He seemed completely comfortable, at ease. Catching Renee's eye, he grinned; she blushed and quickly looked away.

A ballpoint pen in her pocket dug into her upper thigh. She pulled it out and took a napkin from the dispenser on the table. Doodles soon turned into Russ's name, over and over, in various sizes and scripts. Block letters. Bubble letters. Curly letters. Shaded and crosshatched. Russ. Russ. Russ. The paper was black with ink. Renee crumpled it up and shoved it in her purse. *Breathe.*

The waitress brought the cinnamon roll, warm and dripping with icing. She hesitated, looking at the group for guidance on where to put the plate. Neil said, "Middle of the table, Wendy." Instead of passing the plate around, they simply dug in all at once, devouring the pastry in a matter of a few minutes.

As they each took a last mouthful, Judy said, "I was right. Three bites each." She dabbed at her mouth with a napkin. "Yum, that was good!"

"We need some music," Cal said, sliding out of the booth. He stepped over to the jukebox and selected a few tunes. Using exaggerated hand motions reminiscent of Motown groups like the Temptations, the boys sang lustily to the Contours' "Do You Love Me." Savannah leaped up to do the Twist and Mashed Potato, pulling Neil with her. When "She Loves You" came on, they all joined in on the chorus, singing "yeah" over and over in harmony.

"It's so cool that they put old songs in this jukebox," Savannah said, flopping back in the booth. "I love this stuff!"

"You probably screamed at Beatles concerts, didn't you?" Cal asked her.

Savannah blushed. "Yes, I admit it. My girlfriends and I were complete fools. How did you guess?"

"No guessing necessary," Cal said.

"Come on," Alex said. "Let's make a tower—see how high we can get it before it falls." He turned the cinnamon roll plate over and put the napkin dispenser on top of it. Cal added his empty coffee cup and topped that with the saucer. Neil jumped up and went to the counter; he asked for ketchup and mustard, adding the containers to the stack on the table. The tower crashed, sloppily dumping grains of salt, sugar, and pepper, sloshes of coffee, clatters of forks and spoons. They began to build it again, even Judy contributing to the construction, everyone at the table laughing and cheering when it toppled.

The waitress approached the booth, coffee pot in hand, frowning as she looked at the scattered dishes. "All right, children, I'll bring a rag over for you to clean up your mess. And any breakage will be added to your tab."

"Chill out, Wendy," Neil said. "Nothing's broken. You want to deprive the place of entertainment?"

She shook her head. "Not me. I just don't want to have to explain your behavior to the owner."

"Nah, you won't have to. We'll clean it up."

"I know you will." She held up the coffee pot. "Refills?"

"Hey, Wendy," Savannah said, adding cream to her fresh coffee. "Would you take our picture?"

"You really want to be photographed with these guys? I don't know, that hippie you're sitting with—his face might break the camera."

"Yes," Savannah said. "We need a picture. Otherwise no one will ever believe we actually hung out together." She removed a Kodak Instamatic camera from her purse.

Neil made a show of combing his fingers through his hair, pulling it back into a ponytail. "Hey, any of you chicks have an extra hair band? I can look as respectable as Calvin and Alex."

"No, no," Renee said. "Leave it, Neil. It's so you. If your hair is back we won't know who you are in ten years."

"Yep," Savannah agreed. "The hair makes the man, you know."

"You have a flashcube?" Wendy asked. "It's dark in here for pictures."

Savannah snapped the flashcube on the top of the camera,

Alleycat

handed it to the waitress, then motioned for the others to be still. "Let's make it unforgettable!"

Crushed together in the booth, unable to keep quiet, they made comical faces and soon had nearby customers watching and chuckling. Wendy snapped half a dozen pictures before the roll ran out.

"We'll give you one to hang up in here as your most loyal customers," Neil said. "It should have a place of honor."

"Yep, right over this booth," Cal said.

"Sure, I'll bring it up with the owner." Wendy laughed and winked at the girls. "I'm certain he'll be agreeable. If I don't tell him how rowdy you all are."

At midnight, when the Alleycat closed, they helped the waitresses stack the chairs before leaving. The boys insisted on walking the girls back to their dorm.

"Don't ever go out alone," Cal cautioned them.

"Oh, brother," Judy scoffed. "We can take care of ourselves."

Cal smiled at her. "I know you can. Even so, you should be careful. Monmouth's small, but..." He paused, looking directly at each of them. "I've seen some people around who could be trouble. Things can happen. Stay in groups, okay? In fact, you should have one of us with you at night."

The next day, planning to go to the library to study, Renee and Savannah instead went for a walk off campus. They talked about Cal's warning and agreed that he probably had a valid point.

"But I like our late night walks," Renee said. "Sometimes I just have to get away from Judy. Doing something she hates is my only escape."

Savannah nodded and said, "I don't think we have to always have a guy with us. OCE security is out there every night."

"We just stay close to home, that's all."

"The Alleycat's practically on campus. I'm not worried about it," Savannah said.

"Me either. All I know is when I need to get out, I *need* to. Know what I mean?"

"Oh yeah. I understand completely!"

When they neared the intersection of Warren and Knox streets, they stopped.

"Neil told me they live in apartment number eight." Savannah looked at the three tan-colored apartment buildings stretched before them, concrete steps leading to the second level catwalks, five apartments on each floor. Several doors had notes tacked to them; one had a large poster of President Nixon, with a red goatee and devil's horns scrawled in marker, taped securely to the wood panel. Identical beige drapes covered most of the windows. A tie-dyed tapestry with a peace symbol in the center of it hung over one curtain. The parking lots held a scattering of cars. Faint sounds of rock music drifted across the deserted complex.

"Which building?"

"Vine? Village? Something like that. Anyway this is the street." They walked up to the foot of the stairway of the Villa Apartments and paused. "This must be the one." She hesitated, then asked, "Um, do you really think we should go up?"

Renee laughed. "Come on, are you chicken? What've we got to lose?"

"Ha! Think about it!"

"Yeah, you're right." Renee turned to leave.

"On the other hand..." Savannah began. Renee stopped again and Savannah shrugged. "What can it hurt?"

"Good grief! Can't we even visit our friends without a lot of embarrassment? I mean, come on!"

"We're being irrational."

"Acting like twelve-year-olds."

"Pretty immature, considering we're nineteen."

"Number eight you said?"

They crept up the stairs, aware that their footsteps on the concrete and metal would echo in the space between buildings. At the top, trying to look nonchalant, they sauntered along the walkway past doors numbered six and seven. "Here it is," Savannah said. "Number eight. Go ahead. Knock."

"Okay." Renee raised her fist, then paused. "Uh, how about if we knock together?"

Savannah stifled a giggle. "Twelve-year-olds you said?"

"Well, how's it going to look? I mean, me being engaged and all. You knock."

"And look like Husband-Hungry Harriet? No thanks."

"They won't even know which one of us knocked. So what does it matter?"

"They probably aren't home anyway."

Alleycat

"You're right. Let's just go get some coffee and study or something."

"But, Renee, we came this far—"

Renee knocked softly. Complete silence. She rapped more boldly. After a long moment the door opened, but no one was visible. Savannah peeked in. "Oh," she said, her voice almost a whisper. A boy, shirtless, with disheveled hair and half-open eyes, was stretched out on a sleeping bag. He slowly propped himself up, leaning on one elbow, his free hand shading the sunlight from his sleepy eyes.

Savannah spoke up. "Is this where Neil lives?"

"Neil? He's around here somewhere."

From the back of the apartment a muffled voice called out, "Who is it?"

Savannah and Renee backed away. "Uh, that's okay," Savannah mumbled. "Never mind."

"Sure," the boy said, closing the door. The girls fled.

~~ 6 ~~

After a quick early dinner Sunday evening, the girls fast-walked to the Alleycat. Judy, out of breath, raised a hand to signal Renee and Savannah to wait a minute. "Why—do—you have— to walk—so fast?"

Savannah, annoyed, gave a quick shake of her head. "You've griped about something every night. Why did you come with us?"

"Because—I studied all afternoon," Judy answered. "I'm caught up and wanted a break."

"Well, there you go," Renee said, pushing the door open. "I guess if you want to come along with us, you have to walk fast." She started toward the corner booth, but stopped short. The boys were there but six other people also sat at the table, one girl and five guys. Renee led the way to an empty booth and slipped into the seat facing the corner table. Savannah and Judy sat across from her. Fragments of conversation from the corner filtered through the noise of the restaurant. Renee caught the words, "weed" "party at your place?" "need some 'ludes" "foxy chicks this time." Judy sat hunched over, looking grim, as she stared into her coffee cup. Savannah chatted about school, seeming to pay no attention to the sounds from the corner booth.

"How long are we staying?" Judy asked.

Savannah spoke sharply. "We've been here half an hour. That's hardly worth the walk over and paying for coffee."

"You look upset, Judy," Renee said. "What's wrong?"

"Can't you hear what they're talking about? I knew they were druggies."

"So what?" Renee said. "It's not news to us. Almost everyone in town is using some kind of drug or drinking booze. Besides, they're just weekend partiers."

"How do you know that?"

"You might think they're high all the time, but they aren't. I think they mostly smoke cigarettes and drink a little beer."

Savannah nodded. "Neil likes to act stoned but most of it is just

Alleycat

his way of bugging you. He's a guy—he loves to be annoying."

"And you still want to spend time with them?" Judy shook her head.

"Yes," Savannah said. "I've told you before, it doesn't matter what they do. Doesn't mean we're going to do it, too."

"We'd have no friends at all if we excluded anyone who messes around with drugs," Renee said. "There must be ten girls in the dorm who don't drink, us included. And look at all the girls who want you to help them with their assignments. They ask you for help because they know you're smart, but I bet half of them are high when they talk to you, Judy. Are you going to send them away without helping them?"

"No, of course not. But they probably need help *because* they're high."

"Yeah, it's a losing battle no matter what, isn't it?" Savannah said, laughing.

"Savannah! Renee!" Neil called across the diner, waving them over. "We didn't see you come in."

The girls gathered up their coats and coffee cups and walked over to the corner table. "Hi," Savannah said. "How did you suddenly know we were here? We've been sitting over there since six o'clock."

"Oh, come on," Neil said. "Your laugh is like no one else's."

"Why didn't you just come on over when you got here?" Alex asked.

"Um, sure, like there's room for us," Savannah said, tossing her head. "We didn't want to crash the party." She smiled at the group around the table. "Hi, I'm Savannah."

Greetings and introductions were made, then the six people sitting with Cal, Neil, and Alex stood, preparing to leave. "See you guys later," Cal said. "Friday at your place, Chuck?"

"Yeah, man. Neil, you'll bring—"

"No prob, I got it covered," Neil said. "Guess you're splittin', huh?"

"Gotta check out a source across town. I heard he's selling some righteous shit."

"That dealer who works out of the Woods?" Alex asked.

"Yeah, yeah." Chuck laughed. "Gentle Woods Park, dope store. Pretty wild, huh?"

"Well, don't lose all your bread in one buy," Neil said. "Save

67

some for Friday."

Savannah grabbed one of the extra chairs and returned it to an empty spot at another table; Renee followed with the other one. Judy slid into the booth next to Alex. Neil picked a few songs on the jukebox and waved to the waitress, signaling for coffee refills. "We need a plate of fries, too," he told her as she poured coffee all around.

"You got here early tonight," Alex said to the girls.

"I studied all day," Judy said. "I needed a break. We went to dinner at five." She rolled her eyes. "And practically raced over here after. I had a terrible side ache."

"So you're going to a party Friday night?" Savannah asked.

Neil grinned. "Yeah. Want to come?" Savannah shook her head. "Well, if you change your mind I could pick you up at the dorm."

"No, thanks. Remember? We're the boring 'good girls'."

Cal laughed and said, "Good, maybe, but not boring. I don't think you'd like the party much. Actually, *it* will probably be somewhat boring. Same as always, reefer and beer."

"If I didn't have to go home next weekend," Alex said, "we could do something while these two losers are getting passed-out drunk."

Judy sat up straight. "I have to go home, too." Then she frowned, gloomy again. "My parents make me visit every month. I hate it."

"I'm only going home because it's my mom's birthday."

"If you *were* going to be here," Savannah said, "what would you suggest we do?"

"Fly kites or go on a scavenger hunt." He smiled. "Or go out to an elegant, expensive restaurant. I could wear my tux and buy flowers for all of you."

"Ohhh, sounds fun," Renee said. "Stay. Your mom won't care."

"Yeah, sure," Alex said. "I'll just tell her my three girlfriends are more important. She'll be so happy to hear that."

The waitress delivered the fries; Cal put big dollops of ketchup and mustard on a saucer. "Have you ever had this on your fries?" He sprinkled them with salt and used one to swirl the condiments together. "Try it." He handed the french fry to Renee. She ate it, nodding in approval.

Alleycat

"What did you guys do all day?" she asked, reaching for another fry.

"Um," Neil said, scratching his chin. "I think I slept. Don't remember, really."

"You slept, all right," Alex said. "And snored like an old man. Cal and I had to get out of the apartment. We played basketball at the high school."

Alex and Cal began a play-by-play recap of their game and Neil interrupted to tell a dirty joke. A new song on the jukebox caught Savannah's attention and she started humming; a moment later everyone joined in, singing loudly and lustily, banging the table to the beat of the bass. More jokes, more singing, fries devoured and coffee refilled multiple times. They stayed until midnight, again helping the waitresses stack up the chairs.

They began meeting nightly at the Alleycat after dinner; usually Judy went along but sometimes begged off, saying she needed to study. Most of the time Cal, Neil, and Alex had already arrived and the six shouted back and forth across the room, ignoring the stares of other customers. The waitresses greeted them, asking if they wanted coffee, countering the boys' often raunchy teasing with mock finger-shaking warnings. They kept the jukebox going, singing along in loud voices. Their favorite song was "Hey Jude" and when Paul McCartney did what they called "his thing" near the end of the song, they all joined in, shouting along with him, pounding the table like drums. They ignored looks—glares, smirks, amused smiles—accompanied by head-shaking, from other customers. Sitting in the farthest corner of the restaurant gave them a sense of anonymity and isolation.

Renee made a joke about how Russ would be horrified by their behavior. "He would probably drag me away from here to protect my virtue."

"Oh, you have a virtue?" Neil said, with an innocent look on his face.

"Ha ha." She flicked her hand. "He would never do things like mixing up the sugar and salt or jump on the table because he wanted to see across the room."

With an exaggerated British accent, Cal said, "He's very proper, eh?"

"Definitely. If he was here, we would be sitting quietly at a

69

table for two—"

"Gazing into each other's eyes while he felt you up under the table," Neil said, finishing her sentence.

She turned red. "No!"

"Neil," Alex said, "she doesn't do that sort of thing." He pressed Renee's hand. "Pay no attention to him. He's just a crass joker who can't keep a girlfriend."

"Thanks for sticking up for me, Alex." Renee tried to glare at Neil, but ended up giggling.

"Sure," Alex said with a laugh.

"So what do you call him?" Cal asked. "Rusty? Russell? Pumpkin?"

"Very funny," Renee said. "I call him—"

"General!" shouted Neil. "I know you do. You probably salute before you get down on your—"

"Stop!" Renee giggled so hard she could barely get the word out. "You're so bad! I just call him Russ and he calls me Renee. He doesn't like nicknames." She could feel the heat from her face and knew she must be fiery red. She would never admit it, but General was a fitting nickname. He gave the orders and she followed them. Any disagreement was usually met with a hard, quiet look and she would give in, wanting to avoid a confrontation or, worse, his silence.

Judy frowned and looked at Renee. "They should be more respectful."

"Russ is very lucky, you know," Renee said, speaking to the group. "Getting to learn about another culture by living it."

"So are you learning all about geisha girls, Renee?" asked Neil, nudging Cal and grinning. "You know he'll expect you to perform for him like they do when he gets back."

Judy glowered at Neil. Turning to Renee, she said, "He likes the family he's with, doesn't he?"

"Yes, I think so. He talks a lot about his little 'brother', Denjiro. He's ten and really looks up to Russ. There's an older boy, too, Hiroki. He's sixteen."

"Tell these guys what he did on his winter break," Judy said. She turned to Alex. "He had a month off and traveled around. Renee let us read some of his letters."

"He went to Chichibu City for the Yomatsuri Festival. He said it's essentially an all-night party with lantern floats, Kabuki plays,

Alleycat

and fireworks."

"You should bring your pictures to show these guys," Judy suggested.

Renee paid no attention to Neil and Cal as they grimaced and rolled their eyes. "In Tokyo, he attended the Gishi Sai at the Sengaku-ji Temple. He wrote a long letter about that, telling all the history." She smiled. "I can't believe I can remember the names of these things. He'd be proud of me, huh?"

"Of course," Judy said.

"I wish he wasn't gone, though. I wish all of you could meet him."

"Oh, me, too," Neil said. "He sounds like a dream guy."

"You'd like him," Renee insisted. "He knows so much. He's very smart."

"Like us?" Cal looked at her solemnly. "I mean, if he's half as intelligent as me then we'd get along famously."

Renee blushed and fiddled with her ring. "I miss him."

"You're halfway through," Judy said. "July is only six months away."

In a singsong voice, Neil said, "Russ, Russ, a bossy old cuss."

"He orders his girlfriend around," Cal continued.

"She pushed him away and said 'Not today—I'm with better folks than us.'" Neil guffawed as he finished the limerick, giving Cal a hearty slap on the back.

Cal reached over and shook Neil's hand vigorously. "Well done, old chap!"

Renee struggled not to smile. "That's awful."

"But true?" Cal asked. Renee didn't answer.

Savannah reached under the table and found Renee's hand, giving it a quick squeeze. "You okay?" she whispered.

Gripping Savannah's hand in return, Renee nodded. *How do they know how true that is?* She clenched her jaw. *And Judy will be on my case later. Just stop. Don't think about it.* Looking around the table, she said, "I need some ice cream. Anybody want to share a dish of chocolate?" Five hands shot up in the air and Neil yelled for the waitress.

She automatically brought six spoons with the bowl of ice cream, which she had loaded with a double scoop. She also brought a can of whipped cream, raising it in a question. The chorus of "squirt it on!" made her laugh and she pressed the can's tip, releasing a swirl of foam that dripped off the edge of the metal bowl. She pushed the dish to the center of the table. "Will you guys ever order separately?"

"Only on payday," Alex replied. Renee chuckled, liking Alex's deadpan humor.

Judy, clearly annoyed at the childish behavior, off-color jokes and pointed teasing that dominated the conversation every evening, declined to share the ice cream. She sat with her arms folded across her chest, a bored expression announcing her disinterest in the others. She waved her hand in broad sweeps to keep the cigarette smoke away from her face, glaring at the smokers while muttering under her breath. But Renee could feel Judy's eyes following every move she made.

After the boys left them at the dorm, the three girls went upstairs to Renee and Judy's room. Judy settled at her desk and began going through a stack of papers. Renee paced the room a couple of times, chewing on a fingernail, finally taking a seat on the edge of her bed. "Judy, what's your problem?"

"They're so juvenile."

"Oh come on," Savannah said. "Are we any more mature than they are?"

"Well, I should hope so," Judy said.

"It feels good to just be silly." Savannah shook her head. "You're too serious all the time. Can't you lighten up and have some fun?"

"I have plenty of fun," Judy said, frowning. "I just think Cal and Neil's behavior is ridiculous. At least Alex can be serious. He's like a port in the storm."

"He's pretty funny, though, don't you think?" Renee asked.

"But he isn't ridiculous about it. How can you laugh when they call Russ names?"

Renee shrugged. "It's okay. It doesn't hurt anything."

"Doesn't it hurt your feelings?"

"Not really. They don't know Russ so the names don't mean anything."

"Okay," Judy said doubtfully. "But you don't have to go along with it. If it bothers you, I mean."

"I know that. But guess what—Russ *is* bossy and self-centered." *Yep, now I've opened up that can of worms.*

Judy's eyes widened. "What do you mean?"

"Never mind, it doesn't matter," Renee said, shaking her head. "When you meet him you'll see what I mean." She chewed on a fingernail, then shoved her hands in her pockets. "I just want to have some fun, you know? Don't you?"

"I'm trying," Judy said. "I just don't get what you see in them."

"It's lots better than sitting in the dorm, hanging around wallflower girls who don't ever want to do anything," Savannah said. Judy winced and Savannah quickly added, "You know what I'm saying."

"They're rude. Why do you want to spend time with rude, annoying jerks?"

"You're not letting yourself see the real picture," Renee said, a trace of exasperation in her voice. "They're funny. And sweet. And interesting. And different. And—"

"Okay, okay, okay. Fine. As long as I get my papers written and ace my tests, it'll be fine." Judy opened her three-ring binder, picked up a pen, and began going over class notes, pointedly ending the conversation.

In the diner, Alex and Judy usually sat side-by-side, crushed together by the group's rowdiness. Renee watched Judy try to get Alex to talk to her; he listened to her ramblings—discourses on her coursework, complaints about her two brothers, strong opinions on social issues—but Renee could see that he observed and listened to everything going on at the table. He didn't talk much but always joined in with the group's singing or telling jokes. She thought of him as "the thinker" and Cal and Neil as "the Don Juans" as they turned their absurd charm on herself and Savannah, competing for their attention. Savannah, gregarious and flirty, reveled in the spotlight, playing one guy off the other, enjoying the good-natured rivalry. More reserved, especially when Judy was there, Renee seemed to present a certain challenge to Cal and Neil as they tried to get her to "loosen up!" Her reaction usually was a blush and uncontrolled giggles. And that just encouraged them further.

When they walked back to the dorm, they settled into couples—Neil and Savannah, talking quietly, earnestly; Alex and Judy, with Judy's voice dominating the conversation; and Cal and Renee. She felt comfortable with Cal, a feeling that surprised her. He was different away from the Alleycat—less foolish, more serious and thoughtful. They shared an easy companionship, something she hadn't had with a boy in a long time.

The evenings became the focal point of her days and she attended classes sporadically, almost impatiently, watching the clock slowly tick off the hours.

~~ 7 ~~

Since the dorm had an eleven o'clock curfew for male visitors, the boys always left the girls in the courtyard. But on Friday evening, when both Alex and Judy had gone home for the weekend, Cal, Neil, Savannah, and Renee left the Alleycat early, walking slowly back to the dorm two-by-two. Cal and Renee strolled leisurely, falling half a block behind Neil and Savannah.

"Cal, what's your family like?" Renee asked. "You've never said much about them. Brothers? Sisters?"

"I have a sister, that's it. My parents are great, pretty cool actually. Mom helps with the grandchildren—"

"Grandchildren!"

He laughed. "Yeah, Katie's thirty-two. She has two kids, Johnny and Ellen. So I'm an uncle."

"Neat." She tried to picture Cal with children, couldn't quite do it. "How old are they?"

"Six and three. Adorable little bastards. Cute as hell."

"Do you see them much?"

"No, they live in Corvallis but I don't go home much. Katie and her husband both work and Mom babysits and Dad putzes around the house, fixing things and, I don't know—it's not what I want to do with my time on a weekend." He stopped to light a cigarette. Cocking his head and squinting thoughtfully, he watched her face as he took the first drag, the exhaled smoke clouding the air between them. "I'm curious about something. Why are you going to marry Russ?"

"I love him and he loves me," Renee answered, looking away from Cal's gaze.

"From the way you talk about him, he seems a little overpowering."

Her back tightened. "No, not at all. He knows what he wants to do with his life. And he wants to share that life with me."

Cal took her left hand, lifting it so he could see the ring up close. "It's a beautiful diamond."

"Thank you."

"Did you choose it?"

Renee pulled her hand back and shoved it in her pocket. "Why are you asking me that?" Cal didn't answer. "No, I didn't choose it. But it's perfect for me."

They walked in silence for half a block. Then Renee said, "I hope you and Russ will be friends next year."

"If I come back to school here, yeah, sure," Cal replied. "I'd like to get to know the guy you're so crazy about."

Renee hesitated, then blurted out, "He says he's quitting and coming back early. In March."

"That probably makes you happy, huh?"

"Yeah, yeah, of course. I miss him a lot."

"So we'll get to meet him."

"Yes." She had decided to take her friendship with Cal, Alex, and Neil day by day and deal with how it would affect her relationship with Russ when he got back. But she knew it would be tough to manage both. Impossible. Her stomach dropped; a lump in her throat threatened to choke her. *I don't think I can introduce him to these guys. What am I going to do?* She held one hand to her chest as if that would still the quaking. *No. Don't think about it now.*

"That'll be a trip."

"I guess so," Renee said. *Don't think about Russ. Change the subject.* "Hey, it's my turn for a question."

"Ask me anything."

"Why don't you have a girlfriend?"

"Oh, I would, trust me, if the right person was available."

"You know someone you're interested in?"

"Mm, maybe." He dropped his cigarette and crushed it out with his shoe. "I had a pretty serious girlfriend last fall. But things just didn't work out." He laughed. "So now I'm a wolf on the loose! If there's a Little Red Riding Hood out there, I'll find her and ravish her and—"

"You wish!"

Cal chuckled. "I keep hopin' she's out there."

"I'm sure you'll find the right one eventually," Renee said, smiling.

They caught up to Savannah and Neil at the entrance to the residence hall. Neil asked, "So, what's in the upstairs lounge? You have a pool table or anything like that? When we lived in the dorm there were pinball machines and pool tables."

"No, nothing like that," Savannah said. "Just some couches and a TV. The television is really small, not like the big console one in the downstairs living room. No one ever hangs out in the upstairs lounge. Girls come up to do laundry, that's about it."

"Can we see it? I've never been in a girls dorm."

Savannah lifted her eyebrows. "Somehow I don't believe that."

Neil grinned. "You think I'd lie to you?"

Savannah laughed. "All right, we'll show it to you. It's really nothing."

Cal held the front door open for Renee and Savannah, then followed them up the wide staircase to the second floor. He and Neil checked out every part of the deserted room including the laundry facilities, small study area, and rest rooms next to it. Three couches were grouped around the television. One had a metal frame, three bright orange vinyl cushions, and three metal arms—on each end and one separating two seats from the third.

"What's the deal with that couch?" Cal asked.

Renee settled on one of the club chairs off to the side of the television. "The story is that an old housemother from a few years ago made the college put the extra arm on so nobody could lie down and make out. The rooms in Gentle and Barnum Halls have separate living rooms and they all have those couches. I'm not sure how one got in this dorm. Landers doesn't have rooms like that—just your standard bedroom with two desks, two dressers, two beds. No extra seating."

Neil sat on one of the high-backed, upholstered couches and taking Savannah's hand, he tugged gently, pulling her down next to him. Cal perched on the arm of the other club chair and the four of them chatted for a few minutes.

"I thought you guys were going to a party tonight," Savannah said.

"Maybe," Cal said. "At any rate, later is better for things like that. Not much happens 'til eleven or twelve. Midnight, the witching hour."

"Oh, well," Savannah said. "We can't stay out that late, right, Renee?"

"Absolutely not," Renee answered. "You don't want to see us out and about at the witching hour. Might be too scary for you."

"Hmm, sounds interesting," Cal said. "Maybe we should stick

77

around tonight."

"No, no," Savannah said with a laugh. "You go on to your party. We need to keep some things secret, you know."

Cal stood and stretched. "Neil, we need to be detectives. You up for it?"

"Of course, man. PI work is right up my alley."

"And we know it works for you," Renee said, winking at Cal. "Marlowe and all."

"True. I'm going to have to consider how to get my information."

"Savannah, you ever have a back massage?" Neil asked. She shook her head. "Come on, take your boots off, and lie down on the floor."

A slow blush crept across Savannah's face. "Why the floor?"

Before Neil could answer, Cal said, "A hard surface works best. The couch is too soft." He grinned at Renee. "And the other couch has a metal bar down the middle. Come on, Ren, I'll show you."

"Not on your life." Renee shook her head and rapidly waved her hands back and forth, palms out. "Unh-uh. You're up to something, I just know it. Is this how you think you'll get information from us?"

"No, not at all. But I do give good massages."

"Oh, so you're a pro, huh?" She glanced at Savannah who winked at her.

Cal laughed. "I've had a little experience, yeah. But it's all good." He gave her a quizzical look. "Would Russ be mad?"

Renee stiffened. "No—"

"I'm not going to do anything you don't want, Renee. I promise. It's a massage, a back rub, just a nice thing to do. I thought it might help you relax. You always seem so uptight."

"That's right," Neil said. "What's the big deal, for Chrissake?"

"Okay," Savannah said. She unzipped her boots but before she could get them off, Neil reached down to remove them. He set them to the side of the couch. Savannah slid to the floor and stretched out on her stomach. She pulled the hem of her skirt down, adjusting it to cover the backs of her thighs. "He's right, Renee. It's just nice."

"All right, okay," Renee said, laying down a couple of feet away from Savannah. She shut her eyes.

She is in Russ's bedroom, crowded with books and papers, record albums, plastic airplane models from his childhood, a stack of clothes his mother has washed and folded. Heavy curtains, drawn tight, block all the afternoon light. His parents are at work, his sister at volleyball practice. Russ leans against the closed door, arms crossed over his chest, eyes intent on watching Renee. She turns her back to him and quickly gets undressed. She pushes his briefcase off the end of the twin bed and scoots under the covers.
"Such a little priss, aren't you?" he says. He drops his pants and steps out of them as he pulls his shirt off. "Scoot over and you can give me a back rub."

"Yeah, it's not always about sex," Cal muttered as he moved down next to Renee, sitting cross-legged on the floor. Placing his hands on her upper back, he began a gentle kneading. She turned her head to look at Savannah. They smiled at each other and their fingers touched briefly. Renee's heart fluttered as Cal's fingers pressed on her shoulders. Neil switched off the overhead lights and stood over Savannah. Dropping to his knees, he straddled her hips. She drew in a breath, held it, then relaxed.

Renee closed her eyes and allowed her mind to drift, away from Russ, away from Cal, away. She let her limbs go limp and concentrated on releasing the tension in her back and neck. *It is a nice thing to do. Very nice.*

~~ 8 ~~

At two o'clock on Saturday, the mail arrived. Renee waited with other girls while the postman opened up the bank of mailboxes and distributed letters into the appropriate sections, then pushed the door closed. She stood back and let others get their mail first. As the mailroom emptied out, she pushed her key into the slot and opened the little door. She knew there was a letter—she had caught a glimpse of the blue envelope in the stack the mailman took from his bag. Relieved that Judy hadn't joined the throng in the lobby and wanting to read her mail in private, Renee buttoned her coat against the cold and left the dorm, the letter in her pocket.

The misty rain calmed her. Few people ventured out for leisure on the miserably wet days and Renee welcomed the solitude. A mile or so south of town was the pioneer graveyard, on a hill crested with fir trees. A narrow gravel road branching off the two-lane Monmouth-Corvallis highway led to the brick and iron sign at the entrance. Renee often made the trek alone, finding the walk peaceful.

She never went into the cemetery itself but always settled under the immense blue spruce at the outside boundary where she had an unobstructed view of the town sprawled in the distance. The ground was damp; her wool scarf made a thick pad to sit on. With the unopened letter in her lap, she closed her eyes.

When he calls her for the first time, Russ and Renee spend hours talking on the phone. She finds him engaging and respectful. They discover a shared interest in books and find they have read many of the same authors. They both want to be teachers and have large families. Renee is impressed by his strong convictions against drinking and drug use.

"I guess I'm kind of a misfit," he says. "I don't approve of the illegal activities so prevalent in our society. Why do people want to use drugs and alcohol? I don't understand it."

She isn't put off by his formality; in fact, she considers it charming. *"I'm tired of guys asking me to provide transportation for them so they can go to parties and get stoned,"* she says. *"They know I don't drink and then they're just disappointed I don't have a driver's license. They don't care about me."*

"I find that attitude all the time. Other students will ask me to help them with assignments when all they really want is for me to do their work."

Chuckling, she says, "Well, I've heard you're very smart!"

"I like your laugh," he says and she can hear the smile in his voice. *After a moment's hesitation, he asks, "Would you go out with me?"*

They were seniors in high school. Two and a half years ago. Seemed like a lifetime. Things had moved quickly; they began dating and became exclusive immediately. She couldn't even think about seeing someone else—Russ took all her time.

She thought of the walks in the park, picnics with sliced cheese, crusty Italian bread, olives, and apples, a Creedence Clearwater Revival concert they had attended. The Homecoming dance and the Junior-Senior Prom, Russ elegant and chivalrous in his tux, Renee feeling like Princess Grace in her strapless formal and long gloves. The after-dance dinners in candlelit restaurants. Sitting at Arctic Circle eating french fries with fry sauce. Playing croquet and badminton. Trips to the coast and stopping at Mo's for chowder. The ordinariness of studying together on weekends and watching movies on television. Good times. Good memories.

At the end of the summer before they went off to college they announced their engagement. He had chosen a simple solitaire and presented it to her with a pronouncement of love, telling her that they would be very happy together. She opened her eyes, held her left hand out, and gazed at the brilliant stone on her finger. *A diamond is forever. Russ-and-Renee is forever.* He said, "I love you. Marry me." *A husband and a family. What I always wanted. What I've always been afraid I wouldn't, couldn't, have.* She leaned her head against the tree trunk. *Why? Why was I afraid?*

Months later she realized he had never asked her to marry him—no, he *told* her. *Not the way I thought it would happen. I thought he'd be romantic and formal. Down on one knee.* But she loved him. And he loved her.

The first year of college was simple—they spent all their free time together. He made most of the decisions and she went along with them. It was easier that way. He tended toward moodiness and irritation when she disagreed with him. And he radiated self-confidence in direct contrast to her own timidity. *He's usually right and I can't argue with him. There's no point.* She covered her eyes with her palms, sitting perfectly still for a moment, then dropped her hands to her lap. The letter fell to the ground. Reading it could wait.

In August before their sophomore year of college, he went to Japan. People questioned her about his absence. "When is Russ coming home? How does he like it over there? What branch of the service is he in? Will he have to go Viet Nam?"

She clenched her teeth, jaw set. *No, he got lucky.* Head back against the tree, she closed her eyes again.

"The draft numbers have been drawn," Russ tells Renee as they drive back to Monmouth after a visit home in early December, 1969. His voice is calm, businesslike. He waits for her to speak.

"What number are you?" She is hesitant, a flash of fear settling in her gut. The draft lottery system has just been implemented for the first time since World War II, sparking headlines and anti-war demonstrations. Renee wishes she had been paying more attention to national news.

"They draw by birthdays. April 24th is number two." He pulls into a parking space at the back of the dorms, turns off the ignition, and sets the brake. He exits the car, walks around to her side, and opens the door. "I'm not going to Viet Nam."

"Two. I can't believe it." She sits still.

"Well, they aren't taking eighteen-year-olds. Maybe next year my number will be higher and it won't be a problem. But I'm registering anyway as a C.O." He gets his duffel bag and her suitcase from the back seat and starts to walk away. Renee scrambles out of the car and follows him.

"What do you mean?"

"Conscientious Objector. I won't fight."

"Oh, no, you can't. I mean, you can't go to war." She grips *his arm and falls into step with him.*

He looks down at her. "Then you'll go to Canada with me if we have to?"

Renee doesn't answer. Her heart feels like it will shatter if *she opens her mouth.*

Alleycat

"Good, I knew you would."

No, he wasn't in the military; he was in a study-abroad program. She knew it was a wonderful opportunity—how many times had she heard that phrase?—and she was thrilled for him. His parents had the money and he had the grades to make it possible. He said, "But, I won't go unless you agree, Renee." *Not fair. You knew I wouldn't stop you.*

He left in August. When school started in September, classes filled her time. She took eighteen credits that first term, thinking to distract her mind with work. She threw herself into studying. Days were busy, filled with school, fun times, almost like being a freshman again. She made new friends, girls in the dorm mostly, who had never met Russ, knew only what Renee told them. By the middle of November, when he had been gone three months, she found herself imagining herself in close situations with Nathan, her biology lab partner. Chance meetings on campus, planned study sessions, actual dates—the fantasies made her tremble. Maybe Russ was not her entire world. *Not fair*, she told herself. *He's far away.*

Then his letter. Coming home early, at the break in March. Her stomach clenched. She closed her eyes, willing her heart to stop pounding. He would be angry that she had never told him about having a male lab partner, never mind that she actually had fantasies about Nathan. Such a silly thing, but it would matter to Russ. *How will I tell him about Cal? Or the Alleycat?*

She picked up the letter. Carefully breaking the seal on the envelope, she hesitated. *What should I do?* After spring break she would request a different lab partner. Maybe Russ would even take the class with her and they could work together. Or she could drop the class and take it next year. It would work out. She would make it work. *But Cal...*

She unfolded the thin paper. The letter was short. His usual block printing, uneven and hard to read in places. But his message was clear. "I'VE CHANGED MY MIND. I'M SORRY BUT I KNOW YOU DON'T WANT TO MARRY A QUITTER. I NEED TO STICK THIS OUT EVEN THOUGH IT'S HARD FOR BOTH OF US. I'M SURE YOU UNDERSTAND."

Relief poured over her like a waterfall in the summer—sun-warmed, heavy, pressing against her from all sides. *Russ, I'm scared of you coming home. What in the world will we find? Will you know me? I don't think so. Other people have entered my life.*

~~ 9 ~~

Pulling a sheet of thin airmail paper from her desk drawer, Renee wrote, "Dear Russ," then with a grunt, balled up the paper and dropped it in the wastebasket. New sheet, old beginning.

> *My Dearest Russ, I got your letter—what a surprise. But at least we're halfway through the year. Six months to go. July! I don't know how we'll do it. I wish you were coming back early, but I guess we'll survive. I miss you so much! We—Judy, Savannah and I—met this groovy guy—*

"No," she whispered. *Hold on. This is Russ you're writing to, remember? Jealous Russ. The General.* She winced and let out an audible sigh, tapping the pen rapidly on the desk, then resumed writing.

> *—and I think Savannah is stoked about him. Judy, of course, couldn't care less. I think she's afraid of having a boyfriend! If she only knew what she's missing.*

She put the pen down. Elbows on the desk, she put her hands over her face. *I'm crazy about him, too. All three of them. But Russ, you'd never understand. I can't tell you this way. A letter is too hard. Too—iffy. You'd get the wrong idea. I know you would.* She stood and paced the room, chewing on a fingernail. *How do I explain it? What do I tell him about the Alleycat?* Nothing. It could wait. *Things might change anyway. Cal and Neil will probably get* bored soon enough and find some other naïve girls to hang out with. Or real girlfriends. She would tell him in July, when he came home. Ignoring the tremor in the pit of her stomach, she continued writing.

> So I hope it works out well for Savannah. School is going fine but I really miss your help in some of my classes, like math. The professor is great, though, and I've been able to get some clarification on difficult problems. I love my lit class. We're reading John Updike's *Rabbit, Run* right now and then we'll be doing *Catch-22*. It's like a vacation from school! I even like writing the papers. Biology lab is okay, kind of fun. My lab partner is cool. I hate the lecture part, though. Oh well, after this year I'll be done with my science requirement. Then on to ed classes—I can't wait!

She prattled on, filling two pages with dorm life anecdotes, talk about the weather, and questions about his experiences in Japan. She finished the letter, sealed and addressed the blue airmail envelope, then stared at it for a long moment. She always drew hearts across the flap, one for each month he had been away. This time she drew a single heart. It seemed more appropriate, kind of a countdown to when she would have to face him again.

Renee and Savannah flipped through the selection of greeting cards in Crider's Variety store. Judy's birthday was coming up and they wanted to get her a gift. They had already picked out some scented soaps and a paperback novel but also wanted to get a card. With a couple of hours until their next class, they had plenty of time to shop.

"How's Russ?"

"Fine." Renee continued to pick up cards and look at them.

"You sure?"

"Yep."

Savannah took the card from Renee's hand and stuck it back on the rack. "Hey, talk to me. You don't sound like he's 'fine.' What's going on?"

"It's hard having him gone, that's all."

"I know." Savannah chose a card at random. "Come on, let's buy this stuff and get out of here. Judy won't care what card we get her."

Renee smiled at that and followed Savannah to the register. She took a Hershey bar from the shelf and added it to the items on the counter. In a soft voice, hesitant and a little uneasy, she said, "I don't know how to tell Russ about the 'Cat."

The cashier rang up the purchase and waited while the girls divvied up the total and paid. They walked outside; the sunlight was dazzling after their time in the dark store. Shading her eyes with one hand, Renee said, "Look at that! Sunshine in January in Oregon! Maybe it's a sign."

"Yeah, not to say anything to him about the Alleycat."

"I got that sign." Renee smiled at her friend. "He would never understand. I don't know. It feels wrong not to tell him but..." She shook her head, hunching her shoulders.

They cut across the middle of the street to the park and sat at a picnic table. Savannah pulled the candy bar out of the bag, unwrapped it, and gave half to Renee.

Renee took a bite of the chocolate. The smoothness of the candy was soothing as she let it melt slightly on her tongue and she felt a calmness settle over her. "Going to the 'Cat doesn't feel wrong."

"It's not." Savannah studied Renee's face. "He's not running your life now. You're on your own."

"Yeah, well..." Renee's voice trailed off. She shut her eyes, smiling, thinking: *And I'm doing okay.*

"Besides, do you think he's telling you every little thing he's doing, every place he's going, every person he's spending time with?" Savannah shook her head. "No. He's doing all sorts of things that he'll tell you about when he gets home." Turning around, she sat with her back to the table, elbows resting on the scuffed wood. A thin breeze whispered through the pine trees. She closed her eyes, lifting her face to the bright sun. "You know, you talk a lot about him but it's different since Christmas. Before the break you were so quiet and careful. Like you were afraid to do anything. Almost like he was watching you. I was getting worried. Now it's almost like you need to convince people that—that—well, I don't even know what." She rubbed the back of her neck. "I wonder if—if you're afraid of Russ, of what will happen if he finds out about—"

"I'm not scared," Renee protested. "It's just that he has strong ideas about right and wrong. He knows so much more than I do."

"Renee, that's not true. He doesn't know more about right and wrong, about how to be a good person. You're smart, kind—"

Renee smiled. "I know you think that. But Russ, he takes care of me, you know? I never thought I'd find somebody who would do that."

"Do you still think you need taking care of? I wish you could see how incredible you are." Savannah held up one hand, cutting Renee off. "Don't say anything. Just listen. I'm sure Russ is wonderful. But I have to ask—do you have a voice in your life with him? Do you get the things *you* need?"

"I guess so. I think so." Renee gazed across the park, picking absently at a ragged cuticle. "I've never felt I could make the right judgments about anything. My dad always told me I can't make up my mind or make decisions. He's right."

"Renee, that's crazy. Your dad—"

"I know it seems ridiculous, but I really do need someone to be connected to, someone to take care of me. All I've ever wanted was to get married and have a family, a *good* family."

"What do you mean by that?"

"Russ's family is really tight. Very close and loving. My family isn't like that. My dad is the boss. Period. Russ and I have talked a lot about what our family will be like."

"Well, that's good," Savannah said. "As long as you agree on things."

Renee nodded. "I've always trusted Russ to know what we should do."

"But right now you have to trust yourself, right?"

"I'm working on it."

"Good. I'll tell you, since we met the guys, I don't know,

Alleycat

you've been more mellow, I guess. Not so on edge. You smile more, like you're okay with yourself. You know what I mean?"

Renee was quiet. "I feel different," she finally said. "And I'm not as careful as I maybe should be. Russ would be very disappointed in me. I mean, the way we are at the 'Cat is, um, questionable? It's a public place, people see us, but I don't even think about that. It just feels so good to—"

"Have fun? Relax? Let loose? You still seem nervous sometimes—when Judy's there, anyway." Savannah laughed and Renee smiled in agreement. "But at least you're trying to enjoy yourself more." She paused, then asked, "What do you think is questionable or that Russ would think is wrong?"

"Well, you know," Renee said. "We get really loud and the guys are pretty raunchy. There's a lot of flirting going on. Between you and Cal and Neil, mostly," she added quickly. "I'm sure people notice us. I—I just hope none of Russ's friends are there."

"Why would Russ's friends even care? It's not wrong to have a good time."

"But Russ would be hurt, I think. That I'm having fun without him, that I'm managing without him—that worries me." She leaned her elbows on the table and placed her hands on her temples. "With Russ I have to watch everything I say, everything do. Sometimes it's more than I can handle. Now that he's been gone for awhile I guess I—I'm like—on vacation or something." She picked at her thumbnail. "My biology lab partner is a boy. I never told Russ, even though he would want to know something like that. In fact, he would have told me to switch partners. I didn't feel I needed to—so what if I have to work with a guy? But he—" She stopped, took her glasses off, laid them on the table, and rubbed her eyes. "After I'd had a couple of labs with Nathan, fall term, I had a dream and he was in it. It kind of shook me up. I mean, Russ had been gone only, what? Two months. How could I have a dream about some other guy?" She let out a long sigh. Nibbled at a fingernail. Gazed across the park. Hunched her shoulders, sighed again. "I got a letter yesterday. He's staying."

Savannah turned to face Renee, straddling the narrow bench. "What?"

"Uh huh. Guess he doesn't miss me so much after all." She looked at the scratchings on the picnic table, her fingertip lightly tracing the deep lines of strangers' initials. "I'm glad he's not coming back yet."

"Wow. I didn't expect that."

Renee smiled. "I know. Neither did I, to tell you the truth." Elbows on the table, fingers entwined, she rested her chin on her hands. "I kind of like my life right now. Even though it's just temporary."

Savannah finished her piece of the chocolate. She folded the wrapper, pressing hard on the folds to make flat creases. She studied Renee's face. "I think Cal's interested in you."

"What!" Renee's head snapped upward. "No! He isn't. He knows I would never—"

"Of course he knows that. But the way he looks at you sometimes…just be careful, okay?"

"Sure, but he's like a big brother. He teases and pushes and gets obnoxious, then the sweet side comes out. I think he cares about me, about all of us, but that's it." Renee shook her head. "No, I'm sure he thinks I'm a total ditz. He likes *you*."

"Haha, you're funny. He's just a big flirt."

"True! And he's good at it. Judy probably thinks he likes *her*!"

~ 10 ~

When the girls arrived at the Alleycat Tuesday evening, the boys were already there, deep in quiet conversation. The mood had shifted dramatically from the usual absurdity to a subtle tension and greetings were subdued as the boys moved to make room for three more people in the booth.

"What's going on?" Savannah asked, looking from Cal to Neil to Alex. "You're acting so different."

The waitress stopped by, pencil poised over her pad. "What can I get for you?"

"Just a Coke," Savannah said, still watching the boys' faces. Renee and Judy ordered soft drinks, too. As soon as the server left, Savannah repeated, "What's going on?"

"Nothing," Cal said. He smoked his cigarette and sipped his coffee.

"Well, something is," Savannah insisted.

Neil, Alex, and Cal exchanged glances, then Neil spoke. "We just have something to do tonight. We can't stay long."

The drinks arrived. Judy ripped the top of her straw wrapper, put the straw in her mouth, and blew the paper off in Alex's direction. It hit the table in front of him. He picked it up and began folding it, making a small square.

"Hey, maybe we'll be able to get some studying done tonight," Judy said. "That'll be different."

Savannah scowled at her, then turned her attention back to Neil. "What do you have to do?"

"It's not important," Cal said.

"Well, it seems odd," Renee said. "You guys aren't usually so quiet."

Alex dropped the square of paper in the ashtray. He sat back in the booth, arms crossed over his chest. "Have you heard of astral travel?" Savannah sat up straight, a look of interest on her face.

"What in the world?" Renee leaned forward, watching Alex intently. "What do you mean?"

"You know, communication on a psychic level," Neil said. "Cal is expecting an encounter tonight. In Gentle Woods."

"There's a new moon," Cal said quietly. "It's a good time."

Judy rolled her eyes. "That's stupid," she muttered.

"No it's not," said Savannah. "The moon is significant in psychic phenomena. According to what I've read, the new moon can be for beginning something or for removing unwanted influences. Also, when it's moving toward the first quarter, like it is now, it acts as a doorway between worlds or planes. Is that what you're thinking, Cal?"

He nodded.

"We're hoping," said Neil, "to make contact with something or someone but we aren't sure it will happen." He saw the look of concern on Renee's face. "It's not dangerous. Hell, Gentle Woods is a public park."

"We want to come, too," Savannah said eagerly.

Cal shook his head. "No. Not this time."

Savannah started to say something but Neil broke in before she could. "Hey, we don't know what to expect. We just want to check it out."

"We won't get in the way," Savannah said. "Come on—"

"What *is* astral travel?" Renee asked, looking from Cal to Neil to Alex. No one answered her.

"I know something about this kind of stuff," Savannah said. "Maybe—"

Cal shook his head. "It's too many people. I don't—"

"We'll stay out of the way, I promise."

"Don't worry," Alex said quietly.

"What do you mean, don't worry?" Renee said, her voice going up an octave. "This is too s—"

Judy cut in. "Stupid."

Savannah glared at her. "Stop it, Judy."

Judy shrugged and poked at the ice in her drink. Renee chewed on a fingernail, eyes on Alex, waiting. He brushed non-existent crumbs off the table, then moved his coffee cup closer. He stirred the liquid slowly, tapped the spoon on the side of the cup, and placed it on a napkin. Neil slid his arm around Savannah's shoulders; she scooted closer to him. Cal quietly smoked.

Alex took a sip of coffee, then said in a matter-of-fact tone of voice, "We'll be fine. We're armed. I have a knife." Startled, the girls stared at him. A quick half-smile flashed across his face. "Just in case."

"My God, are you guys insane?" Renee's eyes were wide, her face somber and pale.

Neil laughed. "No, just a little loaded." He nudged Judy who sat next to him. "Can you move? I need to use the john." She scrambled from the booth, letting him out. He dug in his pocket and found a quarter. "Here, pick out some songs. Let's lighten up, for Chrissake."

"Good idea," Judy said, going to the jukebox.

"Alex?" Savannah said. He didn't answer.

"Like he said, don't worry." Cal crushed his cigarette out in the ashtray. "It's not a big deal."

"Then why are you so serious tonight?" Savannah asked. "I think it *is* a big deal."

"Me, too," said Renee, her voice tense. "I want to know what's really going on."

Cal sighed, closed his eyes for a second. "I just—"

"Hey," Judy said as she sat down next to Alex. "Guess what my art professor told us today? There's going to be a student show at the gallery and she's going to choose some of the artwork from my class."

"Judy, no one cares right now about your art class," Renee said sharply.

With a pout, Judy slumped in her spot. "Fine," she muttered.

Renee shook her head, chewing on her lower lip. "Cal?"

"I can't talk about it right now," he said.

Neil came back and plopped down in the booth. "When do you want to go, man?"

"Wait a minute," Savannah said. She looked at Alex. "How's a knife going to help you against a spirit?"

Alex shrugged. "Not against an astral body. But if something else comes along…"

"We're coming," Savannah said firmly.

"No," Cal told her. "Next time. Maybe."

Savannah threw her hands up. "I give up. Just be your chauvinist selves."

Cal spoke softly. "It's not like that, Savannah. I really don't know what's going to happen and I don't want you girls in the middle of something I can't control." He reached across the table and touched her arm. "I'm not trying to shut you out, I promise."

"Okay, okay," Savannah sighed. "I understand. I guess." She looked at Alex. "But—"

Alex pulled a penknife out of his pocket. He flipped it open. "Look, here's my knife. See, great protection." With a wide grin, he snapped the knife closed then jabbed unexpectedly at Neil across the table. Feigning a wound, Neil fell back against Savannah who let out a startled shriek.

"Wilt thou provoke me?" Neil yelled, fist in the air. "Then have at thee, boy!" He tried to wrestle the knife from Alex, then with a loud moan, slumped onto the table. He wrapped his fingers around Savannah's soda glass. "'Here's to my love!'" He raised his body up to take a drink. "'O true apothecary! Thy drugs be quick!'" He sat up, kissed Savannah on the lips. "'Thus with a kiss, I die.'" He fell face first onto the table, motionless.

Savannah gasped. "Romeo! Romeo!" Sobbing, she clutched at his hair.

Alex lunged at Renee. "Your turn, shweetheart," he said in a Humphrey Bogart voice.

She let out a yelp, jerking against Cal, hands up to her face. Cal wrapped his arms around her. Anguished, he spoke in a voice thick with tears and anger. "Now you've done it, Alex! Can't you see she's dying?" He wailed, "My God! Why? Why?"

Renee's eyes fluttered. "Ohhh, everything's going dark…" She went limp.

"Way to go, Alex," Cal said in a stern voice, keeping his arm protectively around Renee's shoulders. "Scaring the girls is not cool."

Savannah laughed, breaking the spell. The last song Judy had chosen was playing and they all joined Mick Jagger as he belted out, "I can't get no satisfaction."

When the song faded to an end, Cal stood up. "Let's pay the tab and get going," he said. He headed for the cash register.

"Wait a minute," Judy said. "We don't have to leave just because you are."

Cal came back to the table. "It's dark. We should walk you home."

"We really want to come with you," Savannah said.

"No, we don't," Judy mumbled.

"Sorry, Savannah." Neil said. "I'll tell you all about it

tomorrow."

"How much do we owe?" Alex asked, reaching in his pocket for change. "I'll get the tip this time." Cal showed him the bill; Alex picked out some coins and dropped them on the table.

"It's just a dollar apiece," Cal said. Everyone handed him their share of the money and he walked to the front of the diner. Neil helped Savannah with her coat and walked outside with her. With a loud "Gotcha!" Judy seized Alex's wool cap out of his hand and pulled it over her hair. He reached for the cap with an irritated grunt, but stopped short and turned away from her, shaking his head. He zipped up his leather jacket and pulled on gloves, then joined Neil and Savannah on the sidewalk. Cal struggled with the cigarette machine by the door; a pack of Camels dropped into the tray. He ripped the cellophane off and tapped out a cigarette, then slid the pack into his coat pocket. After lighting up, he held the door open for Renee and Judy and the group headed for the dorm.

The stars sparkled brightly against the moonless sky, the temperature near freezing. Shivering, Renee tightened her knitted scarf around her neck. "You guys are crazy," she mumbled as she strode away from the Alleycat. Cal caught up with her, the others falling in behind. They covered a block in silence. Renee could hear Judy's clinging voice—"Oh, Alex!"— above Savannah and Neil's quiet conversation.

"What's going to happen tonight?" Renee asked Cal.

"I'm not sure. I think we'll be able to make contact with someone in an astral state."

"Is this the first time you've done this?"

"First time with Alex and Neil."

"What do you mean? You've done this before? Isn't it dangerous?"

Cal chuckled softly but didn't say anything, not looking at her but up into the night sky.

In a low voice Renee said, "Explain it to me, please. Don't make jokes."

"Oh, well, I was going to say either it will work out or I'll be dead. Guess I'll keep that to myself."

"Come on, Cal. You're going to talk to some creepy ghost and you're worried—I know you are. I'm scared and all you do is laugh. You thrive on this, don't you? On me and Savannah getting all worked up and—" She broke off.

He still didn't speak but he wrapped his fingers around her hand. She shivered again, but not from the cold. His hand was warm and strong.

"Ghosts," Renee continued. "What do you plan to talk about with this—this thing?"

"Astral body. I'm sorry. I don't know how to explain it to you. Just forget it."

"Cal!" she cried in a low voice. "You're scaring me. I'm supposed to just 'forget it'? How?"

Cal tightened his grip on her hand, giving it a squeeze. "I'm sorry. I didn't want to tell you girls anything about it. I hoped we could just go do what we need to do and you'd never have known." He stopped walking and pulled Renee close, his arms around her shoulders, and rested his chin on her head for a moment. "Don't worry, please."

She stood very still; tears stung her eyes. "Cal..." *I'm scared for you.*

He let go of her and started walking again. She could see the red glow of his cigarette moving as he smoked. He called out, "Come on, let's get you girls home."

She caught up to him. "How will we know you're okay?"

Cal laughed, his serious mood gone. "Hell, we'll be fine. We'll see you tomorrow like always." He paused, then added, "I want you to know I'm not high. I'm not going into this messed up."

"Okay. At least I know you'll be rational out there, right?"

"Yep."

At the entrance to the dorm, Judy simply shook her head at the group and went on upstairs, leaving Renee and Savannah to see the boys off. "Promise you'll be careful," Renee said, her eyes bright. "Don't do anything rash."

"Yes, mother," Neil said, patting her on the shoulder. "We certainly won't do anything that will have ramifications we can't handle."

She pushed his hand off her shoulder. "Okay, be funny. I don't care." She turned away from him, toward Alex and Cal. "Do you at least have a flashlight?"

"Yes," Alex answered. "Hey, don't worry. It's all cool."

Neil wrapped his arms around Savannah in a bear hug. She looked up at him. "You better let me come next time."

"Yeah, I know." He let go of her and backed away. Looking at

Cal, he said, "You heard her, man. She's serious."

Cal smiled at her. "Yep, I see that. We'll see you tomorrow."

Reluctantly, Renee and Savannah said goodbye, watching after the boys as they left for the park on the northeast side of town, about a mile away.

"I better get upstairs," Renee said when they could no longer see the boys in the shadowy light. "Judy will be upset if I don't come in."

But later, unable to concentrate on homework, Renee wrote a note to Savannah: **Can I come down to your room?** She attached it to the clothespin and stomped on the floor a few times then dropped the clothespin out the window. A couple of minutes later she felt a tug on the string. Savannah had written back: **Of course!** Leaving Judy studying at her desk, Renee trotted down the stairs and knocked on Savannah's door.

"I need to talk to you," she said as Savannah invited her in. "Where's Molly?"

"Watching a movie in the lounge. She'll be gone awhile." Savannah plopped down on her stomach on Molly's bed, facing Renee.

Sitting cross-legged on Savannah's bed, Renee pushed her glasses onto the top of her head. "What did Neil tell you about tonight?"

"He said they were going to Gentle Woods to try to make contact with some kind of psychic being because a guy that Cal met one night told him to." Sitting up, Savannah worked her fingers through her hair, stiff from hairspray, then reached for her hairbrush on the nightstand between the beds. She began her nightly routine of one hundred strokes. "Neil wasn't sure when that happened but apparently this guy talked about things that only Cal would know. Based on what was said that night, Cal decided to check it out. Neil wasn't sure what Cal expected, but he was curious. You know how he is—he'll try anything." She smiled. "Cal asked him and Alex to come along, I guess for safety or confirmation or something." She shook her hair out, then continued brushing.

"Oh." Renee gazed across the room. "I couldn't get anything out of Cal. He was pretty evasive."

"Neil said Cal was jumpy, on edge."

"Well, he wouldn't tell me anything. He claims he didn't do any drugs tonight, either." She absently picked at a cuticle. "Do you know what an astral body is?"

"It depends," Savannah said. She put the hairbrush down and pulled her hair into a loose ponytail. "Sometimes it involves an out-of-body experience, like your spirit travels to another plane or even another world. You can communicate and see things and all that. You can make it happen deliberately. Or it can involve an after-death situation where the spirit continues to exist."

"Do you believe all that?"

Savannah hesitated, and then said, "I believe in the possibility."

~~ 11 ~~

The three girls met in front of the dining hall at five o'clock on Wednesday. Before Judy could push the doors open and enter, Savannah said, "Wait a sec, Judy. Renee and I are going to the 'Cat for dinner." She started to walk away, shifting her purse higher on her shoulder as she opened her umbrella. "Come on, I want to get there."

"I'm broke," Judy said. "I should be eating in the cafeteria. That's already paid for."

"Go ahead," Renee said, absently chewing her thumbnail. "You don't have to come with us. But Savannah and I need to make sure the guys are okay." She flicked a shred of fingernail to the sidewalk and shoved her hands in her pockets. "I'm ready, Savannah."

"What makes you think going early is going to make any difference?" Judy's tone was surly. "I'm sure they're just ducky."

"Sometimes they eat dinner there," Renee said. *Just stay home.*

"We don't want to wait until later," Savannah said. "It's been hard enough waiting all day." She frowned, adding, "I'm still ticked off they didn't let us go with them."

"The whole thing gives me the creeps," Renee said with a slight shudder. "Right now I just want to see them."

"Oh, fine," Judy grumbled. She checked her wallet. "I can get a cheese sandwich. That's cheap." She started walking. "Well, come on, let's go. I'm hungry."

The boys wouldn't talk about what happened in the park. Neil said, "Look, we're here. What happened last night doesn't make any difference. Besides it wasn't any big deal."

"Alex?" Renee said.

He shrugged. "Remember I had the knife? I didn't need it."

"Like it would have done any good," Judy said. "Do you believe this spirit stuff, Alex?"

"Hey, I'm open-minded. Show me proof and then I'll decide."

Watching Cal's face, Savannah asked, "Are you satisfied with how it went?"

Cal smiled at her. "Sure. Now let's talk about something else. Okay?"

Reluctantly, Savannah let it drop but Renee could tell she was disappointed. Savannah, quiet, pensive, watched the boys, particularly Cal who sat across from her, next to Renee. Alex and Neil tried to get her to laugh by telling dirty jokes but she only smiled briefly at the punch lines.

The waitress brought menus to the table. Since it was dinnertime, they decided to get real meals for a change, instead of passing one thing around the table. Alex and Cal ordered pancakes, bacon and eggs, Neil asked for a cheeseburger heavy on the cheese. Savannah and Renee decided to split a chef's salad and Judy chose a grilled cheese sandwich with coleslaw. When the food came, the table was crowded with all the plates. Neil eyed the tomatoes on the salad and asked the girls if they were going to eat them. Savannah laughed and put one slice on his plate. She picked up some french fries in exchange. Soon they were tasting each other's food, sharing everything. The night was back to normal.

Renee went over to the jukebox and dropped a quarter in the slot. She picked out three songs, then went down the short back hallway to the restrooms. The ladies room was empty. Leaning on the counter, she studied her reflection in the mirror over the sinks. Her hair was messy and starting to tangle in the back. She dug in her purse for a brush and, tipping her head forward and down, pulled it through her hair from underneath, brushing it until the knots were gone. Tossing her head back, her hair settled around her shoulders, full and shiny. Russ loved her hair when it looked like that. He called her his movie star. She shut her eyes.

Russ sets up the tripod while Renee changes her clothes and fixes her hair. He wants her to wear the black bikini he bought for her but she has resisted and put on a pair of cutoff jeans and the bikini top. "My hips are too big," *she says.* "I can't wear that tiny thing."

"You have a perfect butt," *Russ says.* "Stick out your hip a little and tip your head. Let your hair drape over one eye, like that actress, what's her name? From the forties."

"Veronica Lake?"

"Yes! Sexy and sultry. My movie star."

Alleycat

"I'm no movie actress," Renee said to the mirror. "Just a girl who wants to be a teacher. An ordinary girl." She sighed. Another memory filled her head, late winter of their senior year in high school.

Renee is sitting at the kitchen table, brochures from state colleges spread out around her. "My parents are asking me about college—where I want to go. I'm thinking of Southern Oregon. They have a good teaching program there."

Russ is making sandwiches at the counter. "Why does your mom buy this kind of bread? Balloon bread—nothing good about it."

"We like it."

"We're going to Oregon College of Education, in Monmouth." *He puts the sandwiches on a plate.* "I might need to bring my own bread next time. My mom gets whole wheat."

"I kind of wanted to go farther away. Monmouth is only 20 minutes from here. Besides, Courtney and I want to room together."

"I've already applied to OCE. You better get your application in soon."

"But I'm not sure I—"

"I am."

She considered how different her life would be if she had gone to SOC. Would Russ have followed her there? Would she have met anyone like Cal? *I let him give me a back rub. I let him hold my hand last night.* She felt a shiver go up her spine. She shoved the hairbrush in her purse and went back to the corner booth.

"Man, I dig your hair like that," Neil said. "You wear that scarf thing too much."

Renee laughed, blushing slightly. "Well, thank you." She ran her hand over her hair, smoothing it a little. "It doesn't always cooperate. Guess I got lucky today."

"I wish I could grow my hair out," said Judy. "It takes so long. And now I need a haircut if I'm going to keep it short like this." She pursed her lips. "I can't afford it."

"I can cut hair," Neil said. "I'll do it."

Judy gave him a sideways look. "I don't think so."

"I wouldn't let him near me with scissors," said Cal. "Unless he's sober."

"Which ain't gonna happen," Alex said, chuckling. "Besides, look at *his* hair—it hasn't seen a pair of scissors in a year."

A few hours later, walking with Renee back to the dorm, Cal broke into a jog. "I'll race you!" She sprinted after him, laughing. She could hear the others behind them, yelling encouragement. When she caught up, he slowed down to a walk. "Remember the night we first met?"

"Of course. January eleventh, I think. Second week of the term. Why? Is this some kind of anniversary?" She giggled and spun around in a circle. "Let's see, two weeks?"

He laughed and shook his head. "Girls always want to celebrate something!"

"Well, sure! Anniversaries are important. But two weeks? That's not very significant."

"That isn't what I was thinking about," Cal said. "That night, before you girls came in the 'Cat the first time—remember, when we had that snow?—an older guy walked in and sat at my table. He said he felt a psychic energy coming from me. He talked about the Woods and told me to check it out sometime, that I might find it significant."

"Who was he? Have you seen him again?"

"No. He told me his name was VanAllen. That's all I know."

"And that's why you guys went there last night."

"Yeah. I know it seems pretty lame. However," he said, walking backwards in front of her, "psychic energy compels a person to do things they might not ordinarily do." He grabbed Renee's hand. "Come on, run with me!" Laughing, she tried to keep up with him but his stride was much longer than hers. He stopped running and twirled her around. "Actually, the experience was interesting last night."

"But I assume you don't want to talk about it with everyone else," Renee said, after catching her breath.

He nodded. "Too many questions to answer. I don't want to get into it with anyone. I'm not even sure if Neil saw anything. I doubt Alex did." He paused, reached for his pack of cigarettes, changed his mind. "Last fall I took a walk through town, ended up at Gentle Woods. No one was there. It must have been too early for the kids in school. It was one of those rare sunny, almost-warm November days so I hung out for awhile, just smoking—not weed, mind you—thinking about some writing I wanted to do. I crossed the bridge, wandered around on the other side. I heard a voice but when I looked around, the park was still empty. The voice spoke again, not out loud but in my head. We had, um, a conversation, I guess. It happened a few times. It was pleasant, actually."

"Did you tell the guy, what's his name, VanAllen, all this?"

"Not all of it. I said I'd been there and felt a presence, a spirit or something. He wasn't surprised. He wanted to know more but I didn't really want to share my entire experience with some stranger who just sat at my table. And when he talked about the Woods, I got a different sense. Like something else might be there. I don't know. I can't explain it."

"Savannah said you were worried."

Cal shook his head. "Not worried. Keyed up, I guess. And it was different from the other times. Almost a negative vibe. And, just like the other times, I wasn't high."

"Neil was, though, right?"

"No, he wasn't. I wanted him sober. He plays the part of a stoner more than he actually lives it."

"Yeah, I kind of thought so," Renee said. "But all I want to know right now is this: are you going back?"

"Most likely. Maybe I'll take you next time."

~~ 12 ~~

Thursday afternoon Judy surprised Renee and Savannah by suggesting a walk to Gentle Woods. They wasted no time in taking advantage of her unusually good mood and agreed at once. Renee was nervous but her curiosity was stronger. They set out, Judy's step jaunty, her chatter energetic. But halfway there it began to rain and she wanted to turn back.

"Oh, Judy," Renee protested. "We've come this far, let's keep going."

With a loud sigh, Judy walked faster, reaching the park ahead of the others. She headed directly for the playground. The rain had petered out and the clouds moved to let the sun shine through.

As they neared the park, Renee and Savannah exchanged glances. When the empty parking lot came into view, they craned their necks to see—what? Evergreens, massive oaks and maples, a few bushes. Green, manicured lawn, dappled by the sunlight, dotted with picnic tables. Swings, a merry-go-round, monkey bars. Garbage cans set awkwardly on tree roots, overflowing with empty beer and wine bottles. A double-doored brick and cement restroom. An ordinary park. Deserted, quiet, peaceful.

A broad, gurgling creek split the park in half. Renee and Savannah crossed the grass and stepped onto the footbridge, hewn from thick logs. On one side, shadows blackened the water tumbling roughly over rocks, splashing onto brush-covered banks. As the water flowed under the bridge, toward the open side of the park, bright sunlight flashed off the ripples. *Night and day.*

Renee caught Savannah's eye. "Shall we?"

"Yes."

Silently they crossed the bridge. On the other side, the park was darker, the foliage more dense. Old bent trees, leafless, with thick gnarled branches. The ground underneath evergreens littered with brown needles and pinecones. Mud, a few patches of weedy grass. Tangles of blackberry vines. A soggy field outside the rim of brush and smaller trees. A barbed wire fence. The sound of the creek, muffled, seemed miles away. The chill air felt still and heavy, oppressive. They stopped walking, staying close together a few feet from the field.

Renee felt as though she stood on the edge of something unknown. One hand on her chest, feeling the bump-bump-bump-bump of her heart, her mouth went dry and she shivered. She could hear Savannah's breathing, shallow and quick. Looking at her friend she saw Savannah had her eyes closed, her head back.

"You okay?" Renee asked.

Savannah opened her eyes and looked around. "Do you feel anything?"

"It's like two different places when you cross the bridge. That side"—Renee pointed to the sun-sparkled playground where Judy, on a swing, pumped her legs hard to get high in the air—"feels okay. This side, right here, feels eerie." They stood in the middle of a ring of trees, in a clear spot of dirt and pine needles. To their right a door-wide opening in the brush divided the field from the park.

Savannah pointed to the field. "I think that's where it is."

"Where the break is in the bushes—it's kind of like a portal, isn't it?" Renee said with another shiver. She wrapped her arms around her chest. "My heart is beating so fast!" She tried to swallow. "And my mouth is like cotton." As quickly as the sensations hit her, they disappeared. "Strange. Now I feel okay, I guess."

"I had the same feeling," Savannah murmured. "And it's gone now. Weird, huh? I don't like it. I wonder what happened last night. Neil was kind of evasive. Do you think they connected with a spirit?"

"Astral body," Renee said. "I don't know. Cal said it was interesting. But it doesn't feel right."

"No, it doesn't. It's strange how dark it is on this side."

"Well, there are a lot more trees and it's a smaller area."

"Yeah, but I don't think that's it. There's something else." Savannah gazed across the park toward the field. "I wish they would have let us come."

"I think we should get out of here. And I'm not talking about this with Judy." Renee headed for the creek; Savannah followed. In the middle of the bridge they stopped, looking down at the water as they leaned on the rail. Beneath the heavy planks the creek gurgled and bubbled, pouring out of the shadows into the light.

Savannah turned, causing Renee to jump. They smiled weakly at each other.

"Come on, Judy, let's go!" Savannah yelled. She walked on across the bridge to the brighter side of the park.

Judy slowed the swing to a stop but didn't get off. "It's a pretty park. I bet it's really beautiful in the spring. Come on and try a swing. How long since you've been on one?"

Renee shook her head. "No, let's go. I don't feel like hanging around."

"Scared?" Judy asked, derision clear in her voice.

"No!" Renee snapped.

"I have to study *some*time," Savannah said. Judy gave her a "since when?" look, but jumped off the swing.

"You know they're just putting you on," Judy said as they walked back along the highway. "Ghosts. Spirit bodies or whatever they call them. Drug-induced paranoia. It's ridiculous and you know it. But," she added, with a triumphant laugh, "you fell for it, both of you. Speaking to the dead. I never heard of anything so ridiculous. What a joke. They must have been cracking up!"

"You know, Judy, it's a serious thing to a lot of people," Savannah said, her voice tight.

"Yeah, potheads," Judy said with a sneer.

Savannah let out a sigh. "Not just druggies. I believe in it."

"Well, sorry I said that, then. Have you actually seen a ghost?"

"Astral body," Renee said.

"Oops, sorry, *astral* body." Judy turned toward Savannah. "Have you?"

"No, but I've read a lot about psychic activity. I believe in astrology, you know that. You've seen my books. And Cal's right about the moon. The phases indicate different things in the psychic world—rebirth, regeneration, death. And I read in one of my books that a lifeline that curves around the thumb, like Cal's does, means the person has strong psychic energy." She stopped walking. "I just think it would be interesting to be part of whatever the guys were doing Tuesday night."

"I still think it's stupid," Judy said, hands on her hips, shaking her head. "I'm sorry, Savannah, but I do."

Savannah took a big breath before speaking, keeping her voice light. "Everyone has their own opinions. I don't mind that you don't believe it. But please understand that it *is* something I'm curious about."

"I know," Judy said. "I'm sorry. I am."

"Why did you suggest coming here today if you think it's so stupid?" Renee asked.

"Humph. I thought you would see there's nothing here but a park. No spirits. Guess I was wrong." Judy sighed, resigned. "You'll believe anything they tell you."

"I believe they believe it," Renee said. "That's good enough for me."

Savannah said, "I wish the guys would let us be part of it." With a shake of her head, she added, "I can't think about that any more right now. I have a lousy term paper to write for my World Lit class. I really do need to study."

"Me, too." Judy turned to Renee. "How's Russ doing? Has he had any tests yet?"

"Russ?" *I haven't thought of him all day.*

~~ 13 ~~

Renee sat in the lobby of the humanities building on Friday afternoon, waiting for Savannah to get out of her geography class. A group of students walked noisily down the stairs.

"Oh, God, that was a killer mid-term," she heard one say.

"Dr. Malcolm sure knows how to put the screws to us, huh?" said another.

Renee's stomach clenched and sweat popped out along her hairline. Dr. Malcolm was her history instructor, a bear of a man, intimidating and humorless. *Oh my God. I missed the history exam? When did he tell us about it? What if he comes down the stairs and sees me sitting here?* She didn't know whether to grab her books and purse and run out the door or hide behind a pretended interest in searching through her binder. Frozen to the spot, she couldn't make a decision. When Savannah stopped in front of her, Renee's breath escaped in a great *whoosh*.

"C'mon, let's get out of here," she said, leaping to her feet and crossing the small foyer to the glass doors. She pushed her way outside and immediately headed away from the building, trusting that Savannah was right behind her.

"Whoa, hold up," Savannah said. "What's the matter?"

Renee stopped and leaned against the giant evergreen in front of the science building next door to the humanities building. "My history class just got out." She closed her eyes.

"Yeah, so? Was it a tough class today?" Savannah reached out and touched Renee's arm, wrapped tightly around her stack of books.

"Beats me." Renee flinched, opened her eyes, and peered over at the building they had just vacated. "I didn't go to class. Again."

"Oh, well, big deal," Savannah said.

"Well, it is kind of a big deal. Apparently we had a mid-term. And I missed it."

"Oh, man, that isn't good." Savannah pulled at Renee's sleeve. "Come on, let's go get some coffee. Or we could go to my room and listen to music. Get out of here, anyway."

"Okay, the dorm. I'm not up to running into anyone from my class."

In Savannah's room, she put a Simon and Garfunkel record on the stereo and they sat on the floor with their backs against the beds. Renee put her head down on her bended knees and listened to the music for a few minutes. Then, raising her head, she wiped at her eyes with a crumpled Kleenex. "What kind of teacher am I going to be? I can't even get to my classes."

"It's one test," Savannah said. "You won't miss another one."

Renee nodded. "I really want to be a teacher, Savannah. It's something I've wanted for a long time, before Russ, before high school. But I don't know if I can do it."

"What do you mean? Of course you can. It's one class, Renee."

"My dad told me I should be a secretary. He thinks that's a better job than teaching. Or maybe he just thinks that's all I can do because you don't have to go to college to type." She shifted her position, crossing her legs, pushing her hair behind her ears. "I used to dream about the classroom I'd have, how the desks would be arranged, the things I would put on the bulletin boards. I could see the children's faces." She sniffled and blew her nose. "I did okay last year, my grades were okay. But now it's so hard. I'm just so overwhelmed. All I want is for night to come and I can forget all about responsibility and classes and grades. I want to write poetry, not essays. I want to talk about crazy stuff, not world history. I want to feel happy and have fun but I'm scared and worried all the time. "

"Oh, Renee, I hate that you feel like that. You shouldn't feel scared. You hide a lot of it, but I know how hard things are for you. Maybe I shouldn't say this but don't worry too much about your grades. It'll work out. I think the nights we share with the guys are important."

Renee nodded and lifted her head, looking at her closest friend. "Savannah, I don't know how I'd get through this without you."

Savannah reached over and embraced Renee. "You will," she said. "You are. And I'm right here with you, all the way."

After Biology on Monday morning, Renee had three hours until her next class and even though she knew she should go see Dr. Malcolm about the test, she couldn't face him. She had occasionally skipped a few classes, but missing a test was bad. She had joked about it with her friends, but inside she felt panicky. Next to math, history was her worst class. She couldn't afford to fail. *How would I tell Russ? Or my parents?*

But going to the professor, telling him some lie, then trying to pass a test she was unprepared for? Playing dumb—"Oh, we had a test?"—was one option she could use when she went to class. Or she could bite the bullet and stop by his office right now. With a dejected sigh she reluctantly went to talk to Dr. Malcolm.

February

~ 14 ~

Renee jumped when she felt the pounding coming from Savannah's room below. Judy stepped to the window and cranked it open, reaching out for the string and clothespin attached to the sill. She pulled the string up and opened the note, then read it out loud.

Savannah had scrawled: **I just had a brainstorm! It has to do with Neil's apartment!**

Renee closed her textbook and put down her highlighter. "Okay, I'm done studying. Come on, let's go find out what she's thinking." She and Savannah had been trying to get up the nerve to go back to the apartment since the uncomfortable fiasco the first time they had visited. The boys had never directly invited them; in fact, the apartment seldom came up in conversations. It seemed too brazen to simply go there as they had before, expecting to be welcomed.

Renee and Judy ran down the flight of stairs and rapped loudly on Savannah's door. When it opened, Renee said, "What's your idea?"

"Let's offer to cook a dinner for them. We could fix something like spaghetti. It's easy and not too expensive and everybody likes it."

"Great idea!" Judy said, clearly motivated. "I make the best spaghetti! I put olives and fresh tomatoes in it. And a little Velveeta—that's the secret ingredient."

Renee and Savannah grimaced. "Velveeta!" they exclaimed in unison. Judy frowned. Renee went on, "The olives sound good, Judy. And peppers, onions, mushrooms, all that. Let's do it."

That evening at the Alleycat Savannah said to the boys, "How would you feel about us fixing dinner for you sometime?"

"It would have to be at your place, if that's okay," Renee added, a bit of hesitation in her voice. She put her elbows on the table and clasped her hands together, looking over them at Cal.

He grinned at her. "A home-cooked meal?"

"Man, that'd be great," Neil said.

"When do you want to come?" asked Alex.

Judy spoke up first. "Tomorrow?"

"Wait a sec, Judy," said Savannah. "We have to have time to buy the food. I have classes late on Tuesday. How about Wednesday?"

"Okay," said Alex. "Do you know where our apartment is?"

Renee winked at Savannah. "Yeah, we know. Number 8, Villa Apartments."

Judy stared at her. "How do you know that?"

Blushing, Renee murmured, "Um, I don't know."

"I told you, remember?" Cal said. "Couple of nights ago."

"More like a couple of weeks, man," Neil said. "We kept thinking you chicks would show up."

"Uninvited?" Savannah shook her head. "Not a chance."

"We have better manners than that," Renee said, with feigned indignation.

"Well, you're invited now," said Alex.

After lunch on Wednesday, the three girls went shopping. For once Judy didn't complain about the long walk to the grocery or the cost of the food. They bought ground beef, a large package of spaghetti, tomato sauce and tomato paste, onions, garlic, green peppers, mushrooms, black olives, Italian seasoning, a loaf of French bread and a pound of butter. Judy had to run back for the Velveeta.

At the dorm they showered, fixed their hair and put on makeup, then dug through closets and drawers for just the right casual clothes. They all agreed that jeans and sweaters would be most appropriate and comfortable. At five-thirty, breathless and a little shaky, they climbed the stairs to the apartment. Judy tapped on the door.

Alex answered. "Ah, the chefs are here! Come in, come in!"

"Thank God," Neil said, stepping forward to take the grocery bag from Savannah.

Alleycat

Cal ushered them inside with a slight bow. "Welcome to our castle, ladies."

The girls stepped into the apartment and looked around curiously. The boys had tried to straighten up the living room. Papers, books, all sorts of junk were shoved under an ancient plaid couch and a sleeping bag had been haphazardly folded and put in a corner. The only real pieces of furniture consisted of the couch, a rickety end table, and a bricks-and-boards bookshelf. A couple of rolled up chunks of foam rubber propped against the wall and covered with a tapestry formed a chair. Posters—political, vulgar, funny, and incomprehensible—tacked everywhichway to the walls, doors, and ceiling added color to the otherwise drab room. Half-melted candles, squatty and abstract, sat on the crowded bookshelf and on saucers on the floor. An incense stick in a tray on the end table filled the room with a sweet, pungent odor. Just off the living room was a small dining area with a card table and four chairs.

"Nice decorating," Judy said.

"Thanks. We didn't think we needed a professional designer," Cal told her. "We figured we could do it ourselves."

Alex laughed. "We won't tell you how long it took us to get it cleaned up for you."

"That's a total lie," Cal said. "Neil didn't do a thing."

"I watched you and Alex work your asses off," Neil countered.

"Thank you," Renee said. "We appreciate it, the cleaning up and the watching."

Savannah added, "Neil, I can't believe you didn't at least dust the furniture."

Grinning, he winked at her. "Oh, that's right. I dusted."

"Well, if you ever want to redecorate," Judy said. "I could help."

"Thank you," Cal said. "We might take you up on that offer. The bedroom needs a woman's touch."

Judy blushed and turned toward Alex. "Kitchen?" She followed him around the corner of the living room wall. "Wow, you sure keep this place clean." She glanced around. "We need a skillet, a big pot, a cutting board, and some knives."

Alex called out to the boys. "Uh, you guys know anything about a cutting board?"

"What's it for?" Cal asked, coming into the kitchen.

"Very funny," Renee said. "It's for chopping food. Onions and

113

carrots."

"What, you're supposed to cut that stuff up?" Alex looked at Cal and Neil. "Did you know that? Why are we eating onions whole?"

Neil nodded. "Yeah, it's a lot harder than eating an apple. All those layers."

"Judy," Cal said, "you find us a cutting board in that pile of junk we have, we'll be forever in your debt."

Judy dug around in several cupboards and drawers before finding a smooth, almost-new cutting board and a couple of mismatched knives. She also pulled out a beat-up skillet, a saucepan, and a large serving bowl. "All set," she said, handing the knives to Savannah and Renee.

"We never come in here," Alex said. "We've been waiting for someone to cook for us."

"We're really sick of 'Cat food," Neil said, grinning at his own joke. Savannah slapped him on the arm. He kissed her cheek. "Hey, I gotta split for awhile. But I'll be back. What time is dinner?"

"Mmm, about an hour," Renee said, looking to Savannah and Judy for confirmation. They both nodded. "Does that work for you?"

"Yeah, yeah, I'll be here by then." He looked at the clock on the stove. "Six-thirty." He headed for the door. "Later, kids!"

"I have play tryouts at seven," Cal said. "Sorry."

"That's okay," Renee said. "We'll get going on this right away."

Savannah and Renee unloaded the grocery bags while Judy opened the package of ground beef and broke it up it into the skillet. Cal leaned against the doorframe and watched them bustle around, each taking charge of a separate part of the preparations. Alex sat at the table. He opened a textbook and began reading.

"This is fascinating," Cal said, "but I need to shower. Renee, care to join me?"

She giggled. "No, thank you."

"We need her right here," Savannah said, trying to sound stern.

"Ju-u-u-d-y-y?"

Judy rolled her eyes and turned on the burner under the skillet. Renee and Savannah stifled giggles.

Cal laughed. "Guess that's a 'no'. Okay. It could have been fun." He dropped a hand on Alex's book as he passed the table.

Alleycat

"You're the boss; keep them in line, okay?"

"Hey!" Judy glared at the boys. "What do you think this is? A job?"

"Settle down, Judy," Savannah said with a groan. "He's kidding. He's trying to rile you up."

"I'm waiting for him to tell us to go barefoot," she said, still glaring.

"Only if you're pregnant," Cal said. He stepped close to her and gave her a quick squeeze around the shoulders. "I apologize. It's very nice of you to cook for us."

"You're welcome," she said, softening.

"Change your mind about the shower?" With a merry grin, Cal raised his eyebrows and gestured toward the bathroom.

"No!"

Cal left the room amid howls of laughter. Alex closed his book and sat back, watching the food preparations. Judy stirred the ground beef and added garlic, salt, and pepper. Savannah chopped up the onion and dumped it in the sizzling skillet. She wiped onion-tears from her eyes with the back of her hand, and then held a few mushrooms under running water, rubbing dirt off them. Renee minced a clove of garlic and mixed it into the butter.

"What are you fixing?" Alex asked. "It smells good."

"Spaghetti," Judy said. "Hope you like it."

"I like anything. I usually just have a bologna sandwich or cereal."

Judy made a face. "Yuck. This will definitely be better than that."

"Do you want any help?" Alex went into the kitchen and looked at the ingredients on the counter. "I could butter the bread or something. Or, I could just watch and give directions." He gave them a big smile, his gray eyes shining.

Renee held out a knife and the small bowl of garlic butter. "Here you go. You have to slice the bread about half an inch thick, okay? Thanks." Alex took the knife with a flourish, brandishing it like a sword, waving it around with a karate yell. Renee ducked, giggling, and darted out of his way. "Watch it, buster. You could kill somebody with that!"

"You're a menace with knives," Savannah said with a laugh, moving as Alex jumped toward Renee.

"Hey, it's a butter knife! What's it gonna do?" He pulled

115

Renee's bandana off, ruffling her hair. She tried to grab the scarf but he dangled it just out of her reach. "Why do you wear this all the time? Your hair is pretty."

She blushed and pulled her hair back into a ponytail, wrapping it in an elastic band she had in her pocket. "It's a mess." She smiled at him. "But thanks. Now, better get the bread ready."

A few minutes later, Cal came out of the bedroom dressed in jeans and t-shirt. He sat on a chair at the table and put on tennis shoes. As he tied the laces, he could feel the girls' eyes on him. "What's the matter?"

Renee said, "You're wearing jeans."

"And tennis shoes," Judy said.

"Where's your tie?" Savannah asked. "We didn't know you had regular clothes."

Standing, Cal laughed. He pulled a cable-knit sweater over his head, pushed his arms through the sleeves. "I have all kinds of clothes, regular and irregular."

"So you're not really Marlowe," Renee said. "How disappointing."

"Keep watching—there may be other surprises," he said.

"Oh, we're watching, believe me," Savannah said. "And we like surprises."

"The food's ready," Judy announced. "There aren't enough chairs at the table so where should we eat?"

"How about the floor?" Alex suggested.

"Yuck," Judy wrinkled her nose. "I mean, I know you cleaned, but did you vacuum?"

"Wait a sec," Alex said, holding up a finger. He got a sheet from the hall closet and spread it out on the carpet. Savannah found a book of matches on the end table and lit the candles. Renee put the bread slices in a large bowl and placed it in the center of the sheet.

They heard a crash, then a curse, outside the door. Cal opened it and Neil stumbled into the room. "Sorry, I tripped over that stupid plant the chick next door has on the walk." He squinted at the group and looked around the room. "Mm, a picnic! Nice!"

"Glad you made it back, man," Cal said.

"Where did you go?" Savannah asked.

"Downstairs. I got a connection, a good buddy, in apartment two. Know what I mean?"

"Yes," Savannah answered, shaking her head. To Renee she

said, "Too bad he has to get high to enjoy our cooking."

"Who says I'm high?" Neil sounded indignant. "Are we ready to eat?"

"I'm hungry," Alex said. "Let's get some food. It looks great."

In the kitchen, they piled spaghetti and sauce on their plates and carried them to the living room, settling on the edges of the sheet. Neil balanced his plate on his lap and ate heartily. Savannah laughed when he sucked in a long strand of pasta with a loud slurping sound. He leaned over and tried to kiss her but she turned away.

"You have terrible manners when you're stoned," she said.

"He has terrible manners all the time," Judy countered.

Cal, sitting next to Renee, put a small amount of spaghetti on his fork and raised it to her lips. "Here, taste."

She opened her mouth and ate the bite of food. "Mmm. Yours is better than mine. See what you think." Giggling, she fed him a forkful. He closed his eyes and chewed.

"I don't know," he said contemplatively. "Let's try it again."

Judy watched with narrowed eyes. "How dumb. Renee, I can't believe you're doing that."

"Judy," Renee said. "His really does taste different. Did you put something extra in it?"

The rest of the group burst out laughing. Cal winked at Judy. "You want a bite?"

"What a bunch of screwballs." She tossed her head and turned to Alex. "Do you like the food, Alex?"

"Yeah, it's good."

Renee and Cal continued to feed each other bites, making comparisons. When Cal accidentally tipped his plate over, Renee scrambled to get paper towels from the kitchen to clean up the mess.

"Who has bad manners?" Neil asked.

"Sorry, Ren." Cal took the towel and began cleaning up the spaghetti. "Here, can you take the plate? Thanks." He turned to Neil. "Nothing to do with manners, dude. It's my way of exiting stage left. I gotta go. Tryouts in ten minutes."

Neil stood up. "I'm going to tryouts, too. Wait a sec, Cal."

"You really have to leave?" Savannah asked. "I didn't know you were interested in this play."

"Might as well give it a shot. Dinner was grand. Thanks for doing this."

Cal and Neil left. Renee sat back down on the floor after dumping Cal's plate in the sink. As she resumed eating, she smiled at Savannah. "I don't think he'll make it through tryouts."

"I don't know," Savannah said with a laugh. "I think he's more normal when he's high."

"This is really, really good," Alex said, twirling strands of spaghetti around his fork. "You can come over and cook any time you want."

"Thanks," Judy said, beaming. "It has a secret ingredient that makes it so tasty. I have some other good recipes, too. Do you like fried chicken?"

Alex laughed. "Like I said, any time you want to fix dinner, come on over. But next time, tell me what to buy and I'll have it here for you. You shouldn't be spending your money like that."

Judy gave Alex a puzzled look. "I want to ask you a question. Why do you share an apartment with people like Neil and Cal? I don't get it. You're so different from them."

"They're okay," Alex said. "I know I'm not much like Cal, and Neil can be a pain, but we're friends. Maybe you should be asking them the question." He paused, then asked, "Why are the three of you friends? You're different from Renee and Savannah."

"Well," Judy said, giving her head a toss, "not *so* different."

"Sure you are," Alex said. "Savannah is kind of high energy and spontaneous. Renee's quiet. You're serious and want to study all the time."

Savannah said, "That's right, Judy, you are pretty serious. And I suppose I am kind of impulsive sometimes." She wrinkled her nose. "That's just how I am."

Renee nodded. "You are, Savannah. And we love it." She turned toward Alex. "And Savannah and I like to go for walks, talk—"

"—and talk and talk and talk," Judy said. "Sometimes you wear me out. Don't you feel like that, Alex?"

He shook his head. "No, I like to listen to them. I'm learning a lot." He grinned as Savannah and Renee giggled.

"So why did you choose OCE?" Judy asked.

"I heard the male-female ratio was too good to pass up," he said with a smile. He began clearing dishes off the sheet and carried them to the kitchen. "I'll take care of these later. Let's play a game."

"What kind of game?" Renee asked. Games made her feel

nervous and inadequate; she tried to sound nonchalant but she found herself chewing nervously on a fingernail.

"You'll see," he answered. He wadded up the sheet and tossed it in a corner. From the bedroom, he got a pillow and lobbed it into the living room, high in the air. "You're it!" he shouted as it landed on Savannah's head. She batted it to Renee. Alex grabbed it before Renee could even react and threw it to Judy who ducked as it sailed past her. Renee screamed when Alex dove at her, knocking her back onto the couch. She gasped in surprise, and then started giggling. He scooped the pillow up from the floor and chucked it to Savannah.

"Come on!" he yelled. "Keep it going!"

"Renee!" Savannah called out. "Get it! Don't let him have it!"

Renee caught the pillow and passed it to Judy. Judy held it high, taunting Alex. As he reached for it, she jumped onto the couch and danced around, laughing and dodging his hands. He turned and grabbed Renee, holding her to him like a hostage. Wriggling, she tried to get loose, but he kept a firm grip, his arm around her waist. "Give me that pillow or she's toast!" He put a cocked finger to her head.

"Never!" Judy screamed. She stepped up onto the back of the couch, balancing with her arms out, and held the pillow higher. "Haha!"

"Okay," Alex said in a serious tone. "Get ready to pay, Renee!" She twisted and squirmed, breaking free, and ran across the room to Savannah's side. Alex lunged toward Judy, reached for her foot, knocking her off balance. She tumbled down, giggling uncontrollably as she tried to throw the pillow away from Alex. He snatched it and wrapped both arms tightly around it. "I win!"

Panting, the girls all nodded. "Yes, you do," Judy conceded.

"Okay, let's play crab soccer," Alex said. "But we need a ball." He took the paper grocery bags and wadded them up into a sphere. "Two teams, Savannah and Judy, me and Renee. Goals will be the hallway and the front door."

"Are you crazy?" Renee said, still panting.

"It'll be fun," Savannah said. "Come on, ladies. Jude, you play front and I'll guard the goal."

They got in position. Alex tossed the ball up and kicked it toward the hall. The girls scrambled after it, fighting to reach it. Judy made contact first and tried to pass it to Savannah, who was giggling too hard to respond. Alex scooted in and knocked the ball into the hall with his head.

"Point!"

"Get it, get it, get it!" Judy was screaming as she pushed past the others to get to the ball. She kicked it, sending it skittering along the carpet toward the middle of the living room. "Savannah! Quick!"

Savannah stuck her foot out and nudged the ball sideways. Judy scooted on her bottom, pushing herself with her elbows, and kicked the ball high, bouncing it off the ceiling. Alex launched himself forward and knocked the ball backwards. Renee dove for it, then tried to kick but missed and fell down on her back, laughing, with arms and legs splayed.

"I can't," she gasped.

"I got it," Alex grunted. He picked up the ball with his hands and carried it into the hall. "Point!" He grinned as the girls collapsed, exhausted.

"Game over," Savannah said, trying to catch her breath. "Whew, I'm sure glad we wore jeans tonight!"

Alex sat on the couch, one ankle resting on the other knee. He watched the girls slowly wind down and settle comfortably, Renee on the foam chair, Savannah on the floor under the window, and Judy at the table in the dining room.

Renee tugged the elastic band from her hair and shook out her ponytail. "Oh man," she said, running her fingers through her hair. "I'm sweaty." She looked around. "Where's my bandana, Alex?" He pulled it from his pocket and handed it to her. "Thanks." She put it around her head, knotting it in the back under her hairline, then fluffed her bangs out in front.

Alex, watching her, shook his head. "I still don't get why you wear that."

She smiled at him. "It keeps my sweaty hair off my face."

"Ready for another game?" he asked.

"No, no! No more soccer!" Savannah said, raising her hands over her head.

"I'm worn out!" Judy said, with a groan.

"Hey, let's tell ghost stories then."

"Thank you, Lord," Renee said, clasping her palms as if in prayer. "I can't take much more excitement."

Savannah nodded. "I agree. Stories will be more restful, at any rate."

"That's what you think," Alex said. He gathered the candles into a cluster in the middle of the floor and turned off the lights. They sat close together in a circle, huddled around the flickering candlelight. "Have you heard about The Hook?" He lowered his voice to a gravelly pitch and slowly intoned, "Once upon a time…"

Russ is holding Renee gently as they lay on her bed in the dorm. Her roommate has left so they could be alone. Visiting hours are nearly over and they are savoring their last moments before the time is up.

"Tell me a story," Renee murmurs in his ear.

"Once upon a time, there was a beautiful princess," he begins. "She lived in a rundown castle because her parents had died and there was no one to help her. She was so sad and lonely. One day, a young man came along, riding a black stallion. He stopped for water and saw the princess looking out the window. 'Who are you?' he asked, gazing in wonder at her beauty. 'Princess Renee,' she answered. 'Who are you?' 'Sir Russell,' he replied. And he promised to take care of her always."

Renee wrapped her arms around herself, closing her eyes. She loved the princess stories Russ told even though they were silly and childish. They always comforted her. *I miss that.*

"…as The Hook clawed its way down the hill. The end." Alex finished the story then crawled his fingers over to Savannah's leg, grabbing her shin in a tight clench. She let out a shriek that could have rattled the windows. With a low growl, he seized her ankle and tickled her bare foot.

"Stop! Stop!" She was gasping and laughing as she tried to get free. "That's enough! Stop!" The others chuckled as Savannah patted her hair, making sure it was back in place. She straightened her blouse as she grinned at Alex. "You're nuts!" She turned to Renee and Judy. "Do I look all right? Is my hair a mess? Boy, is he blitzed or what?"

Alex scrambled to his feet. "So, who's next?" He shifted his body back and forth between the girls, watching them with narrowed eyes.

Renee and Judy screamed and ran in opposite directions, dodging Alex as he tried to catch them. Then, as if on signal, all three girls jumped him, pushing him down onto the couch. Renee pinned his legs, Judy and Savannah his hands.

"Okay, okay, I give up! I can't wrestle three of you." After getting sworn promises all around to stop the attacks, the four of them collapsed on the floor, laughing.

"You're crazy, Alex," Renee said, pulling her bandana off and finger-combing her hair. "I never would have expected all that from you."

He grinned. "Good. I don't want to be too predictable." He tousled Renee's hair. "You had a pretty fair attack going there."

"Comes from having younger brothers," she said, laughing.

"Me, too," Judy said quickly. "I had to fight my brothers off all the time."

Alex shook his head. "You girls have my admiration. But next time, I'll be better prepared for it."

On the way back to the dorm, Renee asked Alex if he would help her with math. "You're good at math, right? I'm scared I'm going to fail that class."

"Now why would you think I'm good at math?" Alex grinned. "Because I'm a business major?"

She nodded, blushing. "Well, yeah, I—I just figured—"

"You figured right," he said, with a big smile. "I'll make you a deal. If I help you with math, you can correct my spelling, okay?"

"I can do that."

"I could help you, Renee," Judy said. "You never even asked me."

"But you're always telling us how much you have to do, how busy you are," Renee said.

"Well, hey, I'm not too busy," Alex said. "And I can't spell worth a shit so it's a good trade." He turned toward Renee. "Let's meet tomorrow at the library, okay?"

"That'll work. How about four? My last class is over then."

~ 15 ~

A few minutes before four, Renee stood in the foyer of the library watching for Alex. She had hurried over, concerned he would be waiting. But the lobby was empty. Sitting on a bench, she rifled through her notebook, checking again for her math assignment. The problems were like a foreign language; she suddenly worried that Alex would find her impossible to help and would regret his decision. Nervously she chewed her thumbnail.

"Hey."

She looked up. Alex approached, a smile on his face. "Ready to work?"

Quickly she pushed the papers inside her binder and stood up. "I guess so. I hope you really don't mind—"

"I don't. Come on, let's go find a spot."

They sat side-by-side at a long wooden table in the center of the library's main room, math book and paper between them. Renee listened carefully to Alex's explanations of the problems she had to complete and he patiently walked her through the process of solving them. When she tapped her pencil against her temple in frustration, he waited, then spoke encouragingly. He bent his head toward her, leaning to see what she had written on her paper. His hair smelled like soap, a clean scent, different from Russ who used a dandruff shampoo with a medicinal odor which he tried to mask with a strong aftershave lotion. Alex had a cowlick on the crown of his head; she liked the way it curled counter to the rest of his hair. *Must be why he keeps it short.* She began to relax and focus on the math and found the work easier to understand.

"You're a good teacher, Alex."

"Only as good as the student," he said. "You're catching on. Just remember to slow down and take it step by step."

"I've always had a block with math. Russ never seems to understand that." She started packing up her papers. She put her glasses on, then her hat. "He tends to be impatient." Pushing back her chair, she said, "Thank you. You helped me a lot."

He stood, put on his jacket, and pulled a black knit hat over his ears. "I'm glad to do it. Tomorrow?"

"Yeah, okay."

"Hey, as payment you can sneak me into the cafeteria!" Alex gave her a sideways look. "Or I could fix myself a bologna sandwich." He paused, then said, "I'm not sure when I bought that bologna..."

Renee punched his arm. "Good Lord! Someone has to take care of you. You're going to die of food poisoning or something." Shaking her head, she walked away. "I've never snuck anybody in before. But life's short, right?"

The cafeteria was set up with a large dining area open to the food line and main doors. On two sides were smaller, more intimate recesses with just three or four tables and the exit-only doors. Renee told Alex to wait outside by the exit where she could let him in after she selected their food. She put the tray on a table in a secluded corner then had to run back to the line for a second fork. Glancing around, making sure no one noticed, she pushed the exit door open and Alex slipped in.

"So I finally get to see the new dining hall from the inside," he said. "It's nice. Much better than the old cafeteria in the student center." They settled at a small table for two in the alcove near the door. "Good hiding place, don't you think?"

"New experience for me," Renee said. "I hope you can stomach the food. At least there's chocolate cake."

"It looks great," Alex said. He tasted the meatloaf and nodded. "Mmm. Guys ribbed me last year because I liked the dorm food." He scooped up a forkful of lima beans and corn. "My mom calls this succotash."

Renee giggled. "So does mine. My brothers call it yuckotash—we hated it. The mashed potatoes are probably instant. I hope they taste okay."

"Yeah, they're fine." He motioned for her to eat. "You got plenty for both of us."

She took a few bites, then said, "Alex, what happened at Gentle Woods?"

"I don't know. I'm not a believer, you know." He smiled. "Cal said he could feel a presence but couldn't figure out what it—or he—was trying to say."

"He? What do you mean?"

Alex shrugged. "Cal called it 'he'. Neil told me there was a light of some sort, but I didn't see anything. I went along mostly to make sure they didn't do anything really asinine. I just stood back and let them do their thing."

"Were they high?"

"No," Alex said. "Cal wanted everyone clear-headed. Neil honored that. I don't use anyway so it wasn't an issue for me." He took a few more bites, finishing up the meatloaf. "Cal was really into it before we even went there. He seemed lucid and focused."

"Has he gone back?"

"I don't think so. Why don't you ask him?"

Renee shook her head. "No, he doesn't want to talk about it." *Because he doesn't want to scare me?* "I just thought maybe you could shed some light on it."

"Sorry I don't know more. Neil and Cal are probably trying to freak you girls out a little bit."

"You know, we went there the next day—me and Savannah and Judy. In the afternoon."

Alex smiled. "So, did you see anything?"

"Not really. It was kind of creepy, though. On the other side of the bridge."

"That's what Cal says, too."

"Did you think so?"

"It was all the same to me. Just a park."

"Yeah, you're probably right. They just want to freak us out." *I felt something.* Without warning, the Portland airport, saying goodbye to Russ, flashed in her mind. Her breath caught, eyes widened. *The man watching me! Does this have anything to do with that? Savannah said a person can choose to travel in an astral state. Could it have been Cal? How? Why? No, impossible.* Smell of tobacco. Leather. *Alex? No.* She shook her head, clearing her thoughts. "I am a little freaked out, actually."

"Well, just stick by me and you won't have to worry because I didn't see or feel a thing."

Renee smiled. "Deal!"

After dinner, they walked over to the dorm to drop off her books. Alex waited in the courtyard. In their room, Renee found Judy sitting on her bed reading a book. She looked up when Renee came in.

"Hi! I didn't know when you'd be back so I already ate dinner.

I went with Savannah. I'm sorry we didn't wait for you."

"Oh, it's fine, Judy. I ate, too. Hey, Alex is downstairs. We're heading over to the 'Cat. You want to come?"

"Alex? Of course!" Judy closed her book and reached for the coat on the back of the chair, putting it on. Taking a moment to look in the mirror, she ruffled her hair a bit, finger combing the short strands into place. "How come Alex is here?"

"Remember I asked him to help me with my math? So I snuck him into the dining room as a thank you."

"Oh." Judy frowned slightly. She picked up a textbook and tucked a few sheets of paper inside it. "You taking any books along?"

"Nope. I've studied enough for one day. Let's go get Savannah."

As the four of them walked across campus to the Alleycat, Renee thanked Alex again for helping her with math. He shrugged, like it didn't matter. Renee stopped walking and looked him in the eye. "Alex, you were so patient! In high school, even junior high, my dad would get irritated with me and treat me like an imbecile when I struggled with algebra and geometry. Russ is like that, too." She could feel herself getting agitated. *Calm down.* She took a breath. "Alex, you can't imagine how helpful you were. You understood how I don't get it and you tried to see the problems from my point of view."

"Well, I'm glad I helped," he said, smiling. "You understand more than you think you do. You should give yourself some credit—you're smart and you catch on quick."

"I don't know about 'quick'," Renee said with a chuckle. "But you made it seem easy."

Savannah gave Alex a one-arm hug. "I'm glad you could help her, too. She works so hard at math. And I'm certainly no help. I barely passed math myself."

Judy started walking and the others fell in beside her. "I'm sorry I couldn't help you, Renee," Judy said. "I just have so much of my own work to do."

"I know," Renee said. "Your parents are on your case a lot about your grades. I understand." She glanced at Alex. "Alex said he'll help me as much as I need."

He nodded. "Yeah, it's easy to meet after last class. And the dorm food was great! "

"You're kidding, right?" Savannah asked.

"Well, I could probably do some of it with you," Judy said quickly. "Maybe Alex and I could both help you." She tried to catch Alex's eye. "We could work together, right, Alex?"

"Don't worry about it, Jude," Renee said. "One person dealing with my ineptness is all I can manage. And you *are* super busy."

"But—"

"Nice offer but we're fine," Alex said.

"I still thi—"

Savannah spoke sharply. "They said no, Judy. You're always talking about how much homework you have. There's no way you'd have time to help Renee."

"I suppose you're right." She glanced at Alex. "I bet you're a really good tutor."

"Don't know about how good, but I liked sitting close to a foxy chick who needed my help." Laughing, pretending to be embarrassed, Renee smacked him on the arm.

In the diner, Cal and Neil, along with two other people, were sitting at a table crowded with dinner plates. The corner booth was empty and Alex led the way to it, Judy right behind him. Savannah and Renee stopped to say hi to Cal and Neil.

"Save us seats, okay?" Neil said. "We'll be over in a few minutes. Maybe you could get the jukebox going. It's too quiet in here."

"Put some Beatles on," Cal suggested. "Do you have a quarter or two?"

"I do," Renee said. "Any particular songs you want?"

"Neil is right, this place is half asleep," Cal said. "Something rockin' like 'A Hard Day's Night' or 'Back in the USSR'."

Renee put the money in the jukebox and punched in the numbers but before she could sit down, Alex grabbed her and swung her around in a modified jitterbug between the tables. Giggling, she let out a shriek as he twirled her in a fast circle.

Dodging the dancers, Cal and Neil carried their dinner plates to the corner booth. Neil set his plate on the table then pulled Judy up from the bench and began doing the Twist. She half-heartedly made a few moves then sat back down, rolling her eyes as she looked at Savannah. Neil joined Renee and Alex and they snaked their way through the restaurant doing a fast grapevine step as Cal and Savannah cheered and applauded along with other customers. The

127

song faded to an end and, out of breath, the three flopped into the booth.

As the group became increasingly loud and rambunctious, Judy was more subdued than usual. She opened the textbook she had brought and began to read.

Alex put his hand over the page. "Is that a good book?" he teased.

She pushed his hand away. "I have a test next week."

"Next week! You got lots of time to study."

"Not when we're here every night."

"You get good grades, right?"

"Because I work at it." She tried to focus on the book again.

"If we all go back to the apartment, you can use the bedroom to study if that would work for you."

"At your house?" Judy looked up and around the table at the group. She sighed.

"It's fun to come here and mess around, but we talked about hanging out at our place, too." He said in a louder tone, "You guys want to go over to our apartment later?"

"Sure," Savannah said.

"Can we still dance?" Renee asked, her eyes shining. "That was so much fun!"

"Yeah, you got it, baby," Neil said. "And it's free at our place."

At midnight, they left the diner and walked the three blocks to the boys' apartment. Renee and Savannah sang old camp songs on the way, forgetting how late it was, until someone shouted "Be quiet! Trying to sleep here!" Giggling, they ran up the concrete steps and pushed through the door, not waiting for the rest of the group.

"Let's have some music," Savannah said. "What have you got?"

Cal pointed to the record collection on the brick-and-board bookshelf and she began flipping through the albums. He tossed his overcoat across the arm of the couch and began filling his pipe.

Neil went to the kitchen and pulled a six-pack from the refrigerator. "Beer, anybody?"

Cal accepted the bottle Neil held out, raised it in a salute. "Cheers, buddy."

Alex showed Judy the bedroom and told her she could study there if she wanted to. "Do you want the door shut?"

Alleycat

"No, that's okay. Just leave it open." She sat on the floor, leaned against the bed, and opened up a textbook. "Thanks, Alex."

"Oh my gosh!" In the living room, Savannah squealed with excitement. "You guys have the Stones' *Out of Our Heads!* I've been wanting to hear this for so long." She put the record on the turntable and carefully placed the needle on the first track. The opening beats filled the room. "Come on, Renee, let's dance." She began singing the opening track "(I Can't Get No) Satisfaction."

"Yeah, yeah, come on you guys," Renee said, joining Savannah in the middle of the room. They began a modified watusi, laughing when the boys added their own unique gyrations. Neil partnered with Savannah and Alex grabbed Renee's hand, swinging her haphazardly, nearly lifting her off the floor. He passed her to Cal who pulled her in close for a moment then twirled her in a half-circle. Renee loved the sensation of freedom and flight as she let the boys spin her around. The music no longer drove the movement—she just allowed herself to dance.

~~ 16 ~~

Late Friday afternoon Judy decided to stay at the dorm to work on a term paper instead of going to the Alleycat. Renee and Savannah went early to have dinner at the restaurant. They split a club sandwich and a side of fries. As they ate, they worked on a poem that Savannah had just written. Alex, Cal and Neil arrived and slid into the booth before the girls could put away their work. Neil yanked the sheet of paper from Renee's hand and read it.

"Hey, that's cool," he said. "Who wrote this?"

Savannah grabbed it back. "Don't be so rude. I wrote it."

"Oh, sorry," he said, sounding contrite. "Can I see it?" She handed it to him. He read it then looked at her. "This is good. Do you write a lot?"

"Just about every day. Renee does, too."

"Can I read it?" Cal asked. She nodded to Neil and he passed it to Cal.

<u>night sky</u>

soft focus obsidian sky
silvery silhouetted shadows
baby's breath stars
curved white petals of the
rhododendron moon

"It *is* good," he agreed, handing the poem back to her. "Do you mind if I make a suggestion?"

"Of course not."

"I think you should take out the word sky in the first line because it's already in the title."

"That's a good idea." Savannah made a notation on the paper.

"I'm not sure what you mean by the reference to rhododendron," Neil said. "It's an odd image."

Renee smiled. "If you wear glasses, and you look at the stars without them, you know exactly what it means."

"Say that then," Alex suggested. "End it with 'who needs glasses?'"

"Oh, that's perfect!" Savannah scrawled the line at the end of the poem, then read it out loud. "What do you think?"

"Groovy," Neil said. "I like it."

"Wow, that was really neat." Savannah beamed. "Renee and I talk about our writing with each other but to get a male perspective, that's great. I should show you guys some more stuff." She put the sheet of paper in her folder. "Do you do any writing?"

Cal and Neil looked at each other. "Just about every day," they said at the same time. With a smile, Cal added, "Maybe that's why we met. It's karma."

So Savannah, Cal, and Neil started bringing their poems to the Alleycat. Renee told Savannah she might bring something of hers sometime, but in truth, she felt too self-conscious. Russ had always either ignored her creative writing or tended to be super critical. *Not putting myself out for ridicule.*

They spent a good part of their evenings examining the writing, giving enthusiastic feedback. Alex called them the Literati, which resulted in increased showing-off. Cal often wore a turtleneck under a tweed sport coat with leather patches on the elbows and a corduroy fisherman's cap. He put on what he considered his "professor" persona as he gave his opinions and suggestions in a British accent. Neil, murmuring "Heavy, man," snapped his fingers like a beatnik. Renee perched her glasses on the end of her nose, which made it hard to see the paper but seemed more in keeping with a literary agent. Savannah stuck pens behind her ears and pulled them out with grand gestures. Alex ended each reading and subsequent comments with a numerical rating for the work, holding up a napkin with a written score. The group either cheered or booed in response.

Judy watched the performances with bored detachment. When Alex got caught up in it, she became quieter, sitting stonily in the booth, resisting anyone's efforts to involve her. Renee and Savannah eventually ignored her and stopped the boys when they teased her. Later, when the three girls were alone, she thanked them.

"It meant a lot to me when you told Cal and Neil to leave me alone," she said. "I'm sorry I can't get all excited about poetry. It just doesn't interest me much."

"We wish you could enjoy the time at the 'Cat more," Renee said.

"Some of it's fun," Judy said. "Like when we talk about the war and women's liberation and what we want to do to change the world. Things that make a difference."

"Yeah, that's important stuff," Savannah said. "But not as much fun as singing and reading poetry and sharing food."

"For you, but not for me," Judy said. "But it's okay. Alex and I talk."

"What do you talk about?" Renee asked.

"Lots of things. School, the classes we're taking, the professors we have. I've told him about how I got my scholarship, what I plan to do with my life. He's a good listener and he respects my opinions."

"I'm glad," Renee said. "We'll try to focus more on the serious stuff, at least once in a while, okay?"

Judy looked away. "It doesn't really matter. Alex listens to me."

A couple of days later, as Renee and Savannah walked to the cafeteria for dinner, Savannah asked, "Why don't you let the guys read some of your writing? I'm getting lots of help with mine. You could, too."

Renee shook her head. "I don't think so. It's one thing to let you see it, but Cal and Neil are so—so worldly. I can't compete with them."

"It's not a competition. Besides, look at what I write. Nothing world shattering."

"You write excellent poetry," Renee said. "It *is* really interesting to talk about writing and having more than just one other person to share observations with." She smiled uncertainly. "Maybe I'll bring something for them to read. Maybe."

The next afternoon Renee and Savannah ran into Alex on campus. "Come over to the dorm," Savannah said. "We can hang out there until dinner."

"In your room," Renee said quickly.

"Hmm, is that so we avoid a certain roommate?" Alex asked, grinning.

"Yes," Renee said. "You're so smart!"

"Yes, I am. But I do need to work on my accounting. Is it okay of we study?"

"Yeah, I need to work on some stuff, too," Savannah said.

The room was empty. Taking advantage of the quiet, they studied for awhile, each absorbed in reading and taking notes. Leafing through her binder, Renee came upon a poem she had composed on the back of her history notes. She snapped open the rings of the notebook and removed the sheet of paper. Scrunching up her face, eyes squeezed shut, she held it out to Alex who sat cross-legged on the floor.

"Are you interested in reading something I wrote?" she asked, looking away when he raised his head.

"Sure," he answered, taking the paper and closing his textbook.

mummy

outer layer swirls of patterned color draped over closely woven
vestures hiding wayward sparks

midlayer crackled glass curveshaped to invite touch
but apt to shatter if jostled

inner layer ice frozen around tiny flame
melting crystals into tears

He sat quietly after reading it, resting his hands in his lap, his eyes focused on the sheet of paper. "Renee, is this how you feel?" She shrugged, noncommittal. "I can see it sometimes. That crackled glass ready to break."

She stood, feeling self-conscious and anxious, and crossed the room to look out the window. "You guys want a soda? I'll run downstairs and get—"

"Hey, come here. Let's talk about this. I'm not thirsty."

"I am." She checked her purse for change. "It'll only take a couple of minutes."

"Renee." Alex arched his eyebrows, smiled lopsidedly.

"Okay." Renee sighed, dropped her purse on the bed.

Savannah was reading at her desk; she looked up, marking her place with one finger. "What's he talking about?"

"It's one of her poems." Alex glanced at Renee. "Has

Savannah read it?"

Renee shook her head. "No one's read it. 'Til now."

"Can I see it, Renee?"

"Of course." She sat on the bed, her back to the others. "Alex, you can give it to her." She began rummaging through her purse, trying to keep her hands busy.

Savannah quietly read the poem. "What do you think, Alex?"

"I want to read more," he said. "And I want to talk about this one. Is that okay?"

"I guess so," Renee said, blushing. "It's just, um, kind of embarrassing."

Alex went to the other desk and pulled out the chair, flipping it around to face Renee. He leaned forward, elbows on his knees. "This sounds like you feel you have to hide your feelings. Like you should only show your happy side." He gazed at her for a moment. "You seem so sad."

"No," she said quickly, shaking her head. "No, I'm not. Not all the time."

Savannah gave Renee a hug. "It's good to talk about it, Rennie. You know it is."

Renee let out a sigh. "Yeah, I know. But I can't. It's just too much."

"You really miss Russ, don't you?" Alex asked. "It's only, what? Four, five months 'til he's back? That's not so long."

Renee sat quietly. *How can I explain? Savannah knows. She knows I'm worried about Russ coming back in only five months. It's too fast. I need more time to*—She didn't allow herself to complete the thought. She smiled brightly at Alex and Savannah.

"You're absolutely right," she said. "It's not so long."

"Will you let me read more of your stuff?" Alex asked.

"You really want to?"

"Yeah. If the rest is anything like this poem, I'm hooked."

"Wow, that would be great. I'll bring some of it over. But it's just for you, okay?"

"Of course," Alex said.

She glanced at Savannah. "And I'll think about bringing something to the 'Cat to discuss, I promise." She smiled at Alex and Savannah. "I guess it's not so bad to let somebody read it."

"I think Cal and Neil will be impressed," Alex said. He patted her arm. "Don't be embarrassed. We're all your friends, you know."

Renee left her writing file at the apartment. Over the next few days Alex read every story, every poem, every thought scribbled on paper, finished and unfinished, good and bad, then discussed them with her. His gentle, constructive comments warmed her and she in turn pored over his writing—articles about WWII battles and a few poems—trying to return a little of what he gave her. They began sharing ideas and even joked about writing a book together. But Renee felt a deep sadness inside. *Russ would never allow it. Forget it, even as a joke.*

In the middle of an evening of sharing poetry at the Alleycat, Renee cleared her throat and announced, "Okay, guys, I'm ready to bare my soul." Face reddening, she pulled a folded sheet of paper from her purse, smoothed it out, and passed it over to Savannah. "I can't read it out loud. Just pass it around, okay?" She covered her eyes with one hand, clamped her mouth shut. The table was quiet—only the sound of the paper rustling as it moved from person to person.

"Is it okay if I read it out loud?" Cal asked. "I would really like to."

Renee dropped her hands but kept her eyes downward. "I'm embarrassed enough. Go ahead—it can't be any worse than this already is."

"Hey, it's not to make fun of you," Cal said gently. "Poetry should be read, performed. The way you've spaced this is interesting, unconventional. I want to hear how it sounds."

<u>Simple Things</u>

Tears burn before falling   pricking eyes reddened
and on fire   pools of heat soothe   as they spill
coursing down warm skin puddling on palms raised
dripping through fingers   leaving salt trails

one Touch   skin to skin   silent vibrations transmitting
healing power from one to another
energy sparking arcing leaping   electrical charge signals
of strength and solace   pleasure and trust

> Laughter fills the air with raucous noise
> giggly sniffly sputtery chuckles
> from-the-belly explosions
> tears gushing noses running smiles wide
>
> Simple Things bonding two individuals

When Cal finished, Savannah reached over and gently squeezed Renee's arm. "Beautiful writing. Thank you for showing it to us. I know it wasn't easy for you."

"I suggest one change," Alex said. "Instead of two individuals, it should be six."

"Yeah, man, that's us," Neil said. He smiled at Renee.

Renee looked around at her friends. She picked up a pen and crossed out the word "two" and wrote in the number six. "Thank you."

~ 17 ~

The diner became their meeting place, but the group ended up at the boys' apartment almost every evening. The idea was to get in some study time there, which never happened at the Alleycat. At the apartment, they fell into an easy routine: Alex and Renee worked on her math at the card table, Judy went into the bedroom and sat cross-legged on the floor with books and papers spread out around her, Savannah did her studying on the couch. Cal often sat close to Savannah and read, sometimes sitting with his back against the arm of the couch, feet pressed against her legs. Neil rarely opened any textbooks at all. He played music, drank beer, smoked, waited for the others to get bored with studying. It never took long. Books were put away, stashed in the corner near the door or piled on the card table. Somebody made coffee, the refrigerator was raided, everyone gathered in the living room and rock music filled the apartment. They made up songs to familiar tunes and took turns performing or they played board games or cards or just talked. They liked to create outlandish poetic odes to political figures or raging anti-war rants, everyone contributing to the works. Often, somebody would start a cadence chant and everyone would drop whatever they were doing to join in.

> My big brother went off to war
> I won't see him anymore
> He's got a gun and wants to kill
> Only Cong blood will he spill
> Sound off—1, 2, Sound off—3,4
> Sound off—1-2, 3-4!
>
> Never mind the war is wrong
> U.S. Marines are super strong
> Nixon wants to show who's best
> He won't let Ho Chi Minh rest
> Sound off—1, 2, Sound off—3,4

Sound off—1-2, 3-4!

Renee and Savannah wrote down all the poems and songs and taped them up in the bathroom. Neil joked that everyone who visited the apartment took way too long in the bathroom due to the unique reading material.

One evening, tired of studying, Alex suggested a game of Risk. He set the board up on the card table and passed out the pieces. Neil and Cal knew the game already and helped Alex explain the rules to the girls. Since there were only four chairs, when a player's turn ended, he or she let the next person sit down to play. A constant stream of jokes and wisecracks accompanied the frequent changes at the table and the game quickly disintegrated into confusion.

"It's my turn," Judy grumbled as Alex picked up the dice and pitched them across the table for his roll.

"No, you're losing track," he said. He began placing tiny wooden blocks on his countries.

"Hey," Savannah said. "It *is* Judy's turn." She reached for Alex's pieces.

"Yeah, Judy goes after Cal and before Savannah. *Then* it's your turn," Renee said. "Take your pieces off, Alex."

He palmed the tiny blocks and said, "Shucks, I thought—"

"No way buddy," Judy said. Quickly she took her turn. "Okay, go ahead, Savannah. Good luck." She grinned at Savannah and Renee.

Savannah studied the board, made her move and passed the dice to Alex.

"You cheated!" Neil yelled, throwing one of his game pieces at Savannah.

"Nuh-uh," she retorted, throwing one of hers at him. It missed and struck the wall. "I'm just a better player. You can't stand losing." She winked at Judy and Renee. "We're on top of the world here, ladies!"

Judy laughed, pointing at the board, more than half of it covered with colored blocks. "I know! Look how many countries we have! I think I'm ahead of all of you!"

Alex grabbed a fistful of yellow blocks from the game board and tossed them toward her. A few went inside her loose-fitting blouse. "Hey," she screeched. "Those were mine! You can't take my blocks off the board!" She wriggled around, shaking her shirt to

Alleycat

make the wooden blocks fall through to the floor.

"Sure I can," he said, scooping up more blocks. "This is how the rules say you can take back a country." He studied the board. "I think I want Spain now." He looked at Savannah, a big smile on his face.

"No you don't," she said. She seized a handful of red blocks from the game box and tossed them in the air. "Now you don't have enough pieces left in the bank," she crowed.

Neil went around the table to Renee who stood waiting for a turn. "Can you believe this?" Hands in his pockets, he shook his head. "Such children." Renee laughed then jerked in surprise as Neil pulled the neckline of her blouse out and dropped several blocks inside it. He grinned. "Gotcha!"

"Hey! That's not fair! You tricked me."

Neil dropped a handful inside the back of her shirt. "Look at that," he said. "They aren't falling through!"

Renee blushed. "That's because my shirt's tucked in. That wasn't nice!"

"Hmm, interesting," Cal said. "I wonder what will come after all this foreplay?"

He ducked, but too late, as Renee shot the game dice at him. She chuckled as they smacked his chest. "Oooh, that is really not nice!"

The game was never completely put away. Alex left the box on the floor under the couch, thinking that maybe sometime they would try playing it again. Instead, it became a kind of ritual, signaling the end of serious study time—someone would grab a handful of blocks and toss them in the air like confetti or drop them down another person's shirt. Cal always called it foreplay, sending the girls into gales of laughter every time.

Once in a while Alex didn't show up at the Alleycat. Neil explained that he went to a friend's apartment to play board games, games too complicated for casual play. After he had missed a couple of evenings with the group, Savannah asked Alex about it.

"They're called conflict simulation games and mostly they're World War II battles," he said. "There isn't enough room in my apartment for the boards because you have to leave them set up for hours or even days sometimes, depending on the game."

"What? How big are these things?" Judy asked.

"The game boards are actually maps with grid markings on

them for the pieces. The pieces represent armies, supplies, tanks, et cetera. A mapboard can have several parts that have to be set up together. You need a really big table or a couple of smaller ones."

"Do a lot of people play?" Renee asked.

"Not around here. I have a friend, Doug, who plays. We got his roommate interested. That's why it's easier to set it up at their place."

"Wow," Savannah said. "You just surprise me all the time. You actually have a life separate from us!"

"Don't we all?" Alex asked.

Late one night Neil found Renee perched on the kitchen counter, staring out the window into the darkness, while everyone else played Monopoly in the living room. She had decided not to play but watched the rest of them from the foam chair in the corner. As the game progressed and everyone's attention focused on buying and selling, Neil saw her leave the room; when he realized she wasn't coming back, he bowed out of the game and went to the kitchen.

"Hey," he said softly. "What's wrong? You look bummed."

"Just thinking," she said, giving him a small smile.

"Do you want to talk about it?"

"I don't know."

He went to her and placed his hands on her shoulders. Their eyes met. "Hey, baby, you can talk to me. Is it Russ?" She nodded, looking away, her fingers finding the ring and twisting it absently. "Man, he has you so screwed up. I don't get it. Why do you stay with him?"

"Because I love him." She looked back at Neil. "We've been together over two years."

"Look, I don't know the guy, but I think he's ruling your life. Even from China or wherever he's gone. You get so defensive when you talk about him. I think you'd be a different chick without him." He shook his head. "I'm sorry, babe, but that's what I think."

"He's not ruling my life," Renee said, her voice just above a whisper. "You *don't* know him so you don't know what you're talking about."

"Hey, it's okay," he said softly. "I don't want to upset you."

"Everything is—hard," she said, looking down at the floor. "I

Alleycat

don't know how I feel anymore." *I'm worried. And I'm scared of Russ coming home. Will he even know me? Still love me?* "I miss him so much."

"I'm sure you do."

"The thing is—what if I—"

"Cut him loose?"

She shook her head, eyes down. "No, I don't mean that. Not exactly. What if I don't love him anymore?" She covered her face with her hands, squeezing her eyes shut. "Please don't say anything to anybody. Please?"

Neil reached out to touch her hand. "I just want you to know I'll listen anytime you want to talk. Or whatever." He pulled a pack of Camels from his shirt pocket, tapped one out, and struck a match. He watched her face as he lit the cigarette. "You deserve better, that's all."

Feeling the threat of tears, she blinked, then rubbed her hands over her face. With a tremulous sigh, she said, "I just can't, you know, do anything right now."

"Hey, you can do whatever you need to."

"But I don't even know what that is."

"He won't be back until July, right? You have some time to figure it out."

"Yeah, I guess." She leaned back, resting her head on the cabinet behind her. "Thanks, Neil. I hear what you're saying, I do."

"Outta sight, babe. Come on, let's go watch the corporate killing in the other room."

~~ 18 ~~

As they walked through town toward Gentle Woods, Cal and Savannah sang a duet, "There's a Hole in the Bucket" with wild improvisations, while Neil tried to seduce Renee, making suggestive comments and attempting to hold her hand. She snickered and jerked away from him, grinning as he persisted. Judy corrected Savannah when she sang off-key and tried unsuccessfully to engage Alex in conversation.

"People are sleeping," she admonished the group. "It's the middle of the night. You're all being too loud. Shhh!"

No one listened. Renee giggled and tried to shrug Neil's arm off her shoulders. Well into their song, Savannah and Cal got louder. Alex laughed at the others' antics.

"You guys!" Judy cried. "Quiet down!" They had spread out across the entire street and discussed playing "chicken," but not a single car passed.

Monmouth was a small town, with almost all the stores on Main Street. There were no parking meters and the only parking lots of any size were next to the First National Bank and the Foodland grocery. They walked past the blacksmith shop, a huge and anciently weathered building. In the daytime, barn-sized doors stood open, revealing a smoky inkiness and a small circle of old men around a blackened table; in the moonlight it was a dark hulk looming over the sidewalk. Next door, the grimy, cobwebby window of the tiny secondhand store dimly reflected light from the corner street lamp. A cardboard CLOSED sign dangled from a window shade on the door and a padlock hung heavily from the latch. The neon sign of the Duck-In, a drive-in serving hamburgers and fries, beckoned from across the street, but it, too, was closed. Another block down stood the bright supermarket with flashing neon letters and big reader board advertising the week's specials. It sat on the edge of downtown, haughtily apart from Crider's, the Alleycat, and the florist lined up at the other end of Main Street. Houses were mostly dark; only an occasional light glowed through a

Alleycat

window. A cat streaked across the road, startling them. Using a variety of *meows* they tried to coax it out of the hedge next to the sidewalk but the cat stayed hidden. A dog barked, rushing to the chain link fence surrounding its yard. Concerned that someone would come out of the house to see what was causing the dog to react, the group hurried on down the street.

They reached the Woods. Their singing, talking, and laughing died down. The trees were shadowy black shapes against the sky; the park felt ghostly, eerie. Judy wandered across the grass to the swings, brightly lit in full moonlight, and sat on the canvas seat, swaying slowly back and forth, her eyes on Renee and Savannah.

Stopping near the swing set, Cal told the girls, "Just stay here." The three boys went across the footbridge to the far side of the park, to the place where the dense, tangled underbrush gave way to the field. Savannah and Renee huddled together, watching. Savannah was trying hard to respect Cal's request that the girls stay on the open side of the park.

"Well, they let us come along at least," she whispered. "That's something." She shook her head. "Cal is convinced that something is trying to communicate with him here. I wish he would talk to *me*."

"I'm glad we're here, but at the same time I wish we weren't." Renee squeezed her eyes shut for a moment. *Please don't let anything happen.* "Savannah, what does it mean when the moon is full?"

"Well, people perform rituals and magic, like healing and protection. The full moon is when psychic energy is at its max and everything kind of gets a surge of power. Maybe he's hoping for that extra energy so he can make a stronger contact."

"Can he do that? I mean, is he in control of this or is something else in control?"

"I don't know," Savannah said, eyes focused on the darker side of the park.

The boys stood still, standing in a row in the tiny clearing of beaten down weeds. An age passed. Judy came up behind the girls. Startled, Renee and Savannah screamed softly, clutching each other.

"Oh, you guys," Judy said. They could feel her skepticism as she watched Cal and Neil stare at the barren ground. Alex had moved a few feet away from the clearing, hands in his pockets, head down, shoulders hunched against the chill air. "What are they up to?"

Renee shivered. "I really don't know."

Tossing her head scornfully, Judy said, "Planning a party with their ghost, I guess. They're so high they don't know which way is up. What a bunch of malarkey."

Savannah and Renee said nothing, never taking their eyes off the motionless boys. When Cal and Neil finally came toward them, following Alex across the bridge, Renee let her breath out in a loud *whoosh*. Alex heard it and gave her a reassuring smile.

"Let's get something to eat," Neil said.

Seeing the girls' questioning looks, Cal said, "Nothing going on tonight." He shot a glance in Judy's direction. "Too much interference."

"How sad," Judy murmured.

The following day when Savannah and Renee came out of their nutrition class, they were surprised to find Cal waiting for them in the corridor. He was sitting on the floor and scrambled to his feet when he saw them.

"Want to go to the Woods with me?"

"Just us?" Savannah asked, glancing around for Neil. She didn't see him.

"I thought you might like to see it in the daytime. Are you game?"

Renee hesitated, looking at Savannah. Savannah nodded and said, "I am."

"Okay," Renee agreed. "I have no more classes today."

The walk was peaceful and Renee found herself noticing things she missed when they walked at night. A mix of houses on each block, some rundown with beer bottles stacked in front windows and shiny bicycles chained to railings, others with neatly manicured lawns and rail or picket fences. A set of fourplexes with doors painted different colors. A psychedelic-decal decorated VW Beetle and a sleek new station wagon parked along the curb. A small dog shot out of a doghouse, barking furiously, trying to make up for size with ferocity. His leash pulled him up short and he resorted to low growls. Savannah stopped to talk to him, reaching out to pet his furry head. An elderly woman sweeping her porch waved as they passed. Two children raced around their yard, firing pretend guns and yelling, "I got you!"

Alleycat

A voice called out from a doorway. "Hey, is that you, Renee?"

She turned around and saw Brian, one of the guys Russ had known last year. Her heart skipped a beat. She nodded, waved in greeting, and kept walking.

When they reached the park, Cal stopped just before the bridge. "It's a far out thing," he said quietly. "I just get these feelings—premonitions? ESP? Anyway, I was in the 'Cat one night, alone, and this old dude comes up to me, starts talking. Shit, he knew me, all about me, and I'd never seen him before in my life. He talked about the Woods and said I should check it out sometime."

"You told me about that. It happened the night we first met," Renee said.

"Yeah." He held out his hands to them. "Ready?" Renee felt her body tense. She clutched Cal's hand; he squeezed it and smiled down at her. "Savannah?"

Savannah took his other hand. "What are you expecting?"

"I can feel a force in this park," he said as they started slowly across the bridge. "Something tells me you do, too."

Savannah nodded. "I think so. When Renee and I came here the first time we both felt something odd."

"It's different in the daytime," Cal said. "I'm interested in how you experience it, if you do." He led them to the edge of the field. They stood quietly, holding hands.

Renee closed her eyes. *This spot—Savannah and I called it a portal.* She shivered involuntarily. Cal squeezed her hand, keeping his grip tight, reassuring. Her skin prickled, the feeling sweeping up from her toes to the top of her scalp. A *shush*ing sound filled her head, soft, then louder. Again, her heart rate increased, her mouth went dry, her vision blurred. She dropped Cal's hand and covered her ears, breathing heavily. "I'm gonna be sick!" Her stomach clenched painfully.

Cal grabbed her arm and pulled her away from the field. "It's okay, come on, sit." He pushed her gently down onto a bench on the other side of the clearing. She opened her eyes and gazed around. Savannah was staring at her.

"That's weird," Savannah whispered. She dropped to the bench next to Renee. "Your pupils are really constricted. Are you okay?"

Renee grimaced. The back of her neck was damp with perspiration. She ran her fingers through her hair. "I feel like I'm going to throw up." She dropped her head down between her knees.

Cal and Savannah both rubbed her back lightly. "Can we go over there?" Renee asked, pointing to the other side of the bridge. She stood, wobbling for a second; Cal reached out to steady her. Across the bridge, all three of them breathed easier. Renee's racing heartbeats slowed.

"Better?" Cal asked. Renee nodded, one hand pressed to her chest.

Savannah studied her face. "You look better. Your eyes were kind of odd."

"Things were a little fuzzy for a minute." She sighed deeply, felt her body relax.

Cal smiled. "Great way to get high without the legal problems."

Renee rolled her eyes. "I guess."

"So, can you talk about it?"

Savannah said, "I felt a presence, definitely. Almost like a touch on my arm. Very light, but persistent. I wasn't scared."

"I don't know what I felt or heard," Renee said. "I just felt strange. I wasn't exactly scared but it wasn't normal." She looked at Cal. "I wouldn't want to have been here alone."

"I'm glad you weren't. Don't come here by yourself, okay?"

"That isn't going to happen in this lifetime!"

Savannah chuckled. "But maybe in your next? You'll be the spirit haunting the Woods!"

"A friendly spirit," Cal said. "That's our Renee. Now if it was me..."

"Scary!" Both girls said in unison.

"Ready to head back?" Cal asked.

They passed the house where Renee had seen Brian; she glanced at the doorway. No one was in sight. Surprised at feeling relief, she found herself letting out a long breath.

"Are you all right?" Savannah asked.

"Yeah, yeah. A friend of Russ's lives there." She kept walking, going a little faster. "So was last night different?"

"I felt another kind of entity," Cal said. "Different from the other daytime encounters I had. Something ominous, I guess. I know I said nothing was happening but I did see a light, a shimmer, in that spot where we were today. Kind of like a heat wave. Same thing the first time me and the guys came here."

"What about today?" Savannah asked.

Alleycat

"A voice telling me to get you out of there."
"Jesus Christ," Savannah whispered.

~~ 19 ~~

They lived in an insulated cocoon-like world, as if nothing existed beyond the six of them. They refused to keep a schedule except when necessary, yet always managed to meet at the Alleycat each evening. Night was their time; daylight hours held no magic. They slept, ate, attended classes, accomplished ordinary tasks in the daytime. But darkness meant freedom. Fantasy. Exploration. Shared secrets. They laughed—with each other, at each other, at themselves, at everything. Their world was the diner, the apartment, the streets of Monmouth after dark. Other people barely existed for them. Alleycat customers, neighbors, dorm-mates, students—all were like extras on a movie set, background filler, nothing of substance.

The apartment didn't have a television or even a radio and none of them read the newspaper on a regular basis. They listened to music on the stereo or the jukebox at the Alleycat. They wandered around town in the night, and at the apartment they played board games, studied, cooked, talked—they made their own entertainment. Whatever happened in the outside world had nothing to do with them.

So it was with shock as well as a sense of displacement that they learned about the death, just two days after their trip to Gentle Woods.

Sitting in their booth early in the evening when the Alleycat was crowded and noisy, an abrupt stillness startled them. The patrons had gone quiet, the clatter of dishes and cutlery ceased, the soft movement of air as waitresses swooped through the restaurant stopped. A hushed shuffling of chairs and bodies traveled like a wave across the room, almost imperceptible, but enough to draw attention toward the counter where a uniformed police officer stood, showing a photograph to the waitress behind the register. She shook her head, then arced a thumb toward the cook in the kitchen. She stepped aside as the officer passed her and held the photo above the chrome counter where the cook put the completed meals for service.

Alleycat

The cook studied the picture briefly, shook his head. A loud sizzle and pop from the grill interrupted the quiet; a collective sigh from held breaths followed it.

The officer stood in the center of the restaurant and said loudly, "May I have your attention, please?" The boom of his voice seemed to cause a shiver to pass through the customers. Renee almost laughed out loud, but sucked in her breath, covering her mouth with her hand. *He certainly doesn't have to ask for our attention.* Customers with their backs to the officer twisted around to face him; otherwise there was no movement in the room. "I have a photograph I'm going to bring around. I need to know if anyone knows this man."

One by one, as the people in the room viewed the picture, they shook their heads and the officer moved to the next table. Gradually sound returned to the coffee shop, subdued and minimal. The officer came to the back corner booth last. The 8 x 10 black and white glossy showed a man, probably late sixties, with a bloated, waxy face. His glassy eyes were partially open; disheveled, stringy hair framed his face. Two to three day's stubble covered his cheeks and chin. Part of a frayed shirt collar showed; the rest of the body had not been photographed.

When Cal looked at the photo, his back stiffened just a fraction. He stared at the man's face then said, "I don't know who he is." The officer waited. Cal shrugged and said, "I've seen him before. Around town. Maybe once or twice."

Judy asked, "What happened to him?"

"He drowned." The officer pulled a business card out of his shirt pocket and laid it on the table. "If you remember anything, call me. My name's Benson."

"Got it."

"Your name?"

"Calvin Bishop."

The officer wrote it down in a little spiral pad he took from his shirt pocket. "Hope I hear from you." He caught Cal's eye, held his gaze for a moment. Cal nodded, then looked away. The officer walked toward the front of the restaurant. As he pulled the door open to leave, he looked back at the corner booth. Cal lifted his hands, palms up, as if to say, "Okay, I got it. I'll call."

The door swung shut behind the officer and the noise in the restaurant swelled. The air crackled with excitement and speculation. Somebody yelled across the room, "Hey, Cal, is the guy your economics professor? You can only hope, right?" Laughter followed as Cal raised his middle finger. To anyone who asked him who the man really was, Cal would only say, "Some dead guy."

Savannah put money in the jukebox. The record dropped onto the turntable and the first notes of the Beatles' "Dizzy Miss Lizzie" burst out of the speakers. She turned to Cal and said, "Dance with me?" He smiled, taking her hand, then swung her around and led her through the maze of tables and chairs. When the song ended, Cal tipped Savannah back over his arm in a dramatic finish, and then kissed her mouth as he lifted his hand in a victory fist. She laughed, shaking her head in surprise. "You're a good dancer! Who would have guessed?"

Renee, Savannah, and Cal sat in the student center coffee shop, drinking cherry Cokes and talking. It was late morning and both Cal and Renee had skipped class. Renee felt a twinge of guilt but swept it out of her mind like a pesky fly. Classes could wait; time with friends had to be savored.

"Cal, who was the guy in the picture?"

"Honestly, Savannah, I don't know."

"You said you'd seen him around town, right?" Savannah watched Cal's face.

"Actually..." He shook his head. "No, never mind."

"At night?" Renee asked. "Is that why you told us not to walk around by ourselves after dark?"

"No, not exactly, but it's a good example of why you shouldn't be out alone," Cal said. He changed the subject abruptly. "Hey, you know what I want? In a woman?" He closed his eyes for a moment. "I want a woman who's a writer and a romanticist. We'll have a house high up on a cliff, overlooking the sea. A small house, with lots of windows and natural wood floors and a huge stone fireplace. We'll write all night, by firelight, and we'll drink brandy. In the morning we'll watch the sun come up. Then we'll make love and go to sleep in a bed with a mirrored canopy and down comforters. She'll have long, long hair and be gorgeous. But the most important thing is she'll be a writer. Then she'll be able to understand me."

"Cal," Renee said, surprised. "I didn't realize you were so romantic."

"I see marriage as a sharing—a commitment to share," Savannah mused. "I'm no women's libber but I do think equality is important. I see us doing dishes together, cooking together, tucking the kids in at night."

"Oh, the perfect couple," Cal teased.

"Just equal and nice."

"Renee has it made. She doesn't have to even think about what she wants and if it can be found. General Rusty has it all figured out for her."

Yes, he certainly does, Renee agreed silently. Russ's face, stern and imposing, popped into her mind's eye, large as a portrait of Lenin in Red Square. She blinked, startled, unsettled.

"That's not true," Savannah said. "Renee's making her own decisions."

With a nod, Cal said, "Of course, just because someone has a ring on her finger doesn't mean she's off-limits." He rested his elbows on the table, fingers steepled, as he observed Renee.

"Oh no," Renee said. "It's as good as being married."

Cal snorted. "You're either married or you're not. Until that certificate is signed a person has a choice."

"Russ doesn't see it that way," Renee said, absently fiddling with her ring as she talked. "I don't either. We've made a promise to each other."

"Hey, I never meant *you*," Cal said, sitting back with his hands clasped behind his head. "I'm talking about engagement in general. The universal 'you', not the individual 'you'. I respect you too much."

"I think 'you' and 'respect' are strange partners," Savannah said.

Laughing, Renee shook her head. "You're full of baloney, Cal."

"Well, I need to go," Savannah said, glancing at her watch. "Got a class in ten minutes." Cal stood up to let her out of the booth. She collected her things, smiling as she put on the fedora. "I love this hat!" She and Cal grinned at each other. "See you in Nutrition class later, Renee." She hurried off.

Cal sat back down and studied Renee's face. "What does the General think about you coming to the apartment and carousing around town every night?"

She reddened. "Who cares? I'm not on a leash."

He grunted. "He doesn't know, does he?" He gave her no time to answer. "Don't tell him."

"I'm going to tell him," she said quickly. "We're completely open with each other. Besides, I'm not doing anything wrong."

"Then why haven't you told him?"

"What would I say?"

"What will you say?"

"He'll just have to understand. You guys are my friends and that's how it is. If he can't accept that, well—well, he just has to." She looked Cal straight in the eye, but under the table her fingers laced and unlaced, twisting the ring around.

Cal snickered. "Sure. How come you're so nervous?" She shook her head. "Yes, you are. You're one scared chick. You talk so much about him it makes me sick. And I'll tell you this—I can't stand him. He's a self-important punk. Everything about him tells me he's a pain in the ass." He groaned, shaking his head. "How did you get stuck with him?"

She bristled. "I'm not stuck with him or anyone else. I choose my friends, I'll choose my husband. You haven't even met him."

"Hope I never do."

"Cal, I don't care what you think—"

"Like hell you don't."

"—but give him a chance. He's in Japan, practically all alone—"

"That's bullshit."

"—and he's not used to that. He comes from an extremely close family and it's the first separation he's had from them or me. And as for me—"

"Yeah, let's talk about you instead. Will you go to bed with me?"

"Cal!" She was upset and frustrated. "Cal, things are so hard right now. Don't."

"You afraid of me?" His tone was mocking. He reached across the table for her hand; she jerked away. "What's the matter, sweetheart? Are you a one-man lady? Saving yourself? For a prick?"

"Cal, stop it." She spoke in a low voice, hands tightly clenched.

"Okay, okay, I'm sorry," he said, his voice kinder. "But damn it! I get so sick—"

"I know," she said quietly. "But if I don't talk about him..."

She crossed her arms on the table and put her head down on them. Trying to calm her pounding heart, she closed her eyes.

"I want to tell you something," Cal said, his voice so low she didn't dare move, or even breathe. "You're the closest one to that dream girl."

Silence. When she raised her head, he was gone.

Later, in their nutrition class, as the professor wrote on the board, Renee whispered to Savannah, "I have a problem. Remember you said you thought Cal liked me?" Savannah nodded and leaned closer to Renee so she could hear more easily. "I think you're right. I don't know what to do."

Savannah wrote on her paper and pushed it over for Renee to read. **He knows you're not going to fool around. He might be interested but he won't act on it.**

Renee covered her face with her hands, nodding her head in response to Savannah's words. She dropped her hands down to her lap, fingers intertwined, and whispered, "I like him but I'd never date him even if I was free to. He's too wild for me." She smiled when Savannah grinned at her.

"He is a little crazy and wild," Savannah whispered. "Maybe that's why he doesn't have a girlfriend." They both stifled giggles and then, sensing the instructor's eyes on them, quickly settled back in their seats and tried to look interested in the lecture on food groups.

I have to tell her. I can't keep this inside. She'll know how I should handle it. After class, Renee said, "You know earlier, in the student center? When you and me and Cal were talking?"

"Sure. Did something happen after I left?"

Renee hesitated. "Kind of."

"Well, what? You obviously have something on your mind. Spill it, girl!"

"Remember what Cal said about his, um, the kind of woman he wants?"

Savannah chuckled. "He's such a romantic, isn't he? A house on a cliff with some gorgeous woman. Dream on, Mister!"

"Yeah, pretty silly," Renee said. "But then he told me…" Her voice drifted off.

"What?" Savannah grabbed Renee by the arm. "Did he say you're that woman? Did he?" When Renee didn't answer, Savannah laughed and spun around. "Oh boy, I knew it! He *is* crazy for you!"

"I don't know. He said some awful things about Russ and when I put my head down because I didn't want to start crying, he said it and left."

"What exactly did he say?" Savannah leaned close, her eyes bright.

"I don't know. I don't know." Renee covered her face with her hands. "He said Russ is a pri—jerk—and I talk about him too much. I—I got upset and he said he was sorry. Then he said I am like that woman." Renee took a deep breath and began chewing on her fingernail.

"Did he tell you to break up with Russ?"

"No. But he didn't have to say it."

"I'm going to ask you a hard question—don't get mad, okay?"

Renee nodded. "Go ahead."

"If—*if*—you could, would you be interested in Cal?"

"I don't know," Renee almost wailed. "That's what I mean—he's too unpredictable."

"Rennie," Savannah said. "You should think about—"

"I'm not breaking up with Russ. For one thing, it would be like sending a Dear John letter. And for another, I love him. I'm marrying him."

"I know. Don't start crying, okay?"

Renee wiped her eyes with the back of her hand. "No crying. Promise." She took a breath, let it out slowly. "Savannah, I'm gonna act like Cal never said anything. I can't—I can't deal with it right now and I think he doesn't realize what he's saying."

"Like I said, Rennie, he won't act on it. He *does* respect you."

~ 20 ~

"The guy apparently had a heart attack," Cal said as the six of them sat in the Alleycat. "He had a heart attack and fell in the creek."

"What creek?" Savannah asked.

"The one in the Woods."

"How did you find out?" Alex asked.

"The newspaper. I was curious so I've been checking. I guess they ID'd him through next of kin—his son reported him missing."

"So did you know him?" Savannah asked.

"Name's Thomas VanAllen. I met him once."

Startled, Renee said, "That's—"

Cal cut her off. "The paper said he probably died the night before he was found. Maybe earlier, going by the rigor mortis and the condition of his skin. Some kid found him."

"Poor kid," Judy murmured. "That must have been horrible." She shuddered. Her eyes circled the table, making eye contact with each person. "Can any of you imagine finding something like that? Horrible."

Later, at the apartment, Renee asked Cal to step outside with her. He grabbed a sweatshirt and her pea coat. "Let's walk," he said, zipping the sweatshirt up and pulling the hood over his head. They crossed the parking lot and headed south.

"Am I the only one who knows about the connection between VanAllen and Gentle Woods?" Renee asked after they had covered a block in silence.

"Yeah, you know more than anyone else. I never even told Alex. I'd like to keep it that way."

"Okay." She wanted to ask a hundred questions but kept quiet.

They walked another block before Cal spoke. "That day we went to the Woods, you and Savannah and me, and then ..."

"He's found the next day," Renee said. "You think that had something to do with it?"

"I'm trying to connect the voice I heard with VanAllen's

death."

"Do you feel like you should have known? Like you could have saved him somehow?"

"I don't know. I'm wondering if the entity was VanAllen in an astral state, trying to communicate with me. The aura was strong at night. The next day was just a voice. But the feeling, the atmosphere, had changed from the other times I went there."

"You said it was like a warning."

"Exactly."

"It felt ominous to me. So what do you think was going on?"

"The voice was definitely cautionary. I just can't figure it out," he said, shaking his head. "I swear to you I wasn't stoned."

"Hey, Savannah and I felt something, too. *We* certainly weren't on anything."

"Your reaction, though," Cal said. "What was it like? Tell me again."

"I felt sick to my stomach. My heart was pounding like crazy, my mouth was horribly dry. I mean, I could barely swallow. I heard buzzing in my head. Savannah said my eyes were strange."

"Sounds almost like a bad drug. Have you really never tried any street drugs?"

"No!"

"Okay, I believe you." Cal chuckled softly. "It disappeared right away?"

"Yes, as soon as we crossed the bridge." Renee shuddered. "If it was VanAllen, maybe he was trying to let us know it wasn't safe to be in the Woods."

"Maybe that's why he died. You know, Gentle Woods is a drug buyer's paradise. And the guy who sells there isn't exactly known for being fair and understanding."

"Is that where you—?"

"No. My source is safe. And in Corvallis."

Thursday night, when Alex had gone to Doug's to play games, Neil pulled a six-pack out of the refrigerator and offered beer all around. Cal took two, swiped the bottle opener off the counter, and popped the caps. He took a long drink from one bottle and held the other one out. "Ren?"

"No thanks," Renee said, shaking her head. She crossed the room to sit on the floor by the stereo. She chose an album, *All*

Alleycat

Things Must Pass by George Harrison, and put two of the discs on the turntable spindle. It was her album; she had brought it over to keep at the apartment, feeling a little guilty because it had been a gift from Russ. Turning the volume up, she leaned against the wall, and listened to the familiar music.

"Ah, come on," Neil said. "Go ahead. One drink." Judy, frowning, picked up her science book, and sat on the couch. Neil took the second beer from Cal and another one from the carton. "Savannah, my love?"

"Sure," Savannah said, joining Neil and Cal at the kitchen table.

"Savannah," Judy said. Savannah waved her hand as if to say, "Leave me alone." Judy stomped off into the bedroom and slammed the door.

Catching Savannah's eye, over the noise of the music, Renee said, "I don't care."

Savannah sipped the drink, making it last. Over the next hour, Savannah, Neil and Cal sat at the table and talked, at first quietly, but as the boys downed two more beers each, they became more animated. Cal told stories of encounters he'd had with prostitutes and street musicians on a senior class trip to San Francisco, claiming also that he had been to one of the Playboy mansions.

"I'd drifted away from the group one night when we were walking back to the hotel after dinner. This beautiful woman comes up to me and asks if I want to 'play.' She had on the tightest, shortest hot pants I'd ever seen and a see-through blouse that you could really see through, know what I mean?" He did a quick imitation of Groucho Marx, bobbing his eyebrows up and down and pretending to flick a cigar. "I didn't say anything, just tried to be cool. She asked me if I wanted to go to the Playboy mansion with her." He opened another beer, took a long drink. "She called a taxi and we left. I didn't know what to expect but figured I was due for an adventure."

"Tell her what happened in the car," Neil said.

"Oh, well, a gentleman never tells," Cal said. "Suffice it to say it was—well, athletic and novel."

"And did you actually get to the mansion?" Neil prompted.

Cal smiled and sat back, his eyes closed. "Those bunny outfits are damn hot. They're cut so high on the hip and so low on the top—"

157

"I don't believe you," Savannah said, blushing a bright red. "You look older than your age but not that old!"

"Shit, this guy's been around," Neil said. He offered Savannah another beer but she shook her head. "Would you rather have wine? We have Annie Green Springs, I think. Or vodka? I'm sure we have some." She shook her head again. "Grass?"

"Neil! I don't want anything." She sat back, relaxed.

Renee changed the record on the turntable and the overture from the rock opera *Tommy* filled the room. She carefully moved the needle to another track, then sang along with "Pinball Wizard". Neil and Cal joined in, their deep voices harmonizing with hers. Neil drummed on the table and Cal pretended to hold a mic as their voices drowned out The Who. Savannah took Cal's fedora from the end table and plopped it on her head, then, with a sultry expression, began doing a slow Twist. Neil joined her, grabbing her hands and swinging her around. They switched to other dance moves as Cal played the part of lead singer with exaggerated irreverence. Renee watched with delight, humming along and applauding at the end of each song. They continued their act through the next few tracks; Savannah finally dropped, spent, onto the chair. She took the hat off and shook out her hair.

"Whew! Maybe I need to exercise more!"

Neil straddled a chair and leered at her. "You look bitchin' to me." He reached out and put his hand behind her head, drawing her closer.

She giggled and slapped his hand away. "Stop it." She called over to Renee. "Hey, I need back-up here! The Russian's at it again."

Chuckling, Renee came into the kitchen. She pulled out the fourth chair at the table. "Something tells me you can handle him. Just remember what I told you." She winked at Savannah.

"I remember. I know what to do if—"

Neil leaned back, eyes wide, mouth agape, pretending surprise. "Have you been talking about me? I can't believe it!" He turned to Cal. "I'm shocked that they would discuss things like that."

"Yeah, you'd think she would just fall all over herself, getting to be with you." Cal grinned. "You're such a badass." Chuckling, he went into the living room and retrieved his pipe from the end table. Back in the kitchen, he pulled a pouch of tobacco from a drawer and began filling the pipe bowl. He struck a match and lit the pipe then looked at the girls. "'The Russian', huh? Good name."

Savannah blushed. "Well..."

Renee said, "Just don't ask what we call you."

"Okay. I can live with that—for now."

Neil got up and stood behind Savannah's chair. He placed his hands on her shoulders and began massaging them. "If I'm gonna have a name like that, I might as well take advantage of it."

"Neil, a back rub is good," Savannah said, giggling. "Just keep it there, okay?"

Judy came out of the bedroom. She packed up her books and put on her coat. "I'm leaving," she said, standing in the middle of the living room. Her posture was ramrod straight and her eyes flashed darkly. "I'll see you later, Renee."

"Judy," Renee said. "We don't have to go yet."

"*I'm* going. You don't have to. *I* have classes tomorrow." She strode to the door, yanked it open, and let it slam behind her.

Cal stood and said, "Come on, ladies, we'll walk you home."

"Hey, man, we're just gettin' started," Neil said. "What's the rush?"

The front door opened and everyone turned toward the sound. Disappointment surged through Renee. *Judy's back already.* But it was Alex. He had a look of surprise and confusion on his face. "What's wrong with Judy? She just pushed past me like I wasn't even there."

Neil headed for the refrigerator. "She's bent out of shape 'cuz Miss Savannah was ingesting alcohol."

"She's falling for your bad influences, huh?" Alex grinned as he took his jacket off and dropped it on the couch. "We have anything other than beer? Any soda left?"

Neil rummaged through an assortment of bottles, cans, and odd-shaped foil packages, extracting a can of Pepsi and a bottle of beer. "Last beer, folks. I call it."

"I think we should walk her back," Cal said.

"It's okay, Cal," Renee said. "Let her go. She's ticked off because of the drinking and I really don't want to hear her lecture about it right now."

"Me, either," said Savannah. "She can be such a killjoy sometimes."

"She'll be fine," Renee said. "I wish she would just do what *she* wants to do, instead of always—"

"Tagging along?" Neil said.

"Yeah, you got it." Savannah made a face. "Renee and I struggle with this all the time. We hate to hurt her feelings. She's so lonely it's hard to tell her to get lost. So we have to take advantage of the opportunities we have."

"You know," Cal said. "People like that rarely get the hints. Sometimes you have to be direct."

"Yeah, you try it," Renee said. "Good luck, too."

"If you want me to, I will."

Renee shook her head. "No, I still have to share a room with her."

The five of them moved to the living room. Renee curled up on the foam chair; Cal sat on the floor and leaned against the end table. Neil sprawled on the couch and Savannah and Alex stretched out on the floor. Cal put a Moody Blues album on the turntable; the symphonic music swelled and surrounded the five friends as they talked about religion and politics and music. The mood of the group was peaceful, quiet, relaxed; heavy topics didn't lead into disagreements or even good-natured teasing. Renee listened to the discussion, saying very little, simply enjoying the conversation. She looked around at her friends and felt the warmth of contentment sweep over her. She loved the simplicity of these evenings. And with Judy gone, even for just a few hours, Renee had the freedom to say what she wanted, act the way she wanted, without expectation or pressure. *What is it I want? What do I need?* No answers, but it didn't matter.

A couple of hours passed. Savannah stood, stretched, and yawned. "We should go."

"Judy will be hurt that we stayed so long," Renee said, rising. Her knees cracked; she did a series of side bends to stretch her muscles.

"She's not a baby," Neil said. "Maybe she's having a better time by herself."

"I doubt it," Savannah said. "We do need to get back."

"Let's split then," Neil said, throwing on his fatigue jacket. He wrapped a woolen scarf around his neck.

After the boys left them at the dorm, the girls went upstairs to Renee and Judy's room. Judy was on her bed, laying quietly in the dark.

"Hey, Jude," Renee said softly. "Are you asleep? Savannah's

here with me."

Judy's voice was strained as she said, "I thought you don't drink."

"Once in a while," Savannah said. "So what?"

"It's illegal. We're nineteen."

"Well, I'm sorry." Savannah threw her hands up and turned away from Judy. "Renee?"

"Some people drink," Renee said matter-of-factly. "I don't. That's all. Just don't get yourself in trouble. Don't cross your line." She smiled at Savannah. "I know you won't."

Savannah reached out to Judy, touching her shoulder, but Judy shrugged her off, turning onto her side away from the others. "Really, Judy, I'm sorry."

"Don't worry about it. It's fine. Do what you want." Her voice was unnaturally husky.

Renee turned on the lamp next to her bed. She could see that Judy's sides were shaking. "Judy? Are you okay?" She sat carefully on the edge of Judy's bed. "Are you crying?"

"Someone was following me," she whispered. "I took the back way, the shortcut behind the student center. It was really dark. I don't know why the street lights weren't on." She shuddered and curled up tighter, knees drawn up against her chest. She wrapped her arms around her legs. "I walked faster but—" Her voice broke into sobs. Renee gently rubbed her back.

Savannah went around the bed and knelt on the floor. She reached out and stroked Judy's hair.

"He grabbed me. I could *smell* him. He said something, I don't know what. His hands were so strong, I couldn't move. I tried to scream and his hand—" She gulped in air, then continued, her voice hoarse with tears. "His hand smelled like chicken. Chicken! Greasy, smelly, disgusting. I bit him. Hard."

Renee hugged her, laying her head on Judy's shoulder. "Good for you," she murmured.

"I tried to kick him but he was holding me so tight. He yelled when I bit him, he got really mad. He called me a bitch." She covered her ears with her hands. "I screamed and screamed and screamed."

"It's okay, it's okay," Savannah said tenderly. "Did he hurt you?"

"No, he ran off when I screamed. There was a light and he was gone."

"A light?" Renee asked.

"Campus security showed up. I couldn't even tell what he looked like. I never saw him."

"I'm so sorry," Renee said. "We should have left with you."

"I'm sorry I got mad." She wiped her eyes and sat up. Renee and Savannah put their arms around her. "Don't tell the guys, okay?"

"They should know, Judy," Savannah said.

"They'll feel guilty. I don't want that."

"No, Judy," Renee said. "They won't. But they'll be sure to never let us walk home by ourselves. And that's a good thing, right?"

In the morning, when her alarm went off, Renee was surprised to see Judy still in bed, stretched out on her back, covers pulled to her chin, eyes wide open. "Judy, I thought you have an early class today."

"I'm not going to class."

"Because of last night?"

"I can't." She turned her head, stared at Renee. "I just want to stay here."

"Judy, I'll walk with you. You've never missed class."

"I know." Her breath came out in a shuddering sigh. "But what if he's out there and sees me? He's probably really angry." Turning, she curled into a ball, facing Renee. "He might think I saw him and can identify him."

Renee leaned across the space between the beds and stroked Judy's form huddled under the blanket. "Let's stay together today, okay? You can come to my classes or I'll go to yours or we can just play hooky all day and hang out in the library. I don't want to leave you alone."

Judy nodded and slowly rose out of the bed. She pulled the covers taut, tucking in the ends more out of habit than as a conscious ploy to delay leaving the room. She dressed in brown cords, a white turtleneck, and a heavy black sweater. After finger combing her hair, she pulled a black watch cap over her head, completely covering her hair. With the addition of her bulky winter coat, she resembled a bear.

"I'm not hungry," she said. "Can you pass on breakfast? I just want to get going."

"Sure," Renee said. "But I told Savannah I'd meet her. I'll just drop her a note, okay?" On a scrap of paper she wrote: **S—Judy and I are skipping breakfast and going to the library today. See you later, at dinner. R**—then clipped it to the clothespin, hung the string out the window, and stomped on the floor. Moments later a tug on the string indicated a return message. **R & J—I understand. Maybe I'll see you there after my comp class. Stay cool, it'll be fine. Savannah**

They collected books and paper, pens and highlighters, and headed across campus to the library. Judy was quiet and responded to Renee's comments with single words or grunts, making it clear she did not want to talk. They found a large table in the middle of the upper floor and settled in to study. Renee found the hours passed peacefully as she concentrated on reading and taking notes, staying on task because Judy sat across from her. At four o'clock, she stretched her arms up and then out, twisting her back until it cracked and popped several times.

"I'm starving," she said. "I have to eat something or I'm gonna die."

Judy smiled. "Yeah, I know. We've been here all day. I need a bathroom. Now." She made a beeline for the restrooms behind the stacks and Renee gathered up their books and papers.

"Hmm, I thought Savannah would show up," Judy said when she returned. "Oh well, at least we got some stuff done. I'm caught up in history and ahead in science. Which is good since I skipped class." She winced. "I've never done that."

"Doesn't matter," Renee said. "Come on, let's go to the dorm and get ready for dinner."

The sky was darkening when they stepped outside. Streetlights flickered. Students crowded the sidewalks, most in small groups or occasional single pedestrians hurrying to destinations, wanting to get out of the gloom and chill air. Renee and Judy walked briskly, reaching the dorm in five minutes. Renee could feel tension in Judy's step; Judy had never walked so fast.

"Do you think we'll go to the Alleycat tonight?" Judy asked as they left the dorm and headed over to the dining hall.

Renee nibbled her lower lip. "Do you mind?"

"No, not really. I expected it." She waved to Savannah who waited at the dining hall door. "I mean, we always do. I just don't want to be alone."

That evening, when the boys found out about the attack on Judy, they discussed going to campus security to check on the status of the case.

"They won't find him," Judy said. "If two security guys had shown up, maybe. One could have chased him down. But only one officer came."

"What did this bastard look like?" Cal asked.

"I couldn't see him. He was behind me." She shuddered and put her head in her hands. "It was so fast." She looked up, her eyes wet.

"Hopefully the creep had to check in at the medical clinic for his hand," Alex said. "Biting him was smart."

"It was all I could do. It was kind of funny how he yelled at me." Judy giggled, tears dripping. "Damn, I can't believe I'm crying and laughing at the same time!"

Savannah hugged her. "No more walks alone, right?"

"Right," Judy said. She looked at Renee.

"Right," Renee agreed.

The boys made the girls promise they would stay in groups and have at least one guy walk with them at night. Alex wanted them to practice self-defense moves. They went to the apartment and spent the evening working on different techniques—how to get out of a hold from the back and how to use an elbow or a knee to strike. Neil dug three mismatched old socks out of his dresser so he could make them each something for self-defense. He tied a heavy glass ashtray in each sock.

"Where did you get these ashtrays?" Savannah asked. "They look familiar."

Neil grinned. "From the 'Cat. We needed them for a party." He handed one to each girl. "It's an impact weapon. Just keep it in your hand when you're out walking."

Judy palmed the sock and lifted it like a dumbbell, noting the heft of it. "Good. This will fit in my coat pocket. Thanks."

Monday afternoon Judy got a call from the front desk of the dorm that the police were looking for her. She raced down the stairs, Renee right behind her.

"Did you catch him?" Her eyes were wide and anxious.

"Judith Reynolds?" The uniformed officer asked. "Officer Black."

She nodded. "Did you find the guy?"

"In all probability. We had another student report a similar attack but she was able to see his face and give us a description. We picked him up this morning."

"How do you know it's the right person?" Renee asked.

"She ID'd him in a lineup. Plus he had a pretty good bruise on his palm. Imprints from teeth. It looked like it was about two days old. That fits with your report."

"Who is he? What's his name?" Judy's words came out in a rush. "Is he in jail?"

"You weren't the first girl attacked," the officer said. "We've been looking for him for some time. Haven't you read the papers? People have been talking about this guy for weeks."

Renee and Judy shook their heads. Looking at each other, eyes enormous, they simultaneously reached for each other's hands and held on tightly.

"Well, he's incarcerated. But don't go out late at night anymore. That's—"

"Dumb," Judy said, her voice solemn. "Very dumb."

"I'm not telling you it's dumb," he said quickly. "Just be smart."

Renee said, "We know some guys who will always walk us home. We won't be out alone." She smiled at Judy. "They won't let us."

"Good," Officer Black said. He looked directly at Judy. "You're lucky you weren't hurt. More than one girl was sexually assaulted."

Judy's hand flew to her mouth. "Oh no!"

"People think nothing can happen in a small town." He put his notebook in his pocket. "We may need more testimony from you if this goes to trial. I'll contact you if necessary."

After Officer Black left, Judy stumbled to the sitting room and fell into a chair. "Renee…"

"I know," Renee said. "Cal was right. He said he's seen weird people out there." She sat on the floor next to Judy. "How did your parents react?"

Judy looked away. "I'm not telling them. They'll make me drop out of school. I can't do that."

"You have to tell them!"

"No, I don't. The creep's in jail, we'll stay together, my parents don't need to know." She rubbed her face with her hands. "I'm okay. He's been caught and that's it."

"But if you have to testify—"

"So what? Daddy isn't going to hold my hand." Judy made a sound that was half-laugh, half-grunt. "No, Daddy dear would take me home and make me go to correspondence school and become a secretary. My life would be over."

Renee chewed a fingernail. "Judy, if it comes to having to go to court, you know Savannah and I will go with you." She drew in a breath, let it out in a huff. "I wouldn't tell my parents, either."

Monmouth didn't have a local newspaper so they bought a *Salem Statesman-Journal* from the box in front of the Alleycat. They had to buy papers for two days before they found the article, a small, half-column in the "Around the Valley" section.

> "Monmouth police department made an arrest in the recent attacks on the Oregon College of Education campus. Rex Marshall, 35, was stopped for a traffic violation in Independence and police discovered an outstanding warrant for a parole violation. One of the victims identified him in a line-up as the man who attacked her on the night of February 4. Several other women have reported similar attacks on the OCE campus, all at night, since Marshall was recently released from prison after serving a five-year sentence for assault and attempted rape. Students are urged to travel in groups and be aware of their surroundings at all times."

"Heavy stuff," Neil said, folding the paper in half and setting it on a nearby table. "Are you testifying, Judy?"

"I'm not sure," she said. "Since I didn't see him at all, I doubt it."

"If you do have to go to court," Alex said, "we'll go with you."

~~ 21 ~~

Neil never directly offered them beer again and rarely drank more than one or two in front of them. One evening he and Cal passed a joint back and forth; again, the girls declined offers to take hits. Renee figured Cal and Neil did most of their drinking before the others arrived at the apartment or after they left. Monmouth was a "dry" town—no bars, no public drinking. Students tended to either hold parties at private homes or go out of town to Independence, three miles away, or Corvallis, twenty miles south, where frequent fraternity and sorority parties took place at Oregon State University.

Renee never saw Alex drink or smoke. When she brought it up, he said, "I really don't care about getting stoned any more. The hangovers, the stupidity of getting falling-down plastered doesn't do anything for me." He chucked her under the chin and grinned. "I see you don't either, unless you're hiding it."

She smiled. "Yeah, one time is one time too many. Besides, I'm the kind of person who'd get caught and end up in jail or something. Not worth it. I want to be a teacher some day."

Later she asked Cal why he and Neil didn't pressure the girls into getting high. They were walking back to the dorm, the others a block ahead of them. He looked away for a long moment. "I like to drink. I like the sense of euphoria it gives me. The looseness. And grass helps my creative side come out." Stopping, he lit a Camel. "And, I suppose, it's expected. College students get high."

"True, but that doesn't answer my question."

"Yeah." They started walking again. "There's a moral side, you know."

"What do you mean?"

"I'm not going to make somebody do something they don't want to do. I actually have some capacity to show respect for another person." He gestured with his cigarette. "I'm not a guy who has to make girls do what I want them to."

After a moment Renee said, "Well, what about Neil? He doesn't seem so—moral."

"We talked about it. Alex and I told him to leave you girls alone. No alcohol, no dope. And that's why you don't see that other group around the apartment. We kind of discourage you and Savannah being there at the same time they are." He flicked the ash off his cigarette. "Neil doesn't care if you drink his beer or not. He's fine as long as nobody tries to run his life or tells him *he* can't get loaded."

Renee was quiet. They walked another block. "Thank you." Eyes brimming with tears, she wiped them away with the heel of her hand. She sniffed, then cleared her throat. "It's been a long time since someone treated me that way."

"Hey, it's no big deal." Cal seemed surprised by her reaction. "We have plenty of people to get stoned with. You know that." She nodded. "No worries, okay, Ren?"

Russ wipes the steam off the car windshield and peers out into the gloom. They are parked at the end of a gravel road, a rutted lane really, the front end of the car about ten feet from thick brush. Leaning across Renee, roughly pressing against her bare body, he pulls the door handle and shoves the door open. "Go! Go!" He's smirking as she huddles in the light of the overhead lamp. He gives her a nudge. "Come on, do it!"

"No, I don't want to," she whispers.

He twists away from her, turns the ignition. "Fine." The car slowly moves. She can feel his irritation as she pulls her t-shirt on over her head. Struggling into her shorts, leaving her bra and panties wadded up on the floor of the car, her face reddens at the thought of what he wants her to do.

"It just feels silly," she said. "I'm embarrassed."

"I thought you would do it because you love me."

"I do. I do love you."

"Okay, so do it." He stops the car, but keeps the engine running.

Renee slowly gets out, glances around, then removes her clothes once more. She wraps her arms around her chest and looks at Russ. He waves her on, motioning to the front of the car. She walks around the open door and stands in the clearing. He turns on the headlights, lighting her up like an actress on stage. He raises the volume on the radio and music fills the night. "Go on, dance for me." She twirls around once then runs back to the car, falling in, keeping her tears in check.

Renee blinked, took a breath.
"Okay, no worries," she said to Cal. "Thank you." Impulsively, she stopped walking and gave him a hug, arms wrapped around his neck. They stood that way for seconds, Cal patting her back, Renee's face buried in his chest. Then she pulled away. "You're a very special person, Cal. I'm glad we met."
"I'm glad, too."

The following day Renee and Savannah arrived at their nutrition class early and settled quickly into their seats. The professor often came in late so they knew they had a few minutes to talk.
"Renee, what do you really think of Neil and Cal? Am I leading them on?" Savannah couldn't cover the anxiousness in her voice. "I'm having such a good time. Am I flirting too much?"
Renee shook her head. "We're all having fun, Savannah. The guys are just messing around, trying to outdo each other."
"Yeah, but I—I don't know—do you think—?" She stopped.
"Do I think they're interested in you beyond being obscene and rude?" Renee smiled. "Probably. The real question is are *you* interested?"
"I like to get to know people—guys—really well before I commit. I need to have an emotional connection with a guy, more than just an attraction. Know what I mean?"
"Sure."
"Okay, this is weird. Don't get upset." Savannah paused, then said, "Cal kind of indicated he might like to, you know, go on a date or something."
Savannah's statement took Renee by surprise. "Really? When? What did he say?" The questions tumbled out in a rush. Cal flirted with Savannah but—to ask her out? *He acts as if he's interested in—*
"Last night. When we were alone in the kitchen, getting the chips. Just a vague remark about going to a movie."
"Where? There's no theater in Monmouth."
"I know. And nobody has a car to go to Salem or Corvallis." The professor had come into the lecture hall and the chatter in the room slowly quieted. Savannah whispered, "I don't know what I'd

do if he actually asked me."

It doesn't matter. I am marrying Russ after we graduate from college. I'm going to be a teacher and Russ will be a teacher and we will have seven adopted children. It's all planned. It's what I want. Cal is not an option for me. No one else is an option for me. She began doodling Russ' name in the margin of her note paper. *Breathe.*

After class, as they walked down the hall toward the stairs, Renee said, "I think you should go if Cal asks you."

"Why?"

"Couple of reasons. One, it would be crazy-interesting, you know? Is he a goofball or romantic? What movie would he pick? Two, you like him. He likes you. Three, maybe he's The One. Maybe you're meant for each other. Four, I feel guilty keeping you from dating."

Savannah laughed. "That's more than a couple of reasons." They went down the stairs and outside into the drizzle. Savannah quickly opened her umbrella, shifting her binder and books to the crook of one arm. "Want to share my umbrella?"

"No, that's okay. The rain feels good to me." They headed in the direction of the student center. "But some hot tea would be good. It's chilly out here."

"Good idea," Savannah said. "I don't feel like you're keeping me from dating. I just haven't found anyone I want to date yet."

"Not even Neil?"

"Well, sure, if he asked me. I can't figure out why Cal would ask me out anyway."

"Because he likes you!"

Savannah shook her head. "It's weird because I really think he'd take you out if he could. Remember what he said to you the other day in the student center?"

All too well. "Yeah, and remember the fact that he respects my relationship with Russ?"

"Maybe he wants to make you jealous."

"Or maybe to prove he can get you away from Neil." Both girls burst out laughing. "We will never figure him out," Savannah said.

"Promise me you'll say yes if he does."

"Why?" Savannah looked at Renee with curiosity.

Renee shrugged. "Because maybe he's The One." *And then I'd know he isn't interested in me.*

"Okay, I can take that chance."

March

~ 22 ~

Judy asked Renee every single day about her classes, her grades, her homework. Renee started calling her Little Mother to her face and Judy backed off. However, it was getting harder and harder for Renee to face school responsibilities. Even when they returned to the dorm around midnight, Renee rarely went to sleep. The gooseneck study lamp at her desk had a low light setting and she kept the shade turned away from Judy's bed. While Judy slept, Renee sat up into the night writing, daydreaming, or just trying to keep her mind from spiraling into a black hole.

Often, she slept through the alarm, hitting the snooze button over and over, grateful her bed was across the room from the window and the morning light that grew increasingly brighter each day. After Judy left for breakfast and her classes, Renee would allow herself to wake fully and face the day. She made it to her biology lab, which met only once a week, but she skipped the lecture sessions as often as she attended them. Since missing the history midterm, she tried to get to that class at least two days a week out of the three that it met. She was determined to make up her grade on the final exam so she could override the F she had so far in the class. Dr. Malcolm had been less than sympathetic when she explained that she was sick with the flu on the day of the midterm but he allowed her to take a make-up test with the understanding that her grade would be automatically lowered one level. Unfortunately, she did badly on it and ended up with a D-. Nutrition was her time to see Savannah without anyone else around and they used it to catch up on private conversation, writing lots of

Alleycat

notes back and forth during the lectures. She enjoyed her afternoon lit class and since being tutored in math, she found that subject at least bearable. Grades seemed almost irrelevant in the middle of a term but deep inside, Renee was worried. Her parents expected her to get a decent GPA. *And so do I. But...* But day to day, Renee found it difficult to focus on school; sleepy and bored, she waited for the evenings.

Taking an afternoon off, Renee went alone to the graveyard. A letter had arrived from Russ and she wanted privacy to read it. After settling under her favorite tree, she carefully opened the thin airmail envelope and read the words block-printed on the thin blue paper. Russ was on his four-week spring vacation. If he had followed his Christmas promise he would be home now instead of traveling around Japan, camera slung over his shoulder, eyes on a map. *Would it be better if he were here? Would I feel better? I wouldn't be skipping class. I wouldn't be going to the Alleycat.* She concentrated on the words in the letter. He always wrote lengthy narratives describing all the historic places he visited. But between his bad handwriting and the stuffy terminology characteristic of his letters, they had lost their charm for Renee. This was just a monologue, one of countless others she had received from him since August. He had drawn crude, meaningless maps here and there and arrows shot from sentence to sentence, corralling random thoughts. She reread several passages. Especially the part about his traveling companion.

"IT'S NOT WISE TO TRAVEL ALONE," he wrote. "SINCE I'LL BE GONE FOR A MONTH I ASKED SEVERAL OF THE OTHER AMERICAN STUDENTS TO ACCOMPANY ME BUT ALL OF THE BOYS HAD DIFFERENT PLANS. BARBARA EDWARDS SAID SHE HAD AN INTEREST IN SEEING THE SAME PLACES I PLANNED TO. WHAT COULD I DO? OF COURSE, EVERYONE KNOWS I AM ENGAGED SO SHE DIDN'T HAVE ANY ULTERIOR MOTIVES. I REALLY HAD NO CHOICE. SHE'S A FAT SLOB ANYWAY. AND NATURALLY WE STAY IN SEPARATE QUARTERS. I'M BEHAVING, I PROMISE. THERE IS NO ATTRACTION ON MY PART. YOU WOULD PROBABLY FEEL SAFER WITH ME

TRAVELING WITH A GIRL LIKE BARBARA RATHER THAN A BUNCH OF GUYS LOOKING FOR GIRLS. DON'T WORRY—SHE'S THE WORST OF THE BUNCH."

Well, so what? What do I care about fat slob Barbara? It doesn't matter. I can't do anything anyway. Except cry. And who wants to cry?

Wadding up the letter, she stuffed it in the pocket of her pea coat. Hunching her shoulders against the chilly air, she gazed across the fields stretched out between the cemetery and the town. Every single day he had told her he loved her, that he would always take care of her, that he knew best. She'd believed him. She had done what he told her to, without question. How did it get to be that way? When?

Does a girl really marry a man like her father?

She needed a way to break free of her father and his power over her. She hated the way she stayed a child in his eyes. He made demands she couldn't meet, saddled her with his expectations that had nothing to do with her own dreams and goals, made fun of her innocence and lack of knowledge about world affairs, but did little to encourage self-improvement. He embarrassed her in front of her friends and complained when they sat up in her bedroom listening to music and talking. Her mother, soft-spoken, meek, immersed herself in community work—volunteering at the hospital, playing cards with residents at a nursing home, teaching Sunday School—and gardening, baking, doing arts and crafts projects she loved. Busy mothering four children, she found Renee's quietness a relief. Renee made little extra work for her parents—her rebellion was to stay silent, follow the rules, keep her feelings tight inside, wait for the time when she could escape her father's control. She thought Russ was the way out. *But how is it any different with him?*

She and Russ are walking hand-in-hand in the park, in the spring of their senior year. Taking a deep breath, Renee speaks in a voice barely above a whisper. "When I was thirteen, I wanted to kill myself." Long pause. "I had a letter written to my parents. I kept it under my pillow along with a big plastic bag that would fit over my head. I didn't know any other way to do it."

Russ keeps walking but he drops her hand and looks straight ahead as she talks.

"I never told anyone." She can feel tension radiating from him and she speaks more strongly. "I never did it. Tried it, I mean. Things got better and I ripped up the letter." Regret courses through her and she wishes she hadn't told him. "It's nothing, really. I was just thirteen. A mixed-up kid."

"How will I ever know if you're going to try again?" He stops walking and faces her, hands on her shoulders. "How can I know?"

"Because I'm telling you."

"Do you promise?" His mouth is set, his eyes bore into hers. "Do you promise?"

Tears welled up, her chest constricted, and she began to shake. Alone on the hillside, cold and sad, she sobbed, wailing and moaning, until despair filled her up and wrapped itself around her.

~~ 23 ~~

Savannah and Judy both left for a weekend home on Friday afternoon and Cal and Neil joined a group of friends going camping at the beach. Renee welcomed the solitude. She skipped dinner, snacking on crackers and peanut butter, and spent an hour doing laundry, full of plans for the rest of the weekend. She put a stack of records on Judy's worn stereo, sat on the floor and began work on a term paper for her lit class. Hungry, she munched on an apple. What did the advisors say every term? "Budget your time and plan three study hours for each hour you spend in class." *Right.* Her three hours were more than up. She couldn't help thinking how tiresome and dull this weekend was turning out to be. Not that she needed excitement.

Feeling a little rebellious, she shut off the record player, slipped into her pea coat and without a glance, not one, at Russ's gold framed photograph, walked outside. *I'm a nice, quiet, shy girl who behaves and generally acts quite respectably. So who wants to behave?*

For a Friday night, the dorm was quiet. Stopping in the lounge to sign out, she checked the clock. Nine-thirty. An image of Judy's attack flashed through her mind. *I'll be fine. The guy's in jail.* The weapon Neil had made weighted down the left side of her coat. Hand in her pocket, she curled her fingers around the sock-wrapped ashtray. *Thank you, Neil.* She felt a little trepidation at going out but the thought of sitting in her deadly quiet room in the even deader dorm seemed worse than walking alone at night. Anyway, she was just going to the Alleycat for a hamburger, then straight back. And since the Alleycat was only a few blocks away, the walk was practically nothing.

When she arrived at the diner, she strolled nervously past the glass doors and on down the street, chiding herself. *How dumb can you be? It's only a restaurant. All I want is a hamburger.* She walked by the door again, straining to see inside. As far as she could tell, it was crowded. *Oh, shit. Why am I acting like this?* Turning around, she pushed through the door.

Still nervous, she ordered the hamburger to go. Perched on a stool at the counter, she coolly glanced around. The restaurant was smoky and noisy. No familiar faces. She drummed her fingers on the counter to the beat of the song pulsating from the jukebox.

"It'll be just a few more minutes," the harried waitress said apologetically.

"Oh, no—I didn't mean—" Renee stammered, but the waitress had moved on down the counter.

She thought again about how upset Judy acted when she learned that Renee would be all alone the whole weekend. She almost talked herself into staying, but her parents insisted that she visit them every month. Doubtfully, Judy accepted Renee's assurances that being alone was just what she needed. She wanted to write to Russ and she had laundry, mending, ironing, cleaning, and studying to do. And Judy was the last person she wanted around.

The waitress delivered her hamburger and a thick paper cup of coffee. Renee paid and went outside, not quite sure what to do next. She thought bleakly of her room, the solitude, the unbearable isolation. She considered the tiny park a block away.

"Hey."

The voice startled her; the coffee would have spilled except for the plastic lid the waitress had snapped on the cup. "Alex! What are you doing here?"

"Walking around. I was over at Doug's. Here, let me help you." He took the cup and poked out the opening in the lid with his thumb. "Having dinner?"

She laughed. "Fighting boredom. I don't even really want it."

"How about strawberries and ice cream?"

"Are you serious? Fresh strawberries?"

"Sorry. Frozen. Besides, where would I get fresh strawberries this time of year?"

"I don't know," she conceded. "Oh, man, I love strawberries. You really have some?"

"Come and see for yourself."

He served it in a chipped china bowl at the kitchen table. She protested when he didn't save any fruit for himself, but he accepted the hamburger. "What were you doing out at this time of night? I know it's not that late, but you have to be careful."

"Well, I felt adventurous." She looked at him, then away.

"Actually, I just couldn't take the dorm anymore. I—I was going a little crazy." *And now I'm in a guy's apartment, alone with him. First time without someone else here, too. I am crazy.* She smiled.

"Savannah and Judy went home? You know Cal and Neil went to the coast?" She nodded. He went on, "Guess we're the only ones around then. Where were you today? I looked for you in the library."

"I stayed in the dorm."

"I came close to going over there."

She looked up at him, surprised. "Yeah? Why didn't you?"

"Well," he began a little sheepishly. "I wasn't sure. I thought about going to Savannah's, because I really didn't want to see Judy." They both laughed. "And, uh, I didn't want to cause you any hassle."

"What?"

"You know—talk. Because of Russ."

"Oh."

They finished eating. Renee took the bowl and spoon to the kitchen and began filling the sink with hot water. She added a squirt of soap and swished the water around with her hand to make suds. She washed her dish and the ones stacked next to the sink while Alex heated milk mixed with Nestlé's Quik in a pan on the stove. As they worked side-by-side in the kitchen, Renee marveled at how easy it was being with Alex. She felt no pressure to crack jokes or say profound things or applaud the same efforts from him. She didn't need to watch what she said for fear of misinterpretation; she felt free to be herself. *It's okay to be here. In fact, it's good to be here right now.*

Alex poured two cups of cocoa and washed out the pan. He pulled the plug, watching the water drain from the sink, then handed a mug to Renee. She wrapped her hands around it, feeling the warmth seep into her. The chocolate smelled good. Following Alex into the living room, she sat next to him on the couch.

"Tell me about Neil," Renee said. Passing her cocoa to Alex, she untied her shoes and kicked them off, then took the mug back, sipping the hot drink carefully. "Is he really interested in Savannah or is he stringing her along?"

"I'm not really sure," Alex said. "He has a history of dating girls for awhile, then kind of leaving them all of a sudden. I think he gets bored easily."

"Bored? Then I'm amazed he's stuck with all of us for so long."

"You're not boring."

Renee smiled. "Thank you. But I'm not so sure Neil would say that."

"Come on, don't dump on yourself. You're funny and interesting. Believe me, Neil isn't going to spend time with people who bore him."

"So he's had a lot of girlfriends?"

"Every couple of months, I guess."

"Uh-oh, we've known you guys almost that long."

"I think he genuinely likes her," Alex said. "How does she feel about him?"

"She likes him a lot but she's still in the 'preliminary stage'—you know, getting to know someone. It's lasting a long time, though. Maybe because we're all together all the time."

"So he doesn't try to see her during the day?"

Renee shrugged. "Not that I know of."

"Well, he hasn't talked about anyone else so I think she's his main interest right now."

"I just don't want him to pressure her. She's not a girl who sleeps around."

"I think he knows that. But he may consider her a—conquest, a challenge. I'm not sure. Guys don't talk philosophically about stuff like that."

"Did you know Cal might take Savannah out on a date?"

"No. He never said anything to me. But then—"

"Guys don't talk like that." Renee laughed. "Those two, Cal and Neil, are so competitive. Everything is a game with them. Thank goodness you aren't like that."

Alex feigned indignation. "What do you mean? I think I'll ask Savannah out before either one of them."

"Oh, that would make Judy really sad. Are you up for that?"

"Let's not even talk about Judy." Alex rolled his eyes and shook his head.

Renee drank the rest of her cocoa and set the cup on the end table. Folding her legs up into a criss-cross position, she put one hand to her mouth and absently chewed her thumbnail. "I wrote to Russ today and told him you're my math tutor."

"You sound kind of worried. How do you think he'll react?"

She didn't speak for a long moment. Dropping her hand to her lap, she fiddled with the engagement ring. "I don't know. I wish someone could tell me what to do. I wish I didn't even have to think. I wish it was July and Russ was home and I didn't have to worry about it anymore. I wish—oh, wishing is so pointless! I really think I'm going nuts. What am I supposed to tell him and what should I keep from him? Why do I even have to decide? It's not fair. I get so down..." She shook her head. "Everybody tries to help and I appreciate it but I still don't know what I'm supposed to do."

She shifted position, unfolding her legs and putting her feet on the floor. Then, restless, she crossed one leg over the other, clasped her arms across her chest, and leaned her head against the back of the couch. "Russ would be furious if he knew everything. Do you know what he would do, now, if he knew I was here alone with you?"

"Grab you by the hair and drag you back to his cave?"

Frustrated, she said, "Not funny. My God, when he's around I can't even say hi to friends unless they're girls. He considers it improper."

"That's not fair. He must be pretty insecure."

Renee considered that idea. *Russ insecure?* "He seems very sure of himself all the time. I don't think he's insecure."

"Well, sometimes people like that have to cover it up. You know, boss others around to hide the fact they feel inadequate." Alex tapped his fingers rhythmically against his knee. "That's my take on it. We already know Russ likes to tell you what to do." He paused, looked at Renee. "I hope that doesn't upset you."

She pulled her feet up onto the cushions. Hands in her lap, she fingered the ring, sliding it around, letting her fingertips run over the diamond. She cleared her throat, then took a deep breath. "Okay, this is weird. In high school he made a chart of our outfits that matched, or at least coordinated. He would tell me what to wear each day and he would wear the matching shirt or whatever. His favorite was my gray skirt and pink sweater and his gray slacks and pink dress shirt. I never told anyone about the chart. My friends, at first, made comments like 'You guys are like the Bobbsey Twins'. Then they just acted like it was no big deal. Maybe they were just embarrassed for me, I don't know. My parents were a little crazy over it—you know, the whole 'make up your own mind' stuff. But Russ wanted it, so...Last year we had dorm rooms that faced each other. He lived in Butler and I lived in Gentle Hall. He figured out which room numbers we needed to request on our applications. He bought us walkie-talkies and I had to buzz him every morning like an alarm clock. It got to be sort of a joke—my roomies would make stupid noises and say things like 'This is your wake-up call, Sir—get your lazy butt out of bed', which made Russ mad. He didn't like them listening in."

Realizing she was talking too fast, she slowed down and quieted her voice. "You know what else he did? He burned all the old notes, letters, pictures, cards—everything—from my old boyfriends. Everything, one at a time, like a ritual. Even my diary. And the sad part is I thought it was so loving. Romantic. But it was just dumb! He's a jealous, possessive..." She could feel the anger rising and she stopped, taking another deep breath. "What would he do if he knew I was here now?"

"Renee, it's okay." Alex touched her arm, pressing lightly. "He'd be mad. So what? You can have friends. You can be here and it's okay."

She sighed, nodded, eyes closed. "Thank you. You're right."

Alex's voice was controlled but she could sense his disgust. "What he did was wrong. He should never have burned your stuff. He—" Alex stopped. Rapidly tapped his knee. "Never mind what he did. Things will be different when he comes back."

She wrapped her arms around her legs and put her head on her knees, eyes closed, holding back tears. "Oh, God."

The only light came from the kitchen; the living room was shadowed and she was glad. If she cried she didn't want Alex to know. *I shouldn't be happy. I'm hurting so much. What's going to happen in July? Russ, you don't understand me. And you don't own me.* She felt Alex shifting; he moved closer and put one arm across the back of the couch, resting his hand lightly on her shoulder. She wanted to lean back, into his arm, his shoulder, his side, lay her head on his lap, feel his fingers in her hair, but instead she sat very still. Without speaking, he simply sat with her. Gradually she relaxed. *Just breathe.*

Someone running on the catwalk outside woke her. Sunlight stabbed her eyes; she stretched stiff limbs. Alex stood in the kitchen doorway, watching her. A blanket covered her legs and body. She yawned, sitting up. "What time is it?"

"Noon."

"Oh, no! I gotta get home!"

"Why?"

"Well." She hesitated. "I've been here a long time." She touched her face. "Where are my glasses?"

He smiled. "I put them right there on the table. How about some breakfast?"

She washed her face and used a plastic comb that she found on the bathroom counter. Then she folded the blanket and laid it on his bed. The plaid spread draped over the mattress was pulled up over the pillow. Going into the kitchen she asked, "Where did you sleep?"

"Didn't. Do you like soft-boiled eggs?" He handed her a mug of coffee.

"Hm. I don't know. Try me." She sat at the table and stirred sugar into the coffee. "I only use sugar once in awhile," she explained as he stood at the stove cooking. "On special occasions."

He put a plate in front of her with toast and two eggs. She carefully cracked the shells and scooped the eggs out. She took a bite. "Yum. You're a good cook."

Alex sat at the table with his own plate. "I'm glad you like them."

"When I was a kid, my mom used to make scrambled eggs for dinner. She'd add chunks of potato and grated cheese or pieces of ham to make the meal stretch for the whole family. I would go to my room and cry before dinner, I hated it that much." She laughed. "These are definitely not my mother's eggs!"

"What do you want to do today?"

She groaned. "Study. I have a term paper I have to finish. Luckily it's a subject I know about—a comparison of Updike's *Rabbit Run* and Betty Smith's novel, *Joy in the Morning*—two extremely different views of relationships in marriage."

Alex grimaced. "Sounds like a drag."

"No, it isn't. I love those books. I've read *Joy in the Morning* at least four times. My nickname last year was Annie, after the character in the book. I have the paper halfway done—just have to get it in shape to satisfy Mr. Kelly."

"Well, I'm impressed. When have you had time to work on it?"

"You teaser! I study more than anybody realizes. Math and English, my best subjects!" She giggled when he tilted his head questioningly. "Thanks to you!"

Alleycat

"Come on, let's do something fun. We can study later."

"Enough arm twisting! Got any ideas?"

"Do you play ping-pong? They have tables in the student center game room."

"Ooh, that sounds fun," Renee said. "Sure, I can go for that. Let's clean up here first."

As they washed and dried the dishes, they chatted about school. Alex said his business classes were okay but he hated statistics. "It's confusing and boring. But necessary, I guess. The class I like best is physics."

"Oh, just like Judy!" Renee grinned. "Do you have Dr. Hayes, too?"

He shook his head. "No, too bad, huh?" He grinned back at Renee. "She would like that, wouldn't she?"

"Oh, if you only knew how much," Renee said.

"Sometimes I get the feeling she wants to be my girlfriend."

Renee studied his face. "Do you want that?"

"No! I'm not interested in her, not that way." He shook his head. "Not any way, to be honest."

"Hm, she'll be so disappointed if she finds out."

"Can't you fix her up with somebody?"

Renee frowned. "Since the attack, she never wants to be alone. I can't blame her. But she doesn't really have fun at the 'Cat. I don't know what to do for her. She really wants to be around us—you, me, Savannah. As for Cal and Neil, she couldn't care less."

"I kind of get stuck with her. But it's okay. I'll survive."

"Poor Alex." Renee patted his arm. "Don't *you* know someone to fix her up with?"

"No. I feel kind of sorry for her." He picked up Renee's coat from the back of the folding chair. "Let's go over to Crider's. We should be able to buy ping-pong balls there."

"We have to buy them? Don't they provide them with the paddles?"

"Nah, we went over there once to play pool but it was too crowded so we tried ping-pong. The college won't provide balls anymore because they get trashed."

As they headed down the stairs, Renee said, "You didn't sleep, really?"

"I wasn't tired."

"I didn't stop you, did I?"

"Of course not. Stop worrying."

"Well," she exclaimed in mock despair. "You know that my reputation is now ruined, don't you? I spent the night in a boy's apartment."

"Horrors!"

Alex scrounged around in his pocket, coming up with a dime, two nickels, and three pennies. Renee found two pennies in her pocket and they handed the change to the high school girl at the cash register in Crider's. She punched the keys and the old wooden drawer popped out. She deposited the money and passed the receipt to Alex. "Ya want a bag?"

"No, thanks." Alex pocketed the three shiny white ping-pong balls and followed Renee out the door.

The game room, in the basement of the student center, was not crowded. It was a long room with a couple of pinball machines—half wrecked from being tipped, jiggled, and kicked—against one wall and a black and white television in one corner. The vinyl-covered chairs, supposedly grouped around the TV but mostly scattered all over the room, had peeling strips of colored tape over the rips to hold in the gray foam stuffing. The four pool tables, always in great demand, had a one-hour limit on their use, but the two old ping-pong tables were almost always available. They were in surprisingly favorable condition considering their age and all the times they were used as bleachers for the rooting section of the popular billiard games and as storage for coats, books, candy bars, and Cokes.

Alex put a dime on the counter but the student in charge of the game room merely nodded, never looking up from his *Playboy*. He sat very still, hunched over, eyes and lips barely moving. Alex cleared his throat.

"Uh, could we have a couple of paddles?"

The attendant let go of the magazine to wave in the general direction of nowhere. The edge of the magazine dipped back; the page was print, not photos. *Huh. I guess guys really do read the articles.* Renee went around the counter to look underneath. She found two paddles.

Renee lost one ball to the light fixture directly above them. The ceiling was high and Alex could find nothing to stand on that would enable him to reach it. He lost another ball to the light fixture trying to knock the first ball down. He almost broke the light fixture when he threw one of the paddles at it, hoping to get both balls back. Someone stepped on the last ball but Alex and Renee didn't mind. Their hour was up and Renee was howling with laughter anyway. They turned in their paddles and went into the coffee shop for ice cream cones.

~ 24 ~

"Do you like *Star Trek*?" Alex asked the girls one afternoon. They were in the bookstore checking out the new t-shirts and hats with the school logo. Judy wanted to buy something for her youngest brother for Christmas. She liked to plan ahead and purchase things throughout the year; she had a stash of items in a box under her bed. At Alex's question, she stopped flicking through the rack of shirts and almost jumped up and down.

"Yes! I love it!" she said. "I've probably seen every episode twice over."

He looked at Renee and Savannah. "How about you? Are you as excited about Captain Kirk and Spock as she is?"

Savannah shook her head. "It's not my thing. I've seen it, of course, but I'm not that interested. Why?"

"I found out it comes on every day at three o'clock. There are televisions all over campus. I figured maybe we could watch it sometime."

Renee said, "I like it. I'd watch it again." She thought about how she and Russ used to watch *Star Trek* at his house every week. She hadn't seen it since high school.

Judy's face fell and her arms drooped at her sides. "Darn. I have a class at three every day. Can you believe that?" She started looking through the rack of shirts again. "Gee, I really love that show."

"I'll check again and make sure about the time," Alex said. "I could have made a mistake." Behind Judy's back, he winked at Renee. She smiled broadly. *He knows she has a class.* He turned to Renee. "You want to meet in the TV room tomorrow?"

"You mean here, in the student center?"

"Yeah. Or somewhere else. The humanities building has televisions in every classroom. What do you think?"

"Sure. If we find a classroom, maybe I'll actually go to class first!"

Judy scowled, but Alex laughed. "Good plan. Don't you have

Alleycat

Lit on Monday, Wednesday, and Friday at two?"

Renee smiled, surprised Alex knew her schedule that well. "Yes. And I do go to that class, every time." She glanced at Judy. "You could skip, Judy. What classes do you have?"

"I don't skip class," Judy snapped. She yanked a hanger off the rack and marched up to the cash register. "I'll get this shirt," she said to the cashier. "How much is it?"

Alex and Renee found an empty classroom and started watching *Star Trek* three days a week. Frequently other students, hearing the familiar music and voices of the actors, joined them. Those times a lively discussion would follow, usually a comparison of story lines of various episodes. Renee enjoyed it and looked forward to the time spent in simple entertainment.

She and Alex studied her math every afternoon in the coffee shop or her dorm room, occasionally following *Star Trek* with a study session. After spending a good half hour on her assignment on Thursday afternoon, they dropped their books off at the apartment and walked up to the cemetery. As they went up the last hill, Renee pointed out the huge blue spruce at the top of the slope. "That's where I always sit when I come here."

"What do you do up here?"

"Oh, study—" He laughed and she grinned at him. "Read my mail from Russ. Write letters. Think about things. Imagine a different life." She gazed across the landscape at the farms spread out before them. "I've never told anyone that I come up here."

"Why?"

"I guess I think of it as my private place." She giggled. "Sometimes I sing that Beatles song 'There's a Place' while I'm walking. Do you know the one I'm talking about?"

"Yeah, sure. Where you can go when you feel low, right?" Alex sang a few bars in a deliberately off-key voice.

"Yeah, it's embarrassing that I sing like that. But no one's around." They both laughed.

"You have a good singing voice—I've heard you at the 'Cat."

"Well, in a group, with a record, that's different."

"Hey, it's good you have a place like this. And I'm glad you're sharing it with me."

Renee nodded. "Me, too. Thanks for coming with me."

"Even Savannah doesn't know about it?"

"Nope. I don't tell her everything. This—well, some people

187

wouldn't understand."

"She would, though, don't you think?"

"Of course, but I just haven't wanted to share this place before."

"What makes today different?"

Renee hesitated. "Um, I don't know." *Because you're a safe person, Alex. I trust you.*

"Well, seems like a pretty neat place to be alone," Alex said. They reached the entrance to the cemetery. "Come on, let's look at the graves."

They walked among the cracked and tippy headstones, moss creeping along the chiseled names. They stepped carefully around each grave as if the coffins rested on top of the ground, but some of the headstones were clustered so close together they couldn't be sure what "around" meant. Tree roots had lifted several of the markers clear out of the earth. Noticing one that had fallen face down, Alex and Renee struggled to raise it and prop it against the trunk of the offending tree.

Most of the trees were evergreens, which kept the cemetery dark and covered with fallen needles. The narrow asphalt walk wound among the trees and graves, fractured and messy like the headstones. They read names and dates, corny little verses, and beautiful words of remembrance. Lambs and baby shoes revealed children's graves; intricate crosses, curlicues, crucifixes adorned others. Some of the old markers had been worn almost smooth and others had so many crevices they were illegible. Renee and Alex emerged from the dimness into the sunshine reaching just to the trunk of the old tree, where they settled on the cool ground.

"I was here just last week," Renee said. "I don't come up as often as I used to, before I met you guys."

"I guess we keep you busy, huh?"

"Busy is good."

"Besides, it's pretty far."

"Oh, it's not a bad walk, really." She paused. "I just don't like being alone too much. It leads to thinking. And that isn't always a good thing."

They sat quietly for a few minutes. Alex shifted, moved as if he wanted to put his arm around her, but stopped. Awkwardly he ruffled her hair, then let his arm drop back to his side. "Is Russ on his spring vacation now?"

Alleycat

"Yeah, I just got a letter. That's why I came up here." She fell silent.

"Looks like it wasn't a great letter."

Renee shrugged, eyes down.

Alex spoke softly. "Did he say something that bothers you? Are you upset about it?"

She shook her head. "No, it was okay. The usual. You know—travelogue and so forth. He's on a four-week tour of Japan. With a friend." She stopped, then hurried on. "The friend is a girl." Alex nodded but didn't speak. Feeling agitation starting to build inside her, she wrapped her arms around herself, hunched her shoulders, then concentrated on relaxing her back. "Oh, I don't care. Really I don't. What I don't like is how he goes on and on about it. After he orders me not to ever be alone with you. He claims he had no choice about Barbara. He makes such an effort to make it sound legitimate. Legitimate! Good grief! Who even cares?"

"You do."

"Me? Huh." She sighed. "I trust him. Gosh, marriage is based on trust. It has to be—or should be, anyway. Russ is an open, honest person. He has strong beliefs and ideas, and honesty tops the list. If I couldn't trust him I wouldn't be engaged to him."

"Are you sure about that?"

Renee looked across the meadow that sloped down the hill in front of them. She shook her head. "I'm not sure about anything. You know, I wouldn't have thought a thing about that girl he happens to be traveling with if he just told me and dropped the subject. But he wrote so much about promising to be good that it sounded—" She hesitated.

"Suspicious?"

Reluctantly, she nodded. "Yes, and I don't like getting that kind of impression."

"Maybe he wants you to. Maybe he's worried about you and figures if you're jealous you'll, uh, pay more attention to him." Under his breath, his voice barely a whisper, Alex mumbled, "He's not worth it." He began drumming his knee with one hand.

Renee glanced at Alex, eyebrows knitted. *He does that when he's worked up about something. He thinks Russ is bad for me, too.* She stared at the horizon, trying to calm her shaking nerves. "You want to know something? I'm not jealous. It just doesn't matter to me."

"Does he know that? Have you guys talked about it?"

"He gets so jealous he wouldn't even notice my reactions." Renee clenched her hands together, right hand over the left, feeling the diamond bite into her palm. "He'd be so hurt—no, angry—if he saw us up here. He wouldn't understand our friendship. He hasn't had..." Her voice trailed off. She had started to say he hasn't had a normal friendship as long as she's known him. He had few friends in high school. She had felt sorry for him then. Misunderstood, he did nothing to dispel the rumors that swirled around the school. People thought he was odd and made fun of him behind his back. He was studious, serious, a loner, more at ease with teachers than peers. Her thoughts flashed to a time when someone spit on him from the second floor balcony of the boys' dorm. She heard laughter and running. Russ had no reaction at all. She had felt shock and sadness.

"Hasn't had what?"

"Never mind. I just wish things were different." *Does Russ trust me?* "Do you think he's trying to get a reaction out of me?"

"Maybe. He wants you to think you have a say in things but it's like he has to control you. As long as you do what he expects, everything is cool." He paused. "He has to be in charge."

Russ and Renee are shopping at the mall. Renee sees a red dress that she wants to try on and starts looking through the rack to find her size.

"No red," Russ tells her, pulling her away from the dresses. "Look at these blue ones."

"But I love red!"

"Red is for prostitutes, not for you."

Renee tries on the blue dress, modeling it for Russ, who clearly approves.

"You can wear it on Monday. I have a shirt that's the same color. I'll wear that and everyone will know we're together."

"You're right, you know. It's always his way." She gestured toward her sweater, a deep red color. "See this sweater? I bought it two weeks after he left. He told me I couldn't wear red because—because streetwalkers work in red light districts. He said people would associate me with whores." The last word came out in a whisper. Tears filled her eyes. She raised her voice to a normal level. "But that's crazy. I bought this and a red plaid skirt and I feel really good when I wear them. He's going to be furious when he finds out."

"I don't get why you let him do that." Alex's hands tightened into fists. He shoved them into the pockets of his leather jacket.

"He—he is so definite in what he wants. It doesn't really matter so I do it. I think he just wants me to let him decide everything."

"You're a smart person," Alex said. "You're making decisions all the time. You don't need someone to tell you what to do. Don't you know that?"

She didn't answer. She couldn't answer. Russ knew about Alex. He had written to Renee praising her good sense when she told him that she had asked Alex to help her with math. "No point in flunking a class that important," he wrote back. *Thanks a lot. That's showing real confidence. But what about Cal and Neil? And the apartment?* Russ told her in explicit terms not to go to Alex's room (she didn't mention that he had an apartment) or to ever be alone with him. *Well...besides, we met Cal first.* What would Russ say about him? Was she right in skipping over the details? She thought about her conversation with Cal. *Was he right? Is Russ a—prick?* She cringed at that word. *But I can't just stop my life until he gets back. It all goes on. It always will. If he came along right now, what would he do?* She shivered.

~ 25 ~

"My parents are on my case about my grades," Judy told Renee and Savannah as they ate breakfast one morning. "I have to do well or my dad will have a cow. He might even cut off my money. The scholarship doesn't cover everything."

"Are you having problems with your classes?" Savannah asked.

"Well, no, not yet. But nobody else is studying and that makes it hard for me."

Renee sat back in her chair, arms crossed, forehead furrowed, her mouth turned down in a scowl. "I'm studying. Every day. Alex and I work on my math, my papers for English are always written on time. I don't know what you're talking about." She picked up her fork and began eating.

"Every night we go to the Alleycat," Judy said. "I don't understand why. Those guys are just mindless. Morons. Look at the things they do. I mean, smoking a cigarette from a hole punched in the center, with both ends lit! Who came up with that dumb idea? And they're so crude. Don't they know intelligent people don't have to use swear words to get their point across?" She shook her head. "I know they're high all the time. Drunk or stoned or something."

"Come on, Judy," Savannah said. "That's ridiculous. You need to loosen up, stop being so critical."

"Don't tell me you think they're sober. Or intelligent."

Renee rolled her eyes. "They make us laugh—what's so bad about that?"

"They're pretty crazy," Savannah said, smiling at Renee. "But that's what's so fun. I personally don't care if they're high. It's not a big deal to me. They don't use around us." She ignored Judy's indignant grunt. "Tell me, have you ever met anybody like Neil or Cal?"

"No," Judy said emphatically. "Thank God. And if they want to fry their brains, that's fine with me." She gave a short laugh. "Not much to fry anyway." She glanced at Renee. "I don't mean Alex, though. He's different from the other two."

She can't even say their names. Cal and Neil. Out loud, Renee said, "Alex is quieter. And he doesn't drink or use drugs. But he's just as interesting and fun."

"I didn't say he wasn't interesting," Judy said quickly. "He's nice. I don't understand why he's friends with them." She paused, and then added, "Maybe he comes to the Alleycat to spend time with me."

Savannah burst out laughing, then clapped a hand over her mouth. Her eyes sparkled. "I'm sorry, Judy. Maybe he does." She stifled her giggles.

Judy glared. "I don't think that's so funny."

"I think," Renee said, "Alex likes being with all of us, Cal and Neil just as much as the three of us. Just because he's quiet doesn't mean anything."

"Are you saying he couldn't be interested in me?" Judy shifted in her chair, looking from Savannah to Renee. "I don't think that's so far-fetched."

Savannah raised her hands, palms out. "No, no, I'm not saying that at all. Don't get so defensive."

"Why do you come with us to the 'Cat if you don't like it?" Renee asked. "Just to see Alex?"

"You know I don't want to be alone at night. And it's something to do." She looked at Renee for a long moment. "Doesn't Russ care that you're going there every night with a bunch of guys? And then going to their apartment?"

"Judy!" Renee tightened her hands into fists under the table, working to keep the fire inside. Face flushed, she gritted her teeth. "Russ is fine with it. There is no problem with Russ. Leave it alone."

Savannah's voice drew Judy's attention away from Renee. "It's not a 'bunch of guys.' It's a bunch of friends. If you're uncomfortable with it, you should stay home."

"No…" Judy said, her voice trailing off.

That evening at the Alleycat, Renee excused herself to use the rest room. She stood in the shadow of the hallway and watched the group at the table, particularly Judy and Alex. They sat shoulder to shoulder, Judy on the outside of the booth, as usual. She leaned toward Alex, whispering and smiling, until he shifted away from her and said something to Savannah. Judy scowled, tapping her fingers on the table. Then she nudged Alex, offered him a drink of her soda, frowning when he shook his head. *Hmm. Doesn't look like he really wants to talk to her. No surprise.* Alex abruptly reached across the table and picked up Neil's cigarette smoldering in the ashtray. He put it to his lips and inhaled. Coughing, he laughed as Neil smacked him on the back.

"Lightweight," Neil said. "Man, you need to work on that."

"Yeah, light one for me, will ya?"

Judy's eyes narrowed and she quickly stood up. She gathered her coat and hat and moved to another booth.

"Oh, come on back, Judy," Savannah said. "He's just kidding around."

Renee came out of the shadows and sat in the space Judy had vacated. "What's going on?"

"Judy said she's glad I don't smoke," Alex said, chuckling. He dropped the cigarette back into the ashtray. "If I did, I wouldn't smoke these. No filter. Bad news." He grinned at Cal and Neil. "Maybe I should try a pipe, huh?"

"I think it's way cooler than plain old cigs," Cal said. "Sexier, right, girls?"

Judy's disgusted snort could be heard over Renee and Savannah as they agreed with Cal. "Cigarettes just plain smell bad," she muttered. She moved back to the booth, pulling a chair over from a nearby table. "Fine. I don't care if you smoke or not, Alex." She slouched in the chair, arms crossed. He laughed and stretched across Renee to tousle Judy's hair. She jerked away from him, eyes squinted.

"I'm not gonna take up smoking," he said. His arm brushed against Renee. He rested his fingers on her back for a moment, then moved his hand up and rubbed her neck. His touch was firm and reassuring. She sat very still, pretending she didn't notice. She let her breath out slowly. *Oh, I needed that. Thank you, Alex.* She relaxed and sat back, avoiding Judy's stare.

~~ 26 ~~

Renee lay very still, listening to her roommate breathing unevenly through a dream. Judy claimed she never dreamed but most nights her bed creaked and whispered as she struggled against the restraints of the sheets and blankets. Since the attack, her sleep had been much more restless.

Renee was having a lot of trouble sleeping lately. In bed, in the blessed darkness, late at night, seemed to be the only inviolable private time she had anymore. In only two months her life had turned chaotic and emotional and overwhelming.

Things had gotten so complicated. Russ, traveling around a foreign country with another girl. *Terrific.* Maybe he would decide to stay over there. Or maybe he'd come back and meet Judy and they'd fall for each other. She knew Judy would like Russ. And he would like her. There was something about both of them. Smart and—she hated to say it, really, but it was true—insufferable. Quite often they made Renee feel small, powerless. Judy always said "No one can *make* you feel anything." However…

Russ likes to remind Renee that he has an IQ of over 150. At first she wondered how he knew that. She doesn't know anybody who has had their IQ tested, but when she questioned him, he seemed offended. She doesn't question him anymore but assumes he wouldn't make it up. He values honesty more than anything else. At least, he tells her that all the time. He is *very smart. He can discuss any subject with authority and confidence and effectively argue with anyone who shares a different opinion. His belief in himself is one thing that drew her to him. She admires his self-assurance. He knows what he wants and how to make it happen. She considers her own lack of self-confidence and insecurity about her future. Becoming a teacher is important but more important than that is having a family of her own. And Russ wants the same thing.*

"You know, geniuses marry for one of two reasons," he tells her. "Either for love or because the other person is also a genius. And you know I love you, Renee."

Then there was Cal. Although he could be crude and loud, just as often he showed his kind and thoughtful side, especially to Renee. She never knew what he would say or do, if he would be serious or sardonic, but he treated Renee with respect, sensing when he'd crossed the line and backing off. That unpredictability was exciting; she knew that Savannah felt it, too. He was fun to be with and she looked forward to evenings at the Alleycat and the apartment as much because of him as anything else. She wondered if he was really attracted to her. *Why would he think about asking Savannah on a date?* He clearly had little regard for Russ and had said the diamond ring didn't mean a thing. *But he understands my commitment to Russ.*

And Alex. She was puzzled about the way he kept invading her thoughts, even her actions. She had gone for a solitary walk on Thursday, to think things out, and he showed up out of the blue. Happy to see him, she'd greeted him with a huge smile and almost gave him a hug. *But he's not the huggy type.* They had walked to the campus coffee shop and he bought them cherry vanilla ice cream cones. Unusually talkative, he had told her about growing up as a military kid in a large Catholic family.

"We moved all the time, at the drop of a hat. Sometimes my mom had only a day to pack. It was mass confusion. We could each take only one small box of our toys or books—whatever we wanted to keep. Sometimes the box would 'disappear'. I had a ton of comics my dad threw away. They'd be worth something now."

"We moved a lot, too," Renee said. "But my parents never got rid of stuff like that. My dad just changed jobs or transferred to another place so we had plenty of time to get ready for a move. They still have all my old Nancy Drew books."

"Yeah, well, my dad never reads books or anything except the sports page. He thinks reading is a waste of time." He paused and tossed the paper from the ice cream cone in a nearby trash receptacle. "Luckily I got a scholarship because he pretty much thinks college is a waste of time, too."

"Alex! That's terrible. Is that why you never talk about your family?"

"I guess."

"You'll be a much different kind of father."

"Doesn't matter. I don't think I ever want to get married or have kids."

"Wow." Renee had never considered not having a family; it was strange to meet someone who felt so differently. But that was Alex—different from anyone else she knew. She felt comfortable with him, found him easy to talk to. He didn't brag or show off. He listened and didn't interrupt or tell her things just to make her feel good. He had a gentleness about him that felt safe.

And Judy had her sights set on him.

"Alex is a good prospect for a husband," Judy had said to Renee just a couple of days ago as they got ready for bed. "He's decent, smart, good-looking. He talks to me a lot. Do you know he's never been on a date? Well, a blind date in high school but that hardly counts. That means we have something important in common."

"He told me he doesn't plan on getting married."

Judy had said with a smirk, "Well, people change."

Renee sat up in bed, unable to keep her eyes closed. Three names galloped teasingly across her mind, back and forth, like knights ready to joust. Cal. Alex. Russ. Cal, entertaining, unpredictable. Alex, kind, funny, straightforward. *My friends.* And Russ. *My fiancé.*

She shivered. *I gotta get outta here.* Quietly pushing the bedcovers back, she rose and crept out of the room, taking a bundle of clothes from the desk chair with her. The bright ceiling light in the hallway glared like an interrogation lamp and she winced. In the bathroom she dressed hastily: jeans, sweater, socks, saddle shoes. After stuffing her pajamas in her towel locker, she went back into the hall. Letting herself through the door leading outside she ran down the stairs and walked quickly to Savannah's window. Relieved to see a faint glow under the curtain, she rapped on the glass, shivering. March nights were cold. Savannah's face appeared; she cranked the window open.

"Renee," she whispered. "It's way past midnight! Are you okay?"

"Yeah, I just felt like walking."

"I'll be out in a sec."

"Bring an extra sweatshirt, please?"

They met in front of the dorm. "What were you doing?" Renee asked as they walked briskly along the well-lit main road toward town.

"Rewriting a poem—by candlelight, no less. Molly's asleep so I had to be really quiet. I just couldn't concentrate and I wasn't getting anywhere, either, so I guess I needed a break." She rubbed her hands vigorously. "Brr! It's freezing out here! You and your walks!"

Renee laughed. "You wouldn't have come if you didn't want to and you know it." The crisp, vibrant air and just being with Savannah cleared Renee's head and she felt revitalized. "Are you carrying your keys?" They had promised the boys that if they had to go out at night, they would do what they could to protect themselves. Cal told them to grip their keys between two fingers, ready to jab with them if necessary.

"Of course," Savannah said. "And I have my 'impact weapon' as Neil calls it."

"I have mine, too."

Savannah said, "Do you think it'll be okay to go to their place when they're having other people over? And you know there will be drugs there. Are you okay with that?"

"I think anyone can show up. And you know I don't care about the drugs as long as no one tricks me into taking something—and the police don't raid the place." Renee chuckled. "They're so protective! It was weird to go back to the dorm after we left the Alleycat, wasn't it?"

"Yeah. It was strange to actually go to bed so early."

"Maybe that's why we couldn't sleep."

"Judy had no problem, though, did she?"

Renee burst out laughing, the sound carrying across the night air. "Not a bit! She was really glad to go home for a change."

"Did you tell her you were leaving?"

"No. If she wakes up I'm sure she'll just think I'm down in your room."

As they approached the door to number eight, they could hear the sounds of the party inside. Savannah tapped on the door. No answer. She twisted the knob and pushed the door open. In the crowded apartment no one seemed to notice as Renee and Savannah entered.

The walls reverberated with waves of rock music crashing from the stereo, the living room thick with sweet, aromatic smoke. A collection of candles clustered on the end table sputtered and flickered; the only other light came from the kitchen. A couple slow-danced, arms wrapped around each other, feet barely moving. Renee didn't recognize them. She looked around for a familiar face, finally spotting Neil standing near the bedroom, beer bottle in one hand, cigarette in the other. He was laughing at something someone said, head thrown back, stance wide. He swayed and bumped against the wall, laughing harder. Savannah walked over to him, a tentative smile on her face. Bracing himself against the wall with the hand holding the cigarette, Neil leaned down to kiss her. She turned her head so his lips met her cheek. He offered the beer. She shook her head, then changed her mind and took a sip.

Laughter erupted from the kitchen, so Renee moved in that direction, weaving through the crowd. Cal, drawing in deeply on a hand-rolled cigarette, saw her as soon as she rounded the doorframe. He passed the joint to the girl sitting on the counter, exhaled, and motioned for Renee to stay where she was.

"Hi," he said, coming to her side. "What are you doing here?"

"Just out for a walk." She smiled. "This is more crowded than I expected."

He looked at the clock. "God, it's late. You alone?"

"No, Savannah's with me. She's over there by Neil."

"Come on, I'll introduce you around." Renee followed Cal, almost bumping into him when he stopped at the card table to grab a few chips from one of the bags crowding the table, littered with stray Fritos and cookie crumbs. The dip containers were half-empty and messy; a plate with slightly dried-out cheese slices and Ritz crackers made the centerpiece. "Help yourself to some food," he said.

Renee took a couple of crackers. "Where's Alex?"

"He's at Doug's." Cal stopped next to three people sitting on the floor passing a water pipe. "This is Karen and John and uh—who are you again?" They looked up, said hi, and Cal moved on. "Shelli, Tyler, this is my friend Renee." Shelli was stretched out on the floor with her head in Tyler's lap. Eyes closed, her fingers tapped to the beat of the music coming from the stereo next to them.

Tyler looked Renee over, eyes moving up and down her body, stopping at her chest. "Mmm." He grinned at Cal. "Is she your new girl? It's about time, man."

"Give it up, you two-timer," Cal said with a smirk. "Unlike you, I keep my love life private. Come on, Ren." He took her arm and started to walk away. Tyler extricated himself from Shelli's head and stood up.

"Did you score any dope from that guy I told you about? Shell and I want to drop some acid, maybe next weekend. You game?"

Cal shook his head. "I don't do acid. And I stay away from dangerous people."

"Ah, he's all right," Tyler said. "I know some guy said he got ripped off but I don't believe it."

"No dope is worth going to that guy for," Cal said.

"Hey, man, did you hear about the dude that croaked in the creek last month?"

"Yeah. Think he was a buyer?"

Tyler laughed. "That old man? He probably told the dopers to get out of his nice little neighborhood park and then fell into the creek. Probably drunk out of his mind."

"Maybe."

As Cal continued talking to Tyler, Renee moved a few feet to stand near the wall where she could see the whole room. *Wallflower. That's me.* She smiled a little, letting herself fade into the background as she scanned the room. A few people were scrunched together on the couch deep in conversation. Then a question rang out from the group, "What if we're just a tiny speck—an atom—a miniscule piece of a gigantic, mile-long—coffee table!—in some other universe?" Renee watched eyes widen and heads nod in agreement and she heard the phrases, "Heavy, man" and "That's profound!" *Oh, brother. I guess that's what makes drinking so worthwhile—you get such great insight into life!*

She watched Cal and Tyler, both of them animated and intense in their discussion. She caught the words "Gentle Woods" and wondered if the dealer Tyler referred to was the one Cal had told her about. She shivered. Shelli had shifted position, sitting cross-legged, back straight, hands resting lightly on her knees, fingertips barely touching, eyes still closed. Renee could see her chest rising and falling as she breathed. *Is she meditating? Here? With all this noise? Wow.*

In another area, a skinny, pimply boy with a straggly goatee was telling a story. When he finished the narration, an argument broke out as another guy, taller, beefier, accused the storyteller of messing it up. Their voices got loud and angry as one challenged the other to go outside and settle it. A girl stepped between them, talking softly, pleading. The boys slowly backed off, glaring at each

Alleycat

other. *It's like watching a B-movie. Crazy.*

The music on the stereo changed and Janis Joplin's distinctive voice filled the room. The slow dancing pair did not alter their movements to match the beat and paid no attention as several other couples began dancing near them. They appeared to be oblivious to everything around them. The boy slid his hand downward from his partner's waist to squeeze her bottom and pull her closer against him. She wrapped her arms tighter around his neck. He pushed his knee between her legs and when she tipped her head back, he pressed his mouth against hers. Abruptly they broke apart, a look of shock on the girl's face. Then she laughed. "You bit me!"

In the hallway, Savannah's laugh drifted across the apartment. Savannah stood close to Neil, focused on the small group around her. She had taken her coat off and hooked it on the bedroom doorknob. *Good, she's having fun. We might be here awhile.* Renee slipped out of her jacket and glanced around for a place to put it. Making her way across the room toward the front door, she nodded and smiled as people greeted her, mumbled a few hi's, tried not to trip over anyone. Her eyes stung from the smoke hanging in the air, a pungent mix of tobacco, marijuana, and incense. Her head began to throb with the start of a headache and she felt a little lightheaded. She opened the door a crack, took a gulp of fresh air, then turned back to the room, dropping her coat in the corner after she made sure her room key was in her jeans pocket. Somebody offered her a toke; she raised her hands and shook her head. "No thanks! I'm fine!" She had to shout over the music. A half-empty bottle of Ripple was thrust in her upraised hand. She reflexively grabbed it.

Cal came over to her, smiling, and took the bottle. "Do you want a drink? We might have a can or two of soda in the sink."

"The sink?"

"With ice. It's our cooler."

"Okay, do you have 7-Up?"

"Most likely. Come on." She followed him into the kitchen. He dug around in the jumble of bottles, cans, and ice cubes floating in the sink and pulled out a can of 7-Up. He opened it and handed it to her. She counted seven bottles of cheap liquor on the counter, most uncapped and nearly empty. A stack of paper cups had tipped over and lay precariously close to the edge of the ice-filled sink. She reached over and pushed them back.

"Oops, s'cuse me," she said as a tall, burly boy rammed into her. She sidestepped out of his way.

"Sorry, I just need that vodka over there. Can you hand it to me?" Without waiting for her to do that, he reached across the sink and grabbed the bottle, taking a long swig. "Damn!" He grinned at her. "Hi, I'm Chuck. Who are you?"

"Umm, I'm a friend of Cal's. Renee."

"Oh yeah," Chuck said. "You're that chick that hangs out at the diner."

She ducked her head, not wanting him to see her blush. *Is that how people know me? Yikes.*

"Hey, you want some vodka with that 7-Up? I'll get you a cup."

"No thanks. I'm good with just this right now."

He went to the refrigerator and yanked it open. "There's gotta be somethin' good in here. I've had enough chips." He rummaged around, moving containers, finally pulling out something wrapped in tin foil. He opened a corner and sniffed at the contents. "Ah, ham. Perfect. I need a knife."

Renee looked around for Cal. He had disappeared, so she pointed to a drawer. "The knives are in there." A girl with waist-length hair, granny glasses, and a long peasant dress was perched on the counter above the drawer.

"Ooh, Abby," Chuck said, leering. "I'm so sorry but I just have to dive between your beautiful legs!" He grabbed her skirt and pushed it up. Quickly she moved her legs to the side and reached down to open the drawer, rolling her eyes. Renee couldn't help laughing.

"He's drunk," Abby said to her. "Usually he's pretty decent."

Chuck put the ham on the stove and sliced off a big piece. As he munched on it, he said, "You guys hear about the bombing in Washington?"

"No, what happened?"

"Bonnie," Chuck said, wagging a finger at the girl sitting on the counter across from Abby. "Don't you keep up with your current events?"

She laughed. "Current events are all right here, in this little pill." She held out her hand; in the palm was a tiny blue capsule, which she popped in her mouth. "Give me that bottle," she said to Chuck. He handed her the vodka and she swallowed a mouthful.

"You should keep up on things," Abby said. "The capital was

bombed."

"Why?"

"To protest the war, what else?" Chuck finished off the piece of ham and went to the table for some chips. He scooped up a huge blob of clam dip, catching the drips with another chip. With his mouth full, he said, "It was the Weathermen again."

"It's insanity," Abby said. "Violence doesn't work. It's ineffective."

"But the Underground makes its point," Chuck said. "Nixon is cowering in his tunnel right now, you can bet on it."

"Nixon is a moron." Bonnie slid off the counter. "I need a hit. Anyone have a joint?" She wandered into the other room.

"She's totally looped," Chuck said, leaning against the counter.

Peter, Paul, and Mary had replaced Janis Joplin; sounds of "I Dig Rock and Roll Music" drifted into the kitchen. Renee peeked around the wall. A couple of people were dancing to the music, doing the Twist. The slow dancers were gone. Savannah was still with Neil, standing just a little behind him. Bonnie approached them, said something to Neil. He handed her a joint. Cal was engaged in conversation with several people; he caught her eye and nodded, smiling. She smiled back. He left the group and came over to her side. Glancing at the clock on the stove she was surprised to see that more than forty-five minutes had passed.

"You doing okay?" Cal asked.

"Sure. People-watching."

"This will give you fodder for a poem, right?"

Renee chuckled. "I guess it will!"

"I don't get it," Abby was saying. "Why can't they use peaceful means? Bombing is so senseless."

"But no one is listening," another girl said. "They've tried written manifestos and going on television and radio."

"The Weathermen?"

"Well, no, not them, but others. The bombing was an act of desperation."

"It makes me sick," Abby said. She took a gulp of beer from the bottle in her hand. "Remember Peter Arnett, the reporter?"

"Didn't he say something like you have to annihilate the people to protect them?"

She nodded. "Yes! The exact quote is 'We had to destroy the village in order to save it.' Sad."

"But it's true," Cal said. "For the greater good, you know. Sometimes it just has to be that way."

"Bombing for peace," Renee said, "is just as bad—worse!—as bombing for the purpose of killing in a war."

"You're right," Abby said. "Do you have to join the enemy to make it listen to you? God, I hate this fucking war."

"My boyfriend is a conscientious objector," Renee said, surprised at her ease in talking with people she didn't know. "We met with some guys who were getting ready to defect to Canada. I hope the war is over before we have to make a decision like that."

"Now that makes sense to me," Abby said. "A statement that you won't support the oppression of another country by spilling blood. Way to go, man."

"Hey, Abby. Chuck, you raiding our fridge again?" Alex stood in the arch between the kitchen and living room.

"About time you joined us," Abby said.

"Hi, Alex!"

He looked startled at the sound of Renee's voice. Turning toward her he said, "What are you doing here? I thought we walked you back to the dorm a long time ago."

She grinned. "You did. But me and Savannah were bored."

"Is Judy here, too?"

"No! We snuck out."

Alex laughed. "How did you do it?"

"Well," Renee said, "I waited until she was asleep and I left. I went to Savannah's window and we came here."

Cal slung an arm around Renee's shoulder. He looked at Alex. "I've already reminded her that they should not have been out walking past midnight."

"Hey!" Her eyes sparkled as she spoke. "We had our weapons at the ready. And we walked like we knew exactly where we were going and what we were doing. Exuding confidence."

Cal gave her shoulder a squeeze, then dropped his arm. "What else can anyone expect?"

Alex shook his head. "Women!"

Renee slapped his arm. "Stop it!" She laughed. "We were careful. Promise."

"Uh-huh." He went to the table and scrounged through a rumpled bag of vanilla sandwich cookies. Renee followed him. He offered her a cookie as he took a bite of another one. "Well, are you having fun? Do you want to stay or—" Alex raised his hands questioningly.

"Or what? You have a plan? I'm fine with leaving."

"I have an idea," Alex said. "Come on, get Savannah, and let's go." He grinned at Renee. "Hey—it'll be fun." He zipped up his coat. "I mean it. Trust me!"

"Trust *you*? Ha!" Renee laughed. "Wait a sec, I'll see what Savannah wants to do." She crossed the living room and whispered in Savannah's ear. "Do you want to leave?"

"Might as well," Savannah said. "This isn't that much fun." She tipped her head toward Neil and whispered to Renee, "He's so drunk I don't think he even knows I'm here." She pulled her coat on and smoothed her hair, then said goodbye to Neil. He kissed her briefly on the cheek and finished off his beer in one gulp.

"Later, babe, right?"

"Right," she replied. "Tomorrow."

Renee said goodbye to Cal. He gave her a quick hug, a big smile lighting up his face. "I'm glad you came over. See you tomorrow night?"

"Sure." She paused. "Don't get—"

"High?" Chuckling, he winked at her. She raised her hands in mock surrender.

Alex, Renee, and Savannah walked quickly back to campus, the girls pestering Alex for information about his plan, but he would not say anything until they reached the student center. He jogged across the concrete courtyard, calling over his shoulder, "Tonight's the movie marathon! Let's check it out!"

"Won't it be over by now?" Savannah walked over to the kiosk in the courtyard and ran her eyes across the myriad of notices and cards taped and thumbtacked to the four sides. She pointed to a flyer announcing the monthly movie night: Terror Theater. "Oh! It started at midnight."

"Come on, let's go," Alex said. "It'll be fun."

Renee studied the flyer. The first movie listed was Hitchcock's *Psycho,* followed by *Wait Until Dark* and *Cape Fear.* "We better hurry," she said. "The second movie should be starting just about now."

They trotted up the steps to the student center and pushed through the double doors, then sprinted across the long room and down the stairs to the basement. A crowd filled the hallway outside the small theater; a moment later the doors opened and the students pushed inside the darkened room. Savannah, Renee, and Alex scrambled to find seats together, finally settling down with Alex sitting between the two girls. Savannah reached across him to grab Renee's arm.

"Don't get too scared," she whispered.

"Hey, I'll protect you," Alex said. "You can hang onto me if you need to."

"Oh, our shining knight!" Renee said.

The screen flashed with the opening credits. The audience quieted as the camera followed a young woman carrying a doll through a large airport. Renee scrunched down in her seat and concentrated on the film, trying not to think about the closeness of Alex's hand on the armrest between them. But as the terror built and they watched Audrey Hepburn's character figure out the identities of the men in her apartment, Renee had to fight the urge to grab onto Alex.

In a soft whisper, leaning close to his ear, she said, "This is scary!" A slight movement caught her eye; it was Savannah clutching Alex's arm. Renee almost laughed out loud. She folded her hands in her lap, fingers tightly clenched, and watched the rest of the movie, feeling more at ease. *He would protect us if we needed it.*

At the next intermission, between films, Alex said, "Do you want to see the last movie or do something else?"

"Like what?" Savannah asked. "We live in Monmouth, we have no transportation, it's 4:00 in the morning."

"We could walk over to the park. Or go to the grade school."

"What?" Savannah stared at him.

Renee said, "Yeah, yeah, let's do it."

"Why?"

"Do you really want to go home?" Alex asked her. "Or back to the apartment with the drunks?"

"What are we going to do at the school?"

"I don't know, just check it out. Or we could go to the Woods." He gave them a sideways look, then laughed at their stricken expressions.

"No, not Gentle Woods," Savannah said. "The school is fine."

The elementary school was located in the middle of the college campus on the main street. It stood three stories high, a large brick building surrounded by towering trees. They went around the back and found a playground with equipment set in gravel. They tried out the seesaw and merry-go-round, keeping their voices low. Renee peeked in the classroom windows but found it too dim to see anything. They sat on the swings and talked quietly.

"I was surprised to see you tonight," Alex said.

Renee smiled. "I'm sure you were! We had an opportunity to get out, away from Judy, and we took it!"

"What time did you get to the apartment?"

"Oh, a little after twelve," Savannah answered. "We know—it was a risk going out that late. Please, no lecture."

Alex laughed. "Not from me. But I do have a question for you. Are you two okay with Cal and Neil drinking and all that? I mean, if you're not, we could always go somewhere else in the evenings. Like to the dorm."

Savannah smiled at him. "It's really okay. I like their company."

"Me, too," Renee said. "And they don't usually do it when we're there."

"I just don't want you to get in trouble or be in a place that's not safe for you." He shook his head. "God, my parents are on me all the time about it. Ragging about how the police are watching the apartment and all sorts of paranoid shit."

"Parents always over-react," Renee said. "Hey, I asked Cal why they don't offer us beer and pot anymore—just that one time, when Judy got so mad."

Savannah looked at her, surprised. "Really? What did he say?"

"It's a moral issue for him." Renee nodded. "Yeah, that's what he said. And," she added, glancing at Alex, "he said you both told Neil not to bug us about it."

"That's true," Alex said. "Neil likes to party and he wants to make sure everyone with him is happy. We told him that you girls are happy without booze and grass."

Savannah and Renee laughed. Savannah said, "It's impossible to be unhappy around you guys. Don't worry, Alex, we're okay with it as it is."

Judy gave up on trying to convince Savannah and Renee that their grades were suffering. While the group sat in their booth at the Alleycat, analyzing poetry, singing along with the jukebox, teasing each other, flirting and talking, she sat on the outside edge or sometimes at a nearby table by herself, and studied. The others left her alone after a few attempts to include her in their conversations.

When they bundled into coats and scarves, split up the tab, and paid the bill, Judy always suggested they go back to the dorm, to bed. And almost always they went to the apartment, Judy grumbling under her breath. Once there she tried to get Alex to talk to her, play Scrabble or cards, quiz her for a test, anything. Failing to keep his interest for more than a short time, she slept, stretched out on the couch or on one of the twin beds in the bedroom. When Renee and Savannah felt like leaving, they woke her; if it was the middle of the night Alex or Cal or Neil walked them back to the dorm but if the sun had come up they went alone.

With finals looming, Savannah made a resolution to focus more on school, to make up for lost time. The three girls began studying after dinner in the library before meeting up with the boys at the Alleycat. Often they met Alex in the library, too. Once the four of them used a study room, designed for small groups, but they ended up talking and laughing and wrestling. Someone complained about the noise and the librarian came by with a stern warning. Alex came up with a solution: they each studied in a separate area and met every hour for a five or ten minute break. It worked well for them and they began to take studying seriously again, even if only for a couple of hours each evening. Judy made a point of thanking Savannah repeatedly for the idea of the study time. She complained that it was increasingly difficult to study at either the diner or the apartment. When Renee and Savannah reminded her that she was free to stay at the dorm, she reminded them in return that she was uncomfortable being by herself at night.

Renee did not like the library. She missed the noise, the general excitement of the Alleycat. They still went there, of course, around eight-thirty, but the close silence of the library gave her too much time alone. She felt abandoned. She tried to study but ended up starting letters to Russ. She failed at that, too. So she doodled in the margins of her notes and the unfinished letters, wrote poems, began stories. She waited for the hour to pass, and then hurried upstairs to meet the others.

Cal and Neil were often waiting at the Alleycat, their welcoming act (gleeful whoops, a great scuffling of chairs, gallant chivalry) loud and rambunctious. They ordered coffee or sodas,

Alleycat

sometimes sandwiches or fries, and settled comfortably in their booth. And so the laughter, the fun, the unreal night began and some of the panic left Renee. As long as they sat at their table, she didn't have to think about anything. She wished it would never end.

~ 27 ~

Renee and Judy, studying in their room, were startled by pounding from the floor below. Judy dashed to the window, cranked it open, reached out and pulled up the string dangling from their room to Savannah's underneath them. Savannah had written **RENEE** on the folded slip of paper, but Judy ignored that and opened it.

"Oh, wow," she said, scanning the words. "Savannah has a date with Cal."

At her desk, Renee sat up straight, bewildered surprise on her face. "Really? Let me see." She took the note and read it quickly, then snatched a pen off her desk and scribbled something at the bottom of the paper. She folded it back up and crossed the room to clip it to the string.

"What did you write?"

"Congratulations." She dropped the clothespin and, looking down through the window, saw Savannah's hand reach out and take the note.

"I thought she was, you know, with Neil," Judy said, sounding confused. "What's going on?"

"Savannah likes both of them. Neil is just more aggressive." Renee shrugged, her expression neutral. But her heart thumped and her mouth went dry. *I didn't think he would actually do it.* She thought about the note. **Cal wants to see a movie with me. He has a friend who has a car!** She wondered if Savannah would really go. And if going would change things, if Neil would get upset, if Cal would claim Savannah, if Cal's interest... *Stop. Think about how Cal is. And you are* not *available.* She picked up her key. "I'm going down to her room. See you later."

Judy scrambled after Renee, slipping out the door before it closed. "Wait for me."

Downstairs they knocked on Savannah's door. When she answered, Renee grinned and winked at her. "Cool! A night out with the BMOC. When? What movie?"

Savannah giggled. "BMOC! Yeah, sure. Thursday. That's when he can get the car. He didn't say what movie. With my luck it'll be something like *A Clockwork Orange*." She considered that, then shook her head. "Lord, I hope not! I don't think I could sit next to him in a theater for that. Too strange for me."

"You're really going out with him?" Judy made a face. "He's a jerk."

"It'll be fun," Savannah said.

"Won't Neil be mad?"

Renee laughed. "He should have asked her first."

"Lighten up, Judy," Savannah said. "It's not a boyfriend-girlfriend kind of thing."

"Yet." Judy stood with her hands on her hips. "Can you drive? He might not be sober."

"Oh, stop it," Renee said. "Just be glad he didn't ask you. Then you'd have to worry about all this stuff. And you don't have a driver's license, do you?"

"I'm going back upstairs. I have work to do."

Savannah motioned for Renee to come into her room; she closed the door after her and they sat on the beds. Savannah studied Renee's face. Renee dropped her eyes, sat on her hands to keep them out of her mouth. "Are you sure about this?" Savannah asked.

"Of course," Renee said. "It's not up to me anyway."

"You like him. If you walked away from Russ, he would ask you."

"I told you I wouldn't date him anyway."

"I know, but…"

I wouldn't. If Russ and I break up, I wouldn't want to date anyone for a long time. And Cal would have to change, settle down.

"Hey, he's more your type than mine anyway," Renee said. "You like the bad boys."

Savannah laughed. "I guess so."

"Go on the date and have fun. Leave me with Judy." Renee smiled. "We'll compare notes later."

Thursday evening Savannah, Renee, and Judy waited for Cal in the lobby of the lounge. He arrived right on time. As he came through the doors, he stopped short, then smiled and said, "I should have known you'd all be here." He wore a sport jacket with his jeans and open-necked dress shirt and carried a small bouquet of wildflowers, which he presented to Savannah with a grand flourish.

"Oh, Cal, they're beautiful!" She handed them to Renee, asking her to put them in water. "What movie are we going to?"

"I decided to take you to a play instead," Cal said. "It's *A Thousand Clowns* by Herb Gardner. I hope that's okay. My theater class got free passes."

"Of course! At Pentacle Theater in West Salem?"

"Have you been there?" Cal asked.

"No, but I've always wanted to. A play is so much better than a movie."

He laughed. "I have to agree with that!" He offered his arm; Savannah took it and they walked out to a battered '65 Rambler.

Renee and Judy saw them off, waving and yelling warnings about curfew and picking up hitchhikers. Savannah made faces at them, alternating between mock fright and wide-grinned happiness. Cal made a wide sweep around the parking lot, honking the horn and waving.

Renee and Judy strolled through campus to the Alleycat. Neil and Alex were there with Doug, Alex's gaming friend. They were eating hamburgers, drinking Cokes. Renee listened to the discussion about the battles he and Alex were replaying in the game *Stalingrad*. Alex's expression was animated as he got into a friendly argument with Doug about the size and the thickness of armor on a T34 Russian tank. Judy asked questions periodically, demonstrating her depth of knowledge about World War II, her eyes locked on Alex the whole time.

"I'd like to watch sometime," Judy said. "I like history, especially World War II." She noticed the look Renee gave her. "Well, I do. The timeframe, not the actual war part of it."

"No one's arguing with you."

Judy shrugged. "Okay." She turned to Doug. "Could I come and watch sometime?"

"I guess so. It's probably boring just to watch. We're starting a new game tomorrow night. You could come and learn how to play."

"Great! Where is your apartment?"

"Just meet me here at five," said Alex. "We can walk over together. We usually get pizza and play 'til late."

As Judy continued asking questions about the game, Neil passed his plate to Renee. "Here, you look half-starved." She nibbled on the french fries, dipping them in the swirled mixture of ketchup and mustard. "So, Cal and Savannah are at the movies," Neil said, picking up a couple of fries. He popped them in his mouth.

"No, they went to Pentacle Theater. *A Thousand Clowns* is playing."

"Man, that title sure fits Cal!" Neil laughed, looking relaxed, and not at all bothered that Savannah was out with Cal. "Now you have to be—" he lowered his voice to a whisper, leaning close to Renee's ear—"alone with Jujube."

Smiling at his private nickname for Judy, she nodded. "It's fine. Anyway, we're here—I'm not alone!" She watched his face as she asked, "Does it bother you that Savannah's out with Cal?"

"Nah. It's cool. I dig her and all, but we're not exclusive. He's the one that scored the car, so he's the one that gets to score with the girl." He grinned at Renee's shocked expression. "I mean that in a nice way, not the Biblical sense."

Renee's mouth dropped open, then she chuckled. "I think she can handle herself."

"Oh, no doubt."

When Doug decided to leave for home, the rest of the group left, too, walking the three blocks to the apartment. Right away, Judy took a deck of cards out of the hall linen closet. "Gin Rummy, anybody?"

Neil grabbed the cards and began shuffling them at the kitchen table. "Let's play strip poker." He leered at Renee and Judy, looking them up and down.

"No!" Judy spoke sharply.

Renee laughed. "Dream on."

Neil laughed, too. "All right, I guess not. But I had to offer. Sometimes people surprise me." He fished a pack of cigarettes out of his shirt pocket. "Regular poker, then. Five card stud? We can use cigs for chips." Everybody sat down around the table and Neil dealt the cards.

Judy passed out the cigarettes, dividing the pack among the four of them. With a doubtful look she asked, "Is this going to work? Shouldn't we use pennies or something?"

"It'll work," Alex said. He fanned out his cards. "I'm on the left, I start. One Camel." The betting went around the table with everyone putting one cigarette in the middle, then a second when Alex raised the bet. He called, showed his hand—a flush—and

213

scooped the cigarettes toward him. "See? Now I have plenty to bet with."

They played for more than an hour, eventually adding the contents of a package of stale nuts to the chip pool. At the end, Alex won; he popped a handful of nuts in his mouth to celebrate. Judy picked up another handful and threw them at Neil, giggling. He avoided the flying pieces by dodging behind Renee. Holding her by the shoulders, Neil used her as a shield as Judy kept up the assault. Alex, seeing an opportunity, ran for Renee and started tickling her sides. Her screeches echoed through the apartment and Judy, trying to protect her, went for Alex's middle. He arched away from her, then turned abruptly and tickled her along with Renee. Neil held Renee until she howled for them to stop. In seconds, they were all gasping for breath and rolling on the floor laughing.

"My, my, leave the kids alone and look at the trouble they get into." Cal's voice boomed through the noise.

"Voyeurism is not allowed," Neil roared, seizing Savannah by the leg and pulling her down into the pile. Wrestling began all over again until they collapsed, exhausted. Cal put some music on the phonograph, opened cans of beer for himself and Neil, and the six friends sat up talking until dawn.

At lunch Friday, Renee and Judy asked Savannah about her date with Cal. "It was nice," she said. She continued eating, with a quick glance in Renee's direction.

"Well, how was the play?" Judy asked. "Did you like it?"

"Yeah, it was good. We had a good time. We had dinner at an Italian restaurant in Independence—very romantic, with candles in Chianti bottles on the tables, green-checked tablecloths, and lots of ivy."

"Mmm, sounds wonderful," Renee said.

"Neil wanted us to play strip poker at the apartment." Judy rolled her eyes and wrinkled her nose. "He's so tacky." She studied Savannah. "Was Cal okay with you? Did he try anything?"

"Cal was a complete gentleman."

Later, when Renee and Savannah were sitting on a bench in the dorm courtyard and Judy had gone upstairs to change her clothes before meeting Alex, Renee asked, "Is that true, what you said about Cal being a gentleman?"

Savannah nodded, but she blushed. "Yes, he really was. I kind of thought, well, that he might try to get me in the back seat of the car or something."

Renee drew her legs up to sit cross-legged on the bench. "He didn't?"

Savannah bit her lower lip. "I was worried that he might be all over me, the way Neil is. Like he might figure that's what I want. He held my hand during the play, until the intermission. After that, nothing. I guess he wasn't interested."

"Does that bother you?"

"It just surprises me. I guess I had him pegged for a 'get what I can' kind of guy."

"Are you disappointed?"

"No!" Savannah smiled. "Much easier this way. Neil is enough to deal with, trying to keep his hands where I can see them. I like Cal, but I don't think there's that kind of chemistry between us. He was very chivalrous and polite, not at all crude." She looked over at Renee. "He did kiss me."

"Really? When?" *A kiss is a big deal. Right?* Another voice crept into her thoughts: *Like a backrub?* She picked at her thumbnail, ragged from biting it.

"Just before we came into the apartment. On the cheek. Then he said thank you for going to the play with him."

"Any mention of another date?"

"Nope. I'm not sure I'd want to anyway."

"Because of Neil?"

"Partly that. And Cal is a good friend. I don't really see him any other way. I think he feels the same about me."

Renee was quiet. A feeling of relief swept through her. Savannah and Cal as a couple would change things. *I have enough change going on without that.*

Judy ran down the stairs to the courtyard and the three began walking toward town. Judy tried to hurry Renee and Savannah along. "You can eat at the Alleycat. I don't want to keep Alex waiting. If I'm not there he might think I don't really want to go."

They met Alex by the bench outside the diner. He carried a game box under one arm. Judy smiled shyly at him. "You sure it's okay for me to come?"

"Yeah, it's fine. Ready?"

Alex and Judy set off down the street and Renee and Savannah went into the Alleycat. A family with several children occupied the back corner booth. Renee couldn't help wondering if Cal would have asked them to move. There were several empty booths along the front section of the restaurant; she chose one of them. They ordered sandwiches and tea.

"You think Judy's having fun?" Savannah asked Renee.

"Of course. The real question is how much fun is Alex having? And Doug."

Savannah stirred honey into her tea. "Cal and I talked about Judy a little. He thinks she's trying to get Alex interested in her. Pretty obvious, I told him. He said Alex has no intention of dating her."

"I know. I think she annoys him. And he doesn't even want to get married or anything, at least not at this point in his life." Renee sighed. "Awfully smart, I'd say."

"Did you know that last year Cal was ready to marry his girlfriend from high school?"

Renee shook her head. "Get married? I had no idea he was that serious about her. What happened?"

"He said he realized they were too young. They called it off before they made anything official."

"Was it mutual?"

"Yes. Just last fall. She was going to OSU, he was here, and they decided to break up. Interesting, huh?"

"So why does he flirt so much with me? He should understand about my engagement."

"Maybe he's hoping you'll break up with Russ."

"Well, I'm not."

"Or maybe he just wants to get you to consider other options."

"Well, I'm not doing that, either."

Savannah opened her sandwich and rearranged the leaf of lettuce, then used her knife to spread the mayonnaise to the edge of the bread. "They sure made a sloppy mess of this. Is yours okay?"

"Yeah, it's fine. I don't care if it's all perfect." Renee took a bite of coleslaw, swallowed, ate part of the pickle on her plate. "I really like Cal, you know."

"Why do you think he asked me out?"

Renee shook her head. "I thought he was attracted to you. Or wanted sex."

Savannah nodded. "Yeah, that's what worried me. I was pretty relieved when it didn't come to that."

"He's hard to figure out. Maybe that's what he wants—to confuse us, keep us guessing about him."

"Did you ever think he was testing you by asking me out?"

"What? To see if I got upset or broke up with Russ to stop Cal from dating you? That's crazy."

"I don't know, is it? Has he ever, um, come on to you?"

"No. I mean, he held my hand a couple of times, but it wasn't in a romantic way. It was just because I was upset about the stuff at the Woods."

"Oh, well, that's good, I guess."

"What do you mean, 'that's good'?"

With a smile, Savannah looked Renee in the eye. "You're engaged?"

"Oh, yeah, that." *That.* Her ring had turned; the diamond bit into her palm when she squeezed her hands shut. "Savannah, talk to me about Neil."

Savannah laughed. "I like him a lot. I'm not sure why, though. Strange, huh?"

"Neil's fun but is he really a guy you want to be with?"

"For now. It's nothing serious. I'm fine with the status quo but I don't know if he is." She smiled at Renee. "We just have fun talking. It's good for me."

"What do you talk about?"

"Existentialism, spiritualism, the war—he's well read and has interesting ideas. He does have a serious side, when we're alone. He told me he wishes he could go to San Francisco to Haight-Ashbury, but his parents would freak out. They're paying his full cost for school so he doesn't have a lot of choice."

"Unless he flunks out," Renee said with a shake of her head. "Does he ever see you during the day, like between classes or anything?"

"Not really. Once or twice, I guess, we've run into each other and gotten a Coke or something. By alone, I just mean when we're walking around at night."

"I'm surprised that he was okay with you going out with Cal."

"I kind of am, too," Savannah said. "But that tells me he's not going to make our relationship something it isn't."

Neil and Cal came into the restaurant around six o'clock. Savannah waved them over. "Our booth is taken," she said.

"That's okay." Cal slid into the seat next to Renee. "We're a small group tonight." He called to the waitress. "Hey, Debbie, can we get some coffee? And a short stack with eggs over easy?"

"Alex really took Judy to Doug's?" Neil asked. "I'm amazed. Didn't think he'd do it."

Cal offered a cigarette to Neil, and then lit one for himself. "Kind of hard to avoid, I think. He'll be all right." The coffee came and he thanked the waitress.

"Darlin', you are always welcome. Eggs'll be up in a few." She refilled Renee and Savannah's mugs. "Got crowded out of your booth tonight, I see."

"We're here early," Renee said. "I guess we could have called for reservations, huh?" The waitress laughed.

"I'll get my usual," Neil said.

"Cheeseburger, no onion, extra pickles."

"You're a sweetheart," Neil said. "You never forget, do you?"

"For you, sugar, I keep track." She winked at Neil and smiled at the girls. "You two doing okay?"

"Yeah, we're fine, thanks," Savannah said. The waitress went to the next table. Savannah sipped her tea. "I haven't seen her before. Is she new or are we just here super early?" She smiled at Cal. "You know all the waitresses, don't you?"

Cal grinned. "Yeah, pretty much. She usually works the morning shift. We come in for breakfast a lot."

"Then how does she know about our booth?" Renee asked.

"Everyone knows that's our booth," Neil said. "We're renowned and famous."

"Infamous is more likely," Savannah said.

The four of them spent the next couple of hours talking, mostly about their classes and plans after graduation. Cal hoped to have a career in theater or film and said he might head off to New York in the summer.

"Before graduation or as a temporary thing?" Renee asked.

"I don't know how important it is to have a degree in theater in the long run," Cal said. "If I can get into summer stock, it'll be a step to bigger things. New York is where I need to be. Also, I've been working on writing a play, so I'm hoping to find a producer."

"When do we get to see this script?" Renee asked. "This is the first I've heard of a play. Not fair to keep secrets like that."

Cal laughed. "Sorry. Maybe I'll show you the first act later tonight." He turned toward Savannah. "What about you, Savannah?

Alleycat

What are your post-graduation plans?"

"Oh, the standard English teacher," she said. "I would like to write novels and make a living at it but I'll need a day job. I'd love to teach creative writing in high school."

"When are you and Russ getting married?" Neil asked Renee. "He'll be back in July, right? You must have a date set." He glanced at Cal, then chuckled. "Are we invited?"

Cal shook his head, "No, man, she won't be able to invite us. He won't let her." Renee looked down, shoulders hunched. Cal shrugged. "But that's okay. I don't really like weddings much, do you, Neil?"

"Nah, they're a drag. Not that I've been to any."

Savannah gave the boys a warning look. "Shush. They don't have a date set."

"No, not yet," Renee said. "After graduation, probably. Couple more years." She leaned over the table, hands wrapped around her coffee cup. "If I still know where you are by then, I *will* invite you." She looked at each of them. "I don't know why you think I wouldn't."

Neil snorted, a loud sound that rang through the restaurant. "That's a laugh. The General—"

Cal cut him off. "I think it would be great to come to your wedding, Ren. I wouldn't blame you if you didn't invite me, though." She started to speak but he put his finger to her lips. "No, don't say anything. We know how it is."

She stared across the room. *Yeah, we all know how it is.*

Judy and Alex came back to the apartment around midnight. She was energetic and giggly. Savannah was in the kitchen making cookies with Neil; Renee and Cal were doing a crossword puzzle, trying to come up with inventive words to fill the spaces. Renee watched Alex and Judy out of the corner of her eye, not hearing Cal's word for "alabaster." She thought Alex looked a little tense. He caught her eye and grimaced slightly.

"Boobs," Cal repeated. "Does that fit?"

"What? Oh. Yeah, I mean, no. It's six letters, not five."

"Breast, then. God, I can't believe they want the technical word."

Renee flipped to the back of the book. "Actually, it's gypsum."

"Cookies are ready," Savannah called out. She came out of the kitchen with a tray of warm chocolate chip cookies, nearly dropping the plate as the others crowded around her, grabbing two or three cookies each. "Careful, they're right out of the oven. Hey, Judy, was the game fun?"

"Yes! It was hard, though." She gave Alex a sideways glance. "I don't know if the guys want me to come back."

Alex shrugged. "It's fine if you want to. I know it was hard to catch on to the rules." He went into the kitchen and poured himself a glass of milk. "Anybody want a drink?"

Following him, Renee said, "Yeah, I'll have some milk." As she took a glass out of the cupboard she whispered to Alex, "How was it?"

"Interestingly enough, she and Doug hit it off." He filled her glass and put the carton back in the refrigerator. "What do you think of that?"

"Maybe you can get her to go over there again—without you!" Renee dunked her cookie in the milk and bit off a piece. "Wouldn't that be something!"

A few days later Chuck stopped by the corner booth, pulled a chair up to the table and straddled it, arms resting across the back.

"I remember you from that party," Renee said. "We had a good discussion about the bombing of the capital."

"That's right. You didn't hang around very long, though."

"What party?" Judy asked.

"Um, you were gone home, I think," Renee mumbled.

Chuck, chin on his hands, fixed his eyes on Neil. "So, did you hear the news?" Neil shook his head. "You know Tyler and Shelli?"

Neil grunted. "Yeah. What'd they do now?"

"Went to Gentle Woods this afternoon to score some speed or something," Chuck said. "God, they're a couple of flakes. How many times have we said to stay away from that place? But no, they gotta get whatever shit they can get, no matter what." He sat up straight, tapped his fingers on the chair back, then gestured toward Cal's pack of cigarettes. "Can I bum a smoke?"

Cal passed a cigarette to Chuck. Renee noticed Chuck's hands shaking as he struck the match and lit up. He inhaled, held the smoke for a moment, then exhaled. "Yeah, so, the cops raided the park. Tyler and Shelli are in jail. Possession, most likely. The dealer, well, he jumped the fence and ran into that field."

"Did he get away?" Neil asked.

Chuck shook his head. "Nope. I bet they've been working undercover for awhile 'cause the cops had all sides covered. Anyway, what's that dude's name? Don't they call him Rico or something like that?" He took a long drag on the cigarette, stretched to flick the ash into the ashtray, then rubbed his hand across his face. "We couldn't see very well—goddamn trees. But I heard someone yell about the fence. Lotta running and shouting. A cop yelled, 'Freeze!' A shot, then another. He's howling like a banshee, 'I'm shot! I'm shot!' Dumbass."

"How do you know all this?" Cal asked.

"We were cruising by the park, me and Abby," Chuck said. "We saw the flashing lights so we went around by the swings, parked across the street. A group of people were standing around so we got out of the car. Some old guy told me he noticed the cops watching the park all afternoon. No marked cars." He took another drag. "He probably sits in his window every day watching the world go by. I guess when the deal went down, before we got there, more cops showed up, sirens, lights, all that shit. Some from the sheriff's and some state police. Shelli was in the back of one squad car, bawling her eyes out. Tyler was in another, handcuffed, talking to a cop."

"That's crazy," Savannah said. "Were your friends the only ones there?"

"No," Chuck said. "I think a bunch of people were arrested. Must have been at least four squad cars. Looked like someone was in the back of most of them. Rico has certain times he's around for buys so there are usually a slew of dopers at the park at one time. Man, the cops hit the jackpot, I guess. Like I said, they knew when to strike. Had to be some undercover guys working the area."

"I told Tyler that guy was dangerous," Cal said.

"Didn't we all?" Chuck stood up, flipped the chair around. "I gotta split. Promised Abby I wouldn't leave her alone too long. She's pretty freaked out. But I thought you guys would want to know what went down."

"Yeah, thanks," Neil said. He stood up as Chuck left. "Wow, heavy news. Glad I stopped going to that joker."

Judy snorted. "Serves them right. Too bad the guy didn't die."

Neil leaned over and stubbed out his cigarette, shaking his head at Judy's statement. "It's good he's out of commission. Nothing but trouble. I know a few guys who buy from him. I hope they weren't there."

"Guess you'll hear soon enough," Alex said.

"Man, Tyler is screwed up. Shelli, too."

"Bound to happen sooner or later," Cal said. "They're nothing but a train wreck."

"It's a bummer but no surprise," Neil said. "Man, I feel lucky." He looked over at Cal. "I was there just a week ago to make a buy. Something felt wrong and I decided no more. I'll stick with my regular guy on Clay Street."

No one said anything for a long moment. Renee couldn't help but think about her odd experience at the park. *Is this guy Rico why VanAllen had a heart attack?* She glanced at Savannah; she was gazing into her coffee cup, her expression somber. Cal broke the awkward silence. "Hey, Neil, you gonna pick some tunes?"

"Yeah." At the jukebox Neil dropped in fifty cents, hit the numbers. After a moment, the first song started playing—"All You Need Is Love." Renee froze. Around her, the others joined in singing with the music, at first softly, then more lively. Renee sat perfectly still, her breathing shallow, imagining a wall around herself. Building it higher brick by brick. She closed her eyes, shutting out the music.

Their first date, senior year of high school, is the opening season football game and after-game dance. Russ smiles as Renee cheers at each play that advances their team down the field. He attempts to explain the game to her but gives up in the excitement and instead wraps his arms around her. He kisses her on the cheek then on the mouth. Surprised, she starts to pull away, but he looks so happy she relaxes and returns the kiss. At the dance, a sock hop in the school gym, they stand hand-in-hand watching the other couples, too shy to put themselves in the spotlight. Someone puts on the record "All You Need Is Love," and Russ slides his arm around Renee's waist, pulling her closer to him.

"This will be our song," he whispers in her ear.

Renee shivered. *All you need is love, right? So simple. From that first date I should have seen what was happening. It was too fast.* She concentrated on another song, "Love," one she listened to when she was alone, one that had no connection to Russ. The tune, written by John Lennon, sweet and comforting, reassured her when she felt panic setting in. She closed her eyes and let the song fill her head.

The last note of the Beatles died out and the next record began, "Spirit in the Sky." The heavy bass started the boys thumping the table in rhythm. Renee smiled when Alex drummed his fingers lightly on her head. He leaned over and whispered, "You all right? You kind of went away there for a minute."

"Yeah, I know. I'm okay."

"Hey Alex," Judy said. "Since you're on the end, can you get the waitress over here? I want to get another Coke."

Alex waved to the waitress. "Anybody else want anything?"

Cal, watching Renee and Alex, said, "Judy, get it to go. Let's get out of here."

"Hey, man, I put half a buck in that juke. I'm staying put." Neil lit another cigarette and sat back with his arms stretched out along the back of the bench seat.

With a resigned shrug, Cal pulled his pipe from his coat pocket along with the tobacco pouch. He concentrated on filling and lighting it. Savannah and Judy ordered refills on their drinks and Neil added a side of onion rings. Alex told a joke and the others chimed in on the punch line—someone had told it before. He laughed and suggested somebody else tell a joke. The onion rings were gobbled up and the jukebox played more songs. Conversation, music, laughter—Renee let the sounds wash over her, finally feeling at ease.

28

The term neared its end; finals brought it to a quick halt. Celebration and consolation parties were thrown, suitcases packed, the campus closed down for spring break. Cal went to the coast with some friends, planning to camp for a few days before heading home to Corvallis. Judy and Savannah left for home a day before Renee and she spent the last night at the apartment with Neil and Alex. It was not planned but Alex insisted she stay with them.

"You don't want to be at the dorm all by yourself, do you?"

"Not really. It's a little creepy when so many people are gone already."

"So stay here," Neil said. "You can even use Cal's bed. Or mine. I'll share."

Laughing, Renee shook her head. "I'll sleep on the couch, thanks." *No. Not Cal's bed, not where he slept with his old girlfriends.*

"Hey," Alex said. "I was thinking that maybe you'd be more comfortable..." He paused.

"What, Alex? Just tell me."

"Well, you're skinnier than me and I thought maybe my clothes would be more comfortable for sleeping in. I mean—um, you could borrow some pants or something if you want."

Renee smiled. "That would be cool. I do wear kind of tight jeans, huh?"

He went into the bedroom and came back with a pair of faded, soft denim jeans and a black t-shirt. "These okay?"

"Thanks." She changed in the bathroom; the jeans were long so she rolled up the cuffs. The t-shirt had an earthy scent with a hint of leather—*like Alex.* It was big on her, hanging halfway to her knees. She couldn't help smiling. *I don't even need the jeans!*

She put her folded clothes on the floor in the corner of the living room. Alex had gotten a quilt from the closet and the blanket from his bed which he spread out on the floor beside the couch. Smiling, Renee said, "Are you going to keep me company?"

"Is it okay?" He put on an exaggerated hangdog look.

Renee couldn't help laughing. "You're so funny, Alex! Lay down, I'll get the light."

After a couple of minutes of quiet settling, Alex said, "So, where do you see yourself in five years?"

"What?"

"Think about it. In five years we'll be almost twenty-five. Out of school, taking on the world as real adults. What will you be doing?"

Renee considered his question. *Married to Russ. Living the life he has planned.* "Well, I may be up in Alaska on a homestead. You can get land really cheap."

"What?"

"That's what Russ would like to do. Homestead and home school our children."

"Uh-huh. I can imagine that. Pioneer woman. That is definitely you."

"I can do it," Renee said in a strong voice. "Haul water from a well, chop wood. If you had a fireplace in this apartment, I'd show you how easy it is. Tell you what, when we get back from spring break, I'll bake you some bread. Show you what a pioneer I can be."

"It's a deal. Have you ever made bread?"

"Banana bread."

"Yum. You can make that for me."

"Okay. How about with chocolate chips in it?"

"Even better. We can practice your homesteading skills all term long."

One more term. Turning on her side to face Alex, Renee said, "Where will you be in five years?"

"Living in a penthouse apartment in downtown San Francisco working for a high-powered CPA firm. What did you think?"

"Wife? Kids?"

"No, too much trouble. I need lots of room to spread out for my games. I think I'll have a maid."

"Better get a cook, too."

"Hey, I can cook. And you're going to teach me how to make bread, so food's covered. I don't want a bunch of people in my apartment. Just me and the maid."

"A live-in maid?"

He grunted. "No way. Once a week. She can come in while I'm at work."

"San Francisco, huh? Why?"

"Hills. Running the hills will keep me in shape. And I can go sailing on the bay. Plus there's Alcatraz and the tours they give there."

"You *are* funny."

They didn't talk for several minutes, then Alex said, "I would rather be a scientist."

"What?"

"I don't really like accounting that much."

"Then why are you doing it?"

"Remember when Judy said it's a good reliable profession? That's exactly why."

"Alex, you should do what you love. If you love science—"

"I know. But science is a really broad field and I'm not sure what I would specialize in or what the employment possibilities are. I'm in my second year of college, halfway through. Kind of late to switch now."

"You can," Renee said. "You don't have to be in a rush."

"I'm not anxious to move back home. I need a career sooner rather than later."

"So you're going into a field you feel conflicted about just to get out of the house?" *And I'm marrying a man I feel conflicted about for the same reason?*

"Interesting way to put it."

They talked for hours before they fell asleep. In the morning, Neil awakened them. "I don't believe it," he teased. "Did you stay on the couch all night, Renee?"

She blushed. "Of course." She fixed pancakes for the three of them, then quickly washed up the dishes. She changed into her own clothes in the bathroom and brushed her hair. Alex and Neil packed their bags, then Alex walked Renee back to the dorm. Her father was coming for her around three o'clock. They went directly to her room and she began her packing. "My biggest load," she said, shaking her head, "is dirty clothes!"

Alex sat down on Judy's stripped bed. "Wasn't it great that Judy went home yesterday?"

Renee nodded. "It was close. She wanted to stay until tonight to keep me company." She grimaced. "Just what I need!"

"She sure likes to keep an eye on you."

"Yeah, well, she's lonely. Savannah and I—I guess she thinks we have the key to good times or something. She hates being left out."

"She hates being around Cal and Neil all the time, though, doesn't she?"

"Definitely. But she's more afraid of missing something. She's also afraid, since the attack, of being by herself." Renee worked in thoughtful silence for a few minutes. She glanced at Alex. "But it's not just me and Savannah she wants to be around, you know."

"Yeah, I definitely feel that vibe from her."

"Judy's so cool about it, sort of matter-of-fact. See, with Savannah hung up on Cal and Neil, and me safely engaged to Russ—well, that leaves you and her open for all sorts of possibilities. Exciting, isn't it?" She laughed as she sat on the lid of her bulging suitcase trying to snap the latches closed. "She's chaperoning me and keeping her eye on you, just waiting for her big chance. Aren't we lucky?"

Alex groaned, falling backwards on the bed. He shook his head, eyes closed. "Damn. She's a good reason for not dating." He stood up, stretched, and looked at Renee. "We have a week away from her at least. We need to encourage Doug to act on his apparent interest."

"Well, that's your department."

"Yeah, I know."

"Has Doug talked about her much? Savannah and I have wracked our brains trying to think of anyone we know to fix her up with."

"He just asked me the other day if she planned to play games again. I told him he could talk to her anytime he wants."

"What, is he as shy as she is? Heaven help them if that's true."

"I guess. I just wish he would do *something*, get her off my back. He has a car, too, so he could actually take her somewhere."

"Well, tell him to do that. He probably needs some nudging."

"Sure. I'll get right on it." Alex gestured toward the suitcase. "All packed? Let's get some lunch. It's getting late."

"Look, I have crackers and peanut butter. We can get Cokes in the lounge or I can make instant coffee. I also happen to have—" She opened her closet and brought out a shoebox. "—three apples. Help yourself." She laid the food out on the bed.

"You know, I don't think your parents should see me with you," Alex said as they ate and talked and waited for three o'clock.

"I think it's all right," Renee said. *But probably not. I don't need questions.*

"No, I'll go before they get here. They might wonder about a guy they've never met hanging around their daughter."

"I hate to say it but you're right." She sighed, frustrated. "Everything is just so complicated." She put the crackers and peanut butter away and tossed the crumpled napkins and apple cores in the wastebasket closest to her. It was Judy's; a scrap of blue paper caught Renee's eye. Leaning down, she extracted a wadded-up sheet of airmail stationary. Curious, she smoothed it out on the desktop. Sweat popped out along her hairline. She let go of the paper and backed away from the desk.

"What is it?" Alex asked, concern in his voice.

"It's a letter," Renee whispered, her voice choked. "To Russ. Not from me."

"Can I look at it?" No answer from Renee, just a slight nod of her head. Alex leaned over and picked up the letter. He glanced at it, rubbed the back of his neck, eyebrows knitted together. "Huh."

"What does it say?"

"Do you want me to read it to you?"

"Yes."

"'Dear Russ, I hope you won't think badly of me but I thought you should know that Renee—'" He stopped. "That's all. She must have changed her mind."

"How could she do this?" Renee sank down onto the corner of the bed. "Does she hate me?"

"You have to talk to her about it. You have to." Alex's voice was strong, insistent. To Renee he sounded far away, in a tunnel.

"What if she didn't change her mind?"

"Renee, it doesn't matter. Just tell her you saw this. Ask her why she wrote it."

"What if she did write to him and told him about the Alleycat and the apartment and the Woods and—"

"Don't."

"But—"

"After spring break, ask her. Write to Russ like you always do. Nothing has changed. This doesn't make anything different or wrong."

Renee felt her back go rigid, her shoulders stiffen, her heart beat rapidly. In a hard voice, she said, "If she's writing to him, I'll kill her." Her eyes narrowed. "She has no business messing in my life."

"That's right," Alex said. "Get mad. That's good. You have every right to be mad." He kept his breathing measured but tightened his hands into fists. He worked at making his tone of voice calm so Renee wouldn't feel the extent of his anger. "For some strange reason, she thinks she's helping you. You need to tell her to back off."

With a grunt, Renee let her shoulders droop a little. She inhaled deeply, exhaled quickly. "I will never, ever tell her anything or let her be part of anything again. I can't believe she can be that—that vindictive."

"Talk to her first," Alex said. "It could be that she was fantasizing about how she could save you from the bad boys you hang out with."

Fists clenched, Renee gritted her teeth. "I'm so goddamn mad. Disgusted. We put up with her complaining and whining and refusing to have fun. And since she was attacked, she never wants to be alone and we stay with her, even when she's rude and mean. I try to be a friend to her but it's like she fights against it all the time." She pointed to the letter. "This is the last straw!" Renee picked up her suitcase. She grabbed up the letter and crammed it in her purse. "If she doesn't have a good explanation for this…"

Alex took the suitcase from her and led the way out of the room. Renee locked the door. "Listen," he said as they walked down the stairs. "Try to forget this until you get back."

"Oh, sure," Renee said. "When I talk to her, I'm going to be direct and strong and *angry*. So angry." Fists clenched, she muttered, "I could kill her."

"That's good. You can do it. You want me to be there?"

"Of course I do! I want the whole U.S. Army."

"How about if I recruit the Gypsy Jokers? I know a few of them personally, you know."

"Who?"

"The Gypsy Jokers. A motorcycle gang." He grinned. "They'll treat Judy right."

"Ohhh!" Renee smiled. "Of course! I always thought you were a biker."

"Yeah, you got me pegged."

A red station wagon pulled into the road leading to the dorm parking lot. Renee sighed. "Oh crap. That's my parents." Alex started walking away from the dorm. "Bye, Alex. I'll be back Sunday afternoon."

April

~~ 29 ~~

Renee's family reluctantly brought her back to school early Sunday afternoon at the end of spring break. She struggled to come up with a valid reason for returning so much earlier than previous weekends and holidays but the thought of being away from Monmouth any longer gave her the impetus to figure one out. Finally, she told her parents she wanted to get organized for the start of classes and they accepted that. The worst part of the week had been getting her grades. She had gotten Ds in history and biology, barely pulling a 2.0 GPA and she knew that was pure luck. Her savings account was nearly depleted but to drop out of school now was unthinkable. *I have to go back, see Cal and Alex again. If I don't, we'll lose each other.* After a tearful conversation, she assured her mother and father that she would work hard and bring her grades up and they agreed to make up the difference in her tuition costs for one more term.

They helped carry her luggage to her room; the emptiness relieved her. She stored away the food her mother had packed for her and chatted with her family for a few minutes before walking with them out to the parking lot. Her father gave her a check for tuition for spring term and she tucked it in her jeans pocket, giving him a peck on the cheek with a whispered, "Thank you, Dad." They kissed her good-bye, piled into the car, and slowly drove away. *Go! Go!* She waved until they disappeared from sight, then she strolled away from the dorm across the parking lot, walking faster as she put more distance between herself and the other students returning to school. Her fast walk turned into a jog as she cut through campus, taking every shortcut she knew. She reached the Alleycat, feeling a little lightheaded. *Three more blocks to Alex's.* She broke into a run, laughing even as tears blurred the world around her. At the apartment, she pounded on the door, then, pulling herself halfway together, burst in.

"Hi," she shouted. A rustling came from the back of the apartment, from the bathroom or the bedroom. "Hi! It's me!"

Alex appeared, smiling broadly when he saw Renee. "Alone? We must be the first ones back." He gave her a quick hug. "Whoa— you're out of breath!" He gestured toward the couch. "Sit down. You look like you're going to drop."

Arms extended, Renee collapsed onto the foam chair and leaned back, legs stretched out, crossed at the ankles. "Now I'm home." She smiled. "I ran all the way here! Silly, huh?"

"You ran?" His eyebrows went up.

Laughing, she said, "Yeah! Crazy, I know. I definitely am not a runner." She put her hand to her heart and smiled. "I'm fine. You alone?"

"So far. Cal will get in late. Don't know when Neil will drag in. He's probably hitching from Portland." Sitting on the carpet, facing her, his back against the end table, he said, "It's good to see you. Did you have a good vacation?"

"Don't ask." She grimaced and shook her head. "I missed everybody from here. I didn't realize how nice it is talking to you until I couldn't. How was your vacation?"

"What I expected. My mother kept shoving food at me and moaning about how sick I look and worrying about the police raiding this place. My father yapped constantly about summer jobs. I couldn't wait to get back here." He shook his head. "What I wouldn't give to have a car. I hate having to depend on them for rides."

"Yeah, I feel the same way. My parents talked about grades and money and my future." Interlocking her fingers, she stretched her arms up then put her hands behind her head. "I beat Judy back."

Alex grinned. "That's obvious. Otherwise she would be here with you."

"Touché." She gazed around the living room at the familiar posters, candles, Cal's tobacco lying on the end table. How comfortable she felt here! She rose to her feet and went into the kitchen. After filling a small pan with water and setting it on the stove to boil she hoisted herself up onto the counter to sit where she could look out the window. Neil sauntered past and entered the apartment. He noisily hauled his duffle bag to the bedroom, talking loudly to Alex. Renee half listened, never saying a word, and when Neil entered the kitchen, he jumped back, startled.

Alleycat

"Jesus, you scared me! You could have let me know you were in here!"

Calmly, she replied, "Just wanted to get a reaction out of you."

He took a bottle of beer from the refrigerator, opened it, and flipped the cap at her. She caught the cap and tossed it back. "Where's Savannah?" he asked.

"Not back yet, I guess. She'll probably come over here."

"Where's your shadow?" Neil leaned against the refrigerator, drinking his beer.

"Judy? Not here." Renee smiled.

"Wow, how'd you manage that?"

"I begged my parents to bring me back early." She laughed. "I told them I needed to get started on my coursework."

"Yeah, that's a good one. They believed you?"

"Who knows? The point is, I got back before Judy."

"And Savannah," Neil said. "Do you have any idea when she'll get in? Damn, I wish we had phones."

"That would be too normal," Alex said, coming into the kitchen. "You guys want coffee? I'll make it."

"I was gonna have some tea," Renee said. "The water's almost ready."

Alex got the box of teabags and two mugs out of the cupboard. "That actually sounds good."

"I'll stick with beer, thanks." Neil lit a cigarette, shook out the match, and dropped it in the sink. "How you can stand Jujube around all the time is beyond me."

Renee and Alex exchanged looks. "We can't," Renee replied. "You can't imagine how great it was to get back before her. I tossed my junk on the bed and literally ran all the way over here."

"Good for you," Neil said approvingly. "You going to the 'Cat tonight?"

"I don't know. I have to talk to Judy and I'm not sure how that'll go."

"Oh, well, it doesn't matter." He finished his beer and put the bottle down on the card table. Reaching for his fatigue jacket, he swung it over his shoulder and headed for the door. "Guess I'll split. See ya later."

Alex studied Renee's face. "How do you feel about talking to Judy?"

She wrapped her arms around herself, hunching her shoulders.

233

"Scared. And pissed off. She had no right to contact Russ behind my back. I can't even imagine what kind of explanation she'll have for that letter we found in the trash."

"You want me there?"

"Oh, Alex, I would love for you to be there. But I have to do this alone."

He reached out and touched her arm. "Renee."

She relaxed, letting her arms fall to her sides, hands resting on her lap. "What?"

"Don't let her get out of explaining this to you. You might have to push, know what I mean?"

"Yes." She could feel her heart vibrating, her hands trembling.

Alex poured the boiling water into the cups and dropped a teabag into each. He passed one cup to her, wrapping his hands around hers as she held the mug. She bowed her head; the steam swirled around her face. *Don't let go. Give me your strength.*

"You're shaking," he said softly. "Here, take a sip." He moved the cup to her mouth.

She drank a little and he let go of her hands, stepped back. She smiled at him. "I'm okay. Just dreading talking to her. I'm so afraid she actually wrote to him."

"Come on, let's sit in the other room. That counter can't be very comfortable."

"I'm too keyed up to sit. Let's just take a walk, okay?"

"Will you go to the grocery with me? You can help me pick out whatever we need. We have practically no food here."

They spent almost an hour cruising through the grocery store, picking through bins of fruits and vegetables, choosing a variety of canned goods, and staples like bread, butter, spaghetti, and rice. Renee insisted on reading labels and checking prices and as Alex dumped random items into the cart, she yanked them back out.

"Don't you want to get your money's worth?" she asked. "You're grabbing expensive brands, and stuff you'll never eat."

"What? You don't like—" he checked the front of the small jar she had put back on the shelf. "Pimientos? They're colorful. I thought food was supposed to be colorful."

"I know you won't eat those. Come on, get a couple cans of those tomatoes. We can make chili."

In the checkout line, Alex considered the impulse buy snacks and magazines. "What kind of candy bar do you like?"

Alleycat

"Guess." She smiled broadly.

He pointed to a Baby Ruth; she shook her head. "Mr. Goodbar? Snickers?"

"Yeah, Snickers. What about you? You seem like a Junior Mints kind of guy."

"Ah, you know me well."

On the way back to the apartment, they ate the candy and talked about their spring term classes. Once the food was put away, they walked to the dorm. In the courtyard, Alex stopped and put his hand firmly on Renee's shoulder. Startled, she looked him in the eyes.

"Be strong with Judy, okay?" he said.

She nodded.

"I'll see you later." He turned to leave.

"Alex," Renee said, reaching out toward him. He stopped. "Thank you for this afternoon. I needed it."

"I did, too, you know. I'm glad we had time by ourselves." Smiling, he touched her arm.

His eyes crinkle when he smiles. Flooded with warmth, Renee smiled, too. "You going to be at the 'Cat later?"

"Probably. I'll see you there, right?"

"Yeah, I think so. Who knows if Judy will come but I'm sure Savannah will want to."

They said goodbye and she went upstairs. Steeling herself, swallowing the hard lump in her throat, Renee paused at the door to her room. If Judy was there, she had to figure out a way to broach the subject of the unfinished letter. *Not scared. Pissed off. You have every right to be mad. Furious.* She opened the door. *Breathe.*

"Where have you been?" Judy's voice was plaintive, whiny.

Bristling, Renee said, "Alex's."

"You really shouldn't go there alone."

Renee's mouth dropped open. "Why not?"

"From what you've told me about Russ, he would never approve."

"And just what do you think you know about Russ?" Renee slammed her purse down on the desk and ripped the elastic band from her ponytail. Shaking out her hair, she snatched her brush from the desk and began pulling it vigorously through the dark strands. "For your information, Russ knows all about Alex. Not that it *is* any of your business."

Judy stared at Renee. "Whoa. What's wrong with you?"

"Hmm, interesting question." Renee put the brush down, gathered her hair into one hand, and began to braid it. "Maybe you should tell me about a letter you wrote to Russ."

"I—I didn't," Judy protested. "What are you talking about?" The color had drained from her face and she turned away from Renee.

"I found a letter in the wastebasket. To Russ. From you." Her voice was terse. "At least, it was your handwriting, which I'd recognize anywhere. You make those weird little loops on the end of words. Here, I'll show you." Renee finished the braid and twisted the elastic band around the end. She rummaged in her purse then removed the letter, roughly folded into a small rectangle. She shoved it at Judy. "So, did you send a finished one to him? And what did you tell him?"

Judy did not take the letter. She pushed her hands deep into the pockets of her cords, squared her shoulders, lifted her chin. "I didn't tell him anything."

"I don't believe you."

"I didn't. I—I just was messing—"

"Why would you even think of writing to him?"

"It was stupid. I thought he would tell you to—"

"What? Not have friends? Not have fun? Be miserable and alone until he gets back?" Renee tried to keep her voice level but her eyes blazed and her hands balled into fists, the letter crushed in one of them. "Why? Why would you do this?" Renee tossed the blue airmail paper in the trash. "It's garbage, Judy. Garbage."

Judy sat on the edge of her desk chair, arms crossed. She looked past Renee, focused on the framed photograph of Russ on Renee's desk. Eyes squinted, she tossed her head. "I didn't write to him. But I wanted to. I think he should know that you spend all your time with other guys. You flirt and get moony-eyed over Cal and you let them make fun of Russ. It's wrong."

Renee stalked to the door. "You have no idea," she said. "I'm going out."

Judy jumped up and ran to Renee. "Wait, Renee. I'm sorry. I never should have started that letter. I'm so sorry." She put her hand out, touched Renee's sleeve; Renee flinched. "Please don't be mad. I just worry about you and I know that Russ does, too. We all do."

Renee moved out of Judy's reach. "You need to back off. Not

just this, but everything. My grades, my classes, my *life* is not your problem. Do you understand that?"

"But—"

"No buts. My life is my business. If you want to go to the Alleycat and the apartment with me and Savannah, fine. If you want to go there by yourself, fine. If you want to stay here, that's fine, too. You do what you want and let me do what I want." She looked Judy straight in the eye and held her gaze, her eyes bright with anger. "You stay out of my relationship with Russ."

"Okay, I won't bother you, I promise." Judy's shoulders drooped. She took the few steps back to her desk, sat down. "I'm sorry. I never sent anything to Russ. I wouldn't. I won't."

"Yeah." Renee wanted to press a hand against her chest to still her quaking heart but she focused on keeping her arms at her sides. "Don't even think about it."

"I promise. Please don't be mad."

"Judy," Renee said, her voice rising again. "I am more than mad. Do you get that? I have tried to be a good friend to you and this is what happens?" She took in a deep breath, concentrated on softening her spine. It didn't work.

"You *are* a good friend."

"Then why do you act the way you do? You're trying to run my life. Or live it. Just stop."

"Okay, I'll—I'll try. Just don't—I can't—" She looked at Renee with pleading eyes. "I don't want to be alone. It scares me."

"I know that," Renee said through gritted teeth. "But you have no right to interfere in my business."

"I never thought you'd see that letter. You weren't supposed to. But I just thought maybe Russ would let you know how much you mean to him and you'd stop—"

Anger boiled up again. "I'm *not* going to stop being friends with Cal and Alex and Neil. Not even when Russ gets back." *I hope.* She pocketed her room key and left, letting the door bang shut behind her.

Savannah answered the pounding on her door with a shouted, "Hang on, for pete's sake. Is there a fire or something!" She opened the door and said, "Renee! Man, you look—"

"Furious? I am. Are you ready to go?"

Savannah looked confused. "You mean to the 'Cat? Yeah, I guess. It's early. Judy's not back yet?"

"She's upstairs." Renee stalked down the hall.

"Hey, wait a sec, I need to get my purse." Savannah scrambled for her jacket, umbrella, and purse, quickly checking for her key, and joined Renee. "I've never seen you like this."

"You won't believe what Judy's done now." Renee took a breath. "She wrote a letter to Russ." When Savannah gasped, Renee held up a hand, shook her head. "She didn't mail it. I found it in the wastebasket, just before spring break."

"That bitch! How could she do that to you? I can't believe it, Renee. What is wrong with her?"

"I can't trust her at all," Renee said. "I don't want her hanging around. It makes me want to throw up." She glanced at Savannah. "I can't believe I actually confronted her." She gave a short laugh. "I really told her off. You should have seen her face. Total shock."

"Man, I have wanted to do that for so long," Savannah said. "She makes me crazy. She can't leave things alone. She has no life and can't stand someone else having good things happen to them."

"I would gladly give up my problems right now," Renee said, feeling calmer. "I'd like a nothing life, no drama, no heartache, no decisions to make."

Savannah stopped walking and gave Renee a hug. "No, you wouldn't. I don't like that you have problems, but you do have really good friends to help you through them. Judy doesn't have that. She turns everyone off."

"Maybe it's time we move in together."

"You know I'd love to, but how would we do it? Molly won't trade with you. She can't stand Judy."

"I know. And even with her scholarship Judy can't afford to live by herself." With a loud sigh, Renee said, "The thing is, I can't just abandon her, much as I would like to. She's scared of being alone. Which I completely understand."

"*Tch*. She's going to be alone her whole life at this rate."

"I told her I don't care what she does or where she goes," Renee said. "If she wants to come with us to the 'Cat or the apartment, I don't care. I'm not inviting her and I won't tell her she can't. Is that okay with you?"

Savannah nodded. "Yeah. I can't just walk away from her, either. I know I talk big but when it comes right down to actually telling her off and totally cutting her out, I can't do it. But I will be watching her like a buzzard."

~ 30 ~

Cal returned from spring break with a car. He drove to the dorm on Monday afternoon and told the girl at the desk he wanted to see Renee. She ran up the stairs and pounded on the door to Renee and Judy's room.

"One of those guys is downstairs to see you," the girl said.

"Thanks," Renee said. "I'll be right down." She grabbed her key and a sweater. Sprinting down the stairs, she jumped over the last two steps and swung around the rail toward the lounge doors. "Cal! What are you doing here?" With a wide grin, he embraced her in a hug that lifted her off the floor. Giggling, ignoring the stares of other residents, she straightened the bandana holding her hair back. "I always knew you were crazy."

"Are you doing anything right now?"

She shook her head. "Just reading."

"Can you go somewhere with me? Is Savannah around, too?"

"Sure, I can go. Savannah went to the library to do some research for an assignment. Guess it'll just have to be me." The afternoon air was chilly; she buttoned up the sweater and asked, "Go where? What for?"

"Just a drive," he said, clearly enjoying the look of confusion on her face. They walked to the parking lot and he stopped before the shiny black Chevy Malibu. "Well, how do you like it?"

"Yours? Really?"

He nodded, opening the door for her. She slid in and he gently closed the door, then went around to the driver's side. "What do you think?"

"It's great! It looks new."

"Well, it's a '68 but not a lot of miles. I got it pretty cheap from a kid whose parents made him get rid of it. Something about bad influences and going down the wrong path." He chuckled. "I can't imagine that, can you?" He started the engine and backed out of the parking space with ease. He pushed a cartridge into the 8-track slot and Simon and Garfunkel's "The Only Living Boy in New York" filled the car. Cal lowered the volume. "My parents helped finance it. They're hoping I'll come home more often."

"Will you?"

"No—and they know it." He drove away from town, leisurely taking the country roads past fields, lone farmhouses, pastures. "You don't go home very often."

"No. I don't much like being stuck in a car with my dad. And being home for a weekend isn't any better."

"What's wrong with your father?"

Renee raised a hand, put her finger to her cheek, tapped a couple of times. "Hmm, how do I put it? He's intimidating. Kind of a bully, actually." She kept her voice light.

"Oh, man, I'm sorry."

"No, it's fine. But I'm glad to be here, in college, out of the house."

"Brothers? Sisters? You're the oldest, right?"

"I have a little sister and two younger brothers. That's the hard part, leaving them at home to face him every day."

"What does he do? I mean, how does he threaten you?"

"Oh, just his way of talking—you know, like he's so intelligent and we're all just dumbheads." She sighed. "That's his favorite name for my youngest brother." With a *tch*, she added, "People like him, which is what I have trouble understanding. They're like, 'oh your father is so nice!' Um, yeah, sure thing."

"Is he mean? Has he—"

"Beat us?" Renee looked out the side window. "Yeah, sometimes. Like every other father."

"My dad's cool. I'm sorry yours isn't."

"You'll be a fun dad."

"That's my plan," Cal said with a chuckle. "What about your mom? How does she handle your father?"

"She just goes with the flow," Renee said softly. *Like me.*

"Hey, look at that!" Cal pointed to a field. A hawk was swooping low over the pasture and as they watched, it dove straight down and came back up with a snake struggling in its claws. "Not something you see everyday, right?"

"I kind of hope it gets free," Renee said. "Except it will probably get hurt falling from that high." She watched the hawk until it flew out of sight.

"Hard to know which is better for that snake, isn't it?" Cal asked. "Getting eaten by the hawk or falling to almost certain death with a minuscule chance of survival."

Sometimes I feel like that snake.

Cal changed the cartridge in the eight-track player to a Bob Dylan album, *Nashville Skyline*. "Lay Lady Lay" filled the car. Renee leaned her head against the seatback and closed her eyes. "I love this song," she murmured.

Cal nodded. "He sounds so different on this album. It's one of my favorites." They rode along in silence, listening to the music. Cal's fingers tapped the steering wheel in time to the beat. He sang along with Dylan, making his voice a little gravelly.

Renee glanced at him and smiled. "Nice voice," she said.

"His or mine?" Cal laughed. "Man, it's good to have a car. No more hitchhiking."

"Thank God. I worry when you and Neil hitch. It's not a good idea."

"Ahh, it's okay. Everybody does it." He gave her a sideways look. "Except you. And Savannah. You're the good girls."

"What does that mean?"

"Well, aren't you? No vices, and virginity is all important, right?"

She blushed. "I never said that."

"Aha!"

"Cal, stop. I'm not talking about that with you." She giggled, trying to look mortified and dignified at the same time.

Cal laughed and ran his fingers through his hair. "Oh, I thought we could talk about anything." Taking a baseball cap from the seat between them, he flipped it onto his head, pulling the brim down a little.

"You are such a—"

"Sex maniac?"

"You said it, not me."

With an exaggerated suggestive leer, he leaned toward her and said, "Let's see if it's true. While the cat's away, the mice can play, right?"

"I think not." Laughing, she scooted away, pulling the hem of her short skirt down. "You know, I think we *can* talk about pretty much anything." She smiled at him. "As long as you—"

"Behave? Yes, ma'am. I was just fooling with you." He picked up his sunglasses from the dash and put them on.

"I know that." She raised her left hand. "Commitment here."

"Duly noted. Again." His fingers tightened on the steering wheel and he kept his face turned toward the front of the car. Renee wondered if she had hurt his feelings. She shifted in the seat, unsure what to do or say next. They reached the little town of Rickreall; Cal pulled to a stop in a gravel parking lot but kept the engine running. He didn't say anything for a moment. When he did, his voice was measured. "I told you once that an engagement ring doesn't mean anything. I still believe that. But—" He held one hand up to stop her protest. "I know you don't agree."

She nodded, stared out the window. "Savannah said you were engaged last fall to that girl in Corvallis."

"Yeah, I was."

"Would you have wanted her to fool around with someone else?" She stopped—*Maybe that's what happened.* She wished she could see his eyes, but the lenses of his sunglasses were mirrored.

"Of course not. But that wasn't an issue. We just weren't right for each other."

"I'm sorry it didn't work out for you."

"I'm not." He took his sunglasses off and looked at Renee. "I'm not pressuring you. But I wouldn't walk away if you were willing."

"Is that why we're out driving around? Cal, I'm not cheating on my boyfriend." Renee tried to swallow. She chewed a fingernail. "You, um, I—"

"Yeah, I understand." He sighed. "I'm not coming on to you."

The fingernail ripped and a drop of blood bubbled up. *Small payment for hurting Russ.* The thought startled her. *I haven't done anything wrong.* She grabbed a Kleenex from her purse and let the blood soak into it. "That's good. Because I wouldn't want to have to stop you." *What if—?* Heat poured across her face. Sweat dampened her underarms. *Breathe, breathe.*

"Hmm, does that mean what I think it means?" He grinned, breaking the tension.

She covered her face with her hands, then pushed her fingers through her hair. "I really like you, Cal. I like things the way they are. I like that we can joke around. And talk about serious things. I don't want that to change."

"It won't." He put the car in drive and pulled back onto the highway. "You know, I just had to see if things might be right for us."

"Oh, Cal, I'm sorry if I led you on or made you think I would—"

"No, no you haven't. But hey, I'm a guy. Gotta try." *Like dating Savannah?* "I promise not to put you in this position again." He rolled down the window, letting the car fill with cool air. "And I promise you're safe with me." Smiling, he put the sunglasses back on. *Safe.*

Renee welcomed the breeze and rolled down her window, too. Her hair whipped around her face; she removed the bandana and pulled her hair into a ponytail, securing it with an elastic band she found in her pocket. "I know, Cal." They drove in silence for a few minutes. "Where are we going?"

"The Woods." He had made a wide loop around Monmouth and now headed for Gentle Woods on the edge of town. When they reached it, he parked and turned off the engine. They sat in silence, without moving, staring at the motionless swings and bent, twisted trees just beginning to bud. Renee involuntarily shivered; only slightly, but Cal reached over and squeezed her hand. "Come on, let's get out and walk around."

She nodded and scrambled out of the car. They stood for a moment in the parking lot, and then started across the park. At the bridge he removed his sunglasses, put them in his shirt pocket, and looked at her. "Okay?" She nodded and they crossed the creek in silence. They stopped at a scarred and rickety picnic table under the canopy of old trees. They sat next to each other, shoulders touching.

Renee spoke first, her voice a whisper. "I don't feel anything. Do you?"

"I'm not sure. Not like the other times when it was crystal clear."

"You know, it's strange, but Savannah and I've never talked about what happened."

"Neil and I haven't talked about it, either. Maybe it's just too personal."

"I know there was something here."

"Savannah felt it, too," Cal said. "And she said she wasn't scared. Funny how we all perceived it differently." He gazed around the park. "I still wonder why VanAllen died."

"The drug bust. Maybe that's what the spirit was warning us about," Renee said.

"It makes sense to me," Cal agreed. "VanAllen might have seen something going down with Rico. Maybe he was being threatened but he was old, his heart gave out. For all I know, he was a customer and got some bad drugs. Maybe he thought I was a buyer. I still can't figure out why he approached me in the first place." He shrugged. "I'm speculating."

"He probably felt that vibe coming from you," Renee whispered. "The force that, um, you know—your psychic energy."

"Do you feel it?"

"From you? I don't know." She wrapped her arms around herself. Closed her eyes. *Safe. That's what I feel.*

He shook his head as if trying to clear his thoughts. "I'm not sensing anything right now. Well, maybe a lightness. It's very vague. Nothing evil or frightening." He reached into his shirt pocket for cigarettes, changed his mind. "I haven't been out here in weeks. Not since you and Savannah came with me."

"Why today?" She tried to keep the anxiety out of her voice, but knew he could feel it.

"Compelled, I suppose. One last time."

"Do you mean that?" She waited but he didn't answer. "I'm just a little spooked."

"I understand." He leaned back, elbows resting on the table, legs crossed at the ankles. "I never told you about the first experiences I had with what I think of as an astral body, did I?'

"You told me you had them. You said you came here lots of times and talked with some kind of spirit. But no, you never said what you talked about."

"I can't tell you *what* it was about or even details about the experiences, but every time I went to the student center after being here and—visiting—I saw you."

"What? What do you mean?"

"Just what I said. I came here, heard the voice, conversed, left, went to the student center, and saw you walking or sitting or talking to someone."

"Me?"

He laughed. "Yes, you. I finally decided I needed to meet you. Once I did, I never heard the voice again."

"And that night you met VanAllen."

"Yep. Interesting, isn't it?"

"Why would something want you to meet me? That's really

weird."

"I don't know. But I think our friendship is important."

"Oh, Cal! I know it is. I'm a different person than I was six months ago—no, three months ago. Stronger, more independent."

"I'm a different person, too. You've changed me."

"What? No, I don't think so." Renee laughed, punching Cal on the arm.

"Yes, you and Savannah see things I don't, understand things I don't, bring a new perspective to my thinking. You bring an innocence to things. You aren't jaded like most of the people I know."

"Well, that's what friends do." She smiled. "I feel like we've all known each other a lifetime." She touched Cal's hand. "I saw you, too, before I met you. But not here, not in Monmouth."

"Where?"

"The airport. When I was saying goodbye to Russ. You were there."

"No, I wasn't."

"I saw you, I smelled your pipe, I heard your voice." She stopped, her eyes wide. "I smelled leather, too. Like Alex's jacket. But he doesn't believe in astral stuff."

Cal was quiet. Renee wrapped her fingers around his hand. She could feel his pulse thrumming. After a moment, Cal spoke. "I look at it that TJ—the entity I conversed with—wanted me to expand my thinking, so he brought you to me."

Renee raised her palms to the sky. "Thank you, TJ!" Then she turned serious. "Or maybe he knew I would listen to you and Alex about—things. Maybe it was TJ at the airport." She closed her eyes, remembering the day she said goodbye to Russ. *The voice said, "You'll be all right." It wasn't Cal's voice, or Alex's.* Looking at Cal, she asked, "Does that make sense?"

"As much as anything does."

"But he left and something else was here. And someone died." Shivering, she wrapped her arms around herself. "I'm never coming here again."

Cal stood, offered his hand to Renee. "Me, either."

"Really? Promise?"

"Promise."

~ 31 ~

With the new term, Renee had every intention of bringing her grades up. She had arranged her schedule for more mid-day classes with Tuesdays and Thursdays completely open. Her plan was to get most of her work done on those two days. But somehow mornings came later and later for her and it was hard to feel motivated to attend class, write papers, study for tests. So many thoughts swirled around in her head constantly—most having nothing to do with getting a college degree—that it was sometimes impossible to concentrate. She had no classes with Savannah and she missed having that time to talk. They met up between classes and for meals, grabbing time for quick chats. And evenings spent at the Alleycat and apartment meant she and Savannah hardly ever had time alone.

Even watching *Star Trek* after her lit class had become an ordeal because Judy had planned her spring schedule so her classes ended by three o'clock. For Renee it no longer was a fun hour of television but another hour of watching Judy try to get Alex's attention. The subject of the letter never came up, but Judy stopped asking about Russ or making any comments about Renee's behavior. She joined the group at the Alleycat two or three times a week and made attempts to contribute to the conversations, but mostly she was subdued and detached. Renee and Savannah went to the diner every night and Renee found it easier to relax and enjoy the evenings without Judy's interference, real or perceived. At least Judy still had her study group, which met after dinner twice a week in the dorm lounge. Judy had requested the change in location so she didn't have to be out walking alone in the evening.

Three or four times a week, rather than walk across campus at two or three o'clock in the morning, the girls just stayed at the apartment all night. They borrowed t-shirts from the boys and Renee also changed from her own jeans to a pair of Alex's. The foam chair, unfolded and spread flat, formed a large bed in the center of the room which Savannah and Renee shared. Judy, if she was there, slept on the couch, covered head-to-toe with a quilt she found in the linen closet.

After a couple of nights, Alex plopped down on the makeshift bed, sitting cross-legged between Renee and Savannah. "This ain't too bad," he said. "In fact, better than my crappy mattress in the other room."

"Come on, sleep with us," Savannah said.

Renee sat up, startled. "Savannah!"

Savannah giggled. "Why not? There's plenty of room." She jerked her head toward Judy, already lightly snoring. She lowered her voice to a whisper. "Besides, it'll mess with her head—that will be worth it!"

"Alex, do you have more blankets?" Renee asked. *Oh my God, what the heck am I doing? Russ would—*

"What? We can't share? We're all skinny."

Savannah yanked the blanket away from Alex. "No, this one is mine. Get your own."

"Okay, okay," Alex said, rising. He grinned. "Do you need your own, too, Renee?"

"Please." She was glad the lights were out and no one could see her face. She knew her eyes would give her away. *Am I crazy? I don't care.* When Alex laid back down, she wrapped the blanket he gave her around herself, making sure there were inches between her body and his. Still, she could hear his breathing. Once during the night she woke up and felt his leg against hers. Smiling, she drifted back to sleep.

In the morning, Renee awoke feeling eyes boring into her. Judy sat ramrod straight on the couch, watching the three people on the floor. Renee extricated herself from the blanket and stood up, finger combing her hair and straightening her t-shirt.

"Morning," she mumbled, rubbing her eyes. "Sleep well?"

Judy frowned. "Why is Alex there?"

Renee made a *tch* sound, rolled her eyes. "Why not?" She went into the bathroom and closed the door. Her reflection in the mirror almost made her blush. Hair a mess, a spot of dried drool on her cheek, sleep crust in the corners of her eyes—she couldn't help feeling relief that she had woken up before Alex.

After that, Alex slept on the floor every night when the girls stayed over. Cal teased them but when they offered to scoot over and make room for him, he said no, his own bed was much more comfortable.

"I like to spread out or spoon," he said. "Judy, would you spoon with me?" She looked aghast and he laughed. "See? It wouldn't work. Besides, you're sleeping in your clothes. What's that about? You kids have fun with your campout."

"You don't know what you're missing," Alex said. "Get crazy for once in your life."

"Hey, man, just enjoy your harem and tell me all the dirt later."

Pillows came flying all at once, hitting Cal before he could duck. He chuckled and picked up the pillows, tossing them back to the bed. "Don't get into trouble," he said, laughing as he went to the bedroom.

Skipping dinner on a night when Judy had her study group, Renee and Savannah went to the Alleycat early. It was nearly empty. They ordered sodas and salads and stretched out in the corner booth.

"Hey," Renee said. "Do you and Neil ever talk about that time at Gentle Woods?"

Savannah shook her head. "No, and I never said anything about going there with Cal. Have you?"

"No. I think Cal wants to keep it between us. Oh, he told me he's not going there ever again." She didn't mention driving to the Woods in Cal's car.

"Really? Probably a good thing. Even though I wasn't scared, it still felt negative. And your reaction was really odd." She poked through the salad greens, mixing the dressing in. "Do you know what an empath is?"

"No. I never heard of that."

"It's a person who feels what another person is experiencing. Cal said your reaction was like being high on a drug, didn't he?"

"Like a bad drug."

"I think you were serving as an empath for someone."

A shiver went through Renee. "Someone having a bad trip? Maybe the guy who died?"

"Yeah. That kind of makes sense, doesn't it?"

"But why me?"

Savannah shook her head. "I don't know. I only felt a little bit, you felt a lot more." She gazed intently at Renee. "Do you sense things about other people? You know, like are you sensitive to what someone else is feeling?"

"I don't know. I have a hard time walking away from someone who's having a problem, even if they haven't told me about it—I guess I can kind of sense that they might need me. Is that what you mean?"

"When we met, at the orientation, remember? Why did you pick me out of all those girls?"

Renee considered the question, thinking back on that first day in the dorm when she met Judy and had a feeling—*sixth sense?*—that their relationship might be difficult. Then seeing Savannah, off in a corner of the lounge by herself, looking—awkward. Renee had had to push her way through the crowd to reach her. And the bond between the two of them was instant. "I felt a connection to you, as soon as I saw you."

"And why do you defend Judy all the time?" Savannah paused, then said, "Because you're sensitive to her moods and emotions and you can't walk away from her, even when she's horrible."

Renee shook her head. "I'm such a baby. A chicken. A—a scaredy-cat. I can't stand up for myself."

"That's not true. Look how you handled that stupid letter."

"Yeah." Renee ate a couple of bites of her salad. "I guess I did. But I didn't abandon her. I know she needs us."

"See, I would have if it wasn't for you. And she'd probably shoot herself or something. Shit. Maybe you *are* psychic."

"Gosh, I hope not." *Why would I have seen that person in the airport? No one was there. It wasn't Cal. It wasn't Alex. TJ is only—what? Is he real? I felt strange in the Woods.* She closed her eyes, took a breath. Opened her eyes and smiled at Savannah.

"Isn't it funny we've never talked about this before? You and me, I mean."

With a surprised look, Savannah said, "Huh, you're right. I never thought about that. I wonder why? We talk about everything."

"Cal thinks it's because it's too personal. He and Neil haven't discussed it, either."

"If they hadn't found that guy in the creek maybe it wouldn't be so awful."

"Well, I've never had an experience like it," Renee said. "I think I've wanted to avoid it because it didn't feel good. Talking about it just makes it more, um, real, I guess." She considered telling Savannah about the experience in the airport, but then she would be tempted to break Cal's confidence. "But maybe it was meant to tell us something."

"I'm taking it as a warning."

"Yeah, me, too. I never want to set foot in that park again. And no drugs for me, either! Not if it affects me the way I felt that day." Renee signaled the waitress for refills on their sodas. "Hey, do you want to get tickets for the play? Gosh, I really miss seeing Cal." Cal had been cast as the lead in the spring play and had rehearsal nearly every evening.

"I already checked into it. Tickets will be available Friday," Savannah said.

Alex and Neil arrived and joined Savannah and Renee in the booth. Seeing that the girls had ordered dinner, they asked the waitress to bring them hamburgers. The four talked for nearly an hour before leaving for the apartment. The night was lazy, dreamy. The apartment was dark and rather than turn on lights, Savannah lit the candles on the end table. After taking her shoes off, she settled on the couch and Neil sat on the floor in front of her. Renee sank onto the foam chair, her favorite spot. Alex put several records on the phonograph spindle then stretched out on the floor, hands clasped behind his head. The music flowed around them and the flickering darkness was soothing. No one talked; Savannah ran her fingers lightly through Neil's hair and he gently rubbed her bare feet. Alex shifted, sat up, moved next to Renee. Renee liked that he was so close. *Everything's easy with him.* Her skin tingled. She leaned her head back and smiled. *Nice.*

She could hear him breathing, sense the slight touch of his arm against hers. She felt calm, peaceful, sitting with him. *So different from Cal.* Cal had an energy that kept her off-kilter, a little unsure; Alex's presence was reassuring. She felt that she could share concerns with him and he would listen, really *hear* her words, even the ones she kept to herself. With Russ she had never been able to let her guard down, to shake off her outer shell and reveal her true thoughts. She always had to be cautious not to show too much, to protect herself. *What am I so afraid of?* Savannah's suggestion about being an empath nudged at her. *Am I? No, I feel safe with Cal and Alex because they* are *safe. I don't think Russ is.*

She knew he would never understand her friendship with Cal and Alex. Sex, yes—if she was physically attracted to another man, that Russ could comprehend, even forgive, in his own way. She knew that was peculiar, but for him, sex fulfilled a physical need. It had little to do with intimacy, with caring about someone. He often talked about a "man's needs" and implied that a monogamous relationship was a sacrifice he was willing to make for her. He also shared his ideas for sexual experiences he wanted to pursue with her when she was ready; most made her uncomfortable but she complied as much as she could. She knew his spring break trip with Barbara most likely involved some kind of sexual activity that he would, in his mind, justify. *And I don't really care. What does that mean about me? How can I feel that way? Would he understand a hug from Cal, a cheer-up kiss from Neil? What about me sleeping at the apartment? Wearing Alex's clothes?* Picking nervously at her fingernails, she felt her tension rising. *I never should have let this happen. Russ is the man in my life—the only man.*

She considered Cal's belief that a ring was not necessarily a commitment. *Have I betrayed Russ? Has he betrayed me? I love him, don't I?* They had shared so much and made so many plans, she had to love him. He was her life.

But Alex is my life, too. And Cal. As much as Savannah, and Neil and Judy, as much as my family, as much as—yes, as much as Russ. In despair, she remembered Cal's words: "I can't stand him." Neil felt the same. Did Alex despise him also? She talked about him more openly with Alex than with anyone else. More honestly than perhaps she should. Russ would cut off their friendship. He would deny her part of her life so she could be a "proper" wife. Would he cut her off even from Savannah? Would he blame her for Renee's "indiscretions"?

In the uneven candlelight, Renee watched Savannah and Neil. He had moved to sit next to her on the couch, his arm around her shoulder, his other hand on her knee. He pulled her close, kissing her face, fingers of one hand entwined in her hair. Savannah wriggled away from Neil just a little, then she held his free hand, keeping it in check.

"Alex," Renee said quietly, "do you want anything to eat? I'm kind of hungry." She tilted her head toward the couple on the couch, biting her lower lip.

"Yeah," he said, rising and offering a hand to Renee. "You guys want anything?"

Neil paused, looked at Alex, and put two fingers up in a peace sign. "No, thanks. We're good." He smiled at Savannah, pulling her arm up to his shoulder, keeping hold of her hand.

Eyes closed, Savannah murmured, "I don't need anything, thanks."

Renee and Alex went into the kitchen. He opened the refrigerator and took out a chunk of cheese and a tomato. Renee stood in the shadow of the dining area where she could see both rooms. She watched Alex as he sliced the cheese and put the slices on two pieces of bread. He moved with ease and confidence as he worked on the sandwiches, shaking his head when she offered to help. He had gotten more comfortable and proficient in the kitchen since they all did more cooking now. He turned on the broiler and placed the bread on a cookie sheet. While the oven heated up, he cut the tomato into thick slices and topped the cheese with them. In the semi-darkness she could see his silhouette—tall and lanky, a runner's body with broad shoulders and narrow hips, long legs. *Strong in so many ways. I am incredibly lucky to have him for a friend.*

Across the living room, Renee could see that Neil had pressed his body against Savannah's, his weight pushing her back into a semi-reclining position. Her arms tightened around his neck. He pulled her legs up onto the couch, onto his thighs. Renee heard Savannah say something; it sounded like "stop" but she wasn't certain. Whispers drifted into the kitchen.

Alex slid the cookie sheet into the oven and poured orange juice into two tall glasses. He handed one to Renee and whispered, "Let's sit at the table, okay?" He got two plates out of the cupboard and checked the broiler. Renee slipped into the chair on the far side of the table, facing the kitchen, with the living room to her left.

Neil's hand had moved down to Savannah's hip. "No, Neil," she said in a low voice. "Not now."

"Just relax," he murmured, nuzzling her cheek.

She pulled away, pushing against his chest. "Neil, don't."

"Come on, baby," he said, sliding his hand under her legs. "It's fine."

Savannah pushed harder. "Stop it," she said in a firm voice.

Alex brought the sandwiches to the table, taking the chair facing the living room. His back was rigid, his mouth set, as he listened to the faint words drifting into the kitchen. He watched as Neil pulled Savannah closer and she pushed him back. Alex said, "Neil. Hey man, cool it."

Neil stood and held his hand out to Savannah. "Let's go in the bedroom." He tipped his head toward Renee and Alex. "You'll be more comfortable."

"Just to talk," Savannah said, sitting up, straightening her blouse.

"Are you kidding me?"

"To talk," she repeated. She crossed her legs at the knee, hands clasped in her lap.

"You gotta be kidding." Neil flopped down on the couch with a grunt. He sat on the edge of the cushion and lit a cigarette.

Savannah turned toward him, pulling her legs into a criss-cross position. "No," she whispered. "I'm not kidding. I want to talk to you."

He hissed, "Damn, I don't want to talk. I want to—"

"I don't. Will you listen?"

Neil made a guttural sound. Hands flat on his thighs, elbows akimbo, back rigid, and eyes averted from Savannah's face, he grunted, "Sure. Talk."

Savannah looked at Neil, reached out and touched his arm. "Neil, I don't feel that way."

He jerked his arm away from her touch. "Then don't lead me on. Don't act like you want it then go all pure on me."

She wrapped her arms around herself, shoulders hunched. "I'm sorry."

"Yeah. Me, too." Neil looked over at Alex. "I'm splittin'. Make sure they get back to the dorm." He slammed the door behind him.

Renee got to her feet, crossed the room, and hugged Savannah. "I'm sorry."

"It's okay. I was expecting it, just hoped it wouldn't happen for a little while longer." She wiped her eyes with the heel of her hand.

"I know."

The front door opened and Cal came in, stopping suddenly when he saw the candlelight. He closed the door, careful to do it quietly. "Everything okay in here? I just ran into Neil and he sounded pissed."

Savannah let out a long sigh, leaning her head against the back of the couch. "It's fine. He's mad at me." She looked at Renee. "Do you want to go home?"

"Yeah, it's late. Judy will be freaking out if I don't show up before dawn. Not that I really care, but I don't know if you want to be here when Neil gets back."

"That's true. It would be awkward."

The four of them headed back to the dorm. Cal and Renee walked slowly, letting Alex and Savannah move ahead about a block. Everyone was particularly quiet as they walked across the dark campus.

"What happened tonight?" Cal asked Renee.

"Neil and Savannah were, um, getting pretty involved, if you know what I mean." She glanced at Cal. "You were gone and he—treated her different. He came on to her really strong. And in front of us."

Cal laughed. "She's an attractive chick. He always wants to make out with her."

"But he's never made a real move on her."

He shrugged. "He said she wouldn't do it. Called her a tease."

Renee stopped. "Really? He told you that? What a jerk."

"Why do you think he's a jerk when nothing happened?"

"Because he called her a tease. That he even told you she wouldn't go to bed with him. It's none of your business. Or mine. But he made it our business. "

"She's a nice girl," Cal said. "He shouldn't have put her in that position."

"Are you being facetious?"

"No!" Cal faced Renee, his eyes connecting with hers. "I mean that. She's a decent person and she deserves better. Just like you. You deserve better than what you have."

"That's a matter of opinion," Renee said. "I'm right where I want to be." She started walking. "I don't get why you asked Savannah out."

"Like you said, Neil can be a jerk. I wanted to give her a different perspective." He lit a cigarette as they walked. "The chemistry wasn't there. Not that I really expected it, but sometimes you have to take a chance on something." He smoked the cigarette halfway down, then flicked it on the ground, extinguishing it with his foot. "And sometimes you don't."

~~ 32 ~~

The early morning gray sky was turning pink and a light breeze ruffled Renee's hair as she walked quickly to the apartment. She ran lightly up the steps, then checked her watch. Seven o'clock. The bus to Eugene was due at seven-thirty; she hoped Alex was up and ready to go. She knocked twice, waited, opened the apartment door. The brisk walk had been invigorating and she welcomed the warmth of the apartment. But it was too quiet. Pausing, one hand pushing the door shut, feet stopped in mid-step, she listened. A slow and steady breathing came from the bedroom. She tiptoed to the open doorway. Two beds were empty; Cal and Neil had said they were going to a party. *All-nighter, I guess.* On the third bed, Alex sprawled out on his back, arms flung wide. His thin face held the trace of a smile. The blanket and sheet had tangled around his feet and sometime in the night he had yanked them off the bed into a jumbled heap. He wore no pajamas, only a pair of white briefs. She stared at the angular shape of his legs and trunk, the muscles of his arms, the light hair on his chest. Somehow she resisted her yearning to go in and lay down beside him; she tiptoed back to the front door.

"Alex! Alex, I'm here!" Forcing herself to stand still, she listened to the hushed stirring in the other room. He stuck a sleepy blond head around the doorjamb.

"Are you early?" Grinning, she shook her head. "Is it late?" She nodded and he groaned, disappearing. She heard him pull on his jeans; the squeak of his tennis shoes and the slight ratchet sound as he zipped his jeans were barely audible. He closed the bedroom door and walked into the living room dressed as she saw him day after day, but she still visualized the almost naked man asleep on his bed. After a moment she said good morning.

"I need to shave. I'll be just a couple of minutes," he said and went into the bathroom, leaving the door open. He shaved quickly. She thought of her father, shaving in his meticulous way, standing in undershirt and khaki pants, scraping the soap-beard and winking at her when she was a small child. She thought of Russ, shaving twice a day, driving a buzzing electric razor over his dry skin. She didn't watch Alex. In the kitchen she found a package of crackers and a couple of oranges and stuffed them in her purse.

They reached the bus stop just as the Greyhound coach turned the corner and wheezed to a stop at the curb. Alex hopped on and offered a hand to Renee. The bus was nearly empty but they sat in the very last seat, Alex on the aisle. He yawned and settled back. "You sleep well?"

"I had no choice," she smiled. "You sent us home so early that bed was the only escape from Judy. Were you up all night?"

He laughed, shaking his head. "No. I studied for a couple of hours after getting back from the dorm. Sorry I overslept. I *did* have my alarm set; I wasn't depending on you to wake me." Renee smiled at the reference to her relationship with Russ and the walkie-talkies. "But I forgot to actually turn it on. Sorry."

"I'm excited about getting to shop in an actual department store, not a dinky five and dime like Crider's," Renee said. "I really want to find a good present for Mother's Day. I know it's a month away, but who knows when we'll get another chance like this."

The countryside rolled by like a scenic but predictable film. In about an hour the city of Eugene would surround them. An entire day of relaxed anonymity. In the front of the bus, the driver chatted with two passengers, a washed-out, middle-aged woman in a nurse's uniform and a dyed-blonde woman in her thirties. Renee and Alex talked quietly, feeling almost alone in the big bus. They talked about themselves, bits and pieces of their lives before the beginning of winter term. They didn't mention Russ at all, but he crept into Renee's mind. She thought again of Alex asleep; she felt no guilt. Alex never locked his door, Renee always just walked in—like everybody else. She remembered the day she and Savannah had gone to the apartment for the first time. It seemed so long ago. But only three months had passed. She felt like she had known Alex, Cal, and Neil forever. Russ was untouchable, so far away, for so long. Nearly eight months of letters. Eight months of dreams, of change.

"I hope it doesn't rain," Renee said, eyeing the thick clouds collecting in the early morning blue sky. "But it probably will."

"Yeah, this is Oregon," Alex said with a smile. "So, what'll we do first when we get there? It'll be about eight-thirty."

"How about breakfast? You're probably starving. Then we could just walk around. We can window shop and wait for the stores to open."

"Sounds good, but I'm not really hungry. If we can find a doughnut shop I'll be good with that. We need to catch the five-ten bus. It's the last one."

"Okay. That should be easy to remember. Five-ten." She leaned back, eyes closed. "It's lucky I have no classes on Tuesdays."

"And it's lucky I dropped Statistics."

"Yeah, it is. I didn't want to do this alone."

"I'm glad you didn't have to."

"So am I. Thanks, Alex."

"Any time. I'm kind of surprised you didn't ask Cal to drive you to Corvallis or Eugene on the weekend, though."

"I thought about it. But then I would have had no excuse not to invite Judy and Savannah along."

"Well, that's true." He ruffled her hair, loose for once, instead of held back with a bandana. "This will be great—no Judy, no Neil—"

"Does Neil bother you?" Renee asked curiously.

Alex looked uncomfortable. "No—no, not really. I just don't like for you and Savannah to be there when he and his friends are using dope. Sometimes I don't even go back to the apartment after I walk you to the dorm—hey, don't look at me like that! I won't get mugged or anything." He smiled at her worried expression. "I just walk around, sometimes I go to Doug's place. But I just get tired of the way Neil acts, the way he dropped Savannah so fast, the things he says about—" He stopped abruptly. "Just Neil in general."

"He says things about me?"

"Not about you exactly," Alex said, hesitance clear in his voice.

"Oh. About Russ?" Renee shrugged. "I don't care. Neil's pretty full of himself sometimes, kind of like Russ."

"I don't understand how he can just walk away from Savannah. His ego can't take rejection, I guess."

"You were right about him being a user. He can be fun but Savannah and I knew all along what his trip was." Renee shook her head. "She really loved the talks they had. I hope he wasn't just stringing her along so he could get her into bed."

"He likes living on the edge. She's probably too calm for him."

"I don't think she's overly upset that they kind of broke up,"

Renee said. "I know she was expecting it."

"She's not in a hurry to date or settle down, is she?"

Renee shook her head. "No, she's pretty happy with things as they are. I like her confidence. Wish I had some of it."

"You're getting there."

"I guess." Renee sighed. "Everything's so different now, with Cal in rehearsals and Neil…away." She looked at Alex. "At least some things are the same."

"I'm not going anywhere! You're stuck with me."

"Good! I need you. You're my math whiz."

"And you make my life interesting."

"Really?" Renee blinked and gave Alex a confused look.

"Yeah, sure. You're fun to be around. And you're cute!"

"Oh, come on!" Renee giggled and blushed.

"And you have a great laugh," he added.

"Alex," Renee said, turning serious. "Do you know—um, this might sound weird but it's important. And it's true." She cleared her throat, bit her thumbnail, hesitated. Alex waited. "I have always been shy, hardly ever spoke, like in school or even with friends. I used to get in trouble for not speaking up in class or for even wanting to be alone in my room. I've been afraid to give my opinions or share how I feel. I practiced laughing in front of a mirror because I didn't even laugh out loud. But you've given me my *voice,* Alex. You really have. You listen and make me feel that I *can* talk and it's okay."

"Of course I'll listen to you."

She touched his arm. "I know. That's what I mean. I don't think anyone, except Savannah, has done that for me." She smiled, feeling relaxed. "I feel—free. It's incredible. Thank you."

"I'm glad you feel that way. I wish I could do more. If you—no, I'm not going to tell you what to do."

"Why not? Everyone else does."

He smiled at her. "I'm not everyone else."

"So true! So absolutely true." She fought the impulse to throw her arms around his neck and plant a kiss on his face. "Ah, this is going to be one fantastic day!"

Next door to the bus station was a coffee shop. Alex purchased two apple muffins and two cups of hot chocolate to go. They walked slowly through the downtown section of Eugene, waiting for stores to open. At a jeweler's they looked at the wedding rings on display

Alleycat

in the window.

"I know Russ picked out your engagement ring," Alex said. "If you could pick your own ring, which one would you choose?"

Renee studied the selection. "I really like white gold. And something with color would be nice—just a little, like that one with the garnets on either side of the diamond. You know I love red!"

Alex pointed to a set of rings in the corner. "So, how about those?" The engagement diamond was huge, in a high-pronged setting, with a cluster of rubies in an arc. The wedding ring fit into the ruby arc, extending it with more rubies, making a connected set.

Renee shook her head. "Way too gaudy for me." She raised her left hand and looked at her own ring. "I like this one. It's simple, not too big. I would have liked the white gold, though."

They continued to stroll through stores and Renee found a gift for her mother quickly. For lunch, they bought a day-old chocolate roll cake at a tiny bakery. Sitting on the sidewalk, backs against a department store wall, they stared at the cake box between them. Then, with a snap of his fingers, Alex jumped up and disappeared into a nearby Hickory Farms store. When he emerged, he triumphantly held up a few plastic sticks.

"Here we go! Coffee stir-sticks. But for us, they're forks." He deftly sliced off a piece of cake and tasted it. "Delicious! Come on, dig in!" Returning stares from passers-by with smiles, they ate half the cake, then split an orange. Alex retied the string around the box and they wiped their fingers on a crumpled Kleenex Renee found in the bottom of her purse. Gathering up their packages, they crossed the street and walked leisurely around town.

"What a wedding that would be," Renee mused.

"What do you mean?"

"Oh!" She blushed. "I was just thinking about all the fuss and planning an actual wedding takes and that something like today would be so perfect instead."

"Only kind to have," Alex agreed. "No trouble. Just a quick stop at a justice of the peace, then a day-old chocolate cream cake, at half-price, of course. And we'd eat it all—just the two of us."

"With coffee stir-sticks."

"Nothing else would work."

"Then a nice, long walk, by ourselves," Renee said dreamily. "No Aunt Sally's mushing around or jolly fathers slapping you on the back. No tears. No hand-shaking."

"Where shall we spend our"—he made quote marks in the air with his fingers—"honeymoon?"

"Ha! I'm barely past the wedding part of this fantasy! I'll have to think on it."

"Well, I'm getting you that ring—the one with the rubies, because you deserve the best."

"Okay, and I'm getting you the chocolate cake," Renee said.

"Could you get whipped cream, too? I really like whipped cream."

"Yes, dear," Renee said in a mock-weary voice. "If you get me a real suitcase for our honeymoon."

"I'll get you a steamer trunk, how's that?"

"Ooh, yes! An antique one with leather straps and brass hinges."

"Consider it done," Alex said. "Hey, look, there's a park. Come on! I'll race you!"

The brilliant glare of the high silvery slide reflecting the sunlight attracted Renee. She hadn't been on a slide since grade school. Below her, Alex tugged on the hem of her jeans to hurry her along. Fingers squeezing the railing, she lifted her legs over the flat top and perched on the shimmery, dented metal, sailed down and landed with a soft *bump*. Before she regained her footing, Alex crashed into her; then his strong arms lifted her up and they whirled around and around in a frenetic kaleidoscope of trees, metal, sky, and grass. They toppled to the ground, laughing. They raced to the swings, the merry-go-round, the hopscotch painted on a narrow strip of asphalt. Alex talked Renee into sitting on the teeter-totter, then, grinning, held his end to the ground, leaving her high in the air, kicking and yelling. Later they discovered a small pond surrounded by young trees and leafy bushes with a flock of ducks swimming peacefully among the reeds along the bank. They fed the rest of the cake to the ducks, quacking along with them.

The rain began softly at first, a light drizzle, then became a torrent. They took shelter under a tree until it subsided to a steady shower. They walked back downtown and stopped in a used bookstore where they spent an hour browsing through paperbacks and magazines. At ten to five, surprised by the lateness of the hour, they hurried toward the bus depot. The rain poured down, drenching their hair and sending icy shivers down their necks. They ran through puddles, splashing, curling their toes to make squinching sounds in their shoes. Bursting in the door of the depot they fell into the nearest seats, dropped their bundles on the floor. Alex noticed a gumball machine near the door; he fished a quarter out of his pocket and pushed it into the slot. The machine had plastic balls, each containing some kind of jewelry—rings, bracelets, and necklaces—along with a piece of gum. A turn of the handle and a ball slid down the chute. He caught it, twisted it open, and sat back down by Renee.

"Here, I got you a keepsake." He took out a necklace with a tiny flower-shaped pendant and presented it to her.

She ducked her head to hide her surprise. "Would you help me put it on?" He fumbled with the clasp as she held her hair off her neck. When it was fastened, she felt for the plastic flower and made sure it rested at her throat.

"Hey, it looks good on you!" He pulled out his wallet. "I almost forgot. I have something else, too." From the wallet he took a small photograph; he turned it over and wrote something on the back, then handed it to her. "Remember we talked about giving each other photos?"

Renee nodded. "Yes, but I didn't think—" She took the picture and looked at it, then laughed. "How old are you here?"

"First grade."

"You were so adorable!" She looked at what he had written on the back: **To a very special friend, forever.** "Oh, Alex," she said, feeling her heart beat faster. *I wish...no, I can't think about what ifs and wishes.* "You are, oh my gosh, you are the most wonderful friend I could ever hope for." She impulsively leaned toward him, then stopped, red-faced, and turned away. "Thank you for the picture." She fumbled with her purse, then removed the photo book she had. She slipped the picture of Alex into the front of the book, covering one of her with Russ.

"So now you owe me one," he said, smiling.

As they waited for the bus that would carry them back to Monmouth, Renee said, "I've decided how we'd spend our honeymoon. We'd take a month off and do just what we did today."

~~ 33 ~~

Without a shared class, Renee and Savannah had to purposely make time to meet. Between classes they sat in the student center coffee shop, talking, writing, studying. Sometimes they met Alex or Cal. They never ran into Neil on campus; they weren't certain he was even enrolled in classes anymore. When they saw him at the diner or apartment, he remained as friendly as ever, but detached. He and Savannah always greeted each other warmly, like old friends. *How can some people walk away so easily?*

One afternoon, when they were alone, Savannah told Renee she was worried about her. "You've been so quiet lately. Are you all right?" she asked, her face clearly showing concern.

"Oh, sure," Renee answered brightly.

"Well, you haven't been acting like yourself. I miss the old Rennie."

"Yeah, I know." Renee smiled. "It's just circumstances."

"What do you mean, circumstances? Judy? Russ?"

"Everything. Judy, Russ, Alex, Cal, Neil, you." She ticked the names off on her fingers, one by one, as she said them. "I don't even want to write to Russ anymore. I'm nervous about this summer, when he comes home. I want so much for him and Alex and Cal to be friends but I don't think that will happen."

"What do you mean, I'm one of your problems?"

"No, no, not a problem, Savannah. You're just part of the whole picture. In fact, you're the only part that isn't a problem, thank God. If I didn't have you to talk to I'd go nuts."

"Thank you." Savannah leaned over and gave her a hug. "Now, what is it about your circumstances, as you put it, that's bothering you?"

"Number one, I wish Judy would find another interest. She's driving Alex crazy, to say nothing of me. I'm barely civil to her anymore, after that letter incident, but it doesn't seem to matter. She hasn't got a clue about relationships. Maybe she'll hook up with Doug—I can only hope. Number two, Cal. It would be easier if he found a girlfriend. He and I talked, but I don't know if he really understands that I don't intend to break up with Russ." She smiled as Savannah laughed. "I know, I know—we can't run people's lives." She held up three fingers and said, "Number three, Neil. I'm amazed at how easy you two still are with each other. But he can be so obnoxious—sorry if that bothers you."

"I know he is," Savannah said. "I'm kind of surprised, too, how he's friendly with me after I—"

"Crushed him?" Renee smiled and Savannah laughed out loud.

"You know, he's okay," Savannah said. "He was mad that night but I think he really knew I wouldn't go to bed with him. He's just moving on in his own way."

"Alex said he gets bored easily."

"Yeah," Savannah sighed. "But I hate to think I couldn't hold his interest."

Renee shook her head. "It's all of us. He wants a group to party with and we aren't it. I mean, look at how he spends his time. Even before the big whoop-de-doo about the bedroom he was drinking a lot and skipping class, never studying. I don't know how Judy can be on my case when he's a perfectly good target. *Tch.*" She rubbed her forehead, pushed her hair behind her ears. "It's crazy. Number four, I'm scared to death about the changes that have happened since Russ went to Japan. I mean, I've changed and I'm sure he has, too."

"You knew that would happen."

"Yeah, but I'm not at all sure that Russ is going to like it."

"Renee," Savannah said, keeping her voice gentle. "You do have options. Are you thinking about that?"

When the three girls went to the Alleycat that evening, only Cal and Alex showed up. Their mood was especially upbeat, but they skirted around the girls' questions, making jokes and changing the subject. Renee felt a shiver of apprehension. The more Cal and Alex kidded around, the quieter Renee became. Savannah leaned over and whispered, "What's wrong?"

"Something's up," Renee whispered back. "I'm getting worried."

"They're in super good moods and you're upset?" Savannah shook her head. "You are impossible to figure out!"

"I know," Renee said, nibbling a fingernail.

"What are you two conspiring about?" Alex asked.

"Nothing," Renee said.

"She's freaking out," Savannah said, speaking over Renee. "She thinks you guys are up to no good and she's scared about what you have planned."

"That's not true," Renee said. "I'm not scared."

"Hold up your hands and prove you're not shaking," Cal said in a challenging tone of voice. He grinned at the others.

Renee placed her hands on the table, palms up. "See?"

"We do have a surprise for you," Cal said. "Looks like you might be able to handle it. What do you think, Alex?"

"I think we should take her home and just bring Judy and Savannah back to the apartment. The shock might kill Renee."

"Good point, man. Come on, let's hurry to the dorm so we can get on to the fun part of the night." He looked at Renee, who was blushing bright red. "We'll try to get Savannah and Judy back in one piece by tomorrow morning."

"Just stop it," Renee said, covering her face with her hands. "I know I worry excessively. You don't have to rub it in." Dropping her hands, she revealed her smile. "I just thought it might have something to do with Gentle Woods and I—"

"Was worried," Judy said.

"Okay, you guys are right and I'm sorry." Renee blushed again. "I'm so transparent, it's embarrassing."

"So," Savannah said. "When do we get to see this shocking surprise?"

"No hurry now that Renee has recovered," Alex said. "Let's get some food." He signaled for the waitress.

"No way, boys," Renee said. She stood up and motioned to Savannah and Judy. "We're going *now*."

A short time later, Cal and Alex ushered the girls into the apartment. It was quiet and dark. Alex flipped the overhead light on and the girls looked around curiously.

"What is it?" Judy asked. "Is something going to leap out and try to scare us?"

"Keep looking," Alex said. "Check out the whole place. You'll figure it out eventually."

The living room still had the couch and end table and foam chair. The bricks-and-boards bookshelf looked the same. But noticing a few gaps, Savannah checked out the books and record albums. Renee went into the kitchen, followed by Judy. The refrigerator held the usual—six-pack of beer, a few cans of soda, gallon of milk, leftover salad from a dinner the girls had made one night, pickles, ketchup, mustard, bologna. No surprises. The card table was piled with textbooks and pens, paper, an ashtray.

"Some record albums are missing," Savannah called out. "Most notably, Janis Joplin. That belongs to Neil. Some of his books are gone, too." She looked questioningly at Cal.

"No one has looked in the bedroom yet," Alex said.

The three girls rushed to the hallway and peeked in the room. Two beds.

"Where did he go?" Renee asked.

"He told us he was really sorry but he wanted to move in with his girlfriend." Cal glanced at Savannah to see how she reacted to the word "girlfriend." She didn't. "He was afraid we'd be mad, leaving us with more rent to pay. I know it might surprise you but I'm tired of all his bullshit."

"What do you mean?" Judy asked.

"He was insisting that he could put a grow light in the bedroom and no one would know he was growing pot. Much as I'd like a source that close, I don't want it *in* my house."

"I feel like I can breathe in here now," Judy said, opening her arms wide and spinning in the center of the living room. "It's nice to know what we're walking into when we come over."

"Do you think you'll still hang out with him?" Renee asked Cal.

"Yeah, sometimes," Cal said. "We haven't been doing much lately anyway, but he's not mad if that's what you're getting at."

Renee went into the kitchen and removed the photo of the six of them from the refrigerator. "I miss him," she said. "We had a lot of fun." She yelped in surprise when Alex poked her in the side.

Laughing at her startled expression, he said, "We'll still have fun!"

"Hey, let's go to the beach," Cal said. "We have a car now, we should be going somewhere in it."

"Oooh, great idea!" Savannah said. "That would be so much fun."

"We could go tomorrow," Cal looked at the others. "What do you think?"

Judy hesitated. "Tomorrow is Thursday," she said. "I have

classes."

"I think most of us do," Alex said, laughing. "But hey, we're talking the beach!"

"You don't have to come," Renee said.

"After my eight o'clock psych class I'm free until afternoon," Judy said. "My two o'clock class is just a work day for our projects. Mine is already finished."

"So, Miss Perfect, you're ahead of the game," Cal said.

Judy glared at Cal. "I'm not perfect. I just try to be responsible."

Cal laughed. "We're nineteen years old. We have a whole life ahead of us to be responsible. What's one day?"

"I'm going," Savannah said. "I don't care about being responsible."

"Me, too," Renee said. "I'm tired of being responsible."

"Being responsible is for squares," Alex said.

"Okay! Okay! I'll go. What time are we leaving?"

"Whenever we get up," Cal said.

The next morning, awake before anyone else, Renee decided to go to the grocery to buy some snacks for the beach trip. The thought of a real trip out of town, in a car, excited her. Feeling restless, she took her time walking back to the apartment, enjoying the warmth of the early sunshine, smiling in anticipation of the day ahead.

Two more months of school. Seven or eight weeks. Then trying to fit in again at home. Looking for a job. Writing letters. Routine. It'll be a long summer. I'll see Russ in July—what will we say? What should I tell him about this year—and how? What if I decide to keep doing things with Alex and Cal next year? What if I wanted to visit them, with Russ? It will be my decision—-will Russ accept it?

"Renee!"

She looked across the street. Her roommate from last year waved to her. "Oh, hi, Kim," she called.

"Aren't you going to Biology? We're getting our tests back."

Test? A cold chill coursed through Renee. *First History, now Biology. How did this happen?* She tried to remember when she had skipped Biology. Couldn't. "Nah. I don't need to ruin my day! Besides, some friends and I are going to the coast today. Can't pass up an opportunity for that. Friday's soon enough to find out how I did. See you then."

"Okay. Have a nice time." Kim started off, then turned back. "So, how's Russ liking Japan?"

"Very much. You know him—he's doing everything possible."

"I know he misses you!" She waved. "Bye!"

When she got back to the apartment, Cal was making coffee. Alex had formed the foam back into the chair shape and Judy was folding the blankets. Savannah sat at the table eating a bowl of Cheerios.

"Where were you?" Judy asked. "I thought you chickened out."

Laughing, Renee pulled things out of the grocery bag. "No, I got sustenance for us—chips, cookies, crackers, Cheez Whiz, and M & Ms. All the necessities. Oh, yeah, and Junior Mints for you, Alex."

"Great!" Alex said, reaching for the candy. Renee pushed his hand away.

"Not now. In the car."

"Do we need to stop by the dorm so you can get whatever you girls need?" Cal asked.

"Of course," Savannah answered. "I didn't bring my umbrella or extra shoes. Plus, I'm wearing a skirt."

After a quick stop at the dorm, they shoved blankets, coats, hats, and extra shoes into the trunk of Cal's car. Alex claimed the shotgun seat and Judy, Renee, and Savannah crowded into the back. Renee handed the bag of snacks to Alex.

"You're in charge of food," she said. "We're too scrunched back here."

Savannah leaned forward between the front bucket seats. "Can we have some music? What have you got, Cal?"

They headed out of town, singing along with the Beatles' "Baby, You Can Drive My Car." Cal abruptly swerved to the right, causing the girls to fall against each other with shrieks and giggles. He pulled the car up on the shoulder, tires sending gravel spinning. "Look, Neil's hitching."

Alex rolled down his window. "Get a job, hippie!"

Neil strode up to the car. "Hey, dudes! Got room for me?"

Cal let the car move ahead a few feet and Neil raised his middle finger. Laughing, Cal stepped on the brake. "Sure, we got room."

"No, we don't," Judy protested.

"Alex," Renee said, "come on, get in the back. Move over,

Judy."

"I can't!"

Cal set the parking brake and turned around, eyeing the back seat. "Ah, there's plenty of space."

Alex jumped out and pulled the seat forward so he could get into the back. Giggling, the girls moved closer together and he squeezed in, holding Renee's arm, hitching her halfway onto his lap.

"Hey!" she yelped, then giggled. His grip was strong, secure. She couldn't help leaning into him.

"Sit still," Alex said. "I've got you. You aren't going to fall."

Neil threw his backpack on the floor and sat in the seat vacated by Alex. "Where we headin'?" He picked up the box of cookies and pulled a few out, then he held the box up. "Anybody?"

Judy grabbed the box. "Where are *you* planning to go?"

"Wherever you are."

"The beach, where else?" Cal said. "You guys ready back there?" He hit the gas and sped off without waiting for an answer and got shrieks in return. Renee, pressed tightly against Alex, could barely catch her breath before another set of giggles came over her.

As they drove along the highway through farmland, then hills, then forest, they sang and joked and chatted. After dodging numerous attacks of flying M & Ms, and gulping down a soda, Judy pleaded with Cal to stop at a bathroom. He pulled into a small country gas station. Alex went inside the little store to look around and Cal and Neil stepped off to the side of the road to smoke. Savannah and Renee sat at a rickety picnic table chained to an old oak tree. Savannah asked, "Are you having fun, Rennie?"

"Yes, this is wonderful. To get away from normal life is good right now. Even having Judy along is okay. Funny, huh?"

Savannah reached over and hugged Renee, holding her tightly for a few seconds. "I'm so glad we did this today. We all needed a day out but especially you."

"I'm liking it," Renee said. "I'm looking forward to a nice long walk on the beach."

"Me, too. And I bet Judy won't want to go with us!"

"Come on, let's get hot dogs."

In the little store, Renee and Savannah loaded up six hot dogs with mustard and sauerkraut. The clerk found a discarded doughnut box under the counter and put the hot dogs in it. Alex purchased a pack of gum and another six-pack of Pepsi. Judy returned the rest

Alleycat

room key to the hook on the wall and they all followed her out the door. Cal and Neil flicked their cigarette butts into the road. Everyone headed for the car, laughing and chasing each other. Renee walked quietly behind them, carrying the box of food. Alex dropped back. "You all right?"

She nodded. "Yeah." She smiled a little. "Yeah, I'm fine."

"Okay." He leaned down to look at her face. "Are you having a good time?"

She couldn't help laughing. "Yes, don't worry about me. I'm having fun and I'm really okay." Alex and Renee joined the others who grabbed for the hot dogs, emptying the box quickly.

"Hey, thanks," Neil said, his mouth full.

"Don't get mustard on my upholstery," Cal warned, scooping dripping sauerkraut strands into his mouth. "Did you get napkins, Ren?"

Laughing, Savannah handed a paper napkin to each person. "Eat before you get in Cal's precious car," she said.

"Huh," Judy said, after taking a tentative bite. "This is pretty good. I didn't expect that."

"If you don't want to finish it," Neil said, gazing at her hot dog as he wiped the napkin across his mustache, "hand it over."

She held it close and shook her head. "No, I'm eating it. If you want more, just march on over to that store and get more." She tossed her head and glared at him and he laughed. She finished eating, then collected the wrappers from everyone and dumped them in a nearby garbage can.

After they settled in their places in the car, Cal asked, "What beach do you want to go to? We're coming out at Lincoln City so we could go just about anywhere."

"Agate Beach," Judy suggested.

"Oh, that's so far south," Savannah said. "How about Devil's Punchbowl or up to Road's End?"

"I like Fogarty Creek," Alex said. "It's a great beach, lots of room to walk or run. It'd be great to jog on the sand."

"Yeah, I vote for Fogarty," said Neil.

"All in favor?" Cal asked. A booming chorus of "Ayes!" shook the car and Cal gave a thumbs-up as they roared down the highway. He turned onto Highway 101 and at Lincoln City headed south to Fogarty Creek State Park. The parking lot was deserted although the weather was clear and sunny. Cal parked near the trailhead and everyone scrambled out of the car. Alex had brought a backpack; he stashed a blanket and the snacks in it.

Situated east of the highway, a trail led under the bridge to the beach. Crossing the rocky path, Alex stayed close to Renee, one hand gripping her elbow, keeping her steady.

"Do you think I'm going to fall?" she asked with a grin. He grinned back and nodded. "You're very chivalrous. Thank you." She jumped over the last rock and bowed to him. "We made it!"

The sky was bright but gray clouds hovered on the horizon and the waves crashed high on the beach. The tide was coming in so they found a spot close to the grass and stashed their things. Alex spread the blanket out on the sand and Renee sat on the edge of it, legs drawn up, arms around her shins. She rested her chin on her knees and watched the waves. Savannah sat next to her. Alex moved a short distance away and found a large log to sit on.

"Maybe we could build a fire," Judy said.

"I don't know, maybe," Cal said. "Depends on when the tide goes out. We're too close to the grass right now."

"Yeah, let's wait awhile," Alex agreed. "It's not cold yet anyway."

Cal shook a cigarette from the pack and offered one to Neil. Cupping their hands against the wind, they lit them and stood quietly, smoking and gazing out at the sea.

"I'm going to look for shells," Judy announced. She wandered away, head down, hands in her jacket pockets.

"Want to go for a run?" Alex asked the others.

Savannah stood up and pulled her sweatshirt hood over her hair. "How about a walk?"

"Tell you what," Alex said. "I'll run, you girls walk, and on my way back, I'll do a cool-down with you."

"Sounds like a good plan," Savannah said. "Come on, Renee, you said you wanted to walk on the beach."

Cal and Neil waved as Alex, Renee, and Savannah started off. Neil pulled a baggie of marijuana and some rolling papers from his pocket and Cal took a silver flask from his. They settled on the driftwood.

Alex walked for a few hundred yards, then broke into a run. "See ya!"

Renee and Savannah strolled along the edge of the surf, watching the incoming waves, stopping now and then to check out a shell or piece of driftwood or kelp. The sun didn't do much to warm the air and the wind kicked up now and then. Renee shivered, buttoning her coat and pulling the collar up around her neck. Savannah did the same. They came to a little rivulet that bisected the sand from the water's edge to the beach grass. Renee took off her shoes and socks, rolled up her jeans, and stepped into the chilly water. Even though it was freezing, it felt good, refreshing, cleansing. She walked along the stream, stepping carefully into the deeper areas, mindful of her pant cuffs, enjoying the feel of the water rushing over her ankles.

Across the stream stood a cluster of boulders large enough to sit on. Savannah leaned against the biggest one, stretched her arms up, cracked her back. Renee sat down, raised her face to the sun. "This is the best day," she murmured.

"Not to ruin the mood or anything," Savannah began. "But have you thought about what will happen when school ends?"

Renee shook her head, laughed. "I'm pretty much avoiding that. I can't deal with it."

"Yeah, I understand," Savannah said, her voice soft. "But you probably should think about it. Pretty soon, anyway."

"I know. Here it is April already." Renee pushed her fingers through her hair, pulled it back for a moment, then let it settle around her shoulders. "I just have to get through this term and not flunk out. I'll never finish school if that happens. I won't be a teacher. I'll have to move back home." She hunched her back, pressed her hands together. "Goddammit, Savannah, I don't want to do that." *Just a complete failure in everything.*

"I wish—" Savannah stopped, took a big breath, held it, then exhaled slowly. "I wish you could see what I see." She hesitated. "I don't think you should stay with Russ."

Renee looked down, chewing on her thumbnail. She closed her eyes. "I know you feel that way. So does Cal. And Neil. And probably Alex, although he doesn't come right out and say it. But I—I can't do anything until he comes back. When I see him again, I'll know what to do."

"Are you sure?" Savannah stepped in front of Renee, taking both of her hands, squeezing gently, looking directly into Renee's eyes. "Can you stand up to him?"

"What do you mean?'

"Renee, he tells you what to do. Do you ever make your own

decisions when it comes to Russ?" She let go of Renee's hands and perched on the boulder next to her. "Please, just think about it."

Renee nodded, arms folded across her chest, head down. "All the time," she whispered.

"Look, you did it with Judy. You can do it with Russ."

Alex jogged up, bouncing on the balls of his feet. "Come on, let's race back," he said, pulling both girls to their feet and dragging them with him. Shrieking, they jerked their hands out of his and ran as fast as they could back to the blanket. The girls fell down on the sand, giggling. Cal and Neil were almost out of sight down the other direction; Judy was nowhere to be seen. Savannah decided to meet up with the boys, asking if Renee and Alex wanted to come with her. Alex said sure but Renee shook her head.

"Thanks, but I'm going to sit here for awhile."

Gulls circled and swooped, diving for food, their cries harmonizing with the wind and surf; strutting in clusters on the sand they picked through long strings of seaweed. The fishy smell of kelp mingled with the salty breeze coming off the water. Traffic on the bridge hummed with an occasional eighteen-wheeler adding a crescendo to the symphony of sounds.

Renee dropped her head down on her knees, eyes tightly shut, and put her arms around herself, curling into a ball. *What should I do? How, oh how am I going to explain all this? I should* not *feel guilty about having fun.* She twitched when she felt a hand on her arm. She didn't move, but opened her eyes.

"Hey, Renee." It was Alex.

"I'm fine, it's okay." Her voice barely audible, she closed her eyes again. Tears burned behind the lids.

"We're going for another walk, maybe a short jog. Judy's down that way; she found a bunch of pretty neat shells. Do you want to come?"

She shook her head, pulled her arms tighter around her legs. The tears leaked; she willed herself not to cry.

"We'll be back soon," he said softly, touching her shoulder. "Okay?"

"I'm sorry," she said in a shaky voice. "I—I'm just not feeling well. Don't worry. I'll be fine in a minute." She heard their voices get fainter and she lay back on the blanket, curled on her side, eyes covered with her arm. She couldn't cry. The tears would not fall. She wanted to cry; she wanted to bawl her eyes out. Scream, cry, die—anything to get rid of the constant ache. Everything reminded her of it. She could feel the wail beginning, growing louder, louder, higher. It wouldn't end. It stayed inside her head, an earsplitting sound. The earth beneath her rumbled and trembled; she realized it was her own heart pounding, her own body shaking. Then she heard Alex's voice, soft and soothing, murmuring "It's okay, it's all right, I'm here" close to her ear. His hand was gentle on her back. Her breath shuddered as hot tears streamed down her face.

34 ~~

Late one morning, Renee and Alex lay face to face under a couple of blankets on the foam bedding. They hadn't been awake long and were talking quietly. Savannah and Judy had already left for their classes; Cal had showered and was dressing in the bedroom. The sudden loud knocking at the front door didn't startle them. People came and went at every hour of the day. Alex reached out to brush an eyelash from the corner of Renee's eye as he yelled, "Come on in! It's unlocked!" The door swung open. Alex's hand froze on Renee's cheek. "Mom."

"Alex." Her eyes circled the room and she smiled briefly at Renee.

Alex scrambled to his feet. "What are you doing here? It's the middle of the week. Is there something wrong? Did something happen at home?"

"No, everyone's fine, but we need to talk."

"Mom..."

Renee sat up, frantically combing her fingers through her tangled hair. She shook so violently that she nearly stabbed herself in the eye. *Alex's mother! Shit. What if she notices I'm wearing his clothes?*

Cal came into the room, giving a friendly smile to Alex's mother. "Hi, Mrs. Davidson." He picked up his jacket, three-ring binder, and a textbook. "Later, kids."

She moved out of his way, watching as he clattered down the stairs, a solemn expression on her face. She turned her attention back to Alex. "I'd like to talk to you in the car." He nodded and she went outside.

"Stay here," Alex said to Renee. "It'll be okay."

Renee changed into her own clothes with lightening speed, worried that Alex and his mother—his mother, for God's sake!—might come back any second, then paced nervously around the apartment, only sitting down long enough to put on her shoes. She pulled a brush through her hair, too shaky to bother with the tangles underneath, and brushed her teeth. After folding the blankets and putting the foam rubber back into its chair form, she went into the kitchen to put water on for coffee. She spilled some on the floor as she carried the pan from the sink to the stove and swore under her breath. The apartment was clean; she had nothing to do while the minutes clicked by. The coffee was ready. She poured herself a cup and slid into a chair at the table. Taking a sip, she burned her tongue and angrily tossed the coffee in the sink. She paced. Room to room to room. Each time she passed the mirror in the bathroom she stared at her reflection. *Ugly tramp. His mother is probably asking Alex about me now—who is that slut you're sleeping with? God damn fuck it all to hell.*

"Hey."

She jumped at the soft sound of Alex's voice; her knees jellied and she clutched at the wall for support.

"I'm sorry. Did I scare you?"

She smiled wanly. "Yeah, but I forgive you. Why is your mother—"

"Every time my parents bring me back from a weekend home, they comment on how I'm risking my future by living here. They don't like Neil; they think I'm going to get in trouble because of him. They think he's into drugs! Can you imagine that?" He chuckled. "You know, my bike got stolen in October so they think the police are going to suddenly show up—" he rolled his eyes—"to tell me my bike's been recovered and they'll be suspicious about what goes on in this apartment. Mom is worried I'll be arrested—you know, guilt by association."

"So what does that mean?"

"My parents want to pay Neil's share of the rent if he moves out."

"Did you tell her he already left?"

"Yeah. She was shocked. Then she asked if I can handle it financially. I told her no problem."

"What about Cal?"

"He's okay. My parents like him." He grinned. "You know how charming he can be." He reached out and tucked her hair behind her ears. "Ready to meet her?"

"Oh, Alex, how can I? She must think I'm terrible."

"She doesn't. But she does think you should be somewhere else as long as Neil is living here. She told me it's no place to bring a nice girl."

"Don't kid me. I'm too scared as it is."

"It's the truth. Now come on, she's waiting for us. We'll drop you off at the library, okay?"

"Where are you going?"

"I don't know. You go back to the dorm and wait for me there. I'll be there as soon as I can."

Mrs. Davidson smiled warmly as Alex introduced her to Renee. Renee tried to keep her hands steady as she opened the car door and slid into the back seat. She sat stick-straight, eyes ahead, avoiding the rearview mirror.

"I'm glad to meet you, Renee," Mrs. Davidson said. "Where are you from?"

"S-Salem," Renee stuttered. "I-I'm glad to meet you, too."

"Alex said you live in the dorm. Can I take you there?"

"Oh, no, that's okay," Renee said quickly.

"Mom, just drop her off by the library." He turned to smile at Renee. "Aren't you meeting Savannah there?"

Pretending to check her watch, Renee nodded. "Yes, in about fifteen minutes." The car pulled up to the curb. "Thank you for the ride." She yanked the door handle and pushed the door open. "It was nice meeting you. See you around, Alex."

"I hope I'll see you again soon, Renee," Mrs. Davidson said. When they had driven on, Renee went into the library and limply sagged into a chair at a study carrel. She was astonished that Alex's mother had treated her with such friendliness. *She didn't seem to think I was horrible. But maybe she's good at disguising her true feelings. Why do these things happen to me? God, when I think about how that must have looked!* She suddenly became aware of her engagement ring; although only a small solitaire, it felt incredibly heavy. She twisted and pulled at it until it slid off her finger. She pushed it onto her right hand ring finger. Just in case she happened to meet up with Mrs. Davidson again and they worked at becoming better acquainted. *I'm having a nightmare. Alex's mother did not see us in that bed together. She did not tell Alex to kick his roommate out of his own apartment. She did not say she hoped to see me again. This is a perfectly normal day.*

~~ 35 ~~

Finding herself alone one afternoon and between classes with a couple of hours to kill, Renee stopped in at the campus coffee shop for a Coke. She ran into Eric, a dorm-mate of Russ's from the previous year, and he invited her to join him at his table. They talked about classes and grades and money and summer jobs, before the discussion turned to the subject of Russ. Giving her a quizzical look, Eric asked Renee how she was holding up with Russ gone. She shrugged, not saying anything, not quite knowing what to say.

Eric took a deep breath. "He has people watching you. They write to him and report on what you're doing."

Renee closed her eyes, swallowed hard, then looked at Eric. "How do you know? Are you one of them?" He shook his head. "Who?"

"Some of the guys from last year. Brian. Brandon. He knows better than to ask me."

Renee could barely speak. She felt completely numb. "Are they writing to him?" Eric didn't answer. "Anyone else that you know about?"

"Yeah. Kim."

Renee was stunned. Kim had been her roommate last year. She remembered running into her just a couple of days ago. And Brian the day she and Savannah went to Gentle Woods with Cal. *What did Kim think? Did Brian say anything to Russ?* Her blood ran cold. *What was it Kim said? "I know he misses you."*

He swallowed, clearly uncomfortable. "I don't know if anyone has actually told him anything. He hasn't given you any indication that he knows specifics about you?"

She shook her head. "No. Nothing."

"I've seen you at the Alleycat," Eric said quietly. "You always look really happy. I'm glad." He reached out and touched her arm. "He's paranoid, you know. I don't understand why you—" He broke off in the middle of his sentence.

Neither do I.

That evening, with Cal gone to a party at another apartment, Alex suggested taking a walk through town. Tired of sitting at the Alleycat or the apartment, the girls readily agreed. They wandered along back streets, quieter than usual. It was past midnight. The air was cool and refreshing, the night clear with a quarter moon high in the sky. Occasionally they saw a light in a house but most of the buildings they passed were dark. On Clay Street, they came to the big brick Methodist-Presbyterian church. Savannah peeked in the front window, then pushed against the glass door. It swung open.

No one made a sound as they slowly made their way into the spacious sanctuary. Renee slid into a pew; in a moment, each had taken a seat apart from the others. The faint aroma of flowers permeated the room. Votive candles flickered and the moon glowed dimly through a round stained-glass window high over the altar. After a while, Alex went to Renee and sat beside her. She smiled up at him but neither spoke. A few minutes later Judy joined them, followed by Savannah.

"It's certainly different at night," Judy whispered.

"So peaceful," Renee agreed.

"Doesn't it make you feel like you can overcome anything? I mean, you can get everything into perspective in a place like this. Well, I can, anyway." Savannah chuckled softly and looked around at each of them. "I'm so lucky to have you as my friends."

Renee smiled at her. "We're all lucky."

They explored the church, walking down corridors and peeking into classrooms. Judy discovered a piano and she and Savannah played several duets. Renee and Alex stood in the darkness in the next room, listening.

"I hope they don't get too loud," Renee whispered anxiously.

"Don't worry so much. Just enjoy yourself." Alex switched on the light, revealing a chalkboard. He challenged Renee to a game of Hangman. After a few games, the others joined them. When they were bored with it, they went down the hall to a room with thick carpet and settled there, sitting on the floor.

"What if somebody sees the lights and calls the police?"

"Oh, Renee, don't be silly," Savannah said. "The doors were unlocked. A church is supposed to welcome the outcast." She giggled. "We are outcasts, aren't we?"

Judy yawned and lay down on one side of Alex, as close to him as possible. Renee glanced at him with amusement. He sighed, rolled his eyes.

"Isn't anybody tired?" Judy asked, yawning again.

"Yeah, I am," Renee answered, standing up. "Come on, let's go, okay?"

"We don't have to go," said Alex. "We can sleep here."

"Why? Why sleep on a hard floor in a cold church?"

"Oh, come on, Renee," Savannah coaxed. "Have you ever slept in a church?"

"Of course not."

"Well, let's do it!" Savannah said.

Renee sat back down, outvoted.

"Alex, will you turn out the light?" Judy was already half asleep. Alex jumped up, and Renee knew he was grateful for the chance to put more distance between himself and Judy. He flipped the switch and settled back down, nearer to Renee and Savannah.

"Good night everybody."

"G'night," Savannah said cheerfully. "Go to sleep, Renee. No one's going to throw us in jail. Go on, lay down."

Renee stretched out but she didn't sleep. She listened to the light breathing around her and listened for footsteps in the hall. The moonlight cast eerie shadows on the walls and on Alex's face. His eyes were closed and she realized that this was the first time she stayed awake while he slept. *Oh, Alex, you have all my worries as well as your own.* She wished she could touch his face, smooth his hair, tell him to rest. Sitting up, she wrapped his coat around her shoulders and, leaning against the wall, waited for morning.

~~ 36 ~~

"...I HOPE ALL IS WELL AND I JUST HAVE AN OVERACTIVE IMAGINATION. NEVERTHELESS, I CAN'T HELP FEELING CONCERNED. IT'S BEEN TWO WEEKS SINCE YOUR LAST LETTER AND IT WASN'T UP TO PAR. I'M GOING TO CALL YOU, AT MY PARENTS' HOUSE, SATURDAY AT THREE O'CLOCK YOUR TIME. I'VE ALREADY ARRANGED IT WITH THEM. THEY WILL PICK YOU UP SATURDAY AFTERNOON AT ONE. YOU CAN EXPLAIN..."

Fury was Renee's first reaction. She wadded the letter into a tight ball and hurled it at the wall. *I am not doing this with your parents standing there listening. Goddamn you.* Throwing herself on her bed, she wept, tears streaming down her face, harsh sobs shuddering through her body. Shocked at her rage, she crawled under the covers and pulled them over her head. Curled up, with the blankets drawn close, she concentrated on breathing slowly. Gradually her trembling subsided but her mind would not stop racing. *I can't do this anymore. I can't. It's too much.* She squeezed her eyes shut, felt her muscles tensing. *Breathe. In. Out.* She opened her eyes to the darkness around her. *Oh God.* Her fingers searched for and found the tiny plastic flower pendant that lay against her throat.

Alex. I'm in love with Alex.

She had known for some time now. She couldn't say when she first knew—it had happened so gradually. She didn't regret it but the burden was heavy. She wanted more than anything to tell someone, anyone. But she couldn't, she didn't dare. She would wait until Russ came home, test her feelings for him, decide then what to do. And if she no longer loved him...

Throwing the blankets off, she leapt out of bed and began

Alleycat

pacing the room. Hands clenched into fists, her movements jerky, she stopped in front of her desk. Looking into Russ's eyes in the photo pinned to the bulletin board, she said in a tight, soft voice, "I can't marry you."

It's over, Russ. I never thought I could live without you. But I can. I know it. So what do I do now? How does it look if I walk out on you? Write you a Dear John letter? Pretty lousy, that Renee. A tramp, no better than an alley cat. Didn't have the decency to be faithful...

Tears dripped down her cheeks. She wiped her eyes with the back of her hand. *You have spies watching me? How dare you!* She took several deep breaths, gulping air. *You don't respect me and never will. It's over. I won't marry you. You make me feel inadequate and I'm tired of it. I'm better than that. I have friends who know that, friends who care about me. Two and a half years is a long time, but a lifetime is too long.*

Sitting at the desk, she started a letter, weighing how to tell him. Nothing about Alex, or Cal. They had nothing to do with her and Russ. Trying to put her thoughts on paper proved more difficult than she could handle and she put the unfinished letter away. Dropping her head down, eyes pressed shut, hands restlessly clasped in her lap, she considered what to do. Saturday was only four days away. Not enough time. *What's the fastest way? A telegram. I can send a telegram.* She took a piece of notepaper and scribbled down some ideas, then put the paper in her pocket. She checked her purse for change, having no idea how much money she would need. From the pay phone in the dorm lobby she could call Western Union and find out what sending a telegram would cost. Feeling stronger since she had a plan, she headed down the stairs.

It took some time but finally the wire—"Dear Russ, No need for phone call. Letter coming. Love, Renee." —was on its way to Japan. She'd struggled over how to sign it but decided that continuing to use the endearment was easier until she had the actual letter composed. She returned to her room, grateful that Judy had gone to a class. She pulled the engagement ring off her finger, surprised to find it still on her right hand, and put it away.

In the afternoon she met up with Alex and Savannah; she told them she needed to talk so they went to the Alleycat. Cal was there, sitting alone in a small booth. Renee thought about the first time she and Savannah had seen him in the restaurant. So much had happened in three months. She stopped by the table, letting Alex and Savannah pass by to claim the corner booth.

"Hi, Cal," she said. "How are you?"

"You're here early." He studied Renee's face. "Are you okay?"

"Come on. I want to talk to the three of you."

Savannah and Alex were ordering sodas. When the waitress left, Cal and Renee slid into the booth, Renee next to Alex and Cal across the table next to Savannah.

Cal greeted the others, then looked at Renee. "So," he said. "What's going on? You look—sorry for saying it—lousy."

Renee cleared her throat, leaned forward, and rested her forehead on her arms folded on the table. "Yeah, well," she said. "I'm done with Russ."

Savannah drew in her breath sharply. "Wow. Wow, Rennie. That's good. It is." She cleared her throat, and then said, "I know it's hard, but I'm proud of you."

Alex and Cal exchanged glances. Cal said, "What exactly do you mean, 'done with' him?"

Renee sat up straight and held out her left hand. "See, no ring. I took it off. And I sent him a telegram."

"Shit. A telegram." Cal stretched across the table and grasped her hands. "You finally got wise, huh?" He looked into her eyes and saw the tears welling. "Hey, it's the right thing to do."

Alex, sitting next to Renee, put his arm around her shoulder. She tensed, then softened. *I'm safe.* Savannah put her hand over Cal's as he held Renee's. The three of them sat quietly and let Renee cry.

Composing the letter was easier than she expected. Alone in her room while Judy was in class, Renee paced a few times, then sat at her desk. She wrote down every thought that came to mind, scribbling as fast as she could. Then she went over it carefully, crossing out lines, changing words, paring it down to a page. Pulling a sheet of airmail paper from her drawer, grateful she had purchased prepaid mailers, she rewrote the letter in her best handwriting, making certain it was legible and her message clear. *I am not marrying you.* She said nothing about Alex. Nothing about Cal. Nothing about the Alleycat. *I am not marrying you because we aren't right for each other. I don't love you.* Without any hesitation, she signed the letter with no endearment, simply "Renee."

Alleycat

She walked to the post office on Main Street. Pausing with the letter in one hand and holding the narrow door of the mailbox open with the other, she felt a quickening in her heart. She held her breath, standing still as stone. *Even if nothing comes of loving Alex. Russ is not good for me.* She placed the letter on the metal door and let it slam shut. *It's done.* She stood motionless for a moment. *It's right.* She walked back to campus with a lightness that amazed her. She wanted to sing and twirl, shout to the world, but she kept her steps even-paced and her mouth closed. *I did it!*

May

~ 37 ~

A week later Renee, Savannah, Alex, and Cal were hanging out in Savannah's room talking, drinking tea, and munching on rolls left from dinner. At eleven o'clock there was a knock on the door; Savannah answered it. The girl manning the desk in the lobby stood there, peering into the room.

"Renee? Judy told me I could find her here."

Renee stepped forward. "Yeah, I'm here. Why?"

"You have a phone call." The girl looked at the two boys. "And, it's eleven. Curfew, you know."

"Yeah, yeah," Savannah said, rolling her eyes. "We were just going out anyway."

Renee grabbed her coat and followed the girl down the hall. *Who could be calling me this late at night?* A flicker of fear flashed through her. *Mom?*

In the lobby, Renee went to the phone on the wall. The receiver dangled loosely; the muted voices of Savannah and the boys seeped through the glass doors leading outside. She lifted the receiver, her stomach clenching painfully. "Hello?"

"Renee."

When she heard the voice, her stomach dropped. She clutched the receiver so tightly her knuckles whitened. "Russ," she said softly. "I was just—um, hi, how are you?" *Stupid thing to say. Get a grip!*

His voice was high-pitched and agitated. "Renee, what's going on? First, I get a telegram from you. A telegram! And now I get—"

She heard the door open behind her at the same time Russ made a strange noise. She turned.

"You okay?" Savannah asked, a worried look in her eyes.

Renee nodded, pointed at the phone, and mouthed Russ's

name. Her hand trembled.

"Come on, Renee," Cal said loudly. "We want to get going."

She put her finger to her lips, shaking her head.

"Who is that?" Russ's voice pulled her attention back to the phone. "Is that—" His voice broke and she realized he was crying.

"Russ, what do you want? It's really late."

After a long moment, she heard a loud sniffling, then he said, "Your letter came today."

"Then you know how I feel."

Cal leaned close to Renee in an effort to hear the phone conversation; Renee turned away from him, the phone pressed tightly against her ear.

"Are you with somebody right now?" Russ stopped crying. Renee could picture his eyes narrowed, mouth set, arms crossed over his chest. Interrogator's stance. "Are you with that guy? Your *tutor*?" His callous sarcasm made her bristle.

"That's none of your business."

Cal and Alex grinned, arms pumped over their heads in a silent cheer. Renee put a finger to her lips. She whispered, "Go wait for me outside." Savannah pulled them out the door.

"Are you seeing him? Are you sleeping with him? You must be out of your mind." His voice was clear now, strong and sure. "In your letter you said you're breaking up with me. That's not possible."

"Yes, Russ, it is."

"How can you—"

"Because it's the right thing to do. And it has nothing to do with anyone else. I told you that in the letter." She tried not to grunt into the phone as Cal and Alex made silly faces in the window, distracting her. "Look, I'm sorry I couldn't wait for you to get back."

"Yeah, that's harsh."

"I'm sorry." Her voice, barely above a whisper, wavered. "We can talk when you get home."

"No, we can talk right now. We're engaged. That means we're a couple. That means—"

"I have to go. This is costing you a fortune." Her throat was tight and her eyes burned.

"I don't give a fuck what it costs!" He shouted into the phone; Renee had to yank the receiver away from her ear.

"Goodbye, Russ." She hung up and walked out the door, tears streaming down her face.

~ 38 ~

"What happened to Russ' picture?" Judy asked as she changed her clothes.

Renee shrugged. "We broke up."

"What?" Judy stopped, one leg mid-air, pants halfway on.

"Took you a while to notice the photo was gone," Renee said. "It's been a week."

"Well, I, um, I did notice but didn't want, um, to upset you by asking."

"Thank you." Renee brushed her hair, pulled it back with a bandana, fluffed her bangs.

"What, what happened? Did he—?"

"I did it. Hurry up, finish getting ready so we can go."

They met up with Savannah and the three girls walked across campus toward the Alleycat. Renee and Savannah chatted easily but Judy kept quiet, walking in the street, kicking at stones and occasional dried leaves. Just before they reached the diner, Savannah spoke to Judy.

"He was bad for her. Do you realize that?"

"Why? What do you mean? Russ loves Renee. She always says that. And that she loves him. I thought…"

"That he would break up with her?"

Judy didn't speak, but she nodded, eyes averted.

"She's strong enough to do the right thing."

Renee laughed. "Hey, guys, I'm right here. You're talking about me like I died or something."

Savannah gave her a hug. "You are more alive than I've ever seen you!"

"Come on, let's see if the guys are here yet." Renee pulled the diner door open with such gusto that it banged against the wall. She sauntered inside and, arm stretched up high, waved at the three boys in the corner booth with a big grin, eyes sparkling. "Hi! We're here!"

Neil stood and gave her a hug. "Just heard the news this

afternoon."

"I'm so glad you're here, Neil." Renee slid into the booth, next to Alex. Savannah and Judy joined the table and Neil sat back down. The waitress hurried over.

"Hi, Wendy. We want a pie," Renee said. "A whole pie. Chocolate cream. Six forks. We don't need any plates."

Wendy stared at the group. "A whole pie? What is it, payday?"

Renee laughed. "Guess so. I'm paying."

When the pie arrived, Savannah said, "Wait a minute. I have a request." She dug around in her purse and extracted her camera. "We had you take our picture a while back. Could you do it again?"

"Sure thing."

Cal passed the forks out and they posed for several pictures, documenting the demise of the chocolate cream pastry.

A few days later Savannah brought the developed photographs to the Alleycat. She spread them out on the table alongside the ones that had been taken in January. As they snacked on a plate of fries and their special ketchup-mustard fry sauce, they compared the two sets of photos.

"Savannah," Renee said. "Look. You let your hair go. It has a beautiful natural curl."

"I ran out of hairspray for my purse, that's all," Savannah said. "About a month ago." She squinted at the photo in her hand. "I guess it looks okay like this. A little frizzy, though."

"You'll be a hippie yet," Cal said.

"Ack, my hair is a mess," Judy said. "It's gotten so shaggy. And look at Cal. In the first set he's all dressed up."

"As I told you, I have several kinds of clothes. It's spring now. Time for T-shirts and jeans."

"Alex, you've changed, too," Savannah said. "You look looser, more comfortable, like you're ready to break into song or something."

He grinned. "I don't think you want me to do that." He held up two photos, one "old" and one "new." After studying them for a moment, he put them back on the table and tapped each one, placing his fingers on Renee's likeness. "Check this out."

"That's the biggest change of all," Savannah said softly.

Renee felt a blush coming and ducked her head. *I look happy. I am happy.*

~ 39 ~

Renee laughed hard at something Alex said as the two entered the dark apartment. "I don't feel one bit like studying," she said.

"Neither do I," Alex agreed. "However..."

"Ah, come on," Renee begged. "Let's not, huh? Please?"

Laughing, Alex said, "You don't have to ask me."

"I have to ask somebody. I don't want to take all the blame. Come on, say we don't have to study."

"No, we've got to. We have to sometime. Might as well do it now."

"What if I refuse?" Renee teased.

"You want me to make you?" He took on a Frankenstein stance and started for her, arms outstretched, legs stiff, a maniacal leer on his face.

"You have ice cream on your nose!" she shrieked. He stopped, embarrassed, and rubbed at his face. Laughing, she said, "I was only kidding."

"Pest," he said, grinning back at her. "If we don't study, what shall we do?"

"Flunk our tests." She sighed. "You'd better turn the light on. It's getting dark."

"It's not that dark. What do you want to work on first?"

She leaned against the wall, arms crossed. "I'm sick of math, but since you're my tutor..."

"Okay, we'll take advantage of this time we have together with no interruptions to work on your best subject." He, too, leaned against the wall.

"Well, turn the lights on."

"You turn them on."

She didn't move. "I'm so tired of math. Let's work on something else. Have you finished your English paper?"

"I guess so."

"We'll do that."

He laughed. "How in the world—"

"I'll proofread it and tell you everything that's wrong with it."

"Oh, thanks a lot."

"Well, I guess I could tell you the good parts, too."

"Okay, then what?"

"I could work on my Nutrition. I'll cook something for you."

"Like what?"

"What do you want?"

"Cereal."

"You're crazy! Cereal? It's lucky for you that we met. If Savannah and Judy and I hadn't started feeding you decent meals you'd have wasted away by now. You'd live on cereal, wouldn't you, if we let you get away with it?"

"Sure." He smiled. "It's my insurance against you leaving me."

"I won't leave you. Go turn the light on."

"You keep saying that."

She giggled. "It's getting too dark to study."

"So if we don't turn the lights on we won't be able to study."

"That solves our problem then." She slid down the wall to a sitting position on the floor. He followed.

"No, we'll wait until it's really dark in here, then we'll turn the lights on and have a look at your math." He tried to give her a stern look but the waning light was too dim to reveal his features.

"Aww..."

"Cut it out," he said gruffly, but she could hear the smile in his voice.

"It sure gets dark fast. What time is it?"

He shifted slightly. "I don't know."

"Don't get up. I don't really want to know." She sat quietly for a minute, then asked, "What's the date?"

"May—eleventh? I don't know. Something like that. Why?"

"I don't know."

"Are you okay, Renee?"

"Oh, yeah."

"Stand up for a minute." She did and he gathered the stray pillows scattered around the room and spread the foam rubber chair out into the bed. "Okay, lay down. You sound tired."

"I am, a little." She stretched out. "This is nice. Thank you."

He sat next to her, then, changing his mind, lay down. "As usual, you're right. It is nice."

"You should have the pillows. You're always giving me the

best." She started to move but he stopped her, a hand on her arm.

"I'm fine." He didn't move his hand.

Renee stared at the ceiling. "You know, this has been a good year."

"It's only May. What's this 'has been' bit?"

"Oh, you know." She turned her face to Alex. "Did you know that Savannah and I met Cal on January eleventh? Exactly four months ago."

"Four months is long enough to know someone."

"What do you mean?"

Alex didn't answer. He reached over and softly touched her cheek. *Warm. His hands are warm.*

Renee dropped her gaze. "Hey, if I write to you next year will you write back?"

"Sure. And we'll get together once in awhile."

"Of course we will! You'll meet some wonderful woman and you'll get married—I'll have to warn her about the cereal!—and everything will work out just fine. I'll meet someone and—gee, maybe our children will even grow up together! Why do we worry so much?"

"We?"

"Okay, okay."

The room was very dark. Alex stood and went into the bedroom, returning with a blanket. He sat down and carefully spread it over them.

"Thanks," Renee said. "How did you know I was getting cold?"

"As much as we've been together, I ought to know."

They were silent for a long time, unmoving. They lay face-to-face, his arm resting lightly at her waist. Renee, feeling a lightness she hadn't known in months, perhaps years, had no concrete thoughts, only a pleasant jumble of unrelated things running through her mind. Alex's arm around her was—her heart leaped. *His arm is around me!* She didn't move.

"Renee," Alex whispered, pulling her closer. "I love you. I love you more than anything. I want to spend my life with you." He kissed her softly.

About the Author

Sue Armstrong has been writing short stories and poetry most of her life. She has one book of poetry in print: *Chaos/Chaos*. This is her first novel; she is currently working on a sequel to *Alleycat* and a collection of short stories.

She is the mother to three children, grandmother to three (so far), and a semi-retired preschool teacher. She lives in Western Oregon.